CRUEL PARADISE

ORYOLOV BRATVA

NICOLE FOX

MAILING LIST

Sign up to my mailing list!
New subscribers receive a FREE steamy bad boy romance novel.

Click the link below to join.
https://sendfox.com/nicolefox

ALSO BY NICOLE FOX

Pushkin Bratva

Cognac Villain

Cognac Vixen

Viktorov Bratva

Whiskey Poison

Whiskey Pain

Orlov Bratva

Champagne Venom

Champagne Wrath

Uvarov Bratva

Sapphire Scars

Sapphire Tears

Vlasov Bratva

Arrogant Monster

Arrogant Mistake

Zhukova Bratva

Tarnished Tyrant

Tarnished Queen

Stepanov Bratva

Satin Sinner

Satin Princess

Makarova Bratva

Shattered Altar

Shattered Cradle

Solovev Bratva

Ravaged Crown

Ravaged Throne

Vorobev Bratva

Velvet Devil

Velvet Angel

Romanoff Bratva

Immaculate Deception

Immaculate Corruption

Kovalyov Bratva

Gilded Cage

Gilded Tears

Jaded Soul

Jaded Devil

Ripped Veil

Ripped Lace

Mazzeo Mafia Duet

Liar's Lullaby (Book 1)

Sinner's Lullaby (Book 2)

Bratva Crime Syndicate

Can be read in any order!

Lies He Told Me

Scars He Gave Me

Sins He Taught Me

Belluci Mafia Trilogy

Corrupted Angel (Book 1)

Corrupted Queen (Book 2)

Corrupted Empire (Book 3)

De Maggio Mafia Duet

Devil in a Suit (Book 1)

Devil at the Altar (Book 2)

Kornilov Bratva Duet

Married to the Don (Book 1)

Til Death Do Us Part (Book 2)

Heirs to the Bratva Empire

Can be read in any order!

Kostya

Maksim

Andrei

Princes of Ravenlake Academy (Bully Romance)

Can be read as standalones!

Cruel Prep

Cruel Academy

Cruel Elite

Tsezar Bratva

Nightfall (Book 1)

Daybreak (Book 2)

Russian Crime Brotherhood

Can be read in any order!

Owned by the Mob Boss

Unprotected with the Mob Boss

Knocked Up by the Mob Boss

Sold to the Mob Boss

Stolen by the Mob Boss

Trapped with the Mob Boss

Volkov Bratva

Broken Vows (Book 1)

Broken Hope (Book 2)

Broken Sins *(standalone)*

Other Standalones

Vin: A Mafia Romance

Box Sets

Bratva Mob Bosses (Russian Crime Brotherhood Books 1-6)

Tsezar Bratva (Tsezar Bratva Duet Books 1-2)

Heirs to the Bratva Empire

The Mafia Dons Collection

The Don's Corruption

CRUEL PARADISE

BOOK ONE OF THE ORYOLOV BRATVA DUET

What's more embarrassing than a butt dial?

Butt dialing your boss...

And leaving a dirty voicemail when you're uhh... "thinking" about them.

Working as Ruslan Oryolov's personal assistant is the job from hell.

After a long day spent tending to the billionaire's every whim, I need some stress relief.

So when I get home that night, that's exactly what I do.

Problem is, my thoughts are still stuck on the bosshole who's ruining my life.

That's fine—because of all Ruslan's many sins, being gorgeous might be the most dangerous.

Tonight, fantasies of him are just what I need to push me over the edge.

But when I look down at my phone squished next to me,

There it is.

A voicemail for 7 minutes and 32 seconds…

Sent to Ruslan Oryolov.

I panic and throw my phone across the room.

But there is no undoing the damage done by my very vocal O.

So what can I do?

My plan was to just avoid him and act like it never happened.

Besides, no one that busy checks their voicemails, right?

But when he schedules a one-on-one meeting with me for exactly 7 minutes and 32 seconds,

One thing is for certain:

He.

Heard.

Everything.

CRUEL PARADISE is Book One of the Oryolov Bratva duet. Ruslan and Emma's story concludes in Book Two, CRUEL PROMISE.

1

EMMA

"Do I have your full attention, Ms. Carson?"

I gulp and refocus on my boss. Ruslan Oryolov is glowering —not because I've done anything wrong, but just because that's how he always looks at me.

Actually, that's how he always looks at *everyone*. I'm pretty sure he's that unfortunate case you always hear moms telling their kids about: he made a sour face once upon a time and it just got stuck like that.

To be fair, this time, he has good reason. He's actually caught me in the middle of a somewhat shockingly violent fantasy about stapling his beautiful lips together with the stapler on his desk and then yeeting him out of his gorgeous thirtieth-story office window.

He'd deserve it. And he only has himself to blame.

Because I am all-caps *EXHAUSTED* from tending to his every whim today.

I arrived at the office at the buttcrack of dawn this morning. I haven't had more than ten consecutive seconds to myself all day long. And only now, with the clock nearing 9:00 P.M., am I getting anywhere close to the end of this workday from hell.

Without an IV drip of quad espressos, I would be dust in the wind.

But even *with* my caffeine addiction, I feel frazzled inside and out. In my head, I'm cursing my past self for being dumb enough to buy these heels half a size too small just because they were on sale. The arches of my feet are ready to commit war crimes in order to be freed.

Ruslan, on the other hand, looks as polished as ever. It's actually offensive how good he looks, despite working like a machine for every bit as long as I have today. His suit is impeccable, as is his dark five o'clock shadow, and the intensity in his scorching amber eyes hasn't dimmed one solitary notch.

"Ms. Carson. I asked you a question."

"Uh, yes," I stammer. "Yes, you have my attention." I glance down at my notepad. "Litigation release needs to go to Mark Vanderberg in Legal first thing in the morning. New chairs have been requested for the boardroom on Floor Seventeen and I will check on delivery dates. I'm moving your 2:00 P.M. to your 11:30, moving your 11:30 to your 7:15, moving your 7:15 to next Thursday, and I'm telling next Thursday's meeting to—and I quote—'eat shit and die.' Did I miss anything?"

Ruslan arches one unfairly gorgeous brow. Seriously—if I could transplant those bad boys onto my own face, I really might. They're dark and expressive and communicate half of his threats without a single word. "I detect a tone."

I keep my own face perfectly neutral. "No, sir. No tone. You specifically requested 'no snark' after the lunch salad debacle last month. I wouldn't forget."

"Hm."

Like his eyebrow, one solitary, not-even-a-word syllable from the infamous Mr. Oryolov, CEO of Bane Corporation, is enough to make grown men dissolve into tears.

I've seen it with my own two eyes. Literally. When I first started here, one of the microchip suppliers that Bane uses for our flagship home security product came in for a meeting and tried to negotiate higher prices. At the end of the idiot's hardball pitch, Ruslan simply lofted an eyebrow and said, "Hm." The man started shaking so badly they had to take him out of the conference room in a wheely chair like it was an ambulance gurney.

He's not the only one. Lord knows Ruslan has brought me to the verge of tears and beyond plenty of times in the eighteen months I've been working for him.

Everyone warned me before I took the job that it wouldn't be easy. His last three personal assistants lasted six, four, and zero-point-five months, respectively, before running screaming for the hills. There's a rumor that one of them is still checked into in-patient therapy somewhere up in Vermont.

Suffice it to say, everyone was right. Life under Ruslan Oryolov's scrutiny is not easy. It starts early and ends late. It's harsh. Fast-paced. He doesn't say "please" and he doesn't know the meaning of "thank you."

But I've stuck around for one reason and one reason only: I have to.

That's not quite the whole truth, actually. I stuck around for three reasons. And their names are Josh, Caroline, and Reagan.

I glance down and look at the lock screen of my phone where it rests in my lap. Three smiling faces stare back at me. Five-year-old Reagan just lost her front tooth and the little goober has her tongue sticking out through the gap. Caroline is only six, but she's already practicing her "smizing" and chin-tucked selfie poses. She's going to break *so* many boys' hearts as soon as I let her get an Instagram account. Josh, at eight, is the oldest—but you'd think by looking at him that he's a decade older than that, even. It's something in his eyes. A hauntedness. A chill. A stony sense of responsibility that doesn't belong on a boy who's too young to grow armpit hair.

Losing your mom will do that to you.

I would know—sort of—because losing my sister has certainly done it to me.

I do the math in my head quickly. It's March 9th right now and Sienna died in September three years ago. So that's three years, six months, and four days since I last hugged her or heard her laugh.

Three years, six months, and four days since I went from Auntie to Momma in the blink of an eye.

Three years, six months, and four days since my life changed forever.

Ruslan stands and shoots his cuffs. It's effortless, just like everything else he does. You'd be forgiven for thinking he's a model for *GQ*. He cracks his knuckles, then his neck, watching me the whole time.

I sit in my chair and focus on my breathing.

Eighteen months is long enough that I thought my infatuation would have worn off by now. I'd have thought wrong, though. If anything, he's even more beautiful than he was the day I first walked in.

I still remember how that went. I rounded the corner and stopped, dumbstruck and drooling like a lunatic. *This* man ran the biggest home security enterprise in the world? Were we sure he wasn't a Hollywood body double?

For his part, Ruslan took one look in my direction before asking, "Are you going to make my life easier or harder, Ms. Carson? If it's the latter, don't even bother setting your stuff down; just turn back while you still can."

That pretty much set the tone for our working relationship.

"I'm leaving," Ruslan announces back in the present moment. "Make sure the folders are set out for the department head meeting in the morning." He rounds the desk and strides toward me. My heart quickens when he gets close enough for me to smell his cologne. Today's is woodsy. Smoky. Crisp.

"Yes, sir," I croak quietly.

"Oh," he adds, "I also need my tuxedo brought to the penthouse on 48th. Tonight."

"Tonight?" I balk. "But I have to—"

He's already gone. Swishing out the door without bothering to look back. The only thing left behind is the trailing tendrils of his cologne.

~

An hour later, I am the walking dead. Every nerve ending in my feet is on fire. I trekked my booty across town to Ruslan's tailor, picked up his tuxedo, and trekked back to Midtown to his penthouse.

When the elevators let me out directly into his foyer, I release a sigh. One final task on this Tuesday custom-designed by Satan.

Not that tomorrow will be any different.

My shoes clack as I walk down the marble flooring and emerge into the living room. It's floor-to-ceiling glass windows on three sides, so I can see the entire city wrapped around me, bejeweled and glistening in the night. The furniture and finishes are every bit as gorgeous as the man who owns this place—and every bit as brutal. It's all black matte and sharp edges. Grotesque modern contorted sculptures in the corners. Grotesque modern contorted paintings on the walls.

I once looked up the price he paid for this place and almost threw up in my mouth. It had a few too many zeroes for my comfort level. The most sickening part of all is that he comes here once a month at most, usually with one of his many actress/influencer/model dates on his arm. It's pretty much just the world's most expensive fuckpad.

I drape the suit over the back of his black suede couch. It's weird being here, in Ruslan's personal space. It smells mostly like cleaning product, but I swear, every time I turn around, I catch just a whiff of that cologne again.

It's making my head swim.

I want so badly to curl up on the suede couch and sleep for the rest of my life. But I have to keep moving. People are counting on me. Three little ones in particular.

So sleep is off the list. My next thought is how nice it would be to get some kind of petty vengeance against the bosshole from hell for the wringer he's put me through today.

My sister wouldn't have hesitated for a second.

"Sienna, don't you dare pee on his car!"

But my sister was already clambering up on the hood in her way-too-short, way-too-pink nightclub dress, cackling like a madwoman. I was mortified. Her laugh was infamous across campus, so I had no doubt that someone was going to recognize it, open their dorm window, and look out in the East Campus parking lot to see the Carson sisters up to no good, as per usual.

Correction: Sienna *was the one who was always up to no good. I was the one who was always trying to rein her in. Not that it helped; Sienna did what she wanted.*

Always had. Always would.

And when she saw my dirty, rotten, cheating ex's car gleaming in the primo parking spot, it sparked an idea that she absolutely refused to ignore.

Which is how I ended up holding her hand for balance as she squatted on Tommy's Range Rover and let loose.

I can't say he didn't deserve it; this just wouldn't have been my preferred method of vengeance. "Screw that," Sienna said when I told her that living well was the best form of revenge. "Don't get even; get ahead. That's my *motto."*

When she had relieved herself of a long night's worth of cranberry vodkas, I helped her back down to the asphalt. "You're insane," I informed her. "Absolutely clinical."

"And yet you love me. What does that say about you?"

"Nothing good," I muttered.

"Shut up. Say it. Say you love me." She made kissy faces at me and, when I refused, she tickled me in the spot under my ribs that I'd hated since we were little.

"Fine! Fine! I love you!" I shrieked.

Only then did she relent.

"Good. I love you, too, Em. You're the stars to my moon. Never forget that."

Then, just for good measure, she mooned me. We laughed—her laugh and mine, two sides of the same coin, filtering up and out into the night beyond.

I never imagined a life without her. I never thought I'd have to.

I'm not Sienna; I'm not going to pee on Ruslan's fifty-thousand dollar couch. And, as of three years, six months, and four days ago, she's not here to do it for me.

With a sigh, I turn and slump out.

It's a long subway ride from gleaming Midtown to my dirty, cramped apartment building in Hell's Kitchen. When I get there, it's a long walk up the four flights of stairs because, of course, the elevator is broken yet again. I'm almost literally sexually aroused at the prospect of a REM cycle—but when I open the door, I realize with a molar-grinding horror that sleep is a long way away.

My apartment is an absolute disaster.

Beer bottles are scattered everywhere. The kids' clothes are mildewing in the wash. The kitchen sink is stacked high with dirty plates.

I don't have to look far to find the culprit. Ben, my sister's widower, is passed out in the corner armchair. A half-finished cigarette dangles from between his fingertips and the other hand is clutching the dregs of a lukewarm Bud Light. I march over and pluck both from him, stubbing the cigarette out in the ashtray and hurling the beer into the recycling bin. He startles for a second before sinking right back into an open-mouthed snore.

Ben. The bane of my existence, no pun intended. There's a reason he's not on the lock screen of my phone. A reason I try not to think about him whenever I can help it.

He took Sienna's death hard. That's no surprise; we all did. When someone is that bright of a personality, it's hard not to feel like you're living in the shadows once they're gone.

But the kids and I have soldiered on, no matter how much it hurts.

Ben, on the other hand, is wallowing in the mud. He was fired from his job, so now, all he does is drink and smoke and mutter to himself around the clock—which he does *here*, since he couldn't afford the mortgage on their house with no income. When he deigns to parent his own children, he does it like a fairytale ogre, all spit-flecked bellowing and flying off the handle at the least little thing. He made Reagan cry the other day because her scrunchie snapped while he was trying to do a ponytail for her. As if that was *her* fault.

I keep telling myself to have grace. He's going through a dark time. He'll come out of it.

At least, I hope he will. Truth is, I was never a huge fan of his in the first place. I found ways to tolerate him for Sienna's sake, because there's nothing I wouldn't have done for my sister.

Without her, though... it's harder.

I shake my head. It's not good to let myself dwell on these ruts. Nothing good will come of wondering why this is the hand I've been dealt. I just have to do the work. Silently and unthanked, sure. But the world isn't built to be kind to people like me.

So I drop my purse, roll up my sleeves, and do what I can to make it kind to people like Josh, Caroline, and Reagan.

Beer bottles go in the trash. Clothes go in the dryer. Dishes get scrubbed and toweled and put back in the cabinets, and little by little, the mess dwindles. In the corner, the clock hand ticks past 1:00 AM. I need to be back at Bane by quarter to six. With crosstown traffic, that means I'm looking at three hours of sleep max before I have to be up and running again.

By the time I finish, 1:00 AM has become 2:30. I zombie-walk my way down the hall. My room beckons, but before I can succumb to sleep, I have to check on the littles.

The girls' room is the first one on the right. I open the door and peek in.

Caroline is asleep on the top bunk. Her hand is dangling down, so I tiptoe across the thrifted pink shag rug and tuck it back up on the mattress so the monsters won't get it. I pause and listen, but her breathing is practically imperceptible when she's K.O.'d. The first night I had her under my roof, I was terrified that she'd died in my care.

When I'm satisfied she's comfortable, I crouch down to peer at Reagan. Her hair has fallen over her eyes. I smooth it away. Unlike Caroline, she's a snorer. She's got a real *honk-shoo-honk-shoo-mimimi* pattern to her sleep breathing, like one of Snow White's dwarves. My little angel. Those cherry apple cheeks are so pinchable. Just like Sienna's.

I wonder if Rae even remembers her mom. She was so young when we lost her.

I retreat back out into the hall and pull the door shut silently behind me. Then I step down and slowly push open Josh's.

I frown. His bed is empty, the sheets smoothed over and tucked in neatly at the edges. He does that himself every morning without fail, though no one has ever actually asked him to, as far as I'm aware. But if he's not in bed, where is…?

Ah. I glance over to see him with his face pressed against the desk. He's out cold, his hands still fiddling with something in his lap. I'm confused about what it is until I walk over and pull the bundle out from under him.

When I do, my heart breaks.

It's his basketball shoes. They were in rough shape when we got them from the thrift store, but now, they're straight-up ruined. There are gaping holes on either sole, with wads of paper towels and duct tape fashioned into some kind of stopgap. He must've been trying to fix the damage when he fell asleep.

A tear leaks down my cheek. Since he came to me, he's never done one single, solitary thing for himself. Everything he does is for his sisters. He makes Reagan eat her vegetables and he helps Caroline paint her nails. He does his chores *and* theirs. He checks their homework. He's eight years old and he's the last thing holding this broken family together.

So when he shyly admitted to me that he wanted to play basketball this year, I wanted so badly to make that happen for him.

But the money just couldn't work.

Ruslan pays me well, but New York City is expensive and New York City with three growing children (plus one adult-sized baby drinking all the beer) is even more expensive than that. Money just seems to disappear, leaking out through a million different holes. Clothes for school, utilities, rent, and this and that and the other.

Here one second. Gone the next.

Josh knows that. I don't even have to ask to guess that's why he was trying to fix his shoes himself instead of asking me to buy him a new pair.

I sink to the floor with my back against the wall and burst into tears. I do it silently because I don't want to wake him, but the sobs come from somewhere deep, deep down.

I hate how ashamed I am of these tears. Why should I be? If anyone has a reason to cry, it's me. My boss is an arrogant asshole and my sister is dead and her husband is more of a burden than a help and I have three innocent kids I'm doing my best to raise right but I can't seem to catch a break and I need sleep and food and more coffee and a vacation and a fresh start and—the list just goes on. One reason for each of my thousand tears.

It's only when they start to dry up that I force myself to think optimistically. *What would Sienna say?* I wonder. She can't answer, of course, but I have some guesses.

Things will get better. They have to.

They sure as hell can't get any worse.

2

EMMA

"Auntie Em! Auntie Em, wake up."

I come to with a start. The sun is slanting in through the blinds and I have absolutely no freaking idea what planet I'm on. I feel a sharp line of pain on my cheek. It takes me a long moment to realize that it's because I have a shoelace plastered to my skin. I peel it off with a wince and look up to see Josh standing over me.

"Auntie Em, it's 7:45. We're late for school."

"Shit!"

I leap to my feet—and promptly fall right back on my ass, because my legs are completely numb from sleeping in such a weird fetal position, curled up at the foot of Josh's desk like a dead cockroach.

The next fifteen minutes are a blur. I get the girls up and dressed in the least coordinated outfits in the history of shitty parenting. I hurl random food into their lunchboxes with no regard for nutritional value. And then we're all sprinting out the door.

Ben, needless to say, doesn't so much as lift a finger to help.

I get the evil eye from the receptionist at the kids' school when I drop them off well into first period, but she can shove her judgment up her ass. I just pop a kiss on each of their foreheads and then turn to haul ass to Bane.

I get another evil eye from the lobby receptionist there, too, but I don't quite realize why until I'm in the elevator up to the thirtieth floor and I catch sight of my reflection in the polished bronze.

I look like an absolute shitshow. My hair is a rat's nest on my head and my blouse is on backwards. The fashionable one-shoulder cutout is framing my frayed bra strap instead of a tasteful slice of bare arm.

Wet street dogs are more put-together than I am.

It's way too late to go back now, though. I can already imagine Ruslan's eyebrow. It's probably halfway up his scalp by now. His voice is going to be absolutely frigid when he hears me come stumbling in. Something like:

"You have got to be fucking kidding me."

Wait. That wasn't my imagination. *That was actually his voice.*

I open my eyes and turn around to realize that the elevator doors have opened—and who should be standing there but my beloved, benevolent boss?

Sure enough, his eyebrow is locked and loaded and that cruelly sharp jaw of his clenched so tight that I wonder idly if he has a good dentist on speed dial.

I open my mouth to defend myself, but what is there even to say? "I'm sorry," I blurt. "I fell asleep after—It was a long night and—I'm sorry. I'm so, so sorry."

He doesn't so much as blink. "I expect you to dress appropriately for your job, Ms. Carson," he growls. "Not do the walk of shame through my building."

I frown. "The walk of—? Hold on. No, that's not what this is. I didn't—"

"You're wearing yesterday's skirt and flaunting your undergarments like you think you can seduce your way out of being—" He checks his watch. "—two and a half hours late. I'm not sure if you think I'm stupid or easy. I'm also not sure which of those two would offend me more."

One word snags my attention. "Seduce?" I parrot stupidly.

Out of nowhere, thoughts of what it would look like to seduce Ruslan Oryolov come prancing through my head.

Wrapping his tie around my fist and bringing that smirking snarl down to my lips for a taste.

Lying back on his desk, pencil skirt hiked above my hips, while he shoves my panties to the side and devours me like his last meal.

On my knees on his office carpet as he stands over me and—

"Ms. Carson, I'm not interested in your explanations. Go do your job. Before I find someone else to do it for you."

With that, he brushes past me and gets on the elevator. I turn and look dumbly at him as the doors close on his face. The last thing I see is the arrogant slant of his mouth.

Then that, too, disappears.

My cheeks are burning red for the rest of the day. Luckily, I have an extra cardigan at my desk, so I'm able to cover up the worst of my wardrobe malfunction.

But my phone keeps pinging all day long with messages from Ruslan. *Do this. Send that. Fax this. Email that.* He's as unbearable as ever. Everything from the expiration date on his coffee creamer to the status of the conference room chairs he's so anal about merits yet another scathing comment from him. And after yesterday's nightmare, I'm running on fumes.

My only saving grace is that he has a gala tonight, so he's scheduled to leave the office at 5:00 P.M. sharp. I'm counting down the last ten seconds until the clock strikes five like I'm a Times Square partier on New Year's Eve.

"Seven… Six… Five… Four… Three… Two… One…"

Ping. Another text. I groan and look down to see the devil's name pop up on my phone.

RUSLAN: *My office. Now.*

Goddammit. I was so close.

Sighing, I get up and slink inside.

"Shut the door," he orders. It's dark in here. The curtains are sealed tight and the temperature is Arctic. He's a mass of shadows behind his desk, huge and fragrant. The only thing I can see is the sharp light of his amber eyes.

"Sit." A shadowy hand points at the chair across from his desk.

I perch at the edge of the seat in question. My nerves are buzzing and frayed. I'm so, so tired. But I can't show him that. Matter of fact, I *refuse* to show him that.

I won't give the smug bastard the satisfaction of thinking he's outlasted me.

"I asked you yesterday if I had your full attention," he begins. "I'm not so sure I do. So let me say this: if your priorities lie anywhere other than this company, then I will find a new assistant. I'm not a nice man, Ms. Carson. So believe me when I tell you that this is not the kind of place where you get three strikes before something bad happens. You mess up once—you're gone. Am I making myself clear?"

I swallow. "Yes, sir."

He nods. "Good. Be here on time tomorrow. Dress like you intend to keep your job. Now, if you'll excuse me… there's the door."

He looks down at his phone and *poof,* it's like I don't exist anymore.

But I. Am. Pissed.

He doesn't know what I'm going through. He doesn't know Ben is snoring and farting in my living room, or that three little kids are waiting on me to pick them up from after-school care. He doesn't know that I buried my sister or that I'm barely keeping my head above water. He doesn't know *anything.*

"No." I blurt it before I can think better of it. "No. *No.* I'm not some little worm under your shoe, *Mr. Oryolov.* I'm a—I mean, fuck you, I'm a person! I have a life and hobbies and people who depend on me. I'm real! So I'd appreciate it very much if you'd pull your smug head out of your smug asshole and treat me with some damn respect for once."

Ruslan blinks.

Blinks.

Blinks.

"Is there something else, Ms. Carson?"

That's when I realize that my whole little tirade took place entirely in my head. It wasn't real. All imagined. Just a pleasant little detour to a fantasy land where I give him my two cents and then some.

I swallow past the nasty taste in my throat and stand. "No, sir," I say quietly. "Nothing at all."

3

EMMA

"I'm gonna piss on his car."

Phoebe, my BFF, bursts out laughing on the phone. "You're gonna *what?* Em, I love you to bits, but you wouldn't even remind the bodega guy that you asked for no mustard on your sandwich last weekend. I don't think you have a rebellious bone in your body. You certainly don't have a 'pee-on-your-boss's-car' bone in your body."

I sigh. She's right. I hate it, but she's right. "It's bullshit that Sienna got all the rebellious genes," I mutter. "My whole DNA is wired to be compliant. Even the thought of talking back to him gives me hives."

"Aw, babe, don't sell yourself short. You're a firecracker when you wanna be. You're just sucking it up with Prince Douche Bag because you need this job to keep the kiddos in a good place. Food on the table, roof over their heads, all that. You're a martyr, seriously. They should make statues of you."

I snort and get off the train at my stop. "I'm good without that, thanks. I don't need statues of me. I'd just like to not be treated like I'm a second-class citizen at my place of employment."

"Well, if wishes were fishes, we'd all have something to eat," Phoebe says sagely.

"The hell does that mean?"

I can hear the shrug in her voice. "Beats me. Something my mom used to say. People from Oklahoma are weird; what can I tell ya?"

Phoebe's whole family is Dust Bowl-born and bred. She grew up outside of New York, right across the street from Sienna and me, but she inherited the accent and generations' worth of nonsensical folk wisdom.

"Seems like a pretty reasonable wish, though. It's just insane for him to tell me I'm not dedicated to his job. I'm there from dawn 'til dusk every freaking day. I dream in spreadsheets— did you know that? I literally have dreams about Ruslan's stupid color-coordinated calendar and to-do lists. Even when I'm sleeping, I'm working. It's insane."

"Preaching to the choir, baby girl. But go on; don't let me stop you."

People are looking at me funny as I mount the stairs from the subway station and climb back up to street level, but I don't care. All the things I wish I could tell Ruslan are pouring like word vomit from my lips.

"He's just so freaking smug! Where does he get off on that? Like, do you think he just goes home and looks in the mirror to cackle and twist his mustache like some evil comic book villain? Like, '*Muahaha, another successful day of ruining my secretary's life. Well done, Ruslan, well done indeed.*'"

"He has a mustache?"

"Pheebs. Focus."

"Right. Sorry. It's just that I had a very specific mental picture of him, you know? Tall, dark, that sexy, suggestive sort of smile that's like saying *You wanna get outta here?* without actually saying it… Six-pack abs, forearm veins—oh God, I do love some sexy forearm veins—and like, maybe a hot tattoo somewhere, but in a place where you gotta undress a little bit to see it so it's sorta like—"

"*Pheebs.* Not helpful.*"

"Right. Sorry."

The problem is just how accurate her description is. I've known since the very beginning of my employment at Bane that Ruslan is an asshole. But I've also known that he's a stupidly *attractive* one.

I've seen enough glimpses of his tattoos to want to see more. I've seen enough glimpses of that smile—it's rare, but it exists—to want him to turn it in my direction. Just once. Is that so much to ask?

Apparently, the answer is a resounding "yes."

Wearily, I thump up the stairs to my apartment. It's odd to be getting home before the sun has set. The kids are still in afterschool for another forty-five minutes and Ben is at a "job fair" (which is what they should officially rename the neighborhood bar), so I have a rare chunk of time to myself.

"Tell me something about you," I request as I unlock the front door.

"You're changing the subject," Phoebe accuses.

"I absolutely am. Indulge me."

She exhales. "Let's see, let's see... Went out with that hotshot chef dude last weekend."

"Oh? You do love forearms, don't you?"

"Guilty as charged. It was a good date, honestly. Oysters, as it turns out, are indeed an aphrodisiac."

"I take it you got lucky?"

Phoebe snorts. "*He* got lucky, you mean. It's not everyone who gets a chance to dine on the sweet nectar of my—"

"Yup," I interrupt hurriedly before she gets going too far gone to be stopped. "I get the picture. Also, I'm not saying *everyone* gets to, but by my count, lots of people do. There was the accountant—"

"He helped me do my taxes!"

"The zookeeper..."

"He promised I'd get to see his pet monkey!"

"The therapist, the oil rig worker, the PhD student..."

"Okay, okay, I get it. I'm a filthy whorish witch and I should be burned at the stake," she says hastily. "But one, it's the Year of Our Lord 2023, so slut-shaming is no longer socially acceptable. And two, sue me for living a little. I'm young and hot and I want to see what's on offer. You should do the same."

I giggle. She knows I'm not actually shaming her—it's mostly jealousy talking. I haven't been laid in so long that I'm terrified I'm sprouting cobwebs between my thighs.

"I know," I say with yet another weary sigh. "I should. I just… can't, you know? I mean, I don't have time and even if I did, I don't exactly have prospects beating down my door for a chance to take me out on a date."

"You would if you put yourself out there, babe," Phoebe says in her soft voice. "I know it's hard. I know you miss Sienna. I know you've got the kids to think about and Ben to ignore. But just… try, okay? Promise me you'll try. If there's anyone in your life who you could see yourself trying with, it's worth taking a shot. Tomorrow's never guaranteed, love. You and I know that better than anyone. So you owe it to yourself— and to all the people who love and depend on you—to be happy."

I drop my purse on my kitchen table and plop down on the armchair. Something wet crunches under me, which turns out to be a half-eaten Taco Bell burrito. Ben's handiwork, no doubt, along with the rest of the mess in the house that I *literally just cleaned yesterday.*

Grimacing, I extricate the taco and lob it into the nearby trash can. "You're right. I'll try."

"Pinky swear?"

"Yeah. Pinky swear."

"Okay," says Phoebe, sounding satisfied. "I've gotta go to Hot Girl Yoga. I love you with the white-hot intensity of a thousand suns. Give the little ones my love, too. Ta-ta."

Then she hangs up.

I let my hand fall into my lap. The phone slides into the gap between cushion and armrest, but I let it stay wedged there.

It's silent without my best friend's voice in my ear. Weirdly silent. I can't even remember the last time there was this little chaos in my vicinity. And if I close my eyes and ignore the mess, it's even more blissful.

For a moment, at least.

Then a face pops up on the black screen of my mind's eye.

It's Ruslan because, like I told Pheebs, he haunts me even when I'm off the clock. He's smiling that smile she described. That *come-to-bed-and-let-me-show-you-what-I-can-do-to-you* smile. The camera of my imagination pulls back and floats down.

Imaginary Ruslan is wearing an ivory white button-down shirt with the top two buttons undone. Enough to see a dusting of dark chest hair and the edge of a tattoo I can't quite make out. He flexes his forearms in front of him. Those knuckles crack, louder than I expected, and I let out a surprised little gasp.

I like when you make that noise, he croons. *Shall I see if I can make you do it again?*

I'm nodding before I'm even realizing what I'm doing. "Make me moan," I plead.

I'm also touching the inside of my knee before I realize what I'm doing. But it's not my hands that are doing it—or at least, it doesn't *feel* like it's my hands. It's Ruslan's hands, huge and powerful, palming my thigh and drifting up under the edge of my pencil skirt.

You've been a naughty assistant, he growls, breath minty in my face where it mingles with the woodsy spice of his cologne. There's a faint laugh on the edge of his voice, like he knows that this whole thing is crazy but he's just going with it because it's hotter than it is ridiculous. *You've been so very, very bad. Step into my office and shut the door.*

The rest of the world disappears like I just followed his orders. Gone is my messy apartment and the lingering smell of burrito cheese. *Ruslan* is all I smell now.

That cologne.

That breath.

Beneath it, that musk that sets my nerve endings on fire.

"Are you going to punish me, Ruslan?" I whisper.

You'd like that, wouldn't you? You'd love it if I bent you over my desk and unzipped that skirt until it puddled around your ankles. You'd love it if I spread my palm along your bare ass in a tender stroke before I raised it up and spanked you hard enough to make you yelp again. You'd go fucking crazy if I let my fingers wander down to knock your thighs apart and drag one slow, teasing fingertip through your wetness. You'd love all that, wouldn't you, Ms. Carson?

I'm chewing my lower lip frantically. My own hand dances up and touches the edge of my panties, then dips below and pushes them aside. I'm throbbing wet. Aching wet. The whisper of air-conditioned breeze on my pussy is almost enough to send me over the edge.

But that's the problem, Ms. Carson. You'd love it way, way too much. What kind of punishment would it be if you enjoyed every second of it? I have a better idea.

I'm on the literal edge of my seat, grinding and bucking against my fingers. Imaginary Ruslan has me eating out of the palm of his hand. I'd do anything for him. Say anything. Be anything.

"Yes, sir," I rasp. "You're right, sir. What did you have in mind?"

I'm going to start with what I just described. Bend you, tease you, spank you. Then I'm going to press you face-first flat against my desk while I drop down behind you and put my tongue where my fingers just were. I'm going to lap up every drop of you. At first, it'll be just the tip of my tongue. Just a fluttery light kiss to your pussy lips. I'll graze your clit and you'll push back against me, searching for more. But I'll pin you right back to the desk and snarl, Don't you dare fucking move unless I tell you to. *And what will you say to that?*

"I won't move, sir," I croak desperately. "I'll do exactly what you want me to do. I'll stay there while you eat me."

That's a good answer, Ms. Carson. It's the only way you'll get me to keep going. But if you're a good girl, if you listen and obey, then I will *keep going. My kisses between your thighs will turn into long drags of my tongue over you. Then I'll spread the lips of your pussy apart and go deeper. I'll push a finger between your folds, then another, and crook them to stroke against the deepest parts of you, the parts where just touching them makes you twitch like a live wire. I'll go faster and faster, pistoning in and out of you, while I devour your wetness, until your legs are trembling and those moans are loud music in my ears. How does that sound?*

"It sounds so fucking good, sir." I'm pumping in and out of myself. "Please do that. Please, please."

You're going to be right there. Right on the edge. You can feel it, can't you? The biggest orgasm of your life is right there for the fucking taking. All I have to do is lick you in a certain way while I do my fingers just like this and you're going to come for me like my special little princess, aren't you? I know it. You know it. We're both just waiting for the right moment. And it's coming, I promise you that. That moment is coming closer and closer and closer and closer and I'm licking and fingering and you're moaning and spasming and we're almostrightfuckingthere and then...

"And then what?" I scream. "And then what?"

And then I'm going to stop. I'm going to stand up and back away. I'm going to leave you there, a dripping, ruined fucking mess, as a reminder that, just like your heart and your mind and your body and your soul and your free time and your hopes and dreams... that just like all of that, your orgasms belong to me.

I come harder than I've ever come in my life, even as my lips form the most heart-wrenching "Nooo!" I've ever heard before.

It's like getting hit by a bus, if the bus was aimed directly at my clit and was also a trash compactor squeezing me from the inside out while lighting me on fire and then freezing me to ice from head to toe.

Imaginary Ruslan is every bit the cruel bastard that real Ruslan is. He said he'd keep my orgasms to himself, but I feel like I stole this one from him. The euphoria of it rips through me in one endless lightning bolt after the next, until finally, what feels like an hour later, I come back to something like normal consciousness with drool on my lips and my fingers wet and sticky with my own desire.

I stand on legs that are just as shaky as he said they'd be. My throat hurts from moaning and I'm sore as all get-out. As I stand, my phone clatters to the floor.

I reach down to pick it up—

And freeze in horror.

Ruslan's name is lighting up my screen.

And the call is active.

The reality of what is happening clicks in my gut immediately, but it takes a few delayed moments before my head comes to terms with it.

For seven minutes and thirty-two seconds, I've been on a call with Ruslan Oryolov.

For seven minutes and thirty-two seconds, I've been masturbating to the absolute filthiest fantasy I've ever had, *starring Ruslan Oryolov.*

For seven minutes and thirty-two seconds, my phone has been recording every last moan and gasp and breath and twitch I made while I begged for his mercy and pleaded for him to make me come.

Did Ruslan hear the whole damn thing?

4

RUSLAN

"Nosebleeds?"

"Minor blip. Nothing to worry about. We had a few bleeders in every trial." My lead chemist drags his feet over to the pristine white lab table where sets of test tubes sit in neat arrays, each brimming with a white liquid. He hems and haws, flipping through his notebooks like the answers to my irritation will be found in there.

Fucking scientists. They're brilliant.

They're also a pain in my goddamn ass.

I clear my throat. "Sergey, humor me here. What is Venera?"

His hooded eyes blink in confusion. He knows I know the answer, because Venera is the billion-dollar bet that will secure the future of the Oryolov Bratva; what he doesn't know is *why* I'm asking.

"It's, uh...it's an aphrodisiac with mildly hallucinogenic properties."

"Good job pretending I'm stupid. Keep it up. An aphrodisiac would be…?"

His blinks get faster and faster until I'm starting to worry he might malfunction. "I-it's an erotic st-stimulant. Designed to induce st-strong s-sexual urges."

"Excellent. Now, do nosebleeds strike you as particularly erotic, Sergey?"

He glances at his three labcoat-wearing proteges. They're standing in a neat line, inadvertently mimicking the test tube samples of Venera.

"No, sir."

"'No' is correct," I snarl. "Nosebleeds are *not* erotic. Therefore, it's not a 'minor blip.' It's a fucking problem. What I want to know is, *Is it fixable?*"

He gulps loud enough for me to hear him over the dull thunder of the lab equipment churning all around us. "I will try, sir."

I fix him with the infamous Oryolov glare that makes grown men want to piss their pants when they try to meet it. "Don't try. *Do it.*"

Sergey has a mind for science, but he doesn't see the bigger picture. That's also by design—because if he had any inkling of how much is riding on this drug launch, he'd curl up into the fetal position and never come out.

I've spread out billions of dollars in research and development, in bribes to cops and sign-on salaries to new drug dealers, in territory negotiations and raw material suppliers and this, that, and the other, all to pave the way for

Venera to hit the streets and take over this city like a fucking storm.

Venera is my future.

Venera is my legacy.

Venera is how we win.

A grunt behind Sergey alerts me to the stick-thin lab tech waiting at attention just behind him. His eyes are watery and timid and his lab coat is stained at the hem.

The moment my gaze lands on him, Sergey waddles aside like a well-trained seal. He's seen enough of my temper to know it's best to stay out of reach.

I saunter closer to the man who cleared his throat. "And you are...?"

His eyes twitch. Left and right. Left and right. "Mattias," he says at last.

"Do you have something you want to say to me, Mattias?"

Now, his jaw twitches, too. "We need to focus on correcting *all* the side effects, sir. Not just the ones that will affect your bottom line."

I almost want to laugh. Not very many people have the balls to challenge me to my face.

In my peripheral vision, I catch my second-in-command, Kirill, straightening up. He senses danger. So do the other two lab aides. Like Sergey, they distance themselves from the upstart immediately.

"Seems like you disapprove of my decisions, Mattias."

He holds his soft chin up high. "Maybe I do."

My glare doesn't seem to have much of an effect on him, but the slow smile that curls over my mouth certainly does. Fear flits across his eyes and he takes a half-step back.

"I'm going to offer you one chance to step back in line."

His jaw clicks in place. "I—"

"Too slow."

I pull out a gun and shoot the *mudak* right between his squinty eyes.

Cue screams. Cue chaos. Cue bloodshed. All the usual music.

The other aides go scrambling in every direction, hurling themselves under the lab table and behind flimsy wire shelves. Sergey is the only one who remains standing, but judging from his sheet-white complexion, it's a shock reaction to the fact that one of his underlings is lying on the floor with a hole where his face once was.

When I turn to Sergey, he springs back, nearly upending the table with all the Venera samples. "S-Sir…"

"Calm the fuck down, everyone." Kirill's tone is equal parts impatience and amusement as he addresses the terrified room. "That smug motherfucker had a target on his forehead the moment he decided to sell sensitive intel to our competitors."

Sergei's eyes bug out. "Mattias did *what?*"

The lab techs have glommed onto the workbenches that hug the walls of the lab, chins wobbling like toddlers who've shit their pants.

Good. They'll work harder after this. Fear is an extremely effective motivator.

"Did any of you know about this?" I ask them.

I know they didn't. I've had full-scale background checks done on each of them. I know where their mothers live, where they hide their money, where their childhood pets are buried. I know things about them they've forgotten about themselves. Now that Mattias is dead, the whole crew is squeaky clean, but I need to make sure they stay that way. I can't afford another breach like this one.

"N-no...!"

"I swear, sir. I had no idea."

"We would never."

"Please..."

"Enough!" I barely raise my voice, but both of the stuttering scientists clamp their mouths shut. "Let this be a warning. Traitors will be shown no mercy. I will be judge, jury, and executioner and I'm not exactly impartial. Is that understood?"

I'm met with a desperate silence. Heads bob frantically. Satisfied, I snap my fingers and signal over two of my men. "Take out the trash. I'm sure Sergey doesn't appreciate us contaminating his floors with that traitor's blood."

Sergey looks as though the cleanliness of his floors is the very last thing on his mind. The color still hasn't returned to his face.

"The launch will take place soon. I need everything to go smoothly."

"Of c-course, sir."

"Bane Corp. exists to protect the movements of this Bratva. Without my façade as a respectable CEO, I can't run my empire or protect the people under its wings. You understand that, don't you, Sergey?"

He dips his chin so low that he's in danger of snapping his neck. "Yes, sir."

"One mole is forgivable, but a second would raise questions about your competency to pick your own personnel."

"*Pakhan*, I swear—"

I hold up my hand to shut him down. "I'm not interested in excuses. I want fucking *results*. Now, get back to work and get this drug back on track. We're running up against the clock here."

Sergey nods once more, then disappears into the chemical storage room on the right. I chuckle—he'd rather be cooped up with cyanide than with me.

Good choice.

Kirill watches Sergey's clumsy lope until the poor bastard is gone. "Do you think he's up to the challenge?"

"He better be. I don't have the patience for any more delays."

"Patience has never been high on your list of virtues, brother."

Smirking, Kirill and I head out of the lab, shedding our protective lab coats along the way. More lab rats part like the Red Sea as we step aboveground, into the belly of the sprawling facility I purchased to birth this drug into the world. It cost me a pretty penny, but this investment is about to earn us a colossal return—*if* we can perfect Venera before its launch date a few weeks from now.

"I want eyes in that lab twenty-four-seven," I instruct Kirill. "I want every single chemist on this project to be monitored around the clock. Disloyalty won't be tolerated."

Kirill starts tapping at the screen on his phone. "Got it, boss. I'll get a team on them ASAP."

I frown when I notice the voicemail alert on my screen. It's a name that really pisses me off. *What the fuck does she want at this hour?*

"Seven minutes and thirty-two seconds," I mutter. "Fuck me."

"Something wrong?"

"I may need to get myself a new assistant."

"What for? You have a great one. And, added bonus, she's easy on the eyes."

Kirill may have a point—I just don't like the fact that he's made it.

Correction: I don't like the fact that he's *noticed* her in order to make it.

In my mind's eye, I see a flash of her as she was this morning. Not her usual put-together self, but another version entirely. Nervous, flustered, unkempt. I keep seeing the shoulder of her bra strap, the way her breast peeked out of the cup just enough to give me an eyeful of cleavage.

It was unprofessional. Lazy. Annoying. Distracting.

And *tempting.*

Way too fucking tempting.

"She's been dropping the ball recently."

"Enough said. Just give her a good tongue lashing and she'll pick that ball right back up."

I wince. The mention of tongues has me wondering just how much damage I could do to her with mine.

I imagine myself throwing her onto my desk just so that I can push her skirt up and see what those pencil skirts are hiding. It'd be so easy. She'd gasp and moan so fucking deliciously, I can already tell. I'm hard at the mere thought. Although some of that is just pent-up tension. I've piled a hell of a workload on myself, so it's been a long time since I've been with a woman.

"If she's called to give me some bullshit excuse about why she can't come in tomorrow, I'm kicking her to the curb."

"Your choice," says Kirill with a shrugged shoulder.

I walk over to my SUV while Kirill texts some last-minute instructions to my *vors* carrying out Bratva business across the five boroughs. The chauffeur opens the door and I climb into the backseat. Reluctantly, I start listening to Emma's voicemail, which I'm sure is going to be an unnecessary harangue of half-baked excuses and furtive apologies.

I stop short when a series of muffled sounds hits my ear. No coherent words seem to be forthcoming. Is this some sort of prank? A joke? No—what it is is a waste of my time. I'm just about to cut off the message and text my HR manager to open up a new job posting...

When I hear a single breathy moan.

Is this what I think it is?

Her voice comes through a second later. Heated, aroused, filled with a desperate urgency. It takes me a moment to realize what she's saying.

She moans a name—*my* name.

And just like that, I'm hooked.

5

RUSLAN

"Are you going to punish me, Ruslan?"

Never have I wanted something so bad. My knuckles are white with tension as I grip the phone to my ear, hungry for every last moan and sigh and gasp that pops out of that dirty little mouth of hers.

My cock strains against the fabric of my pants, desperate to be freed. But I have a dozen men spread out across the upper floors of the chem facility and Kirill is walking towards the car, curiosity etched across his brow.

"Yes, sir. You're right, sir. What did you have in mind?"

Jolts of electricity race through my core hearing her play out this little fantasy. I can only imagine what *watching* her would do to me.

In the eighteen months Ms. Carson has been working for me, I haven't gotten so much as a hint of impropriety. Maybe this is my fault. Maybe that dig about her half-assed attempt at seducing me this morning unleashed the siren.

Or maybe this was a mistake. There's a chance she's unaware that she even sent me the voicemail. It *is* an unforgivable seven-and-a-half minutes long. And maybe thoughts of what I could do to her are just *that* distracting.

She groans deeply. Sounds of skin meeting skin. I can actually *hear* how wet she is.

"What's going on?"

I rearrange my expression and pause the voicemail. "Nothing. I'll have Boris drop you off first."

Kirill arches a brow but he doesn't push me as he clambers into the backseat. The surging possessiveness racing through me is not unfamiliar. I'm a possessive man and I don't like sharing my things. But that rule has never really applied to women.

Placing ownership on any woman just gives her a claim over me. That's been an inconvenience I've managed to avoid so far in my life. I'm not in any hurry to change things.

The whole way to Kirill's place, my knee keeps bouncing impatiently.

"You sure you're okay, brother?" he asks.

"Just preoccupied with the launch," I lie easily.

The moment we drop Kirill off at the entrance to his apartment building, I have my phone back in my hand and I'm reopening Emma's voice mail. I press play.

"Fuck me," I mutter.

The woman puts on a show tailor-made for me. Every time she refers to me as "*sir*" in that soft whimper, my cock jumps needily. The little hitches in her breathing mirror my own.

By the time we get to my downtown penthouse, I'm wondering if my dick will ever go down. Not that I've made much of an attempt to help.

"Thanks, Boris. See you tomorrow at six."

"Got it, boss."

I take the elevator up to the thirty-fifth floor after punching in my private access code. The doors open directly into my penthouse.

I'm a busy man, so it helps me to compartmentalize my life. That goes for my properties, too. Some are for business, others for pleasure—and this one on Madison Avenue, the grandest of my skyrise real estate, is just for me.

I come here when I'm craving peace and quiet, when I want to be completely alone with my thoughts.

Or with my assistant's filthy fucking fantasies.

There's no peace and quiet to be found here tonight. The only thing swimming around in my head is Ms. Carson. Her pert little mouth. Those innocent almond eyes. The way her ass moves when it's sheathed in a silk dress.

I'm not blind—I noticed her the moment she stepped into my office for the final interview. Her attractiveness wasn't the reason I hired her, though. In fact, I'd hired her *despite* her looks. No man needs to have constant temptation walking around in high heels and a red lip.

But her credentials and experience were all above board and I was sick of the revolving door of morons that darkened my doorstep with their ineptitude and emotional baggage. The assistant who preceded Emma quit, right before she burst

into tears and called me a "psychopath in Hermes." I had
Kirill get that printed on my business cards.

So when Emma stepped into the role, despite a few freshman
kinks, it was like a breath of fresh air. She was smart,
competent, and she didn't complain.

Not that I didn't know *exactly* when she was pissed off or
frustrated with me. Her blue eyes have this way of darkening
and there is a vein in her forehead that twitches anytime I
order her around or give her a task she considers beneath
her.

It's been my way of keeping her busy and far away—so that
she didn't end up beneath me.

Of course, now, I don't have to imagine what she'd sound like
if I were to pin her to the wall and run my fingers between
her thighs.

I've listened to that damn voicemail twice already. Any more
replays and I'm in danger of doing something stupid.

Like masturbating while I think about all the different ways
I'd ravage her body.

Undressing, I walk to the leather recliner set up in front of
the floor-to-ceiling window.. I manage to resist my phone
for a full three minutes before picking it back up once again.

This time, when I start playing the voicemail, I put it on
speaker.

Her moans fill what was supposed to be a blissful Zen
silence. My cock braces against my pants, but I refuse to
touch myself. I'm happy with the idea that I'm the star of her
spank bank material, but I certainly don't want her in mine.

But the way she cries out my name as she touches herself… *Fucking hell,* it's the most erotic thing I've heard in my entire goddamn life. That and the sound of her fingers making contact with her pussy. The slippery wetness thrums just underneath her moans, getting faster and faster as she delves deeper into the fantasy.

"It sounds so fucking good, sir. Please do that. Please, please."

"Blyat'!" I pause the voicemail mid-moan.

I need to fucking delete it. That's the right move; I know that. But even as my finger hovers over the delete button, I can't bring myself to pull the trigger.

I *should* fucking punish her for this. Impaling her on my cock seems like a pretty fitting punishment right about now.

I fast forward almost to the end of the message and press play again. She's well past moaning now. She's practically screaming. I can easily imagine her tight little body shuddering as the orgasm rips through her. It gives me a perverse sense of satisfaction to know that I'm responsible for that orgasm, no matter how indirectly.

Her breathing flutters a little and then it hitches up again just at the very end. A thump. A shocked gasp. Muffled static— then, two seconds later, the message ends.

I'm willing to bet that my prim and proper little secretary had no intention of sending me that voice message. Hell, she probably had no idea she even called me in the first place.

What an irreversible mistake.

I wonder what else that mouth is capable of.

Leaving my phone on the recliner, I head to the en suite bathroom in the master. I strip off my boxers and get into the shower, cranking the water as cold as possible. I force myself to freeze beneath the hailstorm for ten long minutes, until my erection finally gives up the fight and eases.

There's no way I can avoid addressing this little slip-up tomorrow morning. Which leaves me with only two options: fire her or fuck her.

My cock likes the second option a little too much. "Down, boy," I growl, unwilling to endure another fifteen-minute ice bath.

Ignoring my bed, I sit down at the sleek black desk. The light from my personal laptop illuminates the room with an eerie silver glow. A quick search is all it takes to find Emma's file in my employee database. Her photo gleams at the top of the page. Innocent-looking. White blouse, red lipstick, a self-conscious smile.

But it's impossible to look at her and see her the same way anymore.

Not when I know how it sounds when she comes undone.

Each file includes a full background check on all my employees. Everyone has skeletons in their closet; I just prefer to know how many before I put them on the payroll.

As it turns out, Emma Carson was practically a Girl Scout up until about three and a half years ago, when she abruptly inherited a ton of debt. I give the file a quick scan. The debt is innocent enough, just run-of-the-mill life bullshit. Mortgage. Student loans. Inflation. Funeral home. The kind of shit normal people have to deal with if they don't have rich spouses or rich daddies.

But it gives me an idea.

After all, there's nothing sexier than the air-tight boundaries of a mutually beneficial arrangement. It's like Sergey's lab—nothing can go wrong if you keep it contained. Bottle dangerous shit up in a test tube and it becomes a tool, a weapon, a product.

It's when you let the chemistry explode on its own that shit goes wrong.

I pick up my phone once again and scroll through the contacts. My lawyer Isay's voice is cracked with sleep when he picks up. "Boss?"

I don't bother apologizing for waking him up. I pay my people enough to be able to demand twenty-four-hour attention whenever I need it.

"I need you to draw up a contract for me. Immediately."

6

EMMA

"It's over. My life as I know it is over. R.I.P. to me."

"I'm sorry, who is this?"

"Pheebs!"

She chuckles while I stare at my reflection in the mirror and try not to throw up. My phone is lying on the bathroom counter on speakerphone, mostly because my palms have been sweating since I saw the meeting invite in my calendar for today.

9:00 A.M. – 09:07:32 A.M.: Emma Carson 1-on-1 with Ruslan Oryolov.

"Sorry. Couldn't resist. Anyway, rewind, take a deep breath, then tell me what's going on in your big girl voice. Unburden yourself. Take all the time you need. Just make it quick because I have a 9 o'clock appointment."

I'm bouncing on the balls of my feet now, the same way that Reagan does when she needs to pee really bad. "Yeah, so do I. With *him*."

"Ah. Oh, wait—*oh.*"

I first called Phoebe last night right after realizing what I'd done. Her reaction was a dizzying mixture of pride and horror. I believe her exact words were, "*Sure, it's mortifying, but I'm glad you got your rocks off. Knew you had it in you.*"

She's a little more reassuring now that things are escalating out of control. "That doesn't necessarily mean he heard the voicemail, Em. Maybe this is just a standard, no-big-deal, super-boring-business-stuff Thursday morning meeting."

"It's scheduled for seven minutes and thirty-two seconds. Precisely."

"Hm." There's a beat of silence. "Doesn't look good, does it?"

"Seriously? That's all you've got for me? I'm gonna lose my job, Phoebe!"

"You don't know that for sure. Just take a deep breath and go in there, see what he wants. Play it cool, y'know?"

"And what if what he wants is to kick my ass to the curb with a recommendation letter that claims I'm a dirty whore with mediocre phone sex skills?"

"I mean, there's probably a market for that." I groan as Phoebe's laughter fades into a serious tone. "Listen, boo: whatever happens, you're a strong, smart, confident woman and you're gonna land on your feet. And until you do, I've got your back."

Her words mean everything to me, but I know that Phoebe doesn't have much margin for error in her life, either. She struggles just as hard as I do. If she *is* able to help, it still wouldn't put a dent in all the bills and loans looming over me.

"Thanks for the pep talk. I've gotta go to my doom now."

"Keep your pecker up!"

I blink. "Huh?"

"Oklahoma talk. It means, like, 'break a leg,' but for Midwesterners."

If I weren't worried about losing my job and ending up homeless on the street with three kids, I'd laugh. Instead, I say one more miserable goodbye, then spend a solid three minutes dry-heaving into one of the empty bathroom stalls.

Once I've sufficiently bruised my stomach lining, I slink out of the bathroom and waste the remaining two minutes before the meeting standing outside of Ruslan's door, watching the clock steal my life away one second at a time.

"You okay, Emma?" asks Katie Miller, another of the executive assistants on this floor, as she passes by.

"Dandy," I mumble. "Just waiting for the noose."

"What was that?"

"Nothing. I like your earrings. Have a good day."

She raises her brow a smidge. I'm not usually so dismissive, but I can't concentrate on small talk right now. Not when I'm T-minus thirty seconds away from the end of my career.

Dear God, I know I don't pray to you often. Or, well, ever. But please *help me out today and I'll definitely consider starting on a more semi-regular basis.*

Great. Now, I'm bargaining with God. *New low, Emma. New low.*

I take a deep breath and walk into his office. The shades are tight, snuffing out all the light of the Manhattan morning beyond. It's like a bear cave in here—and the grizzly in question is sitting at his desk, scrolling through his phone. He doesn't acknowledge me until I'm standing in front of his desk.

"Sit."

The moment my rear end is parked, he puts his phone down and looks at me. Just *looks* at me.

In the eighteen months that I've worked for him, he's never once given me the benefit of his full attention. Even during our morning meetings, he's either on his phone, flipping through files, or typing away on his laptop. I used to be annoyed about it. I'm only now realizing I should have been grateful.

Should I say something?

Maybe he wants me to break the silence. Maybe I'm supposed to give him an explanation, an apology, *something*. But the more the silence stretches on, the less I'm capable of breaking it.

I decide once again that those amber eyes of his should be outlawed.

"I heard the voicemail," he says at last.

I can't place his tone. Amusement? Anger? Disbelief?

"Do you have anything to say, Ms. Carson?"

I launch into the apology I spent most of last night practicing in the mirror. "I can't tell you how sorry I am, Mr. Oryolov. I have *no* idea what I was thinking. The whole thing was an accident; I didn't realize I'd dialed you. I was so tired and out of it and… I can assure you that it will *never* happen again. I swear."

My cheeks are flushed with embarrassment, but I try to keep my voice steady. I can't sound too desperate, although that's exactly what I am.

"Tell me, Ms. Carson: what would you do in my place?"

"I would give the plucky, hard-working assistant another chance, maybe?" It's a long shot, but I figure, what the hell? I just wish I'd asked it without my voice rising to an *Alvin and the Chipmunks* pipsqueak at the end.

His mouth twitches with the promise of a smile, but it's gone as quick as it came. "I know what you sound like when you orgasm, Emma. Is that the soundtrack you want running through all our interactions from now on?"

Flushing the brightest of reds, I shake my head. "If we could maybe just forget this whole thing—"

"The way I see it, there are only two options here."

I hold my breath.

"One, I fire you."

There it is. I knew it. I'm done for. I'm going to need to call the welfare office and see what—

"Or two… I give you exactly what you want."

I almost choke on my own saliva. What little is left in my gaping mouth. "W-what?"

Silently, Ruslan offers me the blue folder lying in front of him. I pick it up with shaky hands and open the cover. It takes me a few long moments to figure out what on earth I'm looking at.

A… contract?

I read through the first page, feeling a strange sensation bubble up in my chest. Then, since I'm clearly misunderstanding something, I read through the first page again. And again. And again.

Only then do I look up. "Is this a joke?"

He doesn't blink. "I never joke."

"It's just that, it seems like, from what I read, um—"

"I will offer you money and security in exchange for live encores of the little performance you sent me last night. In addition to meeting my other needs."

"And by 'needs,' you mean…sex?"

He tilts his chin down and regards me solemnly. "How explicit would you like me to be, Ms. Carson?"

What.

"So this—" I raise the blue folder in my hand. "—is a sugar daddy contract?"

His brow furrows. "I'd prefer to call it a 'Friend With Benefits' contract."

"But we're not friends."

He smirks. "Fair enough. No, we're not."

There's a throbbing in my head that reminds me of the first time I got drunk. Sienna and I had snuck into Dad's study the eve of my sixteenth birthday and stolen a 1984 Chateau Latour. We passed it back and forth, taking turns sipping from the bottle like it was cheap bagged wine until the whole thing was gone.

For a moment, I think about what Sienna would say if she were here. Would she be outraged or intrigued? Would she slap the smug asshole and storm out?

Or would she grin and say, *Double the price and I'm in.*

What would you do, Si?

And then it hits me, a bolt of lightning straight to the chest, almost like she's speaking to me herself. I miss her so much, it hurts. But she left little bits of herself behind, in all three of her children. The same kids I'm working my ass off to protect.

That right there is the answer.

Sienna would have done whatever was best for her children.

So I don't slap him. I don't storm out. I sit there and stare at my arrogant, asshole boss who always gets exactly what he wants.

And what he wants… is *me*.

I meet Ruslan's steely gaze. "What happens if I say no?"

He shrugs as though this is just another job interview for him and he has a thousand other candidates lined up behind me. "If you say no, I'll let you go with a generous severance package, a glowing recommendation, and no mention of the phone call."

It's a relief, but it doesn't come close to comforting me.

"But if you say yes…" His eyes turn a dark, liquid gold. "It will definitely be worth your while. I have *many* skills, Ms. Carson, and they're not limited to business."

My cheeks feel like they're on fire. I'm sure he sees it.

He leans against his leather wingback. "It's entirely up to you."

I stare at the contract in my lap. It's not a small decision by any stretch of the imagination. "Can I have some time to think about this?"

"You can have today off. I expect your answer by tomorrow."

He's not really giving me a whole lot of time, but I think we both know more time will only confuse me. Maybe it's better this way.

I start to stand when he says, "One more thing, Ms. Carson."

So I freeze, ass hovering over the seat. "Yes?"

"This stays between the two of us." His expression turns deadly. I've seen that look on his face in the boardroom, right before he pounces on some poor fool who was stupid enough to question him. "If you tell a soul about the contract, the deal is off. No protection, no recommendations, no pension—and I have every means to utterly destroy your chances of employment in any capacity ever again. Am I making myself clear?"

I gulp hard. "Crystal."

"Good. Then you're excused."

It's the normal goodbye routine. He picks up his phone, his gaze drops, and just like that, I go back to being a nobody. No one would guess that a few moments ago, he was propositioning me for sex. For *contracted* sex.

I have a lot to process.

I grab my stuff and race out of the building, trying to remember the last time I had a day off. It still doesn't feel like a free day; it feels like a weight sitting squarely on my chest. A weight that gets heavier and heavier with every passing minute.

I take the subway over to Central Park and find a bench in a shady corner. I pull out the contract folder and stare at the cover, gathering up the strength to start reading. Then, with a sigh, I dive in.

Twenty minutes later, I have a growing headache and a pro-con list that's pulling me at both ends.

Pro: The money is amazing. I'd be able to actually take care of the kids without worrying so damn much every second of every day.

Con: I would be exchanging sex for money.

Pro: I'll be able to pay off the loans faster.

Con: Ruslan Oryolov is an influential man with possible mob connections. All rumors, but in my opinion, there's no smoke without fire.

Pro: He also happens to be a very, very, *very* attractive influential man with possible mob connections.

Con: He's an asshole.

Pro: He's an asshole who's probably *great* in bed.

I close the contract after staring at the Non-Disclosure section of the agreement for what feels like an eternity.

If rumors of Ruslan's supposed mob ties are to be believed, I would be exposing the kids to danger. It just feels like too big a risk. Which is why, when I put the contract back in my bag and get to my feet, I feel like I've made my decision.

It's too crazy, too reckless, too insane of a deal for me to agree to. I can't compromise myself that way and I can't let this decision bleed into the kids' lives. Isn't it more important that they're safe?

Okay. Done. Decision made. Goodbye forever, Ruslan Oryolov.

So why don't I feel right about it?

7

RUSLAN

I've had a single question circulating in my head since seven minutes and twenty-three seconds after the top of the hour, when Emma walked out of my office with the contract tucked under her arm.

Will she surrender?

There's a chance she'll turn me down straight-up. I'm prepared for that. What I'm not prepared for is the nauseating churn in my gut when I consider her walking out my door for good.

Which is fucking bullshit, of course. What do I care about one woman in a city of millions? I could hurl my desk chair out of my office right this second and hit a dozen willing prospects on the way down. A dozen eager *yeses* who'd sign without bothering to read a single line of my love life contract.

Correction: not my love life, my *sex* life. I have no interest in love. I made that decision thirteen years ago when I saw what loving a woman would cost me.

I've dawdled away the evening, left aimless by the lack of an assistant. Without Emma to keep my life in line, I've simply canceled everything on my calendar, clearing a block of empty time to do nothing but obsess over what answer she'll bring back to me tomorrow.

So I'm glad for the distraction when my father and uncle stroll into my office. Both are working members of Bane Corp., with offices in the building, though neither one bothers to actually come in very often.

That's the secret to keeping up the appearance of legitimacy: sometimes, things actually need to be legitimate.

"Where's your assistant?" Uncle Vadim asks, taking the left chair opposite my desk.

"She's taking a sick day."

My father, Fyodor, scans my desk. "You should have two assistants. For just such an instance." He has just a hint of an accent, unlike my uncle, whose Russian bark is anything but subtle.

"It's hard enough finding *one* competent assistant. I can't imagine finding two." I really don't want to talk about Emma any more than I have to think about her, so I change the subject smoothly. "How about dinner? Kirill's on his way here. He can pick something up for us."

I text Kirill and tell him to bring food. Then I turn my attention to the elder Oryolov brothers.

At sixty-five, Vadim is still spry. His piercing blue gaze carries a touch of menace from the old days, back when my father was *pakhan* and Vadim was his second.

Fyodor, on the other hand, who's just five years older than his brother, looks every bit his age. People call time the subtle thief of youth, but they're all wrong. It's not time that's the thief—it's sorrow.

"Why are the two of you darkening my doorstep today?"

Vadim speaks first, which is strange. There used to be a time when Vadim wouldn't even sit until Fyodor gave the word. But that was a different time, a different *pakhan*.

"We signed another client. Williamson something or other."

I loft a brow. "The basketball player?"

"That's the one." There's a note of smug satisfaction in Vadim's voice. "He wasn't happy with his previous security company. Enter Bane Corp."

That's easily a ten-million-dollar account, but I merely nod. I learned a long time ago that my uncle considers praise to be offensive. Or rather, he considers praise from *me* to be offensive. In his eyes, he was the one who was supposed to be handing down orders. He was the one who was supposed to wear the mantle of *pakhan*.

But he got short-changed when Fyodor decided to pass him over in the wake of the accident. Instead, at twenty-one, I assumed the crown and my uncle was forced to fall in line behind me. But fall in line he did, because no one fucks with a *pakhan*'s decision.

By the time Kirill walks in with our food, I'm starving. We spread the takeout boxes across my desk and fall silent as we eat.

I stuff my face with pita and shawarma and try not to think about Emma. But despite the conversation rotating through half a dozen equally irrelevant topics, my mind keeps sliding back to her. She showed up today looking extra put-together. Probably intending to counteract her dazzling lack of professionalism from yesterday. High heels, a moss green skirt, a cheap leather choker around her throat. Her hair was pulled back so tight that it made me want to rip it out of the bun just so I could use it to rein her in.

I can just imagine the filthy things she would whimper to me with those plump, red-stained lips. *Punish me, Mr. Oryolov. Fuck me. Do whatever you want, sir.*

Kirill snaps his fingers in front of my face. The fantasy dissolves. "Yo, bro? Where'd you go?"

"Just preoccupied with the launch." I focus on the last of the meat on my plate, but I can feel their eyes on me.

"You can't let this consume you," Vadim offers sagely. "All work and no play makes for a dull *pakhan.*"

He hides his resentment well these days, but I still hear it, in the sliced edge of his tone any time he mentions my title directly.

"I'll focus on playing after Venera is launched successfully."

Fyodor looks at me, his lips poised to speak before he clamps them shut abruptly. Every year, he seems to recede more and more into himself.

You don't have to believe in ghosts to be haunted by them.

Vadim reaches for another piece of the shawarma with bare, greasy fingers. "Playing is good. You know what's better? *Fucking.* And no one is easier to fuck than a wife."

Kirill nearly chokes on his roast chicken. I fix my uncle with an unruffled stare. I know better than to let him rattle me. "Marriage is not on the table for me."

Vadim sighs like I'm too stupid to understand. "You can't escape your responsibilities forever, Ruslan. You need heirs. Only one way to make that happen."

I take a sip of my beer and wait before answering. "There's still time."

"When you're young, you think life is infinite. It's not. Better to secure your legacy sooner rather than later." My jaw clenches, but Vadim pays no heed to the warning. "An heir is good. Two, three, four heirs are even better. Look what happened to Fyodor: he had two heirs and he lost one to a fucking red light at the intersection."

I don't have to look at my father to know how badly those words wound him. He's carried that loss on his sleeve for thirteen years. It makes me furious that Vadim would bring it up so casually. That he would bring it up at all.

He, more than anyone else, saw how my father unraveled after the car crash.

"At least Otets *had* children. What have you contributed to the Bratva, Uncle?"

Vadim flinches back, pale blue eyes glinting. Fyodor clears his throat awkwardly. Kirill keeps shifting in his seat.

No one says anything for a long time.

Then, finally, Vadim breaks the silence. "I've upset you. I apologize."

Fyodor looks between us. On the one hand, I'm his son snapping at his brother. On the other, I'm their *pahkan* and that sets me apart. No—it sets me *above*.

In the end, my father drops his gaze and leaves it for Vadim and me to hash out.

"There are other ways to secure a legacy," I growl. "You should understand that better than anyone."

I'm extending him an olive branch, but he still squirms in his seat and gnashes his teeth. "No, it's true; my legacy will not be left to an heir." He doesn't meet my eyes when he talks. "A young man's mistake. An old man's regret."

"Your uncle was simply trying to give you the benefit of his wisdom, Ruslan." Fyodor's words are soft.

I sigh and relent. The last thing I feel like doing now is squabbling with my uncle over his petty grievances. "Your wisdom is welcome in all matters of business and Bratva, uncle. You know I value your opinion."

Vadim smiles wryly. He's smart enough to understand exactly what I mean. *Keep your opinions on my personal life to yourself.* "Of course, *pakhan.* I will always be here when you need me."

Fyodor seizes the moment and stands. "We should head home. I've been away from my garden too long."

Kirill shows them out. When they're gone, I stare at the mess of food containers on my desk. Normally, it's something I'd order Emma to handle. I'd hide my amusement, watching as the vein in her forehead throbbed with irritation. I could probably make that vein disappear altogether if I just spread her legs wide and fucked her on top of all the empty cartons.

Make her beg for me to stop. It would take a lot of begging, though...

Fuck me. I need to put that little siren out of my head.

But the conversation with Vadim has me thinking. Marriage is definitely not on my to-do list. Heirs may be on the list, but far, far down. Which means I have time. Time to waste on my pert little assistant. Time to enjoy her whenever I want, wherever I want, in whatever position I want. *Without* the inconvenience of expectations.

But first, she needs to say yes.

8

EMMA

By the time I get to the apartment, I actually feel halfway good about my decision.

Sure, it won't be easy not knowing when my next paycheck will be, but I have one last life raft left that I'm hoping will hold us over until I find another job.

It's gonna be okay, Emma. It's gonna be—

Then I open the door to an apartment that can't possibly be mine. Because this place is an absolute mess. This can't be mine—I just cleaned it top to bottom literally a day ago. Did I walk into the neighbor's place by accident?

But then—

"Auntie Em!"

My heart drops, but I plaster a fake smile on my face and spread my arms as Reagan and Caroline beeline straight for me.

"Hey, you little monsters." I catch them both, a kid under each arm, and squeeze hard, lifting them off the floor a few feet. Reagan squeals, Caroline giggles, and I try desperately not to burst into tears.

You're fine. It's just the stress talking.

The living room is a disaster. The toys I boxed are out of the crate once more, clothes and books are everywhere, and there's a trail of chip dust covering the floor. From the bright orange stain on the carpet, I'm guessing Cheetos are the culprit here.

"So who wants to tell me what happened here, guys?" I ask when I've released them.

Reagan looks around the living room proudly. "Josh had to finish homework, so we played Twister."

"Twister?"

Reagan's head bobs up and down. "Yeah, Aunt Phoebe said they have those in Oak-loma."

"Remind me to thank Aunt Phoebe for that. Where's your dad?"

"He has a headache." Caroline pouts. "So he's resting."

Right. "Headache." Another one of Ben's code words. "Headache" means "hangover," just like "job fair" means "happy hour" and "doctor's appointment" means "I ran out of beer, so I went to the bodega to get more."

"For God's sake," I mutter under my breath, "it's not even six o'clock."

"Aunt Emma! Can we play Twister with you?"

"How about we play Post-Apocalyptic Clean-up Crew instead?"

Reagan starts booing me, though I'm pretty sure she has no idea what "post-apocalyptic" means, and Caroline starts jumping on the couch, singing a steady stream of "no's.

My head spins as I retreat to the kitchen. "Oh God, what's that smell?"

I follow my nose to the stove, where I find my favorite Betty Crocker pan covered in a thick layer of burnt sludge. I couldn't decipher what it was if my life depended on it. I probably should be grateful the smoke alarm didn't go off because the landlady always raises a fuss when that happens, but all I can think is, *There's fifty bucks down the drain.*

"Did you guys try cooking by yourselves?" I ask the girls when they follow me into the kitchen.

"We said we were hungry, so Dad made us some food," Caroline explains.

I should've known. This has Ben's fingerprints written all over it.

"Yeah, but it tasted yucky," Reagan adds, scrunching her button nose up so tight it practically disappears. "So we threw it away."

"You guys haven't eaten anything at all?"

Caroline balances herself against the table and kicks her legs up behind her. "Josh made us peanut butter and jelly sandwiches."

"But that was aaaaages ago," Reagan complains. "I'm hungry again."

I grab the pan and fill it with water and leave it in the sink to soak. Maybe there's some hope of salvaging it. "Let's see what's in the fridge for dinner, shall we?"

I notice that the grocery list I'd made last week is still tacked up on the fridge. *Goodness gracious, the hits just keep coming.* "Um, did your dad go to the grocery store today?"

Both girls shake their heads in unison. "He said he was busy," Caroline offers with a shrug.

Gritting my teeth, I open the fridge and look inside. There's nothing there but stale leftovers that I've neglected to throw out.

And beer. Lots and lots of beer.

If Social Services comes around today, I'm screwed.

I can feel my sanity slipping away slowly. "Okay, you know what? We're gonna have pizza today."

I leave them cheering in the kitchen and walk back into the living room to retrieve my purse. My AmEx credit card is connected to my life raft account, and if ever I needed a life raft, it's today.

I dig through my wallet, but the slot where I usually keep it is empty. "Hm. Where could that possibly have gone…?"

"Aunt Em?"

When I look up, Josh is standing at the entrance to the living room in a t-shirt that's far too tight for him. *When was the last time I took them shopping for new clothes?*

"Hey, bud. Have you seen my silver credit card anywhere?"

He frowns. "It's always in your wallet."

"I know." I rack my brain, trying to remember what I last used the card for. Did I just forget to put it back in my wallet? Then it hits me: back-to-school shopping for the spring semester. The kids all needed new binders. I have a vague memory of sitting at the kitchen table on the phone with Social Services to ask when the stipend was getting sent out when…

"Ben walked in."

Josh looks confused. "Huh? What about Dad?"

I turn my back on him and race towards Ben's room, my heart rate rising rapidly. Ben jerks upright when the door flies open, dried drool leaving a trail from one corner of his mouth down to his chin.

"Where is it?" I practically shriek.

He blinks at me, his eyes rolling sleepily. "Huh? What?"

"My credit card, Ben. Where is it?"

A spark of recognition flits across his eyes. That's all it takes to confirm my suspicion: he took it.

I open my mouth to unleash holy hell on him, but before I can, Reagan's pitiful little voice floats up from behind me. Her body is half-hidden behind the door frame and she's looking at me with those big, beautiful eyes.

"Are you mad at Daddy?"

Caroline is standing behind Josh, looking just as upset as her sister. *Keep it together, Emma. For the kids.*

But before I can say anything, Josh steps in. "Auntie Em's not angry. She just needs to talk to Dad. Come on; let's go play Hide-and-Seek in my room."

If I had the money, I'd buy that kid every pair of shoes in the store. I wait until Josh ushers his sisters away before I close the door and turn to glare at Ben.

"*Where* is it, you… you… you *asshole?*"

His eyes pop open. I'm usually not one for name-calling. But there are just some people who kick the Good Samaritan inside you until there's no goodness left. He's one of them.

"Relax. You barely use that card—"

"Because it's for *emergencies,*" I snap. "Hand it over. Now."

He stumbles to his feet. His belly seems to have doubled in size in the last few months. The rest of us are withering away, but Ben just keeps oozing in every direction.

"Goddammit, Ben, you reek!" I exclaim, stepping to the side as he bumbles past me to the floating shelves opposite his single bed. "Is that what you spent the grocery money on? More booze?"

"What're you, the fuckin' alcohol police? It was a rough night, okay?" He slides his hand over the topmost shelf and produces the card.

"Thank God." I snatch it off him. "Please tell me you didn't use it to buy more alcohol."

"'Course not." I'm in the middle of a relieved exhale when he hits me with, "I needed it for Knicks tickets."

I freeze. "I'm sorry—did you just say *Knicks* tickets?"

He grins as wide as I've seen him do in months. "Season tickets, baby. Courtside."

My stomach plummets. Every organ in my body feels like it's been jolted out of place.

There goes my life raft.

"Ben... How. Much. Did. You. Spend?"

His forehead pinches together. "I mean, they're primo tickets, Emma. They weren't cheap."

I take a step towards him. "How much? I want a number."

"Twenty grand."

My jaw falls open. My eyes bug out. My first and only thought is, *Kill him.*

Some murders are justified, right?

"Twenty thousand dollars on basketball," I gasp. "Ben, you idiot. That was *it*. That was *all* my money. *All* my savings. All *our* savings."

He shrugs, his bloodshot eyes wavering. "Don't be a drama queen. You've got a fancy-ass job. Bane Corp., right? That company pays their employees a boatload."

"Except that even a boatload isn't enough when your expenses are a... a... *ship* load!" I turn towards the door. "I'm calling and getting those tickets refunded!"

"Uh..."

I circle around to face him, eyes narrowing with fear. "Don't say it. Don't you dare say what I think you're about to say."

"They're nonrefundable."

I can only stare at my brother-in-law, wondering what kind of man, what kind of *father,* he might have been if Sienna was still alive. I want to believe that he'd have stepped up. I want to believe it's the grief that robbed him of his sense of duty, his patience, his love for his children.

But there were signs even before Sienna died.

Ben was useless when he got back home after work. He'd sit on the couch with his shirt unbuttoned and a beer in his hand while Sienna ran around, getting dinner ready, taking care of the kids, tidying up the house. *I'm tired, babe. I worked a long damn day.* It never seemed to occur to him that she worked, too.

It's funny, though—those things seemed so petty and minor in the moment. It's only in retrospect that the warning signs are blaring red.

The one good thing I can say about Ben: he loved my sister. And for that, I've spent the last three-and-a-half years picking up the slack for his shortcomings.

"Don't be so fuckin' selfish, Em."

"*Me?!*" I gape at him. I know I shouldn't let myself get sucked in, but my nerves are strung out and so is my patience.

"You had that fucking money just sitting there!"

"That's the whole damn *point*! It was meant to sit there until we really needed it. Which we do!"

He rolls his eyes. "Convenient that you need that money right when I need basketball tickets."

"No!" I snap. "You don't *need* basketball tickets; you *want* them. There's a huge, huge difference. Josh *needs* a new pair of shoes, but now, thanks to you, he's not gonna get them. I get that you don't give a shit about me—but what about your kids, Ben. Huh? What about them?"

His eyes flit around the room and his face screws up like he's almost regretful. Then, just when I think he's going to say something remotely helpful...

He burps.

I close my eyes and take a deep breath. "Okay," I breathe, peeling them back open reluctantly. "This is what's going to happen. You are gonna get a job. You're gonna start helping me around the house and with the kids. You're gonna start *pulling your weight.*"

He turns around and bends over, giving me an unwelcome eyeful of his hairy ass crack. Then he straightens back up with a beer in hand.

"Oh, great." I applaud sarcastically. "Another beer. Glad you've got your priorities in order."

He pops the cap and takes a sip.

"Ben! Did you hear me?"

He takes a long drag of his beer before looking me right in the eye. "No."

My eyes bug out. "No? No to which part?"

"No to all of it. I don't see the point anymore." His lip wobbles when he speaks, but I'm long past the point of sympathy. I'm scraping the bottom of the barrel here.

"Your three *children* are the point, Ben."

He shrugs. "They have you."

"Ben—"

"And I know you're gonna do everything in your power to keep those kids."

Why does that feel like a threat?

"So I'm going out."

He pushes past me, taking his beer can with him. A few seconds later, I hear the door slam. Now that Ben's taken the overpowering scent of booze with him, I smell dirty socks and moldy carpet instead.

I back out of his room, but I misjudge where the door is and hit the wall instead. I let it take me down to the ground, sliding into a knees-to-chest puddle on the floor. It smells worse at this height, but the smell is the least of my problems.

Suddenly, the contract in my purse doesn't seem quite as radical an idea as I first thought. In fact, it's starting to feel very much like a replacement life raft.

I'd be able to provide for the kids. And I'd get a little something for myself, too.

Maybe this is not a desperate choice.

Maybe it's not a choice at all.

It might just be the only option I have left.

9

EMMA

Yeah, okay, I dressed up for him.

But it's for me, too.

The silk red blouse I'm wearing is the injection of confidence I need to feel like I can do this. So are the black heels that are an inch taller than what I would normally wear to the office. Of course I'd gone with a red lip today and, for the first time in my professional life, I kept my hair down.

I stare at my hazy reflection in the elevator doors, nervous butterflies flapping around in the pit of my belly. I expected that. What I didn't expect was to be as *excited* as I am. I've been distracted with fantasies all morning.

Will he take me right there on his desk? Will he put me on my knees? Or maybe he'll go down on me. That mouth of his has to be good for something other than making people question their life choices.

I stride to Ruslan's office, the contract burning a hole in my purse. It feels so much heavier since I signed it late last night, clutching one of Ben's beer cans. I didn't actually drink the whole thing; I just needed a little liquid courage before I scribbled my signature on the dotted line.

I pass Katie Miller in the hallway. She does a double-take when she sees me. "Dang, girl! You look like a different person with your hair down."

I smile self-consciously. "Wanted to try something new today."

"Well, it's working for you."

I smile gratefully at Katie, then turn to face Ruslan's door. I don't pause outside his door this time. If I do, I may never walk in.

He's standing at his desk, his body angled towards the view of the city while he talks to someone on the phone. "... get more test subjects. Up the price per hour if you need to. I want a few more trials done just to be safe... Okay. Yes. Let me know."

He's wearing one of his Tom Ford suits. His dark brown hair curls boyishly over the rich blue collar. His shoulders look intimidatingly large, as do his arms.

All the better to pick me up and throw me around.

"Ms. Carson."

I flinch when he turns to me. His gaze flicks over my outfit and heat rises to my cheeks. His eyes darken. And they linger.

Is he thinking about what it will feel like to slide his cock between my lips? Maybe he's wondering what I'm wearing underneath my skirt...

I pull the contract out of my purse. "I signed it."

Way to bury the lede, Emma.

He nods as though he's not in the least bit surprised. Then he sits at his desk and focuses on his laptop.

He's probably just gonna finish up an email before he ravishes me on the desk. Or maybe I'll have to climb aboard and fuck him in his chair. What if he wants to take me up against the window? To give the whole of Manhattan a good show?

My thoughts are so out of control that I'm already hot and ready where it counts. I can't even remember the last time I've been *this* turned on. All I know is, however he decides to start this, it's gonna be good. I'm so damn ready for—

"Leave it on my desk."

Um... what?

He starts typing, his fingers flying over the keyboard with impressive speed. It makes me wonder how much damage those fingers could do inside me.

"Leave it... here?"

He doesn't so much as glance in my direction. "On the desk, yes."

"Uh, okay. Should I, uh... should I leave?"

Again, he doesn't spare me a peek. "My schedule is not going to arrange itself, Ms. Carson."

I swallow my disappointment—at this point, it's more confusion-based than anything else—and slink back to my desk.

What the hell?

It's a mindfuck to find myself sitting behind a desk instead of being spread out on top of it. It's even more difficult to put myself back in the headspace of a personal assistant when I had mentally, spiritually, and emotionally prepared myself for sugar baby duties.

I keep staring at his door, waiting for him to call me back into his office. Or maybe even send me to the copy room, or the restroom, so he can trap me there and fuck the living hell out of me.

The little green light on my intercom flashes. Ruslan's direct line.

It's happening. Be cool.

I count to five Mississippis and pick up. "Yes, Mr. Oryolov?" It feels weird to call him anything else, regardless of the contract I'd just left on his desk.

"Push my three o'clock meeting to four."

He hangs up immediately and I'm left with dead air. On the bright side? My pussy has finally stopped distracting me with its constant throbbing.

On the not-so-bright side?

I wore this lingerie for nothing.

10

EMMA

I'm texting Amelia, the kids' absurdly expensive part-time nanny, to see if she's willing to stay later if she needs to when Ruslan walks out of his office.

"Ms. Carson."

I put my phone down and stand. "Yes, sir."

"Dinner. 8:30."

Panicking slightly, I glance at the schedule on the side of my desk. "You don't have anything scheduled. Do you need me to make a—"

He sighs. "I'm asking *you* out to dinner, Ms. Carson."

"Oh."

Oh!

He cocks one dark brow. "Are you free to join me or not?"

His tone suggests that he's got plenty of other options if I turn him down. I twist my phone around and spy the text that I've just gotten from Amelia. *That's fine!* It feels like my first real break today.

"Yes! Yes, I'm free."

He nods. "Meet me downstairs in five minutes."

The moment he disappears into the elevator, I throw files and papers, notepads and pens back into my desk drawer, grab my bag, and haul ass into the restroom.

I touch up my makeup and add another coat of seduction-red lipstick. I thank my lucky stars that I remembered to pack perfume, too. It's down to its last few puffs, but I manage to apply a spritz onto the sides of my neck and the front of my wrists. Then I pop out the top button of my blouse, allowing just a peek of my bra and the cleavage it offers, before I head downstairs to meet Ruslan.

He's already in the back of the monstrous black SUV parked right outside the Bane skyscraper. The door swings open on its own as I approach.

Ruslan is on his phone when I slide inside. He doesn't acknowledge my presence apart from hitting the roof of the vehicle with the palm of his hand. As soon as he does, we whisk away from the curb.

I spend the next thirteen minutes shooting him furtive glances, wondering if I should break the silence. Spoiler alert: I don't.

The SUV comes to a stop in front of a tall, thin building so white it shines. *Eleven Madison Park*. I'm pretty sure there's a three-month waiting list to even set foot in the lobby here.

It's just as impressive on the inside as it is on the outside. We walk into a huge symmetrical room with double-height ceilings and a terrazzo floor with inlaid carpets. Hanging pendant lights illuminate the neutral color palette of the upholstered furniture, a mix of blue-grays and copper earth tones.

Everything about this place intimidates me. Including the leggy blonde in a little black dress who shows us to a private room in the back of the restaurant.

The door clicks shut behind the hostess and the hubbub of the general dining area dies away. Heat instantly spreads across my body.

Ruslan brushes past. "Shall we sit?"

I nod, reaching for my chair at the same time he does. I lunge back, only to realize that he's pulling out the chair—*for me*.

Who says chivalry is dead?

I squash the juvenile reaction in my head. "Thanks."

He settles into the seat next to me. My thoughts are going berserk. *This is it. This has to be it. Why else would he have asked for a private room?*

So I sit there and wait for him to touch me under the table. Maybe order me to drop to my knees below the tablecloth. But he does neither of those things. In fact, apart from the setting and the way he pulled my chair out for me, he's neither said nor done anything to suggest that this isn't going to be a very above-the-board kind of dinner.

Except that I've *never* had dinner with my boss.

I start with surprise when the door opens and the hostess returns with what I'm sure is a very expensive bottle of champagne. She pours us both a flute and then bows right back out.

"Emma."

My name slips out of his mouth and instantly, I experience what can only be described as a hot flash. Except, you know, it doesn't suck. It just makes my toes curl and my heart beat a little faster. It makes me *very* aware of my body.

Because *more* self-awareness was exactly what I needed, right?

"Yes, Mr. Oryolov?"

"We're not in the office anymore."

I exhale. "So I'm allowed the privilege of using your name?"

Those amber eyes are scorching. "I detect sarcasm."

"Then you detect correctly." I pick up my flute of champagne and give it a taste. As expected, it's jaw-dropping.

He smirks and a lightning rod of excitement rips down my spine. If that smirk doesn't spell "foreplay," I don't know what does.

"I invited you out tonight to lay the ground rules for our arrangement."

My eyebrows pull together. Call me crazy; somehow, I thought this arrangement would involve a helluva lot more ripped clothes, mind-blowing orgasms, and scandalizing dirty talk. And yet here we are, having an extremely civilized dinner, discussing *ground rules.*

"Okay. Got it. Ground rules."

"You need money to pay off your debts." My skin prickles with anxiety, but I don't bother asking him how he knows that I'm in debt. "And *I* need a woman who'll be at my beck and call without expecting me to fulfill her…emotional needs."

Despite the turn this dinner has taken, I still feel those butterflies every time he says something to me. It's different from the orders he usually barks at the office. Still, I get his message loud and clear.

"I mean, you can certainly *try* not to fall in love with me. I'm warning you though, it's gonna be tough. I'm a hoot and a half."

I swear, I almost manage to squeeze a smile out of that stone face.

Almost.

"I wouldn't worry. There's zero percent chance of that happening."

I scowl. "A gentleman would have at least given me five percent. Two percent, even. Or at least lied entirely."

"A gentleman wouldn't be offering you a contract for sex, either."

I wince. "Yeah, okay. Fair."

"When I require your attention, I will send a driver to pick you up and take you to my penthouse."

"The fuckpad?" I blurt before I can bite my tongue.

He doesn't respond to that apart from a subtle tremor in his brow. "My driver will drop you back home when we're done."

"So… no sleepovers?"

"That is correct."

I nod distractedly, feeling uneasy about one thing in particular. "What about other partners? That is, um, other sexual partners?"

His expression completely flatlines. His mouth turns into a harsh grimace, his eyes narrow, and his jaw clenches.

Makes me feel like maybe I should have read the fine print.

"For as long as this arrangement between us lasts, you will not be permitted to date, kiss, or fuck anyone other than *me*."

I should resent the amount of control he's exerting on my life, but somehow, the possessive snarl in his tone has my body writhing with delight.

"Not what I meant."

His expression doesn't relax. "No? Then what *did* you mean?"

"I need to know if this is a two-way street." I take a sip of champagne to bolster my nerves. "I'm sure we both share the same concerns." It's the only way I can think of to get him to stop glaring at me and see even a sliver of reason. He doesn't want to share me with other men? Fine by me. I don't want him sharing whatever he catches from other women, either.

"Hm."

That freaking *"hm."* It's amazing how one little sound can ride under my skin in the worst way.

"I will agree to keep our arrangement monogamous." His tone is clipped, so I have no idea if he's happy about the concession or not, but *I* certainly am.

I file his answer away under my "victory" column and focus on a more practical point. "How often will I be coming?"

"You'll be coming to the penthouse twice a week. As for how often you'll be coming…" He shrugs mischievously.

"Only twice?"

He smirks at the eagerness that question implies. I wanna kick myself. *Great, Emma. Good job not looking desperate.*

"I'm a busy man, Emma. Discipline is the cornerstone of my life. Twice a week will be sufficient, but you should be prepared to be on call at any time."

"'Any time' doesn't really cut it when you've got three kids with different schedules and different needs. I'm gonna need advance notice. At least…" I quickly calculate Amelia's typical response time. "At least three to four hours."

His jaw tightens. "Very well." He sips his champagne and the southern half of my body is making me wish that I were the flute in his impossibly large hand.

"In addition to your monthly salary, you will be compensated for your time in the form of a weekly allowance."

My eyes widen. "A what?"

"It's simply a way to account for any expenses that might come up as a result of our arrangement. As I understand it, you have three young dependents?" I nod and he continues. "I'm aware that childcare is not cheap. The allowance will make sure they're looked after so that you don't have any distractions when you're with me."

The man is thorough; you gotta give him that. His explanation does go a long way toward making me feel better about the whole exchanging-sex-for-money dilemma. There's still a lot of moral ambiguity, but it's a little easier to ignore.

"One more thing."

I shift in my chair, unease turning my palms sweaty.

"I'm not interested in trapping you, Emma. You're free to break our contract at any time, as long as you give me notice. You will still get your severance package, as well as a good recommendation."

I exhale slowly, pleasantly surprised by the escape hatch he's allowing me.

"*However.*"

I should have known. With men like Ruslan, there's always a "however."

"If you so much as breathe a word about this contract to *anyone*, then—

"Then," I cut in, "the deal is off. No protection, no recommendations, no pension—and you have the means to completely destroy my chances of employment in any capacity ever again. I'll be lucky if I can brew coffee for a living. Did I miss anything?"

He cocks his head to the side. That tiny little smirk is back. "You did not."

I nod. "I pay attention, Ruslan." It's mildly embarrassing that goosebumps fleck my arms when I say his name. I'm lucky I chose long sleeves today.

He leans forward, those arms flexing as they hit the table. "Then you'll have no problem following my rules."

I laugh. "You better hope *you* can follow the rules." I point to myself with both hands. "Hoot and a half, remember?"

Those amber eyes burn a little brighter. Then, without warning, he reaches out and grabs my wrist. His grip is tight, bordering on painful. He meets my gaze with an unflinching glare. "I'm going to make myself very, *very* clear: this isn't a relationship. I'm not your boyfriend. I'm not your anything. Feelings aren't an option."

I swallow a gulp and nod.

He relaxes his grip and sits back in his chair. "Good. Now that we've got that out of the way, we can enjoy dinner."

An hour and a half later, the SUV pulls up outside my building.

I'm very satisfied right now, but not in the way I'd expected. The food at Eleven Madison Park was nothing short of holy. The conversation, however, was extremely lacking. In the most literal sense of the word. After we ordered, he barely said a word to me.

I'd half-expected him to take me back to his fuckpad after we finished dinner, but he gave the driver my address instead.

"Goodnight, Emma."

Of course, he's not gonna walk me to the door. That's a boyfriend's job, and he's my... fuck buddy? Sugar daddy? Casual sex partner? Friend with benefits?

I almost snort at that last thought. We're definitely *not* friends.

"Goodnight, Ruslan."

To his credit, he waits until I'm inside the building before driving off. I watch the SUV go, its engine purring softly in the distance. And all I can think is...

What a waste of lingerie.

11

RUSLAN

"I believe she's what they call a 'hot mess.'" Isay's chuckle comes to a grinding halt when he sees the look on my face. "Uh, um... *ahem,* what I mean is, she has a lot going on, boss."

"Your job is to tell me what she's got going on. I don't need a running fucking commentary from the peanut gallery."

He nods awkwardly, his ears turning beet red while his gaunt face remains comically pale. "Right. Of course. Err, so, she's got a pretty large rent to deal with every month. And it looks like she has student loans that she needs to pay off as well. Then, of course, the funeral expenses.

I frown. "Whose funeral?"

"Her sister's."

There's a question on the tip of my tongue, but I swallow it at the last second. I don't need to know Emma's life story. I don't need to know about her past, her dreams, her fears, or her future goals.

I need to know just enough to make this little arrangement of ours a successful one. Beyond that, her traumas are her own.

Isay hands me the file and I scan through the numbers. "Fucking hell."

I pay her well, but I certainly don't pay her enough to be able to take care of all the shit she's got going on right now. I'm actually impressed by her work ethic, considering how much stress she must be under. The only indication of that kind of pressure was the day she turned up late and I accused her of doing the walk of shame through my building.

"Okay." I hand Isay back the ledger. "Take care of this for me."

His eyes bug out. "Take care... Do you mean—*All* of it?"

"All of it."

Isay looks down at the sheet of paper. "This is a lot of money to spend on one woman."

I turn the full force of my glare on the man until his ears turn as red as the lipstick Emma wore to the other night's dinner.

"I-I apologize, sir," Isay stammers. "It's just—"

"I don't remember asking for your opinion, Isay. It's my fucking money and I'll spend it on whatever I want."

Isay nods so hard that his glasses slip down his nose and clatter on the desk. "I'll get it done, sir."

"See that you do. And inform me immediately after."

Isay backs out of the room with his head bowed in deference. The man lacks a spine, but he has a head for numbers. Which is why he's lasted this long.

It's Sunday, which means Bane Corp. is a sleepy labyrinth of abandoned hallways and empty offices. I could have just had him come to my personal estate or one of my penthouses in the city, but I like the structure of keeping things separate.

Ironic, really, considering I've spent most of this weekend imagining all the different ways I plan on fucking my secretary tomorrow night during our first scheduled "meeting." In every single fantasy I've had of her the last two days, she's wearing that dangerous red blouse, her dark hair floating down to her breasts in an obsidian waterfall.

It took every ounce of my self-control to resist her that night. Those blood-red lips of hers were just begging to be claimed. Tomorrow, I plan to tongue-fuck the color clean off them.

But I refused to let myself lose control until the time was right. If this arrangement is going to work, I need to set boundaries and I need to stick to them.

Paying off Emma's debts is just a way of weeding out the mess so that she can focus on meeting my needs. It's purely selfish.

And yet...

I keep thinking about her reaction when I tell her that she's debt-free. I keep thinking about how relieved she'll feel, how much lighter with that colossal weight off her shoulders.

And yeah, there's a deep-seated, caveman-like sense of satisfaction that comes with knowing that *I'm* giving her that.

Her question about seeing other men pissed me off in the moment, but now? Good luck finding *any* other man who can do this. I'd almost like to see her try.

Of course, I'm not the sort of man who does anything for free. I expect her to make it worth my while with that sweet, delicious body of hers.

Tomorrow.

One more fucking night and then she's all mine.

12

RUSLAN

"What's our budget look like?"

Kirill consults the columned paper lying on the table between us. "We're within our targets. Looks like everything's right on track. Financially speaking, at least."

I nod in approval. "Sergey's running the last few trials as we speak. It shouldn't be long now."

"Well, I'll be damned. I thought we'd never reach the top of this mountain."

I've had my moments of doubt, too, not that I'd ever admit to them. It's been a hell of a long road to get here. Sleepless nights. Endless days.

It'll be worth it in the end.

He punches me in the shoulder playfully. "I should have known, though. You've got the Midas touch."

Except when it comes to family... The unwelcome thought takes me off guard. I almost never go there. Luckily, my phone starts ringing.

"Isay?"

"It's done."

That's all I need. Hanging up, I use the intercom button to summon Emma into my office. Kirill's expression is a carefully curated mask. But I've known him too long to be fooled by the indifference he's trying to pull off.

"You called me, Mr. Oryolov?"

"Come in, Ms. Carson."

She click-clacks towards my desk in her standard black peek-a-boo heels. The woman is in desperate need of a wardrobe overhaul. There are a few boutiques I could call to—

No. Not my fucking problem.

"I wanted to let you know that, as of right now, your debts are paid."

There's pin-drop silence. Emma's gaze flickers to Kirill for a moment and then back to me. She rolls her bottom lip, which is coated in a natural nude gloss today.

"I'm not sure I understand, sir."

Kirill adjusts his position just enough to be able to see Emma properly. It's the first time today that I've been glad she's wearing a conservative flared skirt instead of the hip-hugging pencil style she usually opts for.

"You are debt-free," I repeat.

She opens her mouth. Then closes it. Another lip roll. Another short glance towards Kirill. "Is this... a joke?"

My hackles rise instantly. "Do I strike you as the joking type, Ms. Carson?"

She shifts from her right leg to her left. "Um…"

My teeth grind together impatiently. "Why don't you make a call to your bank? That may help you process this. I'm not in the mood to repeat myself a third time."

She twists around, hesitates, glances at me, and then heads for the door. For once, Kirill's eyes aren't fixed on her as she walks away. They're fixed on me.

Which is only marginally better, really.

"What?" I snap.

He shrugs. "Just in awe of your genius. A contracted sexual partner. I never would have gone there, not in a million years."

"That's why I'm the brains of this operation."

He smirks. "I'm the—"

BANG. Emma doesn't even seem to hear the sound of the door slamming into the wall as she flies back into the office, her face a mask of shock and disbelief.

"Oh my God," she gasps. "You weren't kidding."

Then she does the very last thing I expected. She *thanks* me, with actual fucking tears in her eyes.

"Rus—I mean, Mr. Oryolov, I-I can't thank you enough. You have *no* idea how much this means to me. I just… I can't believe it…"

She keeps up a steady stream of chatter that I'm only half-getting because I'm so distracted by the way her tears are making her irises go from dark cerulean to pale turquoise.

It doesn't help that Kirill is still lurking off to the side, grinning like the fucking Cheshire cat.

"This is going to make a *world* of difference. I'm actually gonna be able to save now. I'll have to make sure *he* never knows. That'll take some work, but I can—"

"He?"

The snap of my voice has her dropping off mid-sentence. Color rushes to her cheeks, turning them pinker than her lips. "Oh, never mind. I shouldn't have—It's nothing. I can handle it."

I could make her tell me, but I see no point when Kirill will supply me with all the answers I want with just a little digging.

What I want right now, however, is to get Emma back to her desk as fast as possible. I was expecting gratitude. I was *not* expecting the blubbering mess that stands before me, looking at me as though I'm the second coming.

I'm not interested in being her hero, and yet somehow, that is exactly what I've managed to do.

The warmth of pride in my chest can go fuck right off, too. I'm not in this to be sentimental.

And she's still fucking going. "Seriously, this means the world to me. I can't believe how gener—"

"Fucking hell, woman. Do you have an off button?"

She freezes, her mouth a perfect oval of surprise. Then her lips come together and hurt pools in those light blue eyes. "I'm just trying to thank you."

"I don't need your thanks. What I need is a presentable secretary who's got her shit together. And currently, you're not ticking either one of those boxes."

The brightness in her eyes snuffs out instantly. *Good.* It's too much. She needs to remember that I'm no knight in shining armor—I'm the fucking dragon.

"Go back to your desk and pull yourself together."

She doesn't move. "What is wrong with you?" The fight in her eyes is much preferable to the hurt. It's oddly titillating, too. "I was only trying to thank you. There's no need to be such a… such a colossal *asshole*."

Kirill snorts, but I doubt Emma hears it because she's preoccupied with lighting up bright red in embarrassment, then storming out, her heels clacking like gunfire as she goes.

The door slams again, in the other direction this time.

"Well," Kirill chuckles, "that was… interesting."

I unclench my jaw. "I want another background check done on her. This time, dig into her personal life. I want to know who the fuck this 'he' is that she's hiding shit from."

"On it." Kirill fixes me with a curious glance. "Gotta be honest: I'm surprised you let her talk to you like that. Most people would never get away with that sort of disrespect."

I raise an eyebrow. "Oh, she hasn't gotten away with anything. I plan on punishing her for it tonight."

My cock is already throbbing with anticipation.

Only a couple more hours and I will remind her *exactly* who I am.

13

RUSLAN

Her knee has been bouncing for as long as we've been on the road. I'm curious to see how long she can keep up the anxious momentum while she's stuck in New York City gridlock.

As it turns out: the *whole* damn time.

We turn onto 48th. That's when her leg finally stops pistoning up and down. Now, she looks like she's barely breathing. I catch a glimpse of her face as she slides out—she's chewing on the inside of her cheek and her cheeks are pale.

Not exactly the enthusiasm I was anticipating.

She stays as far away from me in the elevator as possible. I start to wonder if she's just nervous or if she's still pissed about our little spat earlier. I'd half-expected her to back out of our meeting today, but apparently, giving me the cold shoulder is her preferred method of punishment. It doesn't bother me at all. In fact, I'm looking forward to breaking through her icy exterior.

And I have just the tool for the job.

She's still chewing on her cheek when the elevator doors open into my penthouse. Her complete lack of reaction reminds me that she's been here before. I've had her drop off files, clothes, food. Condoms, once, too—which is probably where she got the idea that I use this as a "fuckpad," to borrow her term.

I take my coat off and she follows my lead. "Make yourself comfortable."

Deciding that what she needs is a little liquid encouragement, I leave her in the living room and head into the kitchen. The bar is connected to the kitchen by a vast marble countertop.

I can't help imagining her spread out on top of it. Will she moan for me like she did in her voicemail? Will she plead with me to fuck her? Or will she be shyer in person? Will I need to coax her out of her shell until the siren is unleashed?

All possibilities are equally tantalizing.

I walk the drinks back to the living room. Emma is standing by the window with her back to me, gazing out over the glittering skyline.

"Drink?"

She wordlessly takes the glass and throws it back so fast that my brows hit my hairline. Her eyes close, her mouth puckers, and her nose wrinkles. "*Fuck*, that's strong."

"It's gin."

"That explains it."

She hands me back her empty glass and I offer her my full one in exchange. "Apparently, you need this more than I do."

She eyes the glass for a moment. "No, I think I'll pass. If I drink any more, I might throw up."

I raise an eyebrow. "Sexy."

"Sorry." She cringes.

"Maybe this time, you could just sip it instead of downing it in one go."

She takes the glass and brings her mouth to the rim. The liquid slides between her plump lips and, just like that, I'm starting to feel an unreasonable twinge of jealousy toward that drink. After she swallows, I watch her tongue peek out just long enough to slide across them, igniting a slow-burning heat that starts at my chest and ends at my groin.

"I actually tasted it that time. It's good."

I make sure to meet her gaze. "Some things are meant to be savored."

The blush that spreads across her cheeks is both endearing and alarming. It brings up the series of doubts that I've been fighting ever since our little spat earlier. Did I pick the right woman? Is she a little too naïve, a little too innocent, a little too emotional for this kind of arrangement?

"Ruslan, I know you said not to mention it, but... I want to thank you, again, for what you did."

If she starts tearing up, I'm ending this fucking arrangement on the spot.

"I don't want to make you uncomfortable or anything, so I'll just leave it at that. But I did want to make sure you know that I am grateful. That I'm not taking you for granted."

Her eyes stay dry. That qualifies as a point in her favor.

"You've thanked me. There's no need to mention it again." I pour myself a shot and, despite my advice to her, knock it back in one gulp.

She frowns, which makes me curious. I'm not usually the sort of man who spends his time trying to decipher what a woman—*any* woman—is feeling. But there's something about this one that's got me asking all sorts of questions in the back of my mind.

"I don't know what I'm supposed to do," she blurts out suddenly. Color floods her cheeks the second she says it. "That's probably not a very sexy thing to admit, is it?"

I force down the smile that's almost on my lips. "Take another sip and come with me."

I rarely ever close the blinds in the master bedroom. One, because I enjoy the view. And two, because I hardly ever spend the night here. But for tonight, I don't feel like sharing the kind of view I'm looking forward to enjoying on my bed, so I take a moment to close them while pretending to not notice the look of relief that passes across her face.

Emma's gaze darts around the room, giving away the fact that she's never been in this part of the penthouse before. I don't know why that thrills me. Maybe because it proves her to be trustworthy—she doesn't snoop around when I'm not here.

I set my glass down and start to slowly undo my shirt buttons. Emma freezes. She looks like a deer caught in headlights. Except in this case, the headlights are my abs.

She turns away abruptly when I glance over at her, acting as though she was staring at the cream wallpaper the whole time.

"When was the last time you had sex, Emma?"

Her eyes widen. She still doesn't look at me. "Is that relevant?"

"Answer the question."

"A while ago," she admits.

I nod. "Take another sip."

She listens, then coughs. "If your plan is to get me drunk, I'm not sure sipping the drink slowly is going to accomplish what you want."

I arch an eyebrow. "What makes you think you know what I want?"

She hesitates for only a moment before she speaks. "I know that… you want me."

If only she was just a little more confident when she said it. That'll come with time and practice.

"And that scares you?"

Her brows pinch together. "I'm not scared."

"Then you'll have no problem giving me a live performance of that voicemail you sent me."

Her mouth pops open. "Y-you want me to—"

"I want you to touch yourself, Ms. Carson." I take a seat on the armchair by the window and look her in the eyes. "And I'm going to sit back and watch."

14

RUSLAN

Her eyes widen more and she gulps. The women I usually bring here are all over me the second the elevator doors shut; sometimes, I'm bored even *before* the sex begins. She's definitely not what I'm used to.

Maybe that's why my cock is already straining hard against my pants.

Emma's eyes keep flitting from side to side without focusing on anything. She's standing just out of reach in front of me, the vein in her forehead throbbing softly.

"Emma." Her eyes snap up to mine. "Take a deep breath." The fact that she follows my orders instantly is a massive turn-on. "Good girl. Do you need another drink?"

"I'm okay."

I nod. "Now, remember: I've already heard you come. More than once, actually."

Her throat bobs with another swallow. "You listened to that message again?"

"I listened to it quite a few times." I can still see her forehead vein, but it's not throbbing quite as much. "Whether you realize it or not, you know how to put on a show."

Every time she blushes, I feel the need to make her blush again. And again. And again. It's become a private little game for me. I win every single time.

She runs her tongue along her bottom lip. I'm not sure she's aware just how many different urges I'm fighting off right now. The caveman in me wants to rip her clothes off and fuck her senseless in every conceivable position known to man. But I haven't honed my sense of discipline for nothing and Ms. Carson needs to be handled carefully.

"I'm glad you enjoyed it," she murmurs shyly.

"I enjoyed it so much that I had a special contract drawn up just for you."

She exhales. Her shoulders relax and the anxious vein disappears altogether. I lean back in the chair and lift my glass to her. "Take your blouse off. Slowly."

She hesitates only for a second before she pulls the blouse up over her head. She removes it a little too fast, but the sight of her high, full breasts peeking out of the half-cup bra she's wearing more than makes up for it.

I clench my jaw, greedy for the plump nipples that are practically poking through the thin fabric of her lacy black bra.

Savor it...

"Now, the skirt."

She reaches her hands back and unzips herself. This time, she makes eye contact with me the whole time. Once she pushes the skirt over her hips, it falls to the floor. She steps out of it, another blush reddening her cheeks.

Well, fuck me.

Who knew that my prudish little assistant was hiding *that* body underneath those billowing silk blouses and pencil skirts? Not that I didn't know she had a great figure, but I certainly wasn't expecting the tantalizing curves that are officially making my mouth water. Soft lines accentuate her firm stomach and lead to the patch of skin covered from view…

For now.

The waistband of her G-string is pulled up, highlighting the sharpness of her hip bones. My gaze travels back to the little triangle of fabric that's covering her mound, and for just a moment, I hear myself think, *Fuck restraint.*

She doesn't wait for any more instructions. She unhooks her bra and pulls it off her shoulders, bearing those pert, juicy breasts. Her nipples are hard and I'm willing to bet that if I slide a finger inside her right now, it'll come back wet.

"Fuck, *kiska*, you have the sexiest body I've ever seen."

Her eyebrows arch. Surely this can't be the first time she's heard that? I don't care enough to ask, though. I'm too distracted by the feast my eyes are dining on.

"Turn around."

I'm close enough to see her eyes dilate at the command. Then she turns and my cock jumps hungrily at the sight of her perfectly round ass. It's a fucking work of art. I actually wince from the effort of *not* coming.

My muscles tighten as she bends over, sliding the negligible bit of fabric down her slim thighs. She reaches her ankles and her smooth pussy winks at me between those ripe, pink cheeks. I start to feel cracks skittering on the surface of my steely sense of control.

She straightens back up and glances at me over her shoulder. Just that motion alone tosses her dark hair over her shoulders. What makes it even more potent is how innocently oblivious she is to her own seductive power.

"Can I turn around now?"

Fuck, when has she *ever* been this deferential? This temptingly compliant?

"No." My voice is gravelly with need. "Lie down on the bed."

I watch her walk away, amused and entranced by the fact that her cheeks blush at both ends. She approaches the bed and lies down on her back with her feet hanging off the edge.

I grab a chair and move it toward her. Far enough away so she can writhe all she wants… but close enough that I won't miss a thing.

"What a good girl you are." Her limbs tremble as she sucks in a sharp breath. "Spread your legs for me."

I can see the moisture pooling between her pussy lips. I grind my teeth and resist the urge to slide my fingers inside her.

"Now—touch yourself."

Goosebumps erupt over her arms as her right hand settles between her legs. Using two fingers, she starts rubbing her clit in slow circles. I watch the dangerously hypnotic movement, enjoying the way her body is spread before me.

Mine for the taking.

Eventually.

Slowly, the tension starts to leave her body. Her jaw relaxes, her eyes roll, and a soft little moan escapes through those sinful lips of hers.

"What are you thinking about right now?"

She bites her bottom lip, stifling a moan in the process. "Y-you," she gasps.

"What about me?"

"I'm imagining your cock… what it'll feel like i-inside…*ahh*—"

Another moan. A flutter of her lashes. Her fingers start moving faster over her clit.

Something primal and possessive shifts inside of me. The thought that any other man might have seen her like this… the thought that some other man one day *might* see her like this… It makes me want to mark her so that she'll always remember exactly who she belongs to.

But mostly, it's a hunger to let every other man out there know that this woman is *off-fucking-limits.*

I remind myself of the contract. Her cleanly slanted signature on several different pages. As long as that contract is in play, I don't need to worry about other men. She belongs to me and me alone.

"Yes, baby. Keep going. Faster."

"Touch me," she begs as her voice hitches up a few notes. "Please."

I shake my head slowly. "You'll have to work for that. My touch is not easily earned."

She whimpers, her bottom lip trembling frantically. "R-Ruslan…"

The faster she moves her fingers over her clit, the more her plump breasts bounce. Her dark hair fans out across my Egyptian cotton sheets, a stark contrast to the immaculate white. She looks like a fucking painting come to life.

"Play with your nipples for me."

Her free hand lands on her right breast and she starts massaging it slowly, rolling the nipple between her fingers.

I grind my teeth hard enough to shatter them. "What a good little assistant you are. So fucking obedient. So fucking sexy…"

An unbridled moan flies out of her lips.

"Do you want to see how much I love what you're doing?"

She nods emphatically. It takes me only seconds to strip off my shirt and free myself of my pants and boxers. I step around to the side and her eyes glide down the paths of my tattoos before they land on my cock. She lets out a strangled little moan that demands my full attention.

I wrap a palm around my shaft and start stroking myself. Emma pushes herself up on one elbow, her tongue snaking over her lips.

"You want my cock, baby?"

She nods. "So much."

"It's pretty big. You sure you can take it?"

She bites down hard on her bottom lip, rubbing her clit harder. "*Mhmm.*"

"Say it. I want to hear you say it."

"Yes," she groans. "I can take it."

I keep pumping my cock. I can feel the release build just at the tip, but I bury the urge through sheer force of will. I don't plan on coming tonight. Not until I've made her come a dozen times over.

"Tell me what you want."

Her eyes flare. The flush on her cheeks has traveled over her entire body. Is this the first time a man has ever asked her that question? Judging from the look on her face, it is. But I can't be sure and it's driving me fucking insane.

"Tell me," I growl. "Tell me while your mouth is still empty."

She swallows hard. And like the obedient woman she is, she doesn't stop rubbing between her legs. "I want *that*. I want your—*ahh*—your cock in my mouth. I want your cock everywhere."

I pump harder still. "Everywhere? Such a dirty little assistant."

"Yes," she gasps. "Yes."

"What else?"

Every time her eyes flicker close, she forces them open again so she can meet my gaze. Shivers roll through her body every few seconds and her breathing grows more and more labored.

"I-I want you to eat me out."

"Mmm…"

"I want you to fuck me so hard I forget my own name."

"What about *my* name?" I demand, moving just a little bit closer. I'm not sure I can hold out any longer. I *need* to fucking touch her.

Her eyes keep sliding down to my cock. "Y-your name?"

"Will you forget my name?" There's a feral menace underlining the question.

"No," she pants. "Never. N-not your name…"

"Good girl. Now, say it. Say my name while you come for me."

"Ruslan!" Her voice trembles violently, her breasts shiver, and her fingers bear down on her gorgeous wet cunt. *"Fu-uuu-ck!"*

I've never seen anything as beautiful as her face when she comes.

Only after she's had her release do her eyes close. As if it's over. As if that would ever be enough to sate me…

"I think you're forgetting something, Ms. Carson."

The mention of her office name has her eyes flying open. Her mouth hitches up on one side. "What am I forgetting, Mr. Oryolov?"

The little minx. She's toying with me.

"You're here to service *my* needs. Not the other way around."

She stretches her body along the bed with a breathy moan. "What can I do for you, sir?"

The question sets my body on fire. The answer to it is: *everything*. I've got an entire lifetime's dirty fantasies ping-ponging inside my head. Picking which one is hard—pun fully intended—but I go with my basest instinct, unable to quiet the covetous throbbing of my cock.

"I want to fucking break you," I growl.

Her eyes flash. Fear? Excitement? Anticipation? I don't allow her to face me long enough to figure out which. Grabbing her by the hips, I twist her around, force her onto her stomach, and pull her hips to arch her delectable ass up to me. Her skin is as soft as my sheets and twice as luxurious. I can't wait to mark her with my teeth, my fingers, my cum.

My hands smooth over her hips while my cock presses between her cheeks, lining up with her dripping slit. I can't help myself—I tease us both, rubbing the swollen head up and down, nudging her clit and making both of us shudder.

She's got fistfuls of bedsheets in each hand, her juicy ass pushing back against my cock. Eager little *kiska*.

I slap her ass. She yelps, jerking forward as my handprint glows against the pale pink blush of her skin.

Before she can recover from the slap, I grab her hips and thrust inside her. She makes a sound that's half-moan, half-scream—and one hundred percent *mine*.

As for me... all the noise disappears. All the tension in my body dissolves. All the stress and duty that weighs heavy on my shoulders fades away into the background.

There's just the *thwack* of skin on skin when I push harder, sink deeper, until every inch is buried inside her and I'm fucking *home*.

She's so hot, so tight, so... fucking... perfect.

Emma may have gone limp on the bed, a mass of shivering, sobbing pleasure as I rock into her— but inside her sweet body, she's on fire. I can feel her ripple tightly along my shaft; the naughty minx is already trying to milk my orgasm from me before I've even begun teaching her what a real fucking orgasm feels like.

I pull her onto me the same time I thrust inside her. Again and again and again, relishing the way her moans melt into grunts that melt into sobs of pleasure bubbling my name between her trembling lips.

This is what I want. What I *need*. I need her to feel me so fucking deep inside her gorgeous body that she'll forget whatever else she's experienced before me. I need her to take it so good, she'll struggle to walk in the morning.

I feel her tighten on me and I grin. I grab her hips harder, pull her onto me deeper, and when I feel her tense on that sweet edge of oblivion, I seat myself balls deep inside her quivering pussy and slide my hands up to caress her sides.

"Come for me, baby."

When she does, my eyes roll back in my head. Feeling her spasm on my cock, wild and wet and uncontrolled, tests every fiber of my self-control beyond anything I've ever experienced before.

Goddamn.

I don't wait for her to calm down through the final spasms— I pull out, roll her onto her back, and bury my cock back inside her. The swiftness makes her gasp and arch into me, and I wrap my arms around her back so I can taste those sweet nipples as I buck into her.

Not enough. It's not enough. I feel her spasm again, hear her cries as I fuck her into oblivion while I feast on her delicious curves, feel her fingers tug my hair… and it's not enough. I want more. I buck into her faster, burying my face in the curve of her neck to lick and suck and taste her glistening skin.

If it weren't for the soundproof walls of this penthouse, I'd stand a very good chance of being suspected of murder. Emma is certainly not the quiet little dormouse she appears to be in the office.

In the bedroom, she's a fucking storm.

Maybe that's why I do something I never anticipated doing tonight—leaning down and capturing her lips with my own. Even in the middle of her falling to pieces, I sense her surprised gasp. She didn't expect a kiss any more than I did.

But now that I'm tasting her, claiming her mouth, it feels so fucking right. She's sweet and warm and soft. I swipe my tongue inside of her mouth, tasting her tasting me. She claws at my back as I continue to drive into her tight pussy. We're a sweaty, entangled mess. Fused together head to toe.

For the briefest moment, it scratches the itch I have for *more.*

Then that moment passes. And I want more again.

Even as I reach the end of my tether and brace for my own release, I find myself still craving more. More of her, in different ways, in different places.

The contract. You have her twice a week for as long as you want.

It's that thought that pushes me over the edge. I cling to her, muffling my roar against her neck, as I feel the orgasm rip through me and pour into her in a searing heat that makes her shudder her own final release around me.

Consistent, convenient, decent sex is what I'd been after with this little arrangement. But what I've got is *great* sex. The kind of sex that calms the mind and soothes the soul.

The kind of sex that makes a man feel invincible.

15

RUSLAN

She's still lying naked across my bed when the phone rings. Kirill's name flashes across the lockscreen, which makes me frown. He wouldn't be calling at this time of the night unless there was something to report.

"What's going on?"

"I'm at Alcazar and, buddy, you won't believe who's here."

Emma turns over and the moonlight catches the curve of her ass. I lose myself imagining biting down on the perfect swell of her cheek, so I miss the next thing Kirill says.

"… was, uh, not the reaction I was expecting."

Emma sighs as she stretches. She's facedown on the bed, but the hint of her breast peeking out from under her arm threatens to distract me again. I sit up and turn away.

"I didn't catch that last part."

There's a beat of silence. "Damn, is she *still* there?"

"Kirill."

"Right. Not my business. What I said was, *Adrik is here.*"

My fist tightens around the phone and I sit up straight. "In *my* club?"

"Yup. Spoke to Venus. Apparently, he's been here about an hour."

"Is he causing trouble?"

"Nah. He and his entourage took one of the VIP booths on the balcony. Seems pretty innocent so far."

I snort. "*Nothing* with that slippery fuck is innocent. Has he seen you?"

"Doubtful. I just got here."

"Good. Keep your eyes on him. I'll be there in fifteen."

When I turn back around, Emma's eyes are closed and a soft, half-formed smile is spreading on her face. I did tell her to make herself comfortable. But she's looking a little too comfortable right now for my liking.

I grab her clothes off the floor and fling them onto the bed. "Get dressed."

Her eyes blink open. "Huh? What? Right now?"

"Do I need to remind you of the rules of our contract?" I ask icily.

She grimaces and reaches for her clothes. "You and that contract," she mumbles to herself as she pulls her panties back on.

My dick, which is exhausted after almost two hours of the most vigorous sex of my life, still lurches upward enthusiastically.

Emma notices and lets out a surprised little giggle. I silence it with a glare, then pull on my pants and zip myself up. "Quickly."

She bends to put the skirt on and her hair curtains her face, hiding her expression. I have no idea if she's resigned or irritated at the unceremonious end to this night. *Not that I should even care either way...*

"My driver will take you home."

She glances at me, her lips parting. I wait for the question, but she just snaps her mouth shut and nods. She keeps to her corner of the elevator as we ride down.

I hold the doors open for her when we reach the main floor. "He'll be waiting for you outside."

She glances at me. "Aren't you leaving, too?"

"I have to go down one more floor. My car's parked there."

"Oh. Okay." She hesitates. "See you tomorrow, then?"

"Something like that." I'm in a hurry, but I'm not a dick. Not enough to literally throw her out of the building no matter how much I need her to get going. And I'm lingering only *partly* because I'm still entertaining fantasies of fucking her up against the mirrored elevator walls.

She backs out of the elevator and the doors close on her piqued eyebrows. The post-sex high is dwindling slowly, but there's a certain focused clarity that I haven't felt in forever. Who knew sex was the solution I needed this whole time?

I slide into my Aston Martin Valkyrie and, in less than fifteen minutes, I'm pulling up outside Alcazar.

I toss the keys to Bruno, who's on valet duty, and head inside. The entry passage is a dark, soundproof tunnel that swallows you into the belly of the club. When I emerge, I see bare walls, unadorned save for old black-and-white street portraits of New York City in its heyday, all exquisite mansions and palatial public buildings that marked the city's Gilded Age in the late nineteenth century.

One of my bouncers, Jeremiah, stands at the end of the passage manning the arched metal door. Constant vibrations run down its heavy surface, caused by the state-of-the-art sound system that cost me a cool half-million.

Jeremiah offers me a deferential nod. "Boss."

He opens the door and I'm immediately swallowed up by the lights and music pulsating through the four-thousand-square-foot venue. Neon lights hit the walls at steep angles and ricochet onto the high ceilings. The dance floor is the centerpiece of the space, but it's the VIP boxes up on the balcony that I have my eyes on.

Kirill comes sauntering up. He's got a lager in hand, though his eyes stay fixed on the corner-most VIP box on the second mezzanine. I follow his gaze.

"Is that Vadim?" I growl.

Kirill's purses his lips. "He came in ten minutes before you. Made a beeline straight for Adrik. I thought the old bear was gonna scare him off, but—"

"They look *way* too fucking friendly for that to be the case."

Kirill nods curtly. My suspicions are on full alert. Uncle Vadim is not the kind of man who would ever go against the family. Still, I prefer to operate under the belief that people are unpredictable. And Vadim certainly has enough resentment against me to justify doing something as desperate as fraternizing with the enemy.

Although *enemy* strikes me as the wrong word. It implies a legitimate threat and there's nothing about Adrik that I find remotely threatening. But since we've been pitted against each other from the very beginning, there's no chance that ingrained sense of competition is going to let up any time soon.

"Should I go up there or do you wanna handle it?" Kirill asks.

I thump him on the back. "I got this."

Both men are so absorbed in conversation that they don't see me coming until I'm right on top of them.

"Ah, Ruslan!" Adrik greets as though we're fucking camp buddies.

I glance at my uncle, whose smile seems stiffer than usual. "Uncle." Then I turn to Adrik. "Pretty sure you're in the wrong club, Makarov."

He smirks and shrugs. "Must have mistaken it for mine."

"The day your club is half this full would be the best day of your fucking life."

He runs a hand through his short-cropped blond hair and scowls. "Mine's just a bigger spot. Makes it look emptier."

"It figures you would be one of those men obsessed with size. Explains a lot."

Vadim clears his throat. "Perhaps Adrik is just here to learn from the best."

Adrik's eyes narrow as he glances between the two of us. "I didn't come here to be ganged up on, that's for damn sure.."

"Why *did* you come, Adrik?"

He shrugs again, but his eyes keep flitting around too much for the gesture to come off as nonchalant. "Why not? I mean, we're practically family."

"Family?" I balk. "Now, you're overreaching."

"Overreaching is how I earned my reputation. *And* my empire."

I crook an eyebrow. "'Empire'? Are you referring to the two failing businesses you own? Or the ghost town you call a nightclub?"

Adrik gnashes his teeth together. "You have no fucking clue—"

"Careful, Adrik." Vadim speaks up finally. "It's a wise man who knows when to defer to his betters."

I spare Vadim a dismissive glance, still annoyed with the buddy-buddy exchange I'd interrupted between them. "Why don't you lead by example and go see to my other VIPs, Uncle?"

Vadim's jaw clenches, but he nods all the same. "Of course. Whatever you need, nephew."

Adrik's nostrils flare as his gaze veers from Vadim to me. "You may have the lion's share of power *now*, but I've beaten you in the past and I can do it again."

I smirk. Now, I'm really amused. "Are you referring to the arms deal you stole off me four years ago? Remind me again. Wasn't that the same company I obliterated by coaxing all your buyers to sell to me?"

His jaw relaxes, then clenches as he breaks eye contact. "I'll keep that in mind while I'm drinking your booze and enjoying your women."

I suppress a scowl, annoyed that he's not taking the hint and leaving. But I'm not about to give Adrik the satisfaction of kicking him out and making a public spectacle. The man loves an audience.

"Let's call it a truce for tonight," Adrik declares. "Right now, we're just old friends catching up. Come—let's drink and enjoy the night."

Two cocktail waitresses enter the box with fresh trays of drinks and Adrik's gaze zones in on the leggy blonde in the pink bustier.

"I gotta hand it to you, Ruslan: you have a great selection." He licks his lip and throws her a wink.

I rest my hand on his shoulder, interrupting his intense leer. "Keep those wandering hands to yourself. I have a zero-tolerance policy for guests who harass my waitresses. Is that understood?"

"Of course." He sneers. "I wouldn't even *think* of crossing the mighty Ruslan Oryolov on his own territory."

I leave him to his entourage and find Kirill in the same spot by the bar where I'd left him. "Well?" he asks the moment he spots me.

I lean against the counter and turn to face the crowd. "I'm not sure what's going on yet, but..."

"Trouble's brewing?"

I scan the second mezzanine. Adrik's entourage remains in the same box, but the man himself is missing.

"Lots of it."

16

EMMA

I smell him before I see him. The rancid scent of sulfur and vomit burns my nostrils as I remove my heels and tiptoe toward my room. *If I just stay quiet enough...*

"Where've you been all night?"

Dammit.

Ben is propped up on the living room sofa, and of course, tonight of all nights, he happens to be wide awake.

"Just... out."

He frowns, his tongue clicking softly. "It's late."

I drop my heels off to the side. "Which is why I'm heading straight to bed."

His eyes narrow and, for a moment, I feel like a teenager who's broken curfew. "The kids were asking for you all night."

"I was *busy*, Ben. What do you want me to say?" He has some nerve, making me feel guilty about this. "I would think you'd be grateful to spend some quality time with your kids."

He ignores that and swings his legs off the sofa to snatch up a can of beer from where it's lying on the floor. "Who's the guy?"

I tense immediately. "What guy?"

"The guy you missed bedtime for. The guy you're clearly fucking."

My lips purse. "Good*night*, Ben."

I leave him to his depressing pyramid of empty beer cans and seek refuge in my room. My body is throbbing with the kind of slow ache that I used to find satisfying.

Except, in this case, all I feel is guilt.

It started way before Ben opened his big, fat mouth. Right around the time Ruslan flung my clothes in my face and told me, in no uncertain terms, that he wanted me out of his bed and out of his space.

Charming.

I would have loved to just fall into my pillows and wipe my thoughts clean. But I can still smell him on me. Musky, oaky, minty. I strip down and jump into the shower. The water is cold, but I don't mind. For a few seconds at least, I'm so focused on my breathing that I forget the way Ruslan ushered me out of his apartment and practically shoved me out the elevator doors.

The building security guard had given me a skeptical look. *You're just one more in his revolving door of conquests, so enjoy it while it lasts and be prepared for when he decides he's had enough of you.*

There's a slight chance I may have been projecting.

It's just that it felt so good—in the moment, at least. I'd been nervous, sure. But he managed to calm me down and put me at ease.

I lost myself in the heat of his gaze and the next few hours became a whirlwind of panting, moaning, sweaty, breathy, intense sex. The kind of sex that you call your best friend about so that you can give her *all* the salacious details because you can't quite believe just how good it was.

I can't call Phoebe, though. Because telling anyone about my arrangement with Ruslan would mean forfeiting both a ton of money and a ton of good sex.

Did I say good sex? I mean *great* sex. I mean *mind-blowing, once-in-a-lifetime, I'll-feed-off-the-memories-when-I'm-old-gray-and-trapped-in-a-boring-marriage* kind of sex.

Still, great sex aside, it's getting harder and harder to ignore the fact that I'm exchanging sex for money. There's a word for it…

Oh, right!

Prostitution.

In other words, I'm a whore. A whore who reeks of the man who just used her body and then discarded her when he was done.

So what does it say about me that I actually *enjoy* the way his scent clings to my skin?

I punish myself by scrubbing said skin raw. By the time I get out of the shower, I'm bright pink from scalp to soles. The lavender body scrub I used has successfully erased his woodsy musk. But I still catch a few oaky notes in the air when I reenter my bedroom.

Stop it. He is not *your freaking boyfriend. You don't get to have expectations. You don't get to have feelings. And you definitely don't get to daydream about him after.*

I turn off the lights and crawl into bed. Compared to Ruslan's foamy, softer-than-air mattress, mine feels like a plank of hard plywood.

My skin stings from my aggressive wash, but it gives me some small measure of comfort. I just have to keep reminding myself why I signed his contract.

Mostly for those kids.

Partly for myself.

The reasoning behind the decision was sound. I just need to remember the rules. I need to adjust my expectations.

Time to be a big girl now.

17

___

EMMA

I'm at my desk at eight o'clock on the dot.

The point is to be here before him, so that I can prove to Ruslan—and to myself—that I can handle this arrangement. While we're at Bane, he's my boss. When we're out of the office, he's my—

Oh God, he's here.

"Be cool, Emma," I snap at myself under my breath.

He's wearing a black Burberry coat over his tailored suit. His briefcase catches the light at his side. I lift my chin as he approaches. His eyes meet mine.

Three... two... one...

"Good morning, Mr. Oryolov."

Stuck the landing. Nice job, girl.

He nods coolly and heads into his office. I let out a heavy breath and sink back against my chair. I'm actually pretty proud of how I'm doing. No one would guess I'd spent half the night tossing and turning, worrying about what Sienna would say if she ever found out I'd sold my soul to the devil.

He's a handsome devil, though...

Focus! You're at the office now. There's no point thinking about the way he jerked himself off while watching you come. Or the way he fucked you over the gorgeous black armchair by the window. Or the moment when he—

Ping!

RUSLAN: *Have the day's schedule on my desk in five.*

I snatch up the schedule I already printed and step into his office. "Here you are, sir."

He takes the sheet of paper without looking away from his laptop screen.

So far, so good. Nothing's been different about our interaction. He's my boss; I'm his assistant. And I'm definitely *not* thinking about the way his jaw clenched every time he thrust into me last night.

Once he's done scanning through the schedule, he hands it back to me. "Push my eight o'clock meeting by an hour. And I'll need you to pick up lunch from Spice Symphony today."

I make a note. "Will do. Did you want something scheduled for one o'clock?"

"No. Raquel will be joining me for lunch."

My pen freezes on the paper. Raquel is one of the rich, beautiful socialite-slash-influencer-slash models that Ruslan keeps in his rotation for parties, events, and charities. Every so often, one of his "dates" shows up at the office to have lunch with him.

I swallow hard and glance up from my notepad. He's not looking at me. His attention is back on the laptop screen.

I could break the invisible boundaries of our agreement right now and ask him just what the hell he's playing at. *Are you having lunch with her alone? Why are you having lunch with her at all? Didn't we agree to be monogamous?*

But the moment I ask any one of those questions, he's going to know I care. He's going to assume I'm getting attached, emotional… clingy.

"Will that be all, sir?" I'm proud of the fact that my voice remains composed and casual.

"That will be all."

I nod and step out, even though my heart is doing stupid, self-pitying pitter-patters in my chest.

This isn't some torrid romance.

It's business.

I need to remember that.

"Pizza?"

Both Reagan and Caroline are looking up at me with wide eyes, their excitement momentarily suspended until they get concrete confirmation that the cheesy goodness I'm holding is indeed for them.

I turn the boxes to the side to give them a glimpse of the logo. "*Two* pizzas!"

It's like I just announced that Santa Claus and the Easter Bunny just teamed up to invent a new holiday. Both girls erupt into a chorus of unintelligible screams. I'm fighting a nasty migraine, but honestly, seeing them this happy is so worth it.

I've been feeling like a failure as an aunt and a guardian lately and, even though all I'm offering them is cheesy dough, it still feels like a victory.

"Auntie Em?" Josh walks over to me from the kitchen.

"Hey, Joshie!" I wrap an arm around his shoulder. "Did you hear the news? We're having pizza for dinner."

He frowns. I hate that he's become so wary of good fortune.

"I felt bad about last week," I explain in a quieter voice. "I promised you guys pizza and we ended up eating cornflakes."

"That's okay. I like cornflakes."

"But you *love* pizza. Am I right?" That gets a small smile out of him. "Come on; let's go unbox these babies."

The girls spread their arms, pretending to be birds, and zoom into the kitchen behind us. Thankfully, the kitchen isn't the disaster area I expect. It looks relatively clean, with the notable exception of the giant human stain sitting at the table.

Ben eyes the boxes when I set them down. "Two?"

I have my fabricated answer at the ready. "It was a buy-one, get-one-free deal."

Josh grabs plates while the girls fill up glasses of water for everyone. Ben is the only one who doesn't move, except to knock back the beer he's palming.

"Thought you were strapped for cash."

I don't like the look in Ben's eye. "I am. But the kids deserve to have a little treat once in a while."

"Mm. So this has nothing to do with the new guy in your life?"

I ignore him altogether and just speak to the kids. "Okay, guys, gather around and sit down. I wanna tell you something."

Ben crosses his arms. "This oughta be good."

I have no idea why he's been all up in my business recently, but I'm too happy to care today. "I'm gonna be putting in a lot of overtime in the next few months, so you might be spending a lot more time with Amelia. Is that okay?"

Ben glares at me. "If they said it wasn't, would it make a difference?"

I. Will. Not. Get. Sucked. In.

"Guys?"

"Sure, Auntie Em," Josh offers for all three of them.

Ben cocks an eyebrow. "Overtime, huh? Is that what you're calling it?"

I spend the whole dinner feeling like I'm playing a game of dodgeball. He keeps lobbing questions at me and I keep avoiding them. I'm prepared to lie through my teeth for the rest of my life if I need to. Because there's no way I'm telling

Ben I'm making more money. Just like there's no way I'm letting his bitterness screw me and the kids over again.

Over my dead body.

Better yet—over *his.*

18

RUSLAN

It was a mistake to fuck her.

I was working under the assumption that sleeping with Emma would get her out of my system. We'd have regular sex, it would eventually get boring, and then I'd terminate our contract. She'd get a fat severance package and I'd be able to walk away without a care in the world.

What I didn't count on was her tunneling her way into my subconscious.

I go to bed thinking about our next meeting. I wake up horny from dreams of her. I spend most of my day trying not to look at her too long or too intensely.

It's fucking ridiculous is what it is. I need to get my head on straight. And I've decided that the best way to do that is to make plans for lunch or dinner with a different woman every day for a week until this resolves itself.

It serves the dual purpose of keeping me distracted as well as keeping Emma in her place—which is preferably right beneath me. Naked and spread-eagled.

But since that can't happen any time between the hours of nine and five, this is a better remedy. She doesn't get to question me about who I have lunch with and I don't need to feel guilty about welcoming a different woman into my office each day.

Sure enough, there's no guilt when I look at the name on my calendar today.

But the dread is real.

"Mr. Oryolov?"

I keep my gaze fixed on my phone. The angelic white blouse that Emma is wearing today is giving me "preacher's daughter" vibes and I've already wasted most of the morning imagining her on her knees in front of me, begging to be corrupted.

"Yes?"

"Jessica Allens has just arrived."

I can't help my sneer. *Jessica fucking Allens.* Trust fund heiress. Socialite diva. Daddy's girl. An all-around goddamned nightmare.

Sometimes, I wonder why I put myself through the indignity of her company. Then I remember: her daddy's not just rich; he's important. Hiram Allens is the city's newly appointed police commissioner, and for a man with my variety of irons in the fire, that's a connection I can't afford to pass up.

"Send her in." I'm forced to look up when Emma stays where she is. "Was there something else?"

Judging from the vein throbbing on Emma's forehead, there most certainly is.

"She asked me to get her a finger bowl because, and I quote —" Emma's face screws up in a haughty expression that's all nose and chin—"she *'doesn't like to use public restrooms.'*"

I press my lips together in a hard line to keep myself from smiling.

"*And* she asked me to get her some weird tea thing that I've never heard of. *Gu-yusu…* something or the other. I told her we didn't have that on hand, and she responded by dropping her fur coat and heavy bag right on my desk. Like she's in *The Devil Wears Prada.*"

I raise my brow. "Is that a euphemism?"

She snorts with laughter but manages to rein herself in fast. Her cheeks are flushed a delicate shade of pink. Of course, that might also be infuriation and rage—pretty common symptoms to have after spending any length of time with the resident princess-bitch of New York.

"It's a movie."

I glance back at my phone for no reason. But it's necessary that I look busy whenever Emma is in the room. It helps me avoid any prolonged eye contact.

"There's some salted sakura tea in the director's lounge. She can make do with that."

"Doubtful," Emma mutters darkly.

"She's difficult," I agree.

"Then *why* are you having lunch with her?"

There's nothing ostensibly possessive about that question, but it rubs me the wrong way regardless. "I'm not sure I need to justify my lunch dates to my assistant, Ms. Carson."

She stiffens instantly and, just like that, the vein in her forehead is back. "Right. I'll just let her in then. Have a *wonderful* lunch."

I suppose I deserve that snark.

Seconds after Emma exits, Jessica enters. She looks like she's going to a fancy cocktail party. Her genetically-engineered body is squeezed into a velvet bandage dress and her makeup is so thick that it almost manages to hide all the plastic surgery she's done to her face.

"Ruslan, darling!" She walks gracefully for a woman in six-inch heels. "You get more and more handsome every time I see you."

My gaze slides to the door, then back to her Botoxed forehead. Pretty sure if I were to facepalm her, she wouldn't feel a thing.

I walk her over to the stainless steel table in the neighboring alcove and pull a chair out for her. We spend a good fifteen minutes talking about her damned acrylic nails before Emma shows up with the tea.

"Here you go, Ms. Allens."

Jessica scrunches up her nose. "No guayusa?"

"We're fresh out, Ms. Allens."

"Disappointing."

The vein seems to have taken up permanent residence on Emma's forehead. But apart from that little tell, her face gives nothing away. "If that's all, then…"

She's backing away from the table when Jessica snaps her fingers. "Hold on. Where did you put my coat and bag?"

"They're on my desk, Ms. Allens. Exactly where you dum— left them."

Jessica is not even looking at Emma when she speaks. "That coat is worth more than your entire apartment. Make sure it's looked after."

Emma's jaw clenches. Now that Jessica is looking away, she lets her professional mask slide right off. If looks could kill, Jessica would be a smoldering pile of ash.

I can't say I'd mind.

The moment the door shuts, Jessica rolls her eyes. "What a ditz, huh? Finding good help is *so* hard these days."

Something inside my chest roars to life. I can't quite put my finger on it, but it's accompanied by a very specific thought: *No one insults my woman.*

On the heels of that thought is pure fucking terror.

What the fuck? My *woman?*

"*Ahem*! Ruslan? Where'd you go, handsome?"

I blink away the little red spots that are honestly a welcome distraction from Jessica's face and do my damned best to appear like I'm actually happy to see her.

We spend the next hour flitting from one mundane subject to the next. The only consistent thing about the conversation is the fact that she bookends each topic with the mention of a friend who's getting married or about to get married; a friend who's pregnant or trying to get pregnant.

I keep my phone close the whole time, but try as I might, some of the stupid bullshit she's spewing still manages to slip through.

"… don't you think?"

Since I've completely missed her question, I fall back on my tried-and-true default. "Hm."

Her eyebrows hitch up with excitement. "I knew it. It's the broody, silent ones that are big teddy bears on the inside."

Okay. So maybe it's not a foolproof response. "Come again?"

"It would be a terrible shame if you didn't have children, Ruslan. I mean, look at that jawline of yours! Those genes need to be passed on!"

I nip that shit in the bud immediately. One: I'm not the fatherly type. Two: I have no idea what this woman's children would actually look like; shit, I've forgotten what *she* used to look like. And three: the thought of procreating with her just made me violently sick to my stomach.

"Children aren't on my radar."

"Oh." Her face drops. "But—"

I make a show of glancing down at my Rolex. "It's been a pleasure catching up, Jessica. But I have meetings to get to."

"Oh. Okay. Shall we schedule another date soon? Maybe dinner next time?"

I nod. "I'll have my assistant contact yours."

I open the door for her and Jessica's eyes veer straight to Emma. She makes a point of placing her hand on my chest, her eyelashes fluttering unnecessarily.

"Thanks for a *mesmerizing* lunch, handsome." She leans in, her lips coming for mine. I turn my face deftly to the side and her kiss finds my cheek.

"Jessica."

I step back into the safety of my office and close the door on her faltering smile.

Well, that was a fucking shitshow. But it *did* get me thinking.

Apparently, everyone has babies on the brain. Everyone except me. I need to make sure that I'm covered with Emma where that's concerned. The contract has a detailed section on contraception that Emma signed, indicating she was on the pill. But that leaves the responsibility squarely in her hands.

I thought I was comfortable with it at the time, but the more I think about it, the more I want to take back some control. Condoms aren't my favorite thing, but I'm willing to wear them if they'll prevent an unwanted pregnancy with my secretary.

It's alarming how fast the image rushes to the forefront of my mind. Emma, wearing a blouse similar to the one she's wearing today—except that it billows over her stomach to accommodate the child she's carrying. *My* child.

No.

That's just the caveman in me talking. I don't even want a child. I certainly don't want one with Emma.

No matter how much my dick is suddenly obsessed with the idea.

19

EMMA

"What's different about you?"

On the inside, I'm wincing hard. I've been terrified of this exact question ever since Phoebe called me up yesterday and suggested we go out for lunch. I keep my face perfectly composed as I answer. "I don't know what you mean."

Even to my own ears, I sound fake as hell and twice as guilty. This might just be the first time I've ever had to lie to Phoebe. It's not as though I'm kicking off this new phase in our friendship with a small secret, either. It's a whopper of one—a six-foot-four, two-hundred-pound secret in a Tom Ford suit and Patek Philippe wristwatch.

"Hm." Phoebe drapes her coat over the backrest of her chair and fixes me with an intense stare. "Is there something I should know?"

"Why do you ask?"

She shrugs. "You just seem a little different. There's, like, a bounce in your step."

Okay, she may have a point, but it has *nothing* to do with Ruslan. At least, not in the sense that I'm catching feelings or anything. I'm just riding the sex high straight into Orgasm Town. It's a nice place to be. Especially with someone who knows his way around the bedroom like Ruslan does.

"Oh my God!" Phoebe gasps. "You got laid!"

She blurts it so loudly that the people sitting at the tables on either side turn around to stare at us. *Fantastic.* Now, the whole world knows.

I avoid all eye contact from the gawkers and lean in toward Phoebe. "First of all—*no*! And second of all—*shhh*!"

Phoebe waves away my horror. "Pshh, please. New Yorkers don't care about a damn thing. And you were blushing just then! What were you thinking?"

Orgasm Town.

"Nothing! I'm just earning a little extra cash, okay? Maybe that's why I apparently have this alleged 'bounce' in my step. It's nice to put a dent in those loans." I exhale sharply. I almost let it slip that they've all been paid, but that would be a huge tipoff I literally cannot afford to make. "You have no idea what a relief it is to know for sure that you won't run out of money at the end of the month."

I might be hamming it up just a little. But I really need to sell this story.

Unfortunately, Phoebe's eyes narrow and she sucks in her cheeks. I know from personal experience that nothing good can come from that expression. "You may not be lying to me, but you're not telling me the whole truth, either."

I avoid her gaze by picking at my almond croissant. "Listen, Pheebs—"

"There *is* a guy, isn't there?" She grabs my wrist and I'm forced to meet her eyes.

I squirm in my seat, feeling the weight of that contract settle on my shoulders. It was *very* clear. But half an hour with my bestie and I'm already cracking under pressure.

"There's a... guy, of sorts," I concede. "But I wasn't gonna tell you because it's not serious." My chest feels super tight and I've completely lost my appetite. And that's saying something, because Choux-Choux Cafe's almond croissant is like manna from heaven with crack cocaine dusted on top.

"Um, hello? I'm the queen of casual sex," she reminds me.

I cringe. "Not the same thing." The monogamy part of the contract flashes before my mind's eye. "It's... complicated."

Phoebe frowns. Those dark brown eyes of hers can be penetrating when she cranks the power up to full blast. "Complicated how?"

"You know how these things are."

"I know how casual sex works, sure. But the whole point of casual sex is that it's not complicated." She raises one eyebrow. "Unless..."

"Pheebs, don't—"

"Unless you have feelings for this guy."

"*No!*"

She sets down her espresso and leans back in her chair. "Well, *that* was certainly emphatic."

"Only because I do *not* have feelings for this—"

Phoebe gasps. "It's the bosshole!"

Fuck. Me.

"I'm right, aren't I?" She laughs triumphantly and punches the air. "I fucking knew it! Something's been brewing between the two of you for a while now. It was only a matter of time."

"That is—"

"One hundred percent true, is what it is. You just didn't want to see it because you hate him so much. Correction: you *hated* him so much."

"Oh, I still do," I admit before I tack on a reluctant, "… sometimes."

Phoebe claps a hand over her heart and gives me a wistful smile. "I am so happy for you. I cannot even put it into words. Now, let's get to the really important stuff: what's he like in bed? He's good, right? He has to be. With that face, that body, those juicy forearms—"

"*Pheebs!*"

"What?"

"You cannot tell a soul!"

Her eyes reach full-on Bambi levels of innocence. "Who would I even tell?"

"Just—*anyone.* This is secret information. As in *top* secret. Classified. Area 51-type stuff."

Phoebe sobers up just a bit. "Why do you sound so scared, Em?"

How on earth do I explain to Phoebe that I've just voided a legally-binding contract I signed a little over a week ago? How do I make her understand that one of the main conditions of my agreement with Ruslan is that I keep my mouth shut about it and that I'm already failing miserably? Of course, I can't do that without mentioning the agreement in the first place.

I'm stuck between a place and a rock-hard—wait, that's not how that goes.

"I just really want to keep this under wraps."

"Was that your idea or his?" Phoebe asks shrewdly.

"We both agreed."

She's chewing on her bottom lip now. "You remember Edward, right?"

My mouth turns down at the mere mention of his name. "Oh, do I remember Edward…"

He and Phoebe were only involved for about a year, but it was an intense year. She was twenty; he was forty-two. At the time, she was a struggling college student and he was the owner of a chain of high-end spas and salons spread across New York. It was a match made in hell.

"He had a habit of making me believe I'd made… certain decisions… when he was the one pulling my strings."

"That's not what's happening here."

At least, I don't think.

She nods. "All I'm saying is, beware of men like Edward. Handsome, powerful, richer-than-God? That's bad news. They'll shower you with luxury—roses, clothes, jewelry, fancy meals in fancy restaurants. But they're stingy when it comes to the things that really count. Men like that can be dangerous to the heart." She points a finger at my chest. "Because they refuse to share theirs."

I suppress a shiver rocking me from head to toe. "I understand what you're saying, but trust me: I'm under no illusions as to what Ruslan and I are. We have sex. No feelings, no expectations, no nothing. Just sex. End of story."

Her forehead wrinkles. "Which is great—if you can keep your feelings out of it. The question is: can you?"

20

RUSLAN

There's something about the symmetry of a boxing ring that centers me.

Which is exactly the reason I had a twenty-four foot diameter ring installed in the massive gym complex I designed for myself and my crew. It's an exclusive membership. Price of entry? Lifelong fealty sealed with the mark of the Oryolov Bratva branded onto your skin.

I pull my gloves on and breathe in the scent of freshly-sanitized leather. They're stitched with my initials on the side so the men know they're off-limits.

What can I say? I'm a possessive bastard when it comes to my things.

Kirill is jumping in place inside the ring. He's the only one I box against consistently because he's the only one who offers me a challenge. We're close to evenly matched. Fifteen years of beating each other to a pulp means he knows my weaknesses and I know his.

Makes the fight so much more interesting that way.

"Ready to eat canvas?"

I smirk. "It always amazes me how cocky you are, considering *I* won the last three rounds."

"I have to throw you a bone every once in a while, don't I?"

We start to circle one another. "You're doing a lot of talking from that end of the ring," I remark.

Kirill laughs as he moves towards me with his elbows tucked to his chest, fists over his chin. I know what to expect. He's an impatient bastard, so he almost always throws the first punch.

As expected, he lunges toward me with a jab. I block it once, twice, three times before Kirill lets up. The moment he pulls his fists back, I swing a powerful uppercut.

"Fuck!" Kirill groans, crunching forward.

He reroutes himself quickly and charges forward again. I see the combination he's planning before it even begins. Jab, jab, cross, big right hook designed to separate my head from my shoulders.

I meet them all—both jabs fly off my mitts, I swerve the cross, and then, before that hook can find my chin, I sink a huge left hand directly into his gut, centered on the liver.

Kirill lets out a huge grunt as he collapses back against the ropes, his chest rising and falling hard. I just smirk at him. "You were saying something about luck?"

His jaw flexes and he cracks his neck from side to side. "So… how was your lunch with Jessica yesterday?"

I suppress a smile. Given how well we knew each other's boxing styles, sometimes the only way to win is to get inside each other's heads.

"She was her usual nightmarish self," I say as we resume.

"So you continue to see her... why? For those new tits she's toting around? Heard Dr. Caviezel did a really great job with them."

He launches another barrage of jabs. I block them all, then return fire, backing him up into the far corner of the ring. "The only part of that woman's body that I'm interested in is the palm of her hand." I throw another uppercut that Kirill manages to narrowly avoid.

"Pardon?"

"Because her daddy is right there, in the center of it."

Kirill snorts. "True." Then he gives me an evil grin. "You know, you could just marry the woman. Then Hiram Allens becomes your daddy by marriage."

He lets his hands drop just enough to give me a window. I take full advantage, rocketing a left cross into his eye socket. It's enough to drop him to the ground.

Looking down at him, I laugh. "This strategy's not working for you, brother. You're just giving me fuel."

Kirill manages to get back on his feet before his ten seconds are up. "It's a serious suggestion." I dance a little closer to him to do some more damage to his body while he tries to bob and weave away from me. "Like Vadim says—you need to make babies. And soon."

"Fucker," I growl.

Laughing, Kirill skirts the edge of the ring. He leans back, arms slung across the ropes, as he waggles his eyebrows at me. "Of course you've already contracted a woman for sex. Why not contract the same woman for a baby?"

"Son of a bitch." I charge him and we get tangled up in a clinch, muscles flexing and sweating as each of us searches for leverage.

"Emma's not gonna be the mother of my children," I snarl as we separate just enough for me to rip off a triple jab that leaves Kirill's nose gushing blood.

He dances away once more. He's bleeding like a stuck pig, but you wouldn't know it from the smile on his face. "Hm, I seem to have got you going there. Could it be that the pretty little assistant is a weak spot?"

It takes more than a hook to the face to shut my best friend up. A Mack truck to the face might not be enough, either.

The moment he gets out of attack range, he grins wickedly. "Bet she's an animal in bed though, right? Tell me: is she a moaner or a screamer?"

That fucking does it.

I combine my arsenal—speed, agility, power—and descend on him like a fucking storm. Kirill does his best to hold his own, but few can withstand the beast that is my possessiveness.

With a handful of hard blows, I have Kirill kissing the same canvas he promised me I would have to eat.

"It's in your best interests to stay down, brother."

Kirill twists around and lies sprawled flat against the canvas. Sweat drips off him and puddles around his body. "Oh, I have zero intention of getting up anytime soon," he chuckles. "Also, you're welcome."

I scowl. "For *what?*"

He lifts his neck up maybe two inches and looks around. "For making you look good in front of your men."

I lift my gaze. An audience gathered during our match and I'd barely noticed. Kirill said her name and all I'd been able to see were red dots blurring my vision. My men are nodding their approval of the fight; I catch satisfied, respectful nods in deference to my victory over my second-in-command.

Kirill is known as an elite boxer within the walls of this complex. He's sparred with most of the men here and come out on top time and time again. Beating him is a mark of skill, a badge of honor.

I offer him my hand and pull Kirill back up onto his feet. "Well played."

He smirks. "*You* have the control, brother. You need to make sure you keep it. Especially when it comes to the girl."

I clap him on the back and he exits the ring.

Kirill's right. My preoccupation with Emma feels dangerous somehow. But the only way it has the power to do any real damage is if *I* let it.

And I have no intention of letting anything or anyone control me.

Not even that intoxicating little *kiska.*

21

EMMA

Best friends have a way of asking you exactly the question you least want to hear. Phoebe's eyes stay locked on mine as her words ring in my ears.

Which is great—if you can keep your feelings out of it. The question is: can you?

That's the question of the year. Of the lifetime, maybe.

Because I've had these nightmares already and I know what would happen if the answer turns out to be "no." I spend as little waking time as possible considering those outcomes.

Luckily, I'm saved from having to actually answer her question by a call vibrating my phone. I turn it over and groan the moment I see the name on my lock screen. "Satan's Right and Left Hands." I hold the phone up to Phoebe so she can see.

"Ugh. Just ignore them."

Talk to the demons who spawned me or answer Phoebe's question? Better the devil you know than the devil you sleep with, I guess.

Or something like that.

I give her an apologetic shrug and accept the call. Phoebe shrugs right back and walks off to the bakery counter to get a danish.

"Hey, Mom."

"Hi, honey!" She's so over-the-top cheerful that I roll my eyes. "You didn't return my calls last week."

"I know; I'm sorry. I've just been swamped at work."

"Mm, yes. Ben mentioned that."

I grit my teeth. "You spoke to Ben?"

"Of course!" She has the gall to sound offended. "He is my son-in-law and the father of my grandchildren. Not to mention the fact that my *daughter* doesn't pick up my calls anymore."

Biting my tongue is the main reason I survived eighteen years under their roof. Well, that and Sienna. But with each passing year that I have to do this without my sister, it becomes more and more difficult to turn the other cheek.

"That's because your daughter is busting her ass trying to provide for those kids. Ben can't bust his ass—he's too busy sitting on it."

"Ben is *grieving*, Emma. It wouldn't hurt you to have a little empathy for the man."

Twenty seconds into the call and I'm already gripping the edge of the table so hard my knuckles have turned white. "A little empathy? Mom, it's been three and a half freaking years! I'm grieving, too. That doesn't mean you shut down and ignore the fact that you have three growing child—"

"Emma Lorraine Carson! My goodness. There's no need to shout."

I close my eyes and practice breathing. In through the nose, out through the mouth. You'd think twenty-six years of practice would be enough to get the hang of it; but if you knew my mom, you'd realize otherwise. I'm gonna pop a blood vessel at the rate I'm going. "I didn't realize I was shouting."

She sniffles. "I'm just saying, honey: he's going through a lot. Sienna was the center of his world."

I shake my head in disbelief. Sienna was the center of *my* world, too. She was my center long before she was Ben's. But I've still been able to pick myself up and do what I can for those kids. Because I loved Sienna enough to protect what she loved most.

"Emma? Are you still there?"

"Yeah, Mom." I dig at the flaking table lacquer with my thumbnail as that familiar tide of grief ebbs and flows in all its usual places. "I'm here."

"So… how are the children? John's birthday is coming up soon, isn't it?"

I scowl at my half-eaten croissant. "First of all, it's *Josh*. And his birthday was two months ago. So no, it's not coming up soon."

She titters self-consciously. "Oh, I must have confused it with the girls' birthdays. They were born in March, right?"

"I'm sorry—do you think the girls share a birthday?"

"Twins usually do, honey. What a silly question."

I press my thumb and index fingers to the corners of my forehead and rub slowly. I *was* busy last week when Mom called. But honestly, even if I wasn't, avoiding her calls is completely justified.

"Except for the fact that the girls aren't actually twins, Mom."

"What do you mean? Of course they are. Sienna used to refer to them as her little twins all the time."

"Sienna referred to them as her *Irish* twins. They were born eleven months apart in the same year."

"Oh." She rallies fast. "See? This is what happens when you don't bring the children over to visit their grandparents regularly."

Wow. I forgot about Mom's famous backhand. There's no issue, big or small, that she can't lob blame back on someone else. She's an artist at it.

"Why don't you bring them over this weekend? Saturday is perfect."

"What's happening on Saturday?"

"What do you mean?"

"I mean that you only ever mention specific dates when you're hosting some sort of event and you want to show the kids off like prize ponies."

"*Emma Lorraine!*" That makes twice in one conversation that she's whipped out the middle name. She's in rare form. "Sometimes, you sound so much like—"

I can hear her breathing hitch up just a little. I wait for her to backpedal or make this out to be my fault, but apparently, she's shocked even herself. Probably by managing to forget one of her two daughters is dead.

I'm tempted to call her out, but Phoebe is walking back to the table and I really don't have the emotional bandwidth to keep this conversation going.

"Listen, Mom, I've gotta go."

"Okay." She actually sounds relieved. "And remember, the offer still stands."

"What offer?"

"To take the kids. You said it yourself: you're struggling to provide for them and you refuse to take our money—"

"I'm not interested in taking anything you try to give me with strings attached, Mom."

Phoebe sits down opposite me, her eyebrows arching.

"Strings? What strings? There are no strings. Your father and I just want to be more involved in the children's lives. We want to be able to introduce them to our circle of friends, expose them to new people, new opportunities."

In other words: strings.

"I'll think about it. Love you. Bye."

The moment I hang up, Phoebe throws me a curious glance. "What selfless gesture is she offering up today?"

I roll my eyes. "Taking the kids off my hands."

"That again? I thought you nipped that in the bud."

"I thought I did, too, but my parents don't give up that easily."

Phoebe frowns. "Still—you *do* deserve to get some help."

"If I accept their help, they'll own me. Beatrice and Barrett may look sweet, but those two are cold, hard gangsters when it comes to their investments. And trust me: the littles are nothing more than investments to them."

Phoebe sighs. "I know. It's just a shame. They have plenty of money."

"They can keep their money. I have my own. And what I don't have, I'll earn. With blood, sweat, and tears if I have to."

And sex.

I'm struggling to keep the blush off my cheeks, so I hide behind my coffee mug. "It's more important to me that the kids are happy. I can't hand them over to my parents. Not after what Sienna and I went through with them."

"Hey, I hear you loud and clear. I'm just worried about you." Phoebe sighs. "I don't want you to give so much of yourself away that you have nothing left."

I smile. That's why I've always loved Phoebe: she thinks of me even when I don't. Sienna was always the bright light between the pair of us, but Phoebe saw me just as clearly.

"Have I told you lately how much I love you?"

She gives me a sly wink. "You could prove it to me by telling me all the juicy details about banging your bad boy boss."

"Ugh."

"Wow, sex was that bad, huh?"

"No—"

"So it was that good?"

I shake my head with a shy smile. I know she won't let up unless I give her *something*. "Let's just say it was... explosive."

Phoebe snaps her fingers and does a little shoulder shimmy for me. "*Yes,* queen!"

It's easy to push away the unease when I'm with Phoebe. It's easy to forget that I'm playing with fire. Just goes to show, really—rules are so easy to break.

22

EMMA

After breakfast, I say goodbye to Phoebe at the subway and cut across Central Park. There's a city's worth of people walking their dogs or lying on picnic blankets or running after their kids. It's a perfect day for a nice walk through the trees.

I'm so lost in my thoughts that I don't realize it until I'm passing right beneath it, but I know this tree. Sienna and I used to bring Josh here right after he was born. We'd lie around, just like all these people are doing today, and we'd talk and laugh and spend afternoons blissfully ignorant of the future that was hurtling down the barrel towards us.

I stop and look up. The tree looks a little barer now. Thinner in the trunk, graying in the leaves. I have that familiar pang in my chest. The deep aching stab that comes with the reminder that she's not here anymore. We will never again sit under those sparse leaves and bitch about all the little things in our lives that we thought—at the time—would be our biggest problems.

Sometimes, I miss her so much I can't stand it. That's when I'm usually hit with memories I didn't even remember I had in the bank.

"Did you see that? Did you see it?" Sienna said, grabbing my ankle. "He did a little twerk!"

I laid back in the grass, hands folded behind my head. I didn't even bother opening my eyes. Sienna was always claiming that Josh did this and Josh did that. More often than not, what she thought was a sign of genius turned out to be gas.

"I'm not surprised. He is *your kid."*

She smacked my leg. "You're not even looking."

"Si, he's one*. I sincerely doubt he's twerking."*

"Just look!"

Reluctantly, I cracked open an eye and glanced over at my nephew. His chubby little hands were planted in the grass as his butt wiggled in the air.

"I think he's just bending over."

She threw me an irritated glare. "Look at that booty shake. Boy has rhythm."

Josh let out a little squawk and pushed himself upright, only to fall back down again. Luckily, he had some squidgy baby blubber and a diaper to keep him safe.

I stifled a yawn. "If you say so."

She grabbed her son and held him up to her face so his pudgy little legs swung around. "Auntie Em doesn't understand what a brilliant, multitalented widdle bunny you are! Yes! Yes, you are! Yes, you are!" Sienna stuck her tongue out at me. "Your Auntie Em is such a square."

I rolled onto my belly and looked up at her and Josh. "Can I ask you a serious, possibly politically incorrect question?"

"Duh. Those are my favorite kind."

"Do you think you'll ever regret it? Getting married and having a baby so young?"

Sienna's smile didn't falter for even a millisecond. "Nope."

"Just like that? You didn't even think about it."

She fixed me with an unblinking stare. "You've known me for nineteen years, Em. Tell me, has there ever been a time when I didn't know exactly *what I wanted?"*

I thought about it. "No, I guess not."

She nods. "I may be young—" She twisted Josh around and placed him on her lap. "—but I will never regret my family. This baby here is my whole entire world. I would die for him."

"You say that about me, too."

"Sure, but I never meant it literally."

I threw my empty Coke can at her while she laughed. Even Josh giggled. Those days felt so ordinary. They got lost in the shuffle of bigger moments, bigger milestones.

I wish I knew then how much I'd miss them.

"Excuse me? Are you Emma Carson?"

I blink at the scrawny man standing in front of me. He's wearing what technically passes for a smile, but nothing about it makes me think he's friendly.

"I'm sorry, have we met before?"

"Well, no. Not technically."

I frown. "Who are you?"

He offers me his hand before he answers the question. "Remmy Jefferson."

I wrack my brain trying to place the name, but I'm coming up blank. I shake his hand just to keep up the polite pretense. "How can I help you?"

"I'm a reporter for *The Brooklyn Gazette*. I like to do my research, Ms. Carson, and I know quite a bit about the man you work for."

"Wait—this is about Rus—uh, Mr. Oryolov?"

He nods and his eyes narrow, but his smile doesn't waver. It makes the hairs on the back of my neck stand on end.

"I'd like to ask you a few questions, if that's okay."

I've always had trouble saying "no" to people. But after Sienna died, it became a whole lot easier. There was something about the finality of her death that made me realize I didn't actually care if people liked me or not. *She* loved me and that was enough.

"Thanks but no thanks. Have a nice day." I try to side-step around him, but he mirrors the movement and blocks me.

"Don't think of it as an interview. Think of it as a public service."

"Excuse me?"

"You're his personal secretary, which means you work closely with him. You know a lot about him. And I'm willing to bet you can find out a whole lot more."

My jaw drops. "You want me to spy on him for you?"

"I'd pay you well." He pulls out a card from the pocket of his light blue jacket and hands it to me. "My details are on the front of the card. On the back is what you'll get paid."

I flip it over. Even before I see the number, I know it's not going to make a lick of difference—but I'm still curious.

More to the point, I'm still adjusting to this new reality where I don't have to scrimp and beg for every penny I can get my hands on. The sticker shock of seeing that much money right there for the taking passes over me.

But even if I was inclined to turn rat on Ruslan, it doesn't come close to what he is paying me to be his—well, his "after-work friend."

I know Ruslan is no Boy Scout. And I'm willing to bet anything he doesn't take kindly to people who cross him. Hell, I *know* he doesn't take kindly to people who cross him. I've watched him make plenty of grown men cry. I even handed one a tissue on his way out of Bane.

I don't want to imagine what he could—or would—do to me.

"Thanks," I say, offering the card back to Remmy. "But like I said: no thanks."

His eyebrows lift and he ignores my hand holding out the card. "Come on. You're a young woman with three dependents living in a big, expensive city. You need this money."

The way he pushes as if he knows better than me only reinforces my decision: I need to get as far away from him and his bad haircut as possible.

"I may need money, but I don't need or want *your* money."

Instead of walking around him, I just turn and walk away from him. He doesn't take the hint though; he follows me right out of Central Park.

"Loyalty is admirable, Emma, but not when it comes to men like Oryolov. He's no good."

"Says the guy stalking a woman through Midtown."

His eyes narrow. "I'm not the bad guy; I'm trying to *catch* the bad guy. Do you really want to clean up after a man who's getting away with literal murder?"

I don't flinch. I don't know Remmy from Adam, but there's something in his demeanor that puts me off. It's the shifty way his gaze travels over my body. The way he's demanding my help like he's entitled to it. The way he thinks it's appropriate in the year 2023 to follow a woman who's clearly not interested.

"Those are some serious allegations you're throwing around," I say coldly. "I'd be careful about slandering the reputation of one of New York's most charitable businessmen."

Remmy snorts. "Those charities are a fucking joke. And they're probably just fronts, anyway. I've already got dirt on him. If you were to help me, Emma, I could expose this fucker. One article. That's all it would take."

I stop walking so abruptly that Remmy has to skid and step back. "Mr. Jefferson, you've told me what you want from me. I've politely refused. I think it's time for you to go."

His bottom lip curls. "This isn't the end of it. I'm going to get what I want, Miss Carson."

I sigh. "That's what most men think. It's the tragedy of the patriarchy."

His scowl only deepens. "One way or the other, I *will* expose Oryolov. And you'll help me."

Before I can tell him to shove it where the sun don't shine, he turns and marches back toward the park.

I glance down at the business card in my hand. I have no doubt that he's found plenty of skeletons in Ruslan's closets. But I'm willing to bet that whatever Remmy has on Ruslan won't be enough to bury him.

Matter of fact, I'd put every dollar I own on Remmy going down first.

23

EMMA

"Is there a problem, Ms. Carson?"

The vibrations of an incoming call have my phone tap-dancing on the top of his desk loudly enough to put my teeth on edge. "Sorry." I snatch it up and decline the call. I don't have to look to know who it is—because it's been ringing off the hook all weekend, as if my parents and Scummy Jefferson coordinated schedules to make sure that one of them was bothering me at all hours of the day and night.

Ruslan arches one dark eyebrow, his lips pursed. "You've been flustered all morning."

Ah, yes, just what every woman wants to hear. And I thought I'd done such a great job of hiding it.

"Oh. Have I?"

"Yes." His voice cuts like broken glass. "It's Monday, Ms. Carson. Most people come back from the weekend with a little gas in their tanks."

"Clearly, those people don't have three children to deal with and a lazy freeloader eating all the snacks in the house. Do you know how important snacks are in a house with three children, Rus—Mr. Oryolov? I'll tell you—*really* fucking important."

On second thought, Ruslan might have a point about the whole "flustered" thing.

I wish I could swallow my words back. Cursing on the job, in front of my boss—my infamously vindictive, short-tempered, maybe-not-maybe-a-mob-boss boss—would normally be a shortcut to getting fired. But I'm really hoping Ruslan will go easy on me.

One, because I really did have a hellaciously stressful weekend.

Two, because I backed him up with the skeezy reporter who wanted me to turn informant for his gossip rag.

And three, because—to put it indelicately—we're fucking.

Well, we *have* fucked, with more contractually-obligated sessions on the horizon. But judging from the way Ruslan is glaring at me right now, that horizon is getting further and further away.

Before Ruslan can kick me out of his office or reprimand me for using inappropriate language in the workplace, my phone starts vibrating yet again.

"I'm so sorry to take up so much of your time, Ms. Carson," Ruslan deadpans. "I didn't realize how busy you were today."

"Sorry, sorry, sorry," I mutter, trying to shut my phone up. "Ugh, how do you turn the damn vibration off?" I almost drop my phone trying to change the settings. In the end, I just shove it into the pocket of my fitted black pants. I glance up to see that Ruslan is still staring at me with those crackling amber eyes.

"If you need the services of a full-time nanny, I can make some inquiries on your behalf. You can certainly afford one now."

It takes a few too many seconds for his offer to compute. While it does, I just blink at him. Is he really trying to be *helpful*? Unless of course he's just being sarcastic and I'm so turned around that it's going right over my head. That would make more sense.

"Um—that's—really nice of you," I manage to choke out. "But the kids already have a nanny. Amelia is good."

"But she's not full-time?"

"No, and I don't want her to be, either." I shift uncomfortably. "I want to be able to spend quality time with them on the weekends at least. I barely get to see them during the week."

I have no idea what he thinks of that. His cheekbones are carved from marble. "At the expense of your own sanity— and by extension, mine?"

I clench my jaw. "I'm not stressed because of the kids. I mean, yes, the weekend was chaotic. Caroline broke a wine glass and Reagan took a marker to the walls. And something's bothering Josh, but I have no idea what because he doesn't—" I clam up when Ruslan's eyebrows knit together. "Well, anyway, my point is that the kids aren't the problem; my parents are."

"Is that who's been calling you?"

"Incessantly."

Among others. I decide to leave all mention of Remmy aside. The less I think of that slimeball, the better.

For a split second, I detect the shadow of a smile on Ruslan's face. But one blink later, he seems just as irritated as ever. "Kindly inform them that you don't take personal calls at work. You're excused, Ms. Carson."

It's a heavy-handed way of saying, '*I don't give a shit about your family drama; just keep it out of the office,*' but I still think I've gotten off easy. I'm almost at the door when he stops me.

"Oh, and Ms. Carson?"

Burying the flinch, I turn back around. "Yes?"

"Be ready at eight tonight."

I gulp and nod. Then I levitate back to my desk.

The world seems brighter and less grim now. A visit to the penthouse is exactly what I need tonight. Between Ben and Remmy and my parents, I'm strung out. I want someone to hit my factory reset button and reboot my brain. And apparently, that button is located inside my vagina.

I glance down at my phone. Thirteen texts from Mother Dearest. Groaning, I open the thread and scroll through the messages. They're all variations on the same old theme: *Bring the kids over so that we can show them off, preferably before we die and you regret forever that you kept us from our grandchildren.*

I mute the thread and put my phone away. I'll deal with Mom and Dad tomorrow. Right now, I have sugar baby duties to prepare for.

～

I feel like a live wire as Ruslan and I ride the elevator up to his penthouse. It's a totally different experience this time around. I'm not nervous; I'm not shy. What I am is *ready*. Ready to forget about all my problems and all my stress. Ready to lose myself in the euphoric haze of heated foreplay and sweaty sex.

Honestly? I don't even really need the foreplay today.

All I want is to have Ruslan fuck me into oblivion, until that urgent sense of pressure in my gut is stamped out altogether. I want his cock so bad I'm actually salivating for it. I want him to give it to me hard. Fast. No holds barred.

Doesn't seem like the feeling is mutual, though.

He's still attached to his phone, his eyes fixated on the screen as he scrolls and scrolls. Even when the doors open, he steps out without lifting his gaze.

The sound of my heels disappears into the plush carpet. I take them off along with my coat. I hear the *click* as Ruslan turns his phone off and something inside me snaps. I'm not interested in playing it cool today. I'm not willing to wait around until he makes the move.

We both know what we're here for. Why beat around the bush?

So I throw myself at him, lips landing hot against his. I didn't expect him to kiss me the first time we did this, but once he ripped that Band-Aid off, all I've been able to think about since then is doing it again.

That kiss was everything.

This one is somehow *more*.

I don't give him any time to react before I'm ripping at the buttons of his shirt. One flies right off and almost pops me in the face. But I'm not willing to let anything slow me down.

My hands slide down his washboard midsection while little shivers run through my body. I trace his tattoos with my fingertips. When I cup his dick through his pants and give it a squeeze, he lets out a soft growl. Then, without warning, I find myself thrown against the wall, hands pinned to the sides of my head, trapped between the wall and the heat of his skin.

"What's gotten into you today, *kiska?*" His lips travel along my jaw and down towards my neck.

"The thought of *you* getting inside me," I gasp. "I can't wait today, Ruslan."

"Hm."

That sound…

"Fuck me," I beg. He pushes his hips against me, his erection stabbing at my thigh. "*Ahh…* please… Just fuck me."

"You want it rough today?"

He knocks my legs apart with his knee and forces himself between them. His cock is right there, pressing at my pussy through my pants.

"Y-yes," I moan. "Oh God, yes."

His lips slide back up to my ear. He circles my lobe with his tongue. "Dirty little *kiska*. You want me to fuck you like the filthy little minx you are?"

I nod frantically as my eyes roll back in my head. Is it possible to have an orgasm just from dirty talk? I'm game to find out.

His tongue sneaks into my mouth and I'm caught off-guard by how harsh it is. It's not a kiss at all; it's a tongue fuck. It's him saying, *You're mine. Every inch of you, head to toe, inside and out.*

My cheeks are flushed and my lips rubbed raw, but still, he demands more. He takes greedily, his tongue demanding payment, his cock threatening to rip through the crotch of my pants.

When he breaks away, I'm gasping for breath. My head is spinning so fast that if he weren't holding me up, I'd be melted into a puddle on the floor.

He captures my gaze for a split second. Those amber eyes are ablaze. "Be careful what you wish for, little *kiska*."

He pushes my hands together and pins them in place over my head. He unbuttons my pants first and then his. His palm presses firmly against my soaked panties before he spins me around and yanks them down around my thighs.

"Ruslan…" I whisper helplessly as his cock teases against my drenched pussy. The head of him parts my lips. One more tease. One more tortured moment of waiting.

Then he thrusts forward. I'm so wet that he slips inside me without any effort. My whole body bears down around him.

I asked for rough and that's exactly what he gives me. There's no easing into things tonight. We've been in the door for all of two minutes and he's already driving into me with every ounce of force he has.

"Yes, *yes!*" I moan. My head keeps banging against the wall every time he thrusts into me, but I can't feel a thing. The only thing I'm capable of feeling is his huge cock, the tension of his fingers cuffed around my wrists, the way my body fires off sparks that feel like electricity every time his hips collide with mine.

He crashes against me until my body clenches into one raw sensation. My pussy contracts violently and then it releases in a series of explosions that set my skin on fire.

"Oh, God," I gasp, falling back against Ruslan's shoulder.

He releases my arms and they fall limp to the sides. Then he slides his hands down towards my ass and grips me a little tighter, before hoisting me into his arms. "You have a habit of coming early, *kiska*. That's going to have to stop or I'll have to punish you."

He carries me into the living room while my body still courses with residual shivers. "Yes," I breathe. "Punish me."

"Such an eager little *kiska.* You'll learn soon enough not to ask for more than you can handle."

He sets me down on the arm of his sofa. A part of me cringes at the thought of my bare butt on the cashmere upholstery, like my peasant ass doesn't belong anywhere near furniture this expensive.

Then he tears off my blouse and all thoughts of that variety go right out of the floor-to-ceiling window.

Ruslan's simmering amber eyes are still fixated on my swollen lips. He passes his thumb across them in one swoop, frowning intently like something about the beautiful damage he does to my body bothers him.

Then he withdraws his touch abruptly and any trace of tenderness I thought I might've seen in his face disappears. That snarling mask snaps back into place.

Grabbing me by the hips, he flips me facedown across the arm of the couch. Suddenly, part of me is afraid.

Be careful what you wish for, kiska.

"Ruslan?"

"Silence."

My mouth snaps shut.

"You've been a bad girl."

Tendrils of pleasure erupt inside me.

"And you know what bad girls get, don't you?"

"Punished?"

His hand smooths over my right cheek. "They get broken."

Thwack! I yelp when his hand makes contact with my ass. The sting makes my eyes water.

"Did that hurt, baby?"

"Y-yes."

"But you know you deserved it. Don't you?"

I find myself nodding. "Yes, I'm a bad girl. I need you to punish me. I *want* you to punish me with your dick."

Ruslan's dark chuckle drips of foreboding. He presses the thick head of his cock into my slit, but doesn't actually penetrate. He's driving me insane, one inch at a time.

Thwack!

This time, I'm a little more prepared. I jerk forward, but I don't yelp. I've never felt the warm, tingling sensation of pain twisting into pleasure before now. And yet, between his large hand landing hot blows before massaging the sting into a quickly-spreading warmth and the way his thick head keeps rubbing over my clit to my ass…

I'm not just wet; I'm fucking *dripping*.

I bite down on my lower lip, bracing myself for more. I can't believe I even want more, but here I am—and truth be told, I can't believe I'm in this position at all. Quivering nerves and aching pussy all screaming for Mr. Oryolov to do whatever deliciously naughty things he wants—including spanking me until I come on command.

"Have you learned your lesson now, my little *kiska*?"

"Yes," I gasp.

"Hm. I'm not so sure."

I'm literally writhing against the sofa. The frame digs into my stomach as I struggle to maintain balance on my toes instead of collapsing onto the floor like I want to.

Thwack!

I suck in a breath and let out a low moan.

"Does it hurt?"

"Yes," I whimper.

"Do you want me to stop?"

"No!"

I hear his dark chuckle again and I can feel my arousal dripping down my inner thighs. My toes curl as they try to grip the shag carpet beneath my feet and my fingers work to clutch the smooth suede of the couch cushion.

THWACK!

I gasp, but the pain lasts maybe two seconds before it's drowned in a flood of endorphins. For a moment, I have no idea what I'm feeling. All my body and mind register is the warm sting of pain swirling with the cooling ooze of pleasure.

Oh, God—he really is gonna break me.

My eyes fly open when I suddenly feel his tongue slide up and down my slit. My knees quiver with the anticipation building between my thighs. I've never been eaten out from this position before. It's primal. It's dirty.

It's also *exactly* what I need.

The moment his lips wrap around my clit and suck, my belly clenches and aches with tension. I'm so fucking close… and when his tongue flicks between the tugging of his lips, I feel myself start to tumble over that sweet, sweet edge.

"*Fuck! Yes!*"

"No."

I freeze. "W-what?" I don't even have the strength to crane my neck to the side so I can see his expression.

"Did I say you could come?"

He slaps my ass again but this time, it's not painful; it's simply a reminder. His tongue returns to my clit with slower, smoother strokes and I moan low, holding in breaths because I'm worried I'm going to lose control and orgasm all over his face.

Oh, wouldn't that be a beautiful sight?

"You like that, baby?"

"Yesss," I hiss. "Please… more…"

"Greedy little kitten."

As his tongue swirls around my clit, I squeeze my eyes shut and try to focus on anything else to keep from coming. Death. Taxes. The way balding old rich guys insist on maintaining that weird ring of hair around their otherwise shiny scalps.

None of it helps. Somewhere, in the midst of all these out-of-control emotions, I find a sense of self that I thought I'd lost. I'm here tonight for *me* and there's no guilt attached to that realization.

"Fuck, Ruslan… please… *ahh…* please… I'm gonna… come…"

His mouth pulls away. But before the disappointment crystalizes, his hands grab my hips and he sinks his dick all the way inside me.

Ruslan smooths a hand along my spine as he rocks into me, making sure I feel every inch stretch me open and fill me to the brim. His fingers thread through my hair at the nape of my neck until he grabs a fistful and pulls just hard enough to make me arch deeper for him. Every thrust is timed with a tug; every resounding slap in the air is the sound of his hips connecting with my ass.

I have no idea what I'm screaming—I just know my lungs burn and my throat is hoarse.

I also know that I'm going to get the first layer of skin slapped off my ass for breaking his rules, because there's no way I can hold the orgasm back anymore.

"Come for me, my little *kiska*," Ruslan growls.

Oh, thank God.

I shudder and sob as the orgasm rips through my body. He's close behind me, pulling me harder onto him and grinding in so fucking deep as he fills my body with his own release.

He doesn't wait long before he pulls out of me. I collapse face-first onto the sofa. I'm not complaining; I'd gladly bury myself inside this couch if I could.

Ruslan grabs a couple of tissues from a fancy metal holder. I think he's going to pass them to me for a second, but before I can respond, he bends down and cleans me up himself. His hands are gentle, his gaze staying fixated on his work. I just lie there in awe and let him.

Then, head still woozy, I watch as he rises back up to his full height. Even after coming, his cock is still a dangerous weapon, nearly the size of my forearm. He turns and pulls his boxer briefs back on, then walks over to the bar in the corner.

"Drink?"

It's tempting. Especially because the offer suggests that he wants me to stay a little longer. The thing is, I feel good. Like, *really* good. But I don't want to burst the bubble by overstaying my welcome. And since I'm almost certain that being kicked out again is going to bring my high crashing down, I decide to stick to my guns and leave immediately.

"No, thanks. Don't wanna risk a hangover. I have work tomorrow and my boss can be a nightmare."

He smirks. "Is that so?"

I nod. "But he isn't all bad. At least he pays me well."

"Hm. As you wish." Ruslan gives me a little smile that makes me suddenly wish I hadn't just turned down his offer to stay.

No. Distance is better. Distance keeps you safe.

"Goodnight, Mr. Oryolov."

"Goodnight, Emma."

I dress quickly, cheeks burning—both sets of cheeks—then leave without looking back. On the way down in the elevator, I let out a low breath that turns into a disbelieving laugh. This whole thing still feels too surreal to be happening to me.

This time, when I pass the guard at the security desk, I give him a huge, confident smile. A smile that says, *Yeah that's right. I had hot, sweaty, nasty sex with a hot, sweaty, nasty man, but I am no one's prostitute. I am my own woman. I protect my own heart.*

And when I do leave one day—whenever that day comes—I'm going to leave Ruslan wanting more.

24

RUSLAN

"You're telling me that it's *all* gone?"

"Y-yes, sir."

I wait for the supplier to elaborate, but he sounds like he's concentrating on not shitting his pants. I wish we were having this conversation face to face. Shitting his pants would be the least of his fucking concerns.

"That container of B47 substrate was marked for *me*. The purchase order was sent. You accepted my motherfucking money."

"I-I understand, Mr. Oryolov, b-but I have no control over—"

"Who stole it from me?"

"Excuse me, sir?"

"Two tons of an extensively manufactured industrial chemical doesn't just disappear into thin air. Someone purchased that container and I want to know who." I'm pacing across my office so chaotically that Kirill has to lunge out of my way.

"I, um… That information is classified, sir."

"What's your name?"

Silence.

And then—dead air.

Did that son of a bitch just hang up on me?

I roar, flinging my phone across the room. It hits the door and flies apart, the cracked screen catching the dying sun and winking up at me.

Breathing heavily, I turn to Kirill, who's already pulling out a brand-new phone from one of the drawers of my desk. "I'll just transfer the SIM and you should be good to go," he explains. "As always."

Suffice it to say, this has happened enough times to warrant a standard operating procedure.

"This has Adrik's fingerprints all over it," I fume. "That *mudak* is retaliating for the beating I gave his ego."

Kirill is busy trying to pluck the SIM out of my broken phone. "You really think he has the balls? Or the resources?"

"That idiot's only goal in life is to take me down. What better way than this? Undercutting the development of a drug that I've already spent who-the-fuck-knows-how-much on?"

He hands me the new phone as it powers to life. "Point taken. My question is, what do we…?" He trails off as I stalk out of the office. "Where are you going?"

"To fucking deal with it," I reply. Emma is sitting at her desk, all wide-eyed and concerned at the sounds of mayhem she must've overheard. "Cancel all my appointments. I'm working out of the office today."

I don't linger to wait for her response.

The journey from Bane to the chemical facility is punctuated by a series of vivid and violent fantasies. All of which involve Adrik suffering a messy and painful death under the heel of my boot.

But as satisfying as those revenge fantasies would be, my first priority is Venera. I need to make sure that this setback doesn't affect the rollout. I can deal with delays if we're talking a few days. But if it stretches into months, that's going to be a significant hit to my bottom line. Which means I need to go into Damage Control Mode.

I don't even bother with the bullshit white coat when I get to the facility. I storm into the lab as I am and bellow for Sergey at the top of my lungs. He stumbles out of the storage room, his face pale and his brow already sweaty.

"We've lost the last container of B47," I inform him icily. "How much Venera have we manufactured so far and how imperative is B47 to the formula?"

Sergey's mouth twists into a strange, crooked shape. "Uh, well…"

"Spit it out, Sergey. I don't have time to waste."

He wipes his brow with the back of his hand. "I may have a solution."

"That's what I like to hear. Go on."

The man doesn't look the least bit encouraged. He shifts from one leg to the other, all his nervous tics pinging at the same time. "I have been... experimenting. I did so without your authorization—and I do apologize for that, sir—but I wanted to see if I could improve on or erase altogether the lesser side effects of Venera."

On any other day, I would have been pissed. But I'm not about to bite off the hand that's throwing me a bone when I need it.

"In one of my attempts, B47 was one of the chemicals I removed from the existing formula. I switched it out with a different compound. Its scientific name is—"

I hold up a hand. "I couldn't possibly care less. What were the results?"

"On the face of it, the new formula that omits B47 performs in the same manner that the old formula did. However, we haven't carried out enough trials to know for sure."

My jaw clenches painfully. "Then we need to start a new round of trials. Immediately."

Sergey actually looks a little animated for a change as he nods. "Yes, sir. Right away."

"How badly is this going to affect our launch date?"

His eyes veer from side to side as though there's some imaginary whiteboard in front of him. "If we can run a few dozen trial sessions in the next week, we might not need to delay the launch by more than a handful of days."

This time, when I clench my jaw, it's out of pure satisfaction. "Good. Do what needs to be done then."

I'm heading for the door when Sergey stops me. "Sir, we have a trial running as we speak. Would you like to observe?"

I pause. *Why the fuck not?*

"Lead the way."

He escorts me out of the lab and across the facility to a sterile clinic room. Each of them is fitted with one-way glass so my chemist teams can observe the effects of their inventions on the test subjects.

The observation room is bristling with Sergey's underlings, who might as well be carbon copy clones for all that I can tell the difference between them. I shove aside the clipboard-toting fucks and muscle my way to the front of the room. I barely acknowledge the technicians I pass—because I'm so fixated on what's happening on the other side of the glass.

Both members of the couple in the observation room are young and attractive.

But I doubt that's the reason they're fucking like a pair of horny rabbits.

The man's pants are down around his ankles and the woman's skirt is hiked up around her waist. He shoves into her rhythmically, his ass clenching with every thrust. She lies on the padded examination table, her hands flung carelessly over her head. Both wear hazy, dreamy expressions that look strangely familiar to me—because I just saw one very, very similar on Emma's face last night.

That one didn't require a single dose of anything illicit.

I clear my throat. "Who's the principal investigator for this session?"

A stern woman with short brown hair steps forward. "That would be me, Mr. Oryolov. I'm Dr. Dahlia Canaan."

"Dr. Canaan. When were these subjects introduced to one another?"

"Just moments after entering the room less than an hour ago."

"And they both ingested a sample size of Venera?"

"Fifteen minutes prior, yes."

My eyes keep going back to the young couple. The man's jaw thrums as he increases the speed of his thrusts. She moans wildly, her hair flipping from side to side. They're both so lost in the sex. They could be fucking in front of the President, the Pope, or their own damn parents and it wouldn't slow them down a bit.

"And they're aware they're being observed?"

"Of course, sir. All our test subjects are informed in advance and required to give their signed consent."

"How long has it been since they entered the room?"

"Approximately... fifty-seven minutes, sir." She consults her clipboard. "We noted flirtatious dialogue approximately thirty-one minutes after ingestion of Venera. Physical contact was established after approximately forty-six minutes. Intercourse was initiated less than eighty-four seconds after that."

Fucking flawless.

I turn to Sergey. "If these results hold, we're golden."

"I see no reason why they shouldn't, sir." He actually looks halfway confident for a change. His face is a slightly less pasty shade of white and there's only a hint of warble in his voice. By Sergey's standards, that's as good as it gets.

My gaze shifts back to the young couple. He's fucking like a jackhammer, but it doesn't matter; she's still coming every fifth thrust. Two strangers going absolutely apeshit over each other while a room full of scientists and doctors watch—it's the type of thing that's only possible when you don't give a shit.

The thought of *anyone* watching Emma and I together makes my blood boil. I would soundly beat to death any person who so much as *looked* at her naked body while I still hold a claim to it.

This couple in the observation room? They don't give a shit.

Must be nice.

∿

RUSLAN: *I need you to check in on Sergey more often. Make sure he has everything he needs.*

VADIM: *Your wish. My command.*

That reply is a little too flippant to be sincere, but I decide to let it go. If throwing some snark my way is how he soothes his wounded ego, I'm willing to be generous.

Only because he's my uncle.

Only because he held my father together after the accident.

I glance at Kirill, who's busy running a red light. "Did you pick up my schedule for the next week like I asked?"

"Of course. It's in the back with the rest of your files. I believe Ms. Carson color-coded everything for your convenience."

I don't like the suggestive lift in his tone when he says her name, but I let that go, too, still high from my eleventh-hour victory over Adrik. I shouldn't be counting chickens just yet, but I have a good feeling about Sergey's revised formula.

"By the way," Kirill adds, "you have the Olsen-Ferber charity gala coming up next week. I'll need to arrange a special security detail for that. Did you pick a date yet?"

My jaw twitches uncomfortably as an unwelcome image pops into my head. Me, at the gala, with Emma on my arm, decked out in a red gown to match her lipstick.

Fuck no. That is *not* happening.

I'm already making stupid decisions when it comes to her. Case in point: the lack of condoms last time we fucked. Just when I'd resolved to wear them, the woman attacked me before I'd barely set foot in the door. By the time I got my head on straight, I'd already filled her.

Feeling that sweet pussy tighten around me was absolutely worth it, though...

I grind my teeth. I need to get a grip and stop thinking with my penis. "I'll take Jessica. You can halve the security detail on my entourage for the gala. She always brings her own men—and even if she didn't, no one wants to kill me bad enough to get within a mile of her."

I don't miss the way Kirill's face scrunches in disgust.

We're turning onto 48th when I make a last-minute decision. "One more thing: add Emma to the entourage for the gala."

Kirill brings the SUV to a grinding halt. "Emma?"

I shrug, feigning apathy. "Just in case I need her."

Yeah. Sure. *That's* why she's coming.

25

EMMA

"For God's sake, Ben, I'm *working*!"

"You wouldn't answer my fuckin' texts," he growls over the phone. "What was I supposed to do?"

"Oh, I don't know—*wait*, maybe? At least until I came back home!" I glance nervously at Ruslan's door. If he comes out here and sees me on yet another personal call, I'm a dead woman. He'll rake my ass over the coals for the sheer thrill of it.

I wince at the mere thought of my rear end. Every time I sit down, I'm reminded of the punishment I received at Ruslan's hand last night. The whole day, I've oscillated between feeling sore and aroused.

I guess, when you're sleeping with the boss, that's just an occupational hazard.

Ben's voice jolts me back to reality. "I don't know how long that'll take and I need money *now*!"

I bite my tongue to stop the steam of expletives from bubbling over. "You already have courtside Knicks tickets and a fridge full of beer. What could you possibly need money for now?"

"I have fucking *needs*, Emma."

I have no idea what that means and I have no intention of asking. "I'm hanging up now, Ben."

"If you hang up, I'll just keep calling."

"Then I'll just keep hanging up."

"Don't make me come down there."

I nearly gag with fear. "You wouldn't!"

"Just watch me. I will—"

"*Okay*," I hiss. "You blackmailing bastard. How much do you want?"

"Two hundred bucks."

I answer automatically. "I don't have that."

"Bullshit."

"I'm serious—"

"Okay, see you at the office, in like, half an hour?"

"You're an asshole."

"Just transfer the money directly into my—Caro, Rae! Shut the hell up, I'm on the phone—into my account."

"Don't swear at them!" I hiss.

He just ignores me. "Go ahead and do it now. I can stay on the line with you while you make the transfer."

You have got *to be kidding me.*

The thing is, I can't afford to have Ben come down here and stir up shit. So I cave, which is probably the worst thing to do, but I can't really see another way out.

I open my work laptop and pull up my personal banking page. "I'm transferring the money now. But seriously, this is the *last* of my cash for the month."

"Sure, sure." His voice goes muffled as he holds the phone away from his mouth. I hear mumbling, a few punctured screams in the background, and the sound of skittering footsteps. Then the line clears and his voice comes through again. "Are you doing it? The money hasn't come through— Caro, stop crying, I barely touched you... I don't know... just ignore him—shit, where was I? Oh, right, the money. Done yet?"

I click the transfer button and it starts to process my request. The screen is hijacked by a big rotating circle that informs me not to close the page.

"What is Caroline crying about?"

"Huh?"

"Ben, what is your daughter crying about?" I ask through gritted teeth.

"Um... dunno, something about this creepy guy following them."

"*What* creepy guy?"

"Fuck if I know. Just kids being kids. Josh probably made it up to scare the girls."

For goodness' sake, does this man know his kids at all? "This is *Josh* you're talking about, Ben. That boy wouldn't scare a fly, let alone his sisters. And he doesn't lie."

"Bingo. Just got the payment. Later, Em."

"Ben, hold on! I need to know who this guy—"

But it's too late. The line goes dead and I'm left staring at the picture of Josh, Caroline, and Reagan on my screen, wondering if I should be panicking.

No need to panic. Just stay calm and gather more information.

Knowing that Ben is a lost cause, I call Amelia. She picks up immediately, but she's not her usual chipper self. I want to ask what's wrong, but I need to check in on the kids first.

"Amelia, can I talk to Josh, please?"

"Of course. Hang on."

My knee is bouncing wildly when Josh takes the phone. "Auntie Em?"

"Hey, bud, I was just on the phone with your dad. He mentioned that Caroline was crying because some guy was following you? Is that right?"

Josh hesitates. "Yeah…"

My heart drops. "Are you sure he was following you?"

"He was watching us from outside the gate at school yesterday. And he followed us home today. He tried saying something to Caro at recess, too. I don't like him."

Okay, I'm very close to full-on Panic Mode. "What did he look like?"

"Um, I dunno, normal? Skinny and blonde. He just didn't look nice, though."

I want to vomit. That's that reporter. Remmy something.

"The next time you see this man," I say as casually as I can, "I want you to call me immediately, okay?" He's quiet for a moment. "Josh? Did you hear me?"

"He's standing out on the street, Auntie Em. He's been watching the apartment since we got home from school."

Panic.

Panic.

Panic.

I jump to my feet. "I'll be home soon, honey, okay? Now, can you hand the phone back to Amelia?"

I arrange with Amelia to make sure she will stay with the kids until I get there. Then I grab my purse and beeline for the elevators.

"Where do you think you're going, Ms. Carson?"

That icy snarl freezes me in my tracks.

Of course he chooses *this* moment to step out of his office. I'm starting to think he has a security camera aimed at my desk so he can keep track of my every movement.

"I'm leaving." The panic is eroding all my more diplomatic sensibilities. "I've got a family emergency. The kids need me."

I expect him to go all "Hm" on me and threaten to fire me if I walk out in the middle of a workday. But instead, his eyebrows pinch together. "What's the emergency?"

"It's nothing. Just this reporter. Remmy. He's been bothering —look, it doesn't matter. I just need to handle it really quickly and I'll be right back."

The moment I mention his name, recognition flickers across Ruslan's eyes. "Remmy Jefferson. Of *The Brooklyn Gazette?*"

I inch back towards the elevators. Something in Ruslan's face is scaring me. "Yeah, I think. He approached me a few days ago, asking if… well, he actually asked if I would spy on you for him. I turned him down, of course."

Ruslan's eyes narrow into slits. "Why didn't you tell me?"

"Because I shut him down and told him to take a hike. I thought that was the end of it. But now, he's stalking my kids! He's watching the house right now. The kids are all freaked out. I'm sorry, I gotta—"

"I'll drive you there."

I gape at him. "What?"

He walks fast towards the elevators. "Let's go. We're wasting time."

I keep glancing at him in the elevator on the way down. Letting me leave the office during working hours is one thing, but actually coming with me? Why would he do that?

"Um—you have meetings all evening," I remind him as the doors whoosh open.

He pulls out his phone and starts tapping at the screen. "I'll have Kirill cover for me."

I'm so worried about the kids that I barely register the sleek Aston Martin that pulls up right outside the skyscraper. On the drive home, I keep picking at my cuticles, trying to calm my frayed nerves.

Ruslan glances at me out of the corner of his eye. "I know Remmy. He's a fucking leech. But nothing I can't handle."

I nod, but I'm not going to relax completely until that creep is far away from the kids. Still, something registers in the recesses of my consciousness.

Was that... a gesture of comfort? From Ruslan Oryolov? I look out the window, wondering if I'm going to see pigs flying around the skyscrapers.

There are a handful of cars parked on the opposite side of the street when we pull up. I scan through the lineup, but I can't figure out which one is Remmy's. I'll figure that part out later; right now, I need to make sure the kids are okay.

I'm on the second flight of stairs up the apartment when I realize that Ruslan is right behind me.

My first thought? *He's gonna see the apartment.*

My second thought? *He's gonna meet the kids.*

My third thought? *Oh, fuck.*

I push it all out of my head and use my key to get inside— except it's been chain-locked. I peek in through the two inches of space the chain allows.

"Amelia? Josh?"

"Sorry!" Amelia calls. "Hold on a sec."

I step back as the door closes shut. Then I hear the chain unlatch and Amelia throws it open for us. "Sorry, the kids were really scared, and—" She stops short, her eyes veering to the behemoth of a man behind me. "Um, yeah, so we… um… used the chain."

Her cheeks flush bright scarlet. I have a pretty good idea as to why. Honestly, I don't blame her. We women are only human, after all.

"Where are they?"

Amelia focuses on me. "They worked themselves up into a panic. The girls are hiding in Josh's room underneath his blanket. And—"

"Auntie Em!" Josh yells as he enters the living room. He bolts towards me, his arms wrapping tight around my waist.

I kiss the top of his head. "How are the girls?"

"Scared," he admits without letting go of me. "They think that man is gonna kidnap them."

I'm immediately furious. Josh would never admit to being scared himself, but the fact that he's clinging to me like he hasn't done for years proves that he is, too.

"Amelia, would you mind staying with the girls?"

"Of course." She stumbles away, her cheeks still mildly flushed.

"Listen, J—that man is a weasel." I stroke his head the same way I used to when he woke up from a nightmare and had trouble going back to sleep. The eight or nine months after we buried Sienna held a lot of nights like that. "You have nothing to worry about."

He swallows hard. "Why is he even here?"

Because of what I got myself involved in.

"Because he's bored and jobless," I assure him. "Now, you're gonna stay here with your sisters and I'm gonna go down there and talk to him, okay?"

"But—"

"I won't be more than five minutes. Hold down the fort, okay?"

I let go of Josh. But when I turn to the door, there's a human-shaped boulder in my path. "Excuse me."

Ruslan doesn't move. His gaze skirts past me to Josh. I glance over my shoulder to see that Josh's mouth is hanging open, his eyes wide and awed.

"Emma, you haven't introduced us. This must be your nephew, Josh." He offers his hand.

Josh snaps his mouth shut. He flushes, but his shoulders square and he straightens up as if he's trying to make himself look as tall as possible. "I don't know you."

I raise my brows, taken aback by the stilted, angry way he's talking. "Um, Josh—"

"It's okay," Ruslan says to me before turning back to Josh. "I'm Ruslan, your aunt's boss."

"Why are you here?"

"Josh!" But I can't be too mad at him. He's just trying to be the man of the house, the only way he knows how.

Ruslan just smiles.

Whoa, the famous Oryolov smile. It's even more dazzling up close. But it doesn't seem to have any effect on Josh, who most definitely does not return it.

"I'm here to help," adds Ruslan.

The furrow in Josh's brows eases, but only a little. "How?"

"I'm going to go out there and talk to that man. I'm going to make sure he never bothers you or your sisters ever again."

"And Auntie Em?"

Ruslan nods. "And your Auntie Em, too."

Josh gives him a tiny, begrudging nod. He watches Ruslan straighten up and head toward the door and he doesn't so much as blink the entire time.

I get it—there's just something about Ruslan. Quite apart from being an imposing man, his sheer presence takes up space the way no one else really can. He exudes that "take charge" aura that Josh has rarely seen in the men around him. Ben mostly just radiates "sad and lazy."

"You'll take care of everyone?" Ruslan is asking Josh, not me. He's deadly serious, too. No trace of that smile.

Josh's jaw tightens as he nods.

"Good." Ruslan heads out the door as though everything is settled.

I follow him out into the dimly lit corridor and close the apartment door behind me. He's already halfway down the stairs by the time I get it locked. "Wait!" I call ahead. "I—"

He stops on the landing and turns to look up at me. "You stay. I'll handle this. I'm the one he wants."

The tenderness of his voice throws me for a loop. I'm used to hearing him angry, annoyed, frustrated, or just completely impassive.

But this? He actually sounds halfway compassionate.

"Yeah, but it's *my* kids he chose to stalk. Like some creepy fucking predator. And he's scared the living hell out of them. So I'm gonna go down there and—"

"Emma." His voice may be less harsh than it usually is, but it's no less commanding. "Those kids are scared. They need you right now more than you need to kill him."

That gets through to me.

Dammit. He's right.

Suppressing a frustrated sigh, I gesture for him to go ahead. I wait until he's disappeared down the stairs before I head back into the apartment.

Josh is waiting for me by the door. I take his hand as we head towards the girls' bedroom. He gives me a shy glance. "Your boss is cool," he breathes.

I force a smile. To an eight-year-old boy with no male role model, of course Ruslan is cool. But to a twenty-six-year-old woman with three young dependents, he's nothing but dangerous.

Not for the first time, I begin to question all the choices I've been making recently.

Am I making a mistake?

Am I putting the kids in danger?

Is it too late to go back?

I'm afraid all the answers are "yes."

26

RUSLAN

The sleazy motherfucker is leaning against his rundown Buick LeSabre when I step out onto the street. He straightens up when he sees me, his eyes sharp, his fingers twitching. "What a pleasure running into—"

"Cut the shit, Remmy." My voice is low with menace, but that's only because I don't want to draw attention to this little exchange. The kids are terrified enough as it is. "What the fuck do you think you're doing?"

He shrugs nonchalantly, but his fingers keep twitching and he fidgets around a little too much. "Was just in the neighborhood."

"And you make a habit of prowling around the streets, looking for... what, exactly?"

His crooked smile isn't the least bit intimidating, no matter how much he might wish otherwise. "A story."

"You're not going to find one here."

"Oh, I beg to differ. That pretty little secretary you have knows more than she's letting on."

My hands clench into fists as I take a step closer to him. "My secretary is an employee. She knows only what I tell her. So unless you want to write an exposé on my coffee preferences, get the fuck away from here."

He turns his sleazy smile onto the windows of Emma's apartment. I follow his gaze to see four faces at the window. Josh and Emma are at either side of the frame, with two little blonde heads peeking out from the bottom of the lower pane.

"You know, Ruslan, it strikes me as odd that you would be here at all. Considering she's *'just* an employee.' Seems rather... *protective* for an infamously hardened employer like you."

I gnash my teeth. The most efficient way to get my point across would be to beat the living shit out of him. Except there's no ethical way I can do that with Emma and the kids watching. So instead, I switch to Plan B.

"I take my employees' safety *very* seriously, Jefferson. It's the reason you won't be able to find one person on my payroll who will agree to speak to you."

His eyes narrow. "All that proves is that you've bought their silence. How easy it must be to get what you want when you have cash pouring out of every hole in your body."

"Careful there. You're looking a little green with envy."

He scoffs. "I would be as wealthy as you if I murdered and stole and broke the law as a daily habit."

"Is this you fishing? I expected better."

"I'm gonna crack this story one way or the other."

"Tell you what," I suggest. "Let's take a little drive. Just around the corner. You can ask me as many questions as you want in that time."

His nostrils flare. "I'm not getting in your car."

I shrug. "Then I'll get in yours. Unless, of course, you're scared to be alone with me?"

The easiest way to get to a coward is through his ego. Fyodor taught me that, back when he was more than just a walking shadow.

Sure enough, Remmy bristles on the spot. "Fine. My car, then."

While Remmy gets into the driver's seat, I drop Kirill the location I plan to have Remmy stop at. Then I slide into the cramped passenger seat of his LeSabre.

Ping. Ping. I glance at my screen. Two messages, sent within seconds of each other.

KIRILL: *:thumbs-up:*

EMMA: *Ruslan, what are you doing?*

I put my phone away, conscious of the fact that Remmy keeps glancing at me. His knuckles are bright white as he shifts gears and starts driving, though he makes a big show of whistling like he doesn't have a care in the world.

"You've got 'til the empty lot on 58th," I tell him.

He scowls. "That's not very far."

"Then I suggest you talk fast."

He leans to the side and pulls out a small recording device. "On the record?" he ventures.

I shrug. "Go for it."

"Is it true that you're in the process of launching an illegal, highly dangerous, possibly addictive drug that's funded by Bane Corporation?"

I don't falter. "Of course not. I'm not in the pharmaceutical industry. Nor am I a drug dealer. I run a high-end security tech firm. That is my primary source of revenue."

Remmy grinds his teeth. "I have it on good authority—"

"Do you have a name?"

He grimaces. "Not as such, no."

"So then it's hardly 'good authority,'" I dismiss with a chuckle.

"I've heard people refer to you as '*pakhan.*' Is it true that you are the head of a Russian crime syndicate?"

I lace my fingers in my lap. "I'm a businessman, Mr. Jefferson. That is all."

"And what about the disappearance of Mattias Helva?"

The name rings a bell, but I feign ignorance. "Who?"

"A young man on your payroll. He disappeared a few weeks ago."

Ah, right. The skinny scientist with the smart mouth. The one who ate a bullet for his betrayal. "I'm sure the Bane teams in charge of that sort of thing are working diligently to assist the authorities in whatever ways necessary. But I don't keep track of every single one of my employees on a personal basis, Mr. Jefferson."

"Just the pretty ones?"

I jut my chin toward the parking lot. "We're here. Pull over."

"I have more—"

"Unfortunately, you're out of time."

I get out of the car and he follows, slamming the door behind him. I notice he doesn't bring the tape recorder with him. Pity. It might've saved him some pain.

"That wasn't a legitimate interview," he sneers, jabbing a finger in my face. "You lied about everything."

"I agreed to talk to you. I kept my word. It's not my fault or my problem if you don't believe me."

His jaw clenches. "Well, then you leave me no choice but to make *her* talk."

I check over each shoulder to make sure we're alone. When I'm sure the coast is clear, I lunge forward, palm his throat, and pin him to the brick wall at his back. "You go within a fucking mile of her or her family and I will *destroy* you."

He splutters, pawing uselessly at my arms. I hold him there for one more beat, his feet flinging in every direction, before I set him back down with a grimace.

"Well, well," he croaks, trying to clear his throat a few times. "I can't imagine what I'll find if I dig into *that* relationship."

Great. I overreacted. The last thing this smarmy fuck needed was a reason to keep poking around.

Time to backslide into Plan A.

He's standing there, smirking, at the perfect angle when my fist connects with his face in a quick jab. He goes down so easily that, as I feel cartilage crunch under my knuckles, I start to wonder idly if he'd even survive a full-on beatdown.

"*Fuck!*" His hand reaches up to assess the damage. "You—you broke my fucking nose!"

"Trust me: it's an improvement."

Blood runs down his hand and he keeps touching his nose, the bridge of which is pointing in a different direction than it was a moment ago.

"Fuck," he groans nasally. "My nose. My fucking nose!"

"You're lucky I broke *only* your nose," I snarl, grabbing him by the collar of his shirt and hauling him toward me. "Stay the fuck away from her. You hear me?"

His eyes widen and he nods hard. I shove him back just as Kirill rounds the corner in his silver Maserati.

Remmy trips on the parking block and lands on his ass in the gravel. He's shaking hard and clawing at the rocks, tainting the dirt with his blood. He gulps as Kirill gets out of the car and walks over.

"Started the party without me, did ya?" my second-in-command asks.

"W-what are you g-gonna do to me?" Jefferson stammers. Blood keeps pouring down his upper lip in a thick stream.

Kirill throws him a disgusted look, then glances at me. "Excellent question. What do you think, sir?"

My gaze slides over the runty reporter. Honestly, he's too fucking pathetic to kill. And I'm pretty sure he's got the message loud and clear. Still—I didn't earn my reputation by being lenient.

"Let's give him a new zip code, shall we?"

Kirill raises his eyebrows. "That all?"

"Y-you can't do this. There are people who will look for me!" Jefferson insists.

"I very much doubt that." I squat down in front of him. A brilliant purple bruise has already started to form around his nose and beneath his eyes. "Although, to be fair, if you *ever* go near her again, I will most certainly be looking for you."

Now, even his bottom lip is quivering. A second later, the stench of ammonia stings my nostrils. I look down between his legs.

"Fucking hell," I mutter.

It isn't the first time a man has pissed himself out of fear of me. It might be the most pathetic, though.

I pull my fist back to knock him out just so I don't have to hear him whimper anymore, but the fear suddenly becomes too much for him to handle. His face freezes for a moment, then his eyes roll. He faints back against the concrete before I lay so much as a finger on him.

Disgusted, I get to my feet. "At least he should be easier to transport now. And quieter."

Kirill just scowls. "You couldn't have done that *before* he pissed himself? That car is brand new!"

"Put him in the trunk. Hell, put him in the glove compartment. That little fuck will probably fit."

My second-in-command sighs again. "How did this happen, by the way?"

"Fucker was prowling after Emma, trying to get a story out of her. When she refused, he started stalking her kids." I'm still simmering with anger over the image of Remmy sniffing on her trail.

Kirill lofts a brow. "You sure dumping him in Bumfuck, New Jersey is all you want me to do?"

"For now, yes."

I wait until Kirill stashes Jefferson into his trunk and drives away before I get into Remmy's LeSabre.

I'm very aware of the fact that I'm the one who created this fucking mess. If I hadn't overreacted to his wild guess that I was fucking Emma, Jefferson wouldn't have caught on.

So the least I can do now is protect her.

The least I can do is make sure she's alright.

At least, that's the reason I give myself for driving back to her street and walking up to her door.

I clean up my messes.

That's all this is.

27

RUSLAN

"You're so… *big*."

"Like a giant."

I assumed they were twins from the window. But now that I'm looking right at them, I realize that the one with a missing front tooth must be younger. With her dark blonde hair, round apple cheeks, and prominent dimples, it's hard not to smile just looking at her. Her sister is maybe an inch taller, slightly skinnier, with just as much energy.

"Reagan! Caroline! That's not polite," Emma scolds.

I'd be lying if I said it wasn't strange to see her in her mother mode. She's rushing around the living room, trying to subtly clean up without looking like that's what she's doing. She shoves a dirty t-shirt underneath one of the cushions on the armchair when she thinks I'm not looking.

The boy, Josh, is sitting opposite me. His eyes haven't left my face since I walked in. I've made enough grown men piss their pants to know that looking me dead in the eye is no easy feat—just ask Remmy. And yet here he is, all of eight years old, staring back at me as though he's ready to take me down if I make so much as one wrong move toward the women in his family.

He's definitely a leader in the making.

"What did you say to the man?" he asks.

"Josh," Emma chides gently, "maybe now's not the time?" She glances pointedly at the girls, both of whom are still fixated on me.

Reagan wriggles out of her brother's reach and plops down on the coffee table in front of me. "Why are you wearing that?"

I look down at my Hugo Boss suit. "This is what I wear to work. You don't like it?"

She cocks her head to the side and thinks about it. "It's… too much."

"Reagan!"

I grin. It's quite entertaining seeing Emma this flustered. She still hasn't sat down.

"*I* like your suit," Caroline offers as a shy blush creeps up her cheeks. "And your tattoos." Apparently, she's spotted my neck tattoo, judging from the direction of her gaze.

"Kiddos!" The nanny calls from the kitchen. "Dinner's ready."

Emma kicks a lumpy thing under the sofa. "Go on, guys."

Caroline's upper lip juts out as she turns to me. "Are you coming for dinner? I don't mind sharing."

I smile at the selfless offer. "Thanks, Caroline, but I'll have to come back another time."

"Oh." Her mouth turns down at the corners. "Okay."

Emma comes up behind the girls and puts a hand on each of their shoulders. "Go on. I'll be right in."

"Auntie Em, can you help me wash my hands?"

"Reagan, you already know how to wash your hands."

"But I want *you* to do it. You're never home for dinner. Please? Pretty please?"

Emma's face breaks into a tired smile. "Of course I'll help." She sneaks me an apologetic glance and ducks into the kitchen with both girls trailing behind her.

Josh, however, stays exactly where he is. When I get to my feet, so does he.

"The reporter agreed that he will leave you guys alone," I remind him. "You have nothing to worry about anymore."

Josh frowns as he sticks his hands into the pockets of his pants. They're way too small for him. His ankles should definitely not be on display. It doesn't take a lot to notice that as cozy as this apartment is, it's also on the verge of crumbling.

The carpets are threadbare and stained. The upholstery is barely hanging on. The coffee table is propped up on makeshift coasters to keep it level and one wall is gradually losing a fight against an encroaching water stain. None of it can possibly be healthy for Emma or the children.

"Thank you," he says, so quietly that I barely hear him. Josh shifts in place for a moment as his eyes drop down. He gets a steely sheen in them as he mumbles, "One day, I'm gonna be big enough to protect them myself."

I don't do him the indignity of smiling or talking down to him. I just nod. Solemn. Man to man. "I know you will."

Funny enough, I actually do believe him.

He nods. Then his gaze veers to the side and he starts with surprise. I follow his eyes to find Emma standing by the doorway, tears in her eyes.

She swallows hard and clears her throat. She's about to say something when the girls run back into the living room.

"You're still here? Are you staying for dinner?" Caroline asks, grabbing my hand and pulling on it.

"Yeah!" the little one shouts, imitating her sister and grabbing my free hand. "Stay for dinner!"

Emma's soft voice manages to cut through the clamor. "You can, you know. If you want."

"Thank you, ladies, but I have a late evening meeting I need to get to."

The girls let out a long, disappointed chorus of, "*Awww.*"

Emma claps her hands. "Okay, guys, let's give Mr. Oryolov some breathing room. Come on, dinner's gonna get cold."

She gestures for them to come, but none of them bother looking at her. I squat down in front of the two girls. "You know how I got to be as big as I am?" I chuckle when both their heads bob excitedly. "I ate my dinner. Vegetables and all."

Reagan scrunches up her nose. "Ew! Even the brock-lee?"

"Especially the broccoli."

She looks severely disappointed in me. "Aw, man."

I muss up her downy golden mop and she giggles. Caroline glances shyly at me, so I offer her a low-five. She gives my palm a hearty whack and then scampers off to hide behind Emma.

One look at Emma's face and I know I need to get the fuck out of this house. She's staring at me with this look in her eye —all soft and tender and sentimental.

Hell no. She's got it all wrong. I'm not *this* guy. I'm not a family man. I don't like to spend my evenings with a bunch of screaming kids.

And yet... that's exactly what I've done for the last half hour, and honestly? It wasn't all that bad. In fact, a part of me actually *enjoyed* it.

No. That's not the right word. It can't be the right fucking word.

Abort. Get the fuck out! Now!

"Goodnight."

Emma gives the girls a little shove into the kitchen. "You guys get started. I'll be there in a minute."

Caroline's pout is strong. "But Auntie Em, why do *you* get to stay with him and we don't?"

Josh shushes his sister and shepherds them out of the living room.

Emma chuckles self-consciously as she walks over to me, an attractive blush turning her cheeks pink. "Sorry about all that."

I nod stiffly. "All good."

"You were really great with all of them." Her voice wobbles with all the things she's not saying. "Thank you for being so patient with the girls. And for what you said to Josh."

I nod again. This time, more from discomfort than anything else.

She clears her throat. "So what happened with Remmy?"

"He won't be bothering you or the kids again."

"Okay—but what about you?"

That takes me aback. "Me?"

"He was looking for dirt on you. He mentioned that he knew a lot already." She glances back over her shoulder before moving even closer to me. Close enough that I can smell her perfume.

Citrus, honey, and *danger*.

"I just…" She gnaws at her lip. "I know there are things that you might not want getting out there. I'm worried that Remmy might make good on his threats. He just seemed really determined."

She's genuinely worried about me. After basically being my errand girl the last year and a half. It's enough to boggle my mind…

And arouse the rest of me.

I take a step back. "Don't worry about me. You have your own shit to deal with." She flushes, but she doesn't look angry. "In fact, I'm canceling our meeting tonight."

"What? Why?"

The disappointment in her face reinforces my need to put some distance between us. Especially tonight. Today has been a little too involved.

"Missed a lot today. I need to catch up."

"Right." She forces a stiff smile onto her face. "I guess I'll see you tomorrow then?"

I nod. "Goodnight, Ms. Carson."

On my way out, I notice the shoe rack sitting next to the entrance door. Not one pair is even halfway presentable. One set of basketball shoes in particular looks to have been taped up under the soles time and time again.

I stop and think.

She desperately needed my contract. Which is probably the only reason she agreed to it in the first place. That was fine back then—leverage is leverage, after all. But now that I've been here, reflecting back on that tidbit leaves me feeling fucking *strange.*

I'm assuming I'll feel better outside of her presence, but those citrus notes stay with me long after I've descended the stairs and stepped back out into the funk and mayhem of the city. Before I drive back home, I send Kirill one last directive for the night.

I want a background check run on Emma's brother-in-law.

I'm just doing my due diligence. That's all. Nothing more, nothing less. Nothing that means a damn thing.

28

EMMA

Reagan has been on my lap now for almost half an hour, her head permanently wedged under my chin. I keep rocking her back and forth, hoping that at some point, she's going to relax enough to close her eyes. Caroline is sitting next to me on the carpet, leaving both their beds abandoned.

"How about we sing a song?" I suggest.

"Okay," Reagan agrees, peeking out from underneath my chin for a second. "But I still don't want to go to sleep."

"Oh, honey, the bad man is gone."

Caroline picks at the carpet with one hand while the other stays firmly attached to my knee. "Yeah, but we'll have nightmares now."

"Mhmm." Reagan's muffled agreement comes from somewhere near my collarbone.

Sighing, I kiss Reagan's head and then pat Caroline's hand. I hate that fucking reporter for scaring them like this. And I hate that I can't seem to do anything to reassure them.

If Sienna were here, she'd know what to say.

The door pushes open from the outside and Josh enters with—

"J, is that a sleeping bag?"

He nods. "I'm gonna sleep in here with the girls tonight. To protect them."

My heart trembles with love for my nephew. *There you are, Si. At least you left some of yourself behind.*

Reagan stays on my lap, but she sits up at least. "You're really going to sleep with us?" she asks her big brother.

He nods. "All night."

Reagan and Caroline exchange a glance. The two of them adore Josh. They really do look at him with stars in their eyes and I pray to God that never changes. Everyone needs a big brother like Josh.

But as he rolls out the sleeping bag and positions his pillow, his gaze keeps flicking to the windows. Maybe this sleeping arrangement is as much for him as it is for the girls.

"You know what?" I say.

"What?" they chorus together.

"How about—just for tonight—you guys all bunk with me in my room?"

Caroline's eyes immediately brighten. "Like a sleepover?"

"Exactly like a sleepover." I turn to Josh. "I think I'd like some protection, too. Is that okay?"

Josh cracks a tiny smile and nods.

Ten minutes later, Caroline, Reagan, and I are crammed onto my narrow bed and Josh is stretched out on top of his sleeping bag on the floor with a pillow tucked under his head.

"Can you sing to us, Auntie Em?" Reagan mumbles. Her voice is already heavy with sleep.

I start humming. The moment I do, she cracks a yawn that sounds like whale song. Caroline scoots a little closer, spooning Reagan, and before I even finish the second chorus, they're both fast asleep—Caroline in her cold-and-dead slumber and Reagan with her noisy little freight train snoring.

Josh, however, is far from asleep. He's still in the same position, staring wide-eyed up at the ceiling. I slide carefully out of bed and join him on the carpeted floor. He shifts to the side to let me in.

"Trouble sleeping?" I ask as I lay my head right next to his.

He just nods. I don't ask for permission; I just take his hand. "You know, your mother would have been so proud of you for being brave when your sisters needed you tonight."

He turns his face to the side so we're nose to nose. "Really?"

"Big time. You're a lot like her, you know."

He smiles shyly. "Like how?"

"Like this right here. She used to get in my bed at night when I had nightmares. She used to hug me really tight and sing me songs 'til I fell asleep. She used to protect me all the time. Just like you protect your sisters."

His smile flickers and falters. "Sometimes, I have to think really hard to remember stuff about her." He licks his chapped lips and grimaces as he sighs. "I don't know if what I remember is because I actually remember it or just 'cause I've seen pictures."

I swallow back my own grief so that I can focus on Josh's. "Time is funny like that. It makes things unclear. But trust me: when you least expect it, you'll remember something about her that you've forgotten you know."

His big brown eyes flit back to the ceiling. I don't see the tears on his cheeks until the siren light of a passing ambulance sets the room aglow for a moment. "Can *you* remember her?"

"I can," I assure him. "Don't you worry. I'll remember her for the both of us."

I move a little closer to him and start whispering little stories in his ear. I tell him about Sienna and her short-lived breakdancing career: three of the longest weeks of my life. I tell him about the bejeweled ballet flats she saved for half a year to buy because our parents refused to get them for her. I tell him about the time she baked me a cake for our thirteenth birthday using salt instead of sugar.

"Your mother was a lot of things, but a good baker? She most definitely was not."

"What did it taste like?"

I wrinkle up my nose. "Horrible. Speaking of things I still remember, actually, I don't think I'll forget that taste as long as I live. But we didn't want it to go to waste, so we mashed it up with ice cream and chocolate syrup and then it tasted pretty damn good."

Tears are pricking at my own eyes now. She made me that cake because Mom and Dad had been skiing in Geneva the weekend of my birthday. They sent a postcard and signed it, *Best Wishes from Your Mother & Father.* Sienna said, "Fuck that —" which was only the second time I'd ever heard the word —and stayed up all night baking. I wasn't allowed in the kitchen until morning, when she proudly presented me with that cake, all gorgeously frosted with pink and white buttercream.

I still remember her smile when she took my blindfold off.

"Your mother was marvelous, Josh. Even if you forget everything else, never forget that."

When I get no response, I glance to the side only to discover that his eyes are closed and he's breathing softly. Smiling, I pop a kiss on his forehead and crawl toward the door. I leave it open a crack and head into the living room, which is only marginally disastrous thanks to my panicked attempts at cleaning up when Ruslan was here. Pretty sure he saw me kick Reagan's ratty soccer ball under the armchair.

I fish it out and collapse onto the sofa, squishing the ball to my chest. "Ugh," I groan as the smell of mothballs hit my nostrils. I drop it onto the floor and reach for my phone instead.

Phoebe picks up mid-yawn.

"Shit, sorry—did I wake you?"

"Nah, just oozing into the couch."

I sigh longingly. *When was the last time I'd had the freedom to do that?* "Lucky."

"You sound exhausted. Did you just get home?"

"No, I've been home for a while, actually. Just got the kids to bed."

"Only *now?* Isn't it way past their bedtime?"

I stop short. *Damn it.* This whole "secrecy clause" of the contract is really fucking me over with Phoebe. Maybe I should have tried to negotiate a "best friends only" carve-out exception under the NDA section of the contract.

I'll have to remember that for next time my rich, mob boss employer propositions me for clandestine sex.

"Um, yeah—there was a whole thing today. The kids were being followed by this guy and they were really freaked out, so I left work early to go check on them."

"Hold up. Start from the beginning. A guy was following the kids?"

"It's nothing. Just some sleazy tabloid reporter trying to dig up dirt on Ruslan. I handled it. Or rather, Ruslan handled—"

"*Ruslan?*" Phoebe practically shrieks. "Whoa. Hold on again. Rewind and start from the *real* beginning."

I chuckle. "He insisted on coming home with me and dealing with the reporter himself."

"Wait—did he meet the kids?"

"Yes."

There's a beat of silence. "And?"

I groan. "He was *great* with them, Pheebs. He was nice and patient and downright *sweet.* You should have seen it. Josh was trying to play it cool, but you could see how totally in awe he was. And the girls! Reagan was so interested and Caroline's half in love with him already."

"Girl's got taste. And lemme guess: you're sitting there thinking, *'Just put a couple more babies in me and we'll be a better-looking version of the Brady Bunch.'* Am I right or am I right?"

"Oh, God!" I wince as Phoebe laughs sympathetically. "I can't believe I'm already messing this up. The one rule of this contract is no feelings and I'm breaking it to bits already!"

"Contract?"

I freeze. *Fuck. Me.* "Oh, you know, the unspoken fuck buddies contract you enter into when you agree to start having sex without strings."

Smooth, Em. Real smooth.

She seems to accept that. "Well, hon, you're only human. Plus, let's face it: you've totally outgrown casual sex. That stuff is fine and dandy when you're in your early twenties. But you lost your sister and inherited three children. Life made you grow up fast. You need more than just sex now; you need connection. Support. Why else do you think the dry streak lasted so damn long?"

I close my eyes and wince. Truth hurts. Best friend truth hurts twice as bad sometimes. And Phoebe has never been one for pulling punches.

"I guess I just thought I was safe from this kind of thing. He was—*is*—a freaking brute. An asshole—a *boss*hole, you know? I didn't think there was any chance I'd actually start, you know…"

"Fantasizing about carrying his babies and baking cupcakes in his kitchen while you're booty-ass naked beneath your sunflower-print apron?"

I groan loudly.

"Oh, stop being so hard on yourself," Phoebe scolds. "I mean, he's drop-dead gorgeous. Now that you've confirmed he has a heart, it makes sense that you'd fall in love with the man."

"Whoa, whoa, whoa—*whoa!* No one said anything about love. That is not where I'm at. I'm feeling *something* for Ruslan, but it's definitely not love."

"Methinks the lady doth protest too much."

I know she's teasing, but panic bubbles up inside me all the same. Love is not an option for me. Especially not with Ruslan Oryolov.

Sure, I felt a little somethin'-somethin' when I saw him with the kids today, but that was just natural. Biological. It was *appreciation* more than, you know, the *L* word.

He's my boss. And my fuck buddy. That is all he is.

It has to be.

29

RUSLAN

Emma shows up on time, but she looks like she barely slept last night. There are bags under her eyes and her usually immaculate bun is loose and unkempt. When she walks in with my schedule for the day, her eyes skim over me without seeming to process what she's actually seeing.

Is she self-conscious? Embarrassed? Annoyed?

And why the hell do I need to know so badly?

"Good morning, sir." She hands me the schedule, which is neatly color-coded as per usual. "The Santino people called and asked if they could postpone the meeting to next week. What would you like me to tell them?"

I scan through dates and times without absorbing any of it. "Yeah. Reschedule."

She nods. "Should I get your coffee now, sir? Or would you like it at ten during your meeting with the finance department?"

For some reason, the "sir" is bothering the hell out of me today. It was okay before, when we were just fucking. But now, I've been in her ramshackle little apartment. I've met her kids. I *like* her kids.

Which also begs the question—how the fuck did *that* happen?

My voice is gruff when I answer. "At the meeting is fine."

"Yes, sir. Will there be anything else?"

"How are the kids?"

Her eyebrows lift instantly. Her gaze slides over my face, but again, it refuses to stick. "The kids are…" She sighs and, as she does, that mask cracks just enough to show me the human beneath it. "It was a hard night. Rae had a nightmare and she ended up waking the other two. When I finally managed to get them all back to sleep, Caroline was up with a nightmare of her own."

"And Josh?"

She hesitates, her eyebrows lifting even higher. "Josh is… Josh. He wants to be strong. He slept on the floor of my room the whole night because he wanted to protect us."

I frown. "He's eight. He shouldn't have to protect anyone."

Emma bites her bottom lip. "I know that. But I think he feels an urge to step up and be the man of the house because his father—" She breaks off mid-sentence, her cheeks flushing with color. "I'm sorry. This is not your problem."

I want to remind her that I'm the one who asked, but she's already retreating toward the door. She turns on the spot, freezes, then turns back to me. Before I can figure out a way to ask her what I truly want to know, she cuts off any hope of further conversation. "Did you want anything else, Mr. Oryolov?"

Hell yes. So many things. I want to know why she clams up every time her deadbeat brother-in-law is mentioned. I want to hear how she ended up in this mess and how it feels to have gone through what she's gone through. I want to see, yet again, what it looks like when she comes.

And most of all, I want to know why she's so damn determined to hide all that from me.

"No. That's all for now."

The redness on her cheeks recedes as she walks out of my office. Gritting my teeth, I lean back and swivel my chair toward the view of the city through my windows. The overwhelming question that I find myself faced with is, *Why do I even care?*

I already know enough about her life. Between my glimpse of it yesterday and all the information Kirill dug up for me, I have most of the story.

And yet the fact that all this information has come to me secondhand bothers me. I want *her* to tell me. I want her to *want* to tell me.

Yes, I want her body. But there's a gnawing in my gut that's hungry for more.

When did sex stop being enough?

And if sex is really not enough… what more do I want?

"Do you think the owner will tell us who this other competing buyer is?"

I purse my lips. "I don't give a damn if he confirms it or not. It's Adrik. I know it is."

Kirill doesn't seem to like that answer. "I've had eyes on Adrik since the night he crashed Alcazar. Doesn't look like he's up to too much of anything apart from whoring his way around New York."

The streets are always unnaturally quiet whenever we break out from the chaotic snarl of Midtown traffic. It's a long drive to the manufacturing plant, but my negotiating tactics have always been more effective in person.

"Or that's what he wants us to believe," I growl. "First, he shows up at my club uninvited. Then there's a missing container of B47 substrate. Now, we might lose the manufacturing plant to someone else. All of it feels too on the nose to be a coincidence."

The manufacturing plant rises up on the horizon a quarter-mile before we reach it. It's a monstrously large facility, concentric rings of glazed white buildings and corrugated iron operating with ruthless efficiency. Kirill drives past the generator turbine. We can hear the massive engine cranking long after we've passed it.

Rolf Sunderland is standing outside the entrance of the main plant building as we park and get out, just in front of a row of gleaming windows with tinted glass. Two men stand at his back, one in a suit and the other wearing a lab coat.

"Mr. Oryolov, we're delighted to host you at Sunderland Plant." He grins broadly and spreads his hands wide. "Would you like a tour? Mr. Hadassy here will gladly show you around. He's the—"

"Mr. Sunderland, do I strike you as the type of man who has time to waste?"

His mouth snaps shut. "Pardon, sir?"

I stalk closer. He's no small man, but I still tower over him. The two employees at his back retreat instinctively, abandoning their boss to whatever I might do to him. "My team received a call this morning informing me that the sale might be delayed by a few weeks because you were reopening the bidding process and entertaining other buyers."

He pales, washing out what little color remained in his already-anemically pale complexion. "I… um, that is… I am a businessman, first and foremost. I must consider other deals, Mr.—"

"And this competing buyer? Did he give you a name?"

Sunderland's eyes bulge. "I'm afraid it wouldn't be ethical to divulge that kind of information. With all due respect. Sir. Mr. Oryolov."

I roll my eyes and glance at Kirill, lounging off to one side. He smirks and cracks his neck.

I turn my attention back to Sunderland, who seems to wish I would direct it at anyone else but him. "Lucky for you, I don't give two fucks about his name—I already know that information anyway. I *do* give a fuck about securing this manufacturing plant. But if you turn down the offer I'm about to give you, I can assure you, I will walk away and build my own fucking plant while you struggle to salvage what's left of yours from the mountain of ashes and rubbles that'll pile up right where you're currently standing."

Sunderland gulps. The suit and the lab tech take another couple of steps back. One bumps into the row of windows and nearly screams.

"Here's the deal: you agree to sell to me right now and I'll tack on another twenty percent."

His eyes widen even more. "Twenty percent?"

"You have exactly ten seconds to make your decision. Starting right—"

"Done!"

I nod curtly and glance at the suit. "I take it you're the lawyer?"

"Yes, sir."

"Draw up the paperwork. Today's as good a day as any to sign."

Sunderland gestures to his lawyer to do as he's told. Then he turns back to me with a wobbly smile. "Why don't you join us inside for a drink? To, ah, commemorate your new purchase."

My eyes narrow. "I'm not in the habit of drinking with men who go back on their word, Mr. Sunderland."

That wipes the smile clean off his face. "I-I do apologize, but—"

I take a step forward and the words die on his lips. "If it happens again, our next meeting won't be quite so pleasant."

I look him right in the eye when I say it. Sunderland only nods, his skin taking on a sickly sallow tint. "I-is there anything else I can do for you, Mr. Oryolov?"

"As a matter of fact, there is." I pluck the employee badge from his lapel, drop it on the ground, and grind it into the dust with the heel of my shoe. "You can get the fuck off my property."

30

RUSLAN

I'm high on adrenaline when I get back to the city in time for tonight's meeting. But Emma is chewing on her bottom lip as we enter the penthouse. Instead of looking excited or nervous with anticipation for the night ahead of us, the way she did before, she seems... complacent. Resigned. Like she's just here to work.

Then again, I suppose to her, this *is* work.

I'm suddenly not sure how I feel about that.

My hands clench as I walk toward the bar. "Drink?"

She blinks at me, her face still devoid of any genuine interest. "I shouldn't."

"Why not?"

Her jaw flexes and the vein in her forehead thrums softly. "Tomorrow's a workday."

"I'll put in a good word with your boss," I drawl sarcastically as I pour the drink anyway.

She accepts it hesitantly, her gaze sliding over to the windows. Her shoulders are tense. It's as if she's been holding her breath for far too long and she's afraid to start inhaling again. We stand there in silence for a while, but it doesn't seem to matter how many sips of her drink she takes—she's still stiff as a board.

A gentleman would excuse her tonight. Send her home early so that she can get a good night's sleep.

Too bad I'm the farthest fucking thing from a gentleman.

"It is beautiful up here," she observes. "So quiet."

I take the half-empty glass out of her hand and set it down on the marble side table next to the sofa. "It won't be for long."

She blushes. It reminds me of the first night we spent together. She was shy and unsure then, too, constantly blushing and glancing away from me to focus on the twinkling city lights.

But this isn't actual shyness holding her back. Is it discomfort, maybe? Wariness? Uncertainty? I've been so focused on making sure she doesn't get too close to me that it had never even occurred to me that she might be worried about the same damn thing.

For tonight, though, I want to make her forget everything. Her problems, her brother-in-law, her dead sister. Most of all, her own inhibitions. I want to chip away at the walls she's built around herself until she can't feel anything but pleasure.

I have a plan for exactly how to do that, too: I'm gonna give her so many orgasms that she'll forget her own name and only scream mine.

I glance down below my belt. Just like that, I've worked myself into the hardest erection of my life.

"Come here," I growl.

She turns to me and softly pads her bare feet across the floor, what little distance there is between us. She stops a few inches away. Still too far for my liking.

"Come here," I repeat, doing my best to resist the playful smile tugging at the corners of my mouth. Even in her current state, she's still so deliciously stubborn.

She takes another quarter-step forward. My gaze drops to her collarbone, then to the dip of her neckline. She's wearing a jade-green blouse today and it's doing wonders for those blue eyes of hers.

I caress the back of my hand along her jaw. Then down to the buttons of her blouse. She sucks in a breath and that delicate pink blush spreads to the tops of her breasts.

I tilt her chin up with my other hand to make sure she looks me in the eyes. I want her full attention and I'm going to get it one way or another.

Starting with ripping her blouse open.

Buttons scatter across the floor, not that I give a shit. I'll buy her a new shirt if I have to, as long as she keeps looking at me like she is now while I toss her scrap of a shirt aside.

She's *definitely* not tired anymore.

I pull her even closer to me until there's no space at all between us. I love the way she gasps when I manhandle her. When I smooth my hands up along the curve of her back, she shivers and presses herself into me.

Goddamn, her plump lips are so tempting. I can practically taste her as I flick the clasps of her bra open and let the straps slide down her arms until it falls to the floor.

I turn her around and unzip the skirt she's wearing, and again, I'm tempted to devour her creamy skin, starting with the curve of her neck. But I'm quickly distracted by the other curves of her body. She's wearing panties in the same shade of green as her blouse. They're modest, nothing skimpy, but for whatever reason, that's ten times hotter than if she'd been wearing the skinniest dental floss thong known to man.

I'm tempted to leave them on her. But I want her bare. Warm, bare, and *mine*.

I circle her like a caged beast, trying to figure out where to take my first bite. So many options.

That juicy ass.

Those perky breasts.

Her dripping wet pussy.

Fuck yes.

I hook my fingers in the waistband of her panties and drag them down as I kneel in front of her. The silky fabric clings to her mound, and it's all I can do to not immediately dive between those thighs like a starving man. I drape her leg over my shoulder and breathe her in. *Fuck.*

When I slide my tongue over her slit, she shudders, her fingers gripping my hair. "Ruslan…"

Her moan snaps the last string on my self-control. Grabbing her ass, I pull her sweet slit against my mouth and start eating her out. I lick, suck, and fondle every delicious fucking inch between her juicy thighs, milking out what I'm determined is going to be the first of many orgasms tonight.

Emma's legs are already shaking desperately, her fluttering little gasps turning into throaty moans.

"Fuck, Ruslan!" she mewls as her fingers tug harder on my hair.

I don't go easy on her. I tongue the orgasm out of her until her body collapses into me. Then I wrap my arms around her legs and hoist her over my shoulder, carrying her to the massive dining table that I don't think I've ever used.

Guess I was just waiting for a special occasion. This certainly qualifies.

I drop her down on the table and her eyes widen with surprise. "Ruslan! Not here!"

"Why the fuck not?"

"Because… because people *eat* here."

Adorable. By the end of tonight, she's not going to give a damn about anything other than trying to walk. I doubt she'll be able to do even that.

"Are you saying you're on the menu, *kiska*?"

She flushes bright red. "No—that's not what I—*ah!*"

I grab her legs and pull her forward so her back slides along the table. Emma leans up on her elbows as I free my cock and line it up with her slit.

"Unless you're hungry, too?" I tease her as I rub her clit with the tip. "I'd be more than happy to fill your mouth, your throat…"

She bites down on her bottom lip as I tease her, sliding my cock against her wetness, pushing in just enough to give her a taste of what's to come. Her breasts quiver and those peaked nipples of hers are making my mouth salivate all over again.

A new idea flashes through my mind: spinning her around so I can push those breasts together and fuck my cock between them.

But as much as I want to erupt all over her cleavage, I have a goal tonight. I need her to let go. I need her to forget everything and everyone—except me.

"R-Ruslan," she moans. "Fuck me… oh, God… just fuck me…"

I smirk. "Since you asked so nicely…"

Her eyes flare and she trails her tongue over her bottom lip. I don't look away when I slide inside her to the hilt.

She is so fucking *wet.*

My balls are ready to burst, but I push back the desire and concentrate on her. I grab her hips and start thrusting into her, mesmerized by the way her tits bounce. Even when she starts bucking and sobbing my name in broken, desperate syllables, I don't let up. I don't slow down. I don't go easy on her. I fuck her like a man possessed.

Arms flexing. Jaw clenching. Hips jerking. Sweat drips off my skin onto hers and with it, my own stress starts to melt away.

Her palms slam against the cool teak as she begs between cries. "Ruslan, *fuck…!* I can't… I can't take it anymore… please… yes, yes, *YES!*"

"Take it," I snarl between thrusts. "Take it, baby."

Her nails dig into my forearms and sharp stings of pain run up my arms as she applies pressure. It feels incredible. "That's it, *kiska*," I grunt. "Come for me... come on my cock... yeah, that's it baby..."

Her back arches, her lashes flutter, and her pussy convulses around my dick. Little crystal beads of sweat form between her breasts. I lean down, still buried to the balls inside her, and lick them off. She tastes every bit as good as she smells.

Citrus and sweat. And something else... oaky, spicy vanilla. *My* scent.

I like that a little too much.

I'm still hard when I pull out of her. Her eyes are closed, her chest rising and falling rapidly. I grab her legs again and hook them around my waist, using the leverage to carry her off the table. She instantly wraps herself around me, nestling her head on my shoulder, her body still trembling from her release.

Does that make me feel strong, powerful, *really* fucking entitled?

Absolutely.

Having her at my mercy makes me feel like the only real man who's ever lived.

"Ruslan..." she whispers. Her voice is unsteady and so, it seems, are her legs. "I don't think I can walk."

"You want my help? Then you're gonna have to earn it."

I have just enough time to see her eyes flicker with alarm before I twist her around and press her up against one of the floor-to-ceiling windows overlooking the city. Goosebumps race across her smooth skin as she trembles. And when I rub a possessive hand over the curve of her ass, she stiffens. "Y-you're gonna punish me again?"

I smile, adding a squeeze to the rub. "No, baby. You've been a good girl today, so you've earned a reward."

She moans. "I don't think I can take another orgasm."

I shake my head and nip her shoulder. "Unfortunately, that's not up to you."

Her body arches so fucking beautifully when I push into her. The way she immediately pushes her hips back and her ass up, spreading her legs wide… I probably have ten thrusts left in me at most, but I grit my teeth and force myself to keep going. The need to come is buried under the need to make *her* finish first.

I slide a hand around her neck and pull her up against my chest. Wrapping my arms around her, I grab a handful of those breasts and rock into her, making every hard thrust count. I can feel the vibration travel up my body before it's lost in hers. It's addictive.

Emma has completely surrendered herself to me, her body moving only where I allow it. She's just this side of limp in my arms, writhing only when I tease her nipples and slide a hand down her stomach to rub her clit in small circles.

I tongue the inside of her ear and she cranes her head back against my shoulder. "*Fuuuck*, Ruslan," she moans desperately. "I-I can't… I'm gonna…!"

And when she does, I explode inside her, reveling in the triumph of her body milking me into her.

When it's finished, she melts back against me, her legs officially limp, her body turning to putty. I pick her up again and carry her to the sofa.

"God," she sighs, rubbing her hands against the upholstery. "I can't feel… anything…"

Good.

"I'll get us some water."

It's amazing how satisfied I feel after my nights with Emma. It's not something I've ever experienced before. The revolving door kept spinning and women came—literally— and went. But none of them ever made an impression. Not even while I was inside them.

I stop short when I approach the couch with two glasses of water in hand. Emma is sprawled out across the cushions, fast asleep.

I set the glasses down and watch her for a few moments.

I should wake her.

I will *wake her.*

But maybe… not right away.

I end up on the loveseat facing her, staring at the way her breasts tremble with every breath she takes. She looks so damn peaceful that even an hour later, I can't bring myself to wake her. Instead, I carry her tenderly into my room and settle her on one side of the bed.

This bed has seen a lot of things, none of which involved sleep. That realization sends a little chill up my spine. But it's still not enough to convince me to wake her.

Mainly because that chill isn't exactly bad, per se.

I take the armchair by the window, but at no point do I actually appreciate the view of the city. I'm focused on the view of Emma in my bed.

I watch her for so long that my dilemma doesn't become obvious until long after the moon has risen. It's not that I don't want to wake her up.

I just don't want her to leave.

The way she writhed on my cock; the way she screamed my name... I thought I'd done what I set out to do tonight. But watching her asleep in my bed, it hits me—

This victory may not be mine at all.

31

EMMA

I wake up feeling like I've been swallowed by a cloud.

I stretch against the velvety soft sheets and moan into my pillow. This pillow might just have superpowers. Which is good timing, too, because when I roll onto my side, I realize with a grimace that everything *hurts.*

My thighs? Agony. My ass? Like I got branded with a cattle prod. Between my legs—

My eyes fly open. "Oh my God," I gasp, looking around the massive, sleek, bachelor pad that I should have been out of a long time ago. "Oh my God. Oh my God. Oh my God."

I jerk out of bed so fast that I trip on my own panic, collapse in half like a folding chair, and end up with my face smack dab in the carpet. Luckily, like everything else in this apartment, it cushions my fall with its plush luxuriousness.

"My clothes!" I stammer, running naked around the room like a headless chicken. "Where the hell are my clothes?"

And where is Ruslan?

I imagine his deep, gravelly voice booming through the penthouse. *Fee, fi, fo, fum—I smell the blood of a lazy bum.* I cringe at my own rhyme. I'm blaming *Jack and the Beanstalk* for that one. I read it to the girls a couple of weeks ago.

"Focus, Emma!" I snap at myself.

I'm very well aware that I'm dissociating so I don't focus on the terrifying fact that I'm awake in the penthouse, all by myself, after breaking the contract and potentially ruining everything. If I spend even a nanosecond dwelling on that, I'll have a full-on meltdown, so I just concentrate on the immediate next step.

First up: getting dressed.

Since my clothes are nowhere to be found, I grab the fluffy white bathrobe in the bathroom and scramble into it as I sneak into the living room. I move gingerly, terrified that he's going to be lurking behind every corner, every closed door, ready to bellow at me for overstaying my welcome.

But honestly, why would he let me sleep in? Hell, why would he let me sleep at all?

Wasn't he the one who insisted the contract needed to be upheld? Wasn't he the one who had insisted on the 'no sleepovers' rule? All of that was fine with me! I don't exactly have the time to languish around my fuck buddy's palace like a kept woman. I have a life. A job. *Kids.*

Oh my God, the kids!

He doesn't seem to be around but I do spot my clothes. They've been folded up neatly and left on the white sofa.

I can't find the green blouse he ripped off me but I do see a small white note sitting on top of the pile of clothes, right next to my phone. Ruslan's handwriting matches his personality. Confident, powerful, surprisingly elegant.

Be at the office at noon. There are coffee vouchers on the kitchen table if you're interested. And since I ripped your blouse, feel free to borrow whatever you need from my closet. The driver will be waiting for you outside when you're ready to leave. –Ruslan.

I'm genuinely stunned. He's giving me the morning off? Not just that—he's giving me permission to go into his closet and take one of his shirts?

I have officially checked out of reality.

I sit down next to my stack of clothes and take a deep breath. Then I fold the letter up and grab my phone. I've got a bunch of texts and calls from Amelia.

AMELIA: *Hey Emma. Just wanted to check if you needed me to spend the night with the kids. It's eleven now and neither you nor Ben are home.*

AMELIA: *I'll take your silence as an affirmative.*

AMELIA: *I'm gonna have to charge you an extra 10% for the last-minute notice. I hope that's okay.*

AMELIA: *Anyway. Goodnight. :smiley face:*

I groan, feeling like a complete moron. Amelia probably thinks I'm the world's worst guardian. And who can blame her? She might be right.

Quickly, I dial her number. "God, Amelia, I'm so, so, so sorry!" I blurt as soon as she answers. "It was just a crazy night. I was working late and then I—" *Got fucked into literal unconsciousness by my sex god boss*— "… ended up falling asleep at my desk."

"It's okay," she says with an unfazed laugh. "I didn't actually have plans last night, so it's all good. I won't even charge you that extra ten percent."

"No. Not a chance. You are getting every last cent of that extra ten. You deserve it. I'm so sorry about the terrible communication."

"You fell asleep. It happens."

I grimace. She's being way nicer than I deserve. "Is Ben around?"

Just like that, her politeness vanishes. She'd never say a cross word about anyone, but even she can't seem to muster up anything nice to say about my brother-in-law. "He didn't show up last night."

Ah. That explains her good mood.

"Uh, okay. Copy that. Weird. I'm actually coming back home now. I'll be there within the hour. Are you okay to stay with the kids 'til then?"

"No problem, Emma."

I thank her again and hang up. Grabbing my clothes, I duck back into the master bathroom. The giant tub beckons but I already feel guilty enough for forcing Amelia to pull an all-nighter without notice. So I settle for a quick shower and then step into Ruslan's walk-in closet, which is double the size of my bedroom.

Man, does it smell good in here.

When I start pressing each shirt to my nose, breathing in that deep, oaky scent, I start to catch creepy stalker vibes—from myself.

Get out now, Emma!

Quickly, I pick out a simple white button-down. It's about four sizes too big but after I roll up the cuffs and tuck in the front, it actually looks sorta chic. I spend a minute longer than necessary in front of the wall-mounted mirror, trying to avoid all the juvenile thoughts circling around in my head about the fact that I'm wearing Ruslan Oryolov's shirt on my way to do the world's boujiest walk of shame.

When I slide into the back seat of the tinted SUV parked out front, my legs bump against a large leather duffel with a note written on a piece of cardstock pinned to the handle.

"Um, hey, Boris?" I ask the driver, who'd introduced himself in a monotone, accented grunt when I stepped out of the penthouse building. "Do you know what this is?"

Boris glances at me over his shoulder. "Boss told me give to you."

Frowning, I unzip the bag and peek inside. There are three brand new shoeboxes staring back at me, each marked with a name across the front.

Josh.

Caroline.

Reagan.

Could it be...?

I open Josh's package first to find the most amazing pair of green and black basketball sneakers. Caroline's pair of leather sneakers are pink and silver. Reagan's are sequined and multicolored. And the sizes are all perfect.

I have a billion questions I'd like to ask, starting with, *How did he know?*

But I'm too dumbfounded to bother asking, not that I think Boris was about to be particularly forthcoming with additional details. I spend most of the drive back home just gawking at the shoes. The Debbie downer in me keeps wondering how I'm going to explain such expensive purchases to Ben.

But the optimist in me—the stupid, naive, ever-hopeful optimist—just can't stop smiling long enough to care.

32

EMMA

I feel ridiculously well-rested as I walk the special artisanal coffee blend in my hand towards Ruslan's office.

I was tempted to wear his shirt into work today. The whole oversized-shirt-plus-pencil-skirt combo was really doing it for me. Well, that, and the fact that it was very exciting to imagine myself walking around Bane wrapped in Ruslan's oaky-scented button-down.

It just felt... I dunno. Kind of like I'd be broadcasting the obvious. Flaunting it. In the end, I decided not to push my luck.

Ruslan doesn't look up from his paperwork until I've put the coffee down in front of him. When he does look at me, his expression is impassive—and that throws me for a loop.

Last night, we broke one of his rules. A big one, in my opinion. Are we just supposed to pretend like it never happened? Am I supposed to back out of the room without addressing the giant elephant in it?

"I used the coffee voucher you left for me."

God, I sound awkward.

He raises one eyebrow and nods. I keep twisting one of my beige heels into the dark laminate floors. There'll be a scuff here if he keeps up this stony silence. A testament to me being so cringey it hurts.

"I just... I know you're uncomfortable with gratitude, but I have to say thank you. I can't remember the last time I slept so well. Or so long."

He clears his throat. "Don't mention it."

I know he's not being polite. He means that literally. *Do not mention it.*

"And as for the kids' shoes... you have no idea how much it means to me. Or how much it'll mean to them."

"They're good kids," he says gruffly. "They deserve a decent pair of shoes."

"I'll reimburse you for them."

His eyes snap to mine. "Don't you dare. They're gifts."

"But—"

"They're gifts, Ms. Carson. End of discussion."

My mouth clamps shut. There's this weird, piercing sensation in the center of my heart and I don't like it one bit.

Why? *Why* does he have to go all inhuman on me now?

"If you insist," I concede. "Anyway, yeah, they'll be over the moon. Almost as over the moon as I was to actually get a decent night's sleep."

I give him a self-conscious smile that he doesn't return. *Welp, seems like my time here is done.* I'm about to turn towards the door when he speaks. "I'm glad you got some sleep. You've been running on fumes lately."

I'm not sure if that's meant to be a reprimand or a peace offering, but he looks neither pissed nor annoyed. His signature eyebrow furrow is absent, too.

"Is it that obvious?" He arches his brow again and I let out an embarrassed chuckle. "I'm sorry. It's just that it's not so easy to juggle everything all the time. I do have help. Amelia's a godsend, but she's been getting restless lately and I just know that, at some point, it doesn't matter how much more I agree to pay her; she's going to want to leave."

I have no idea why I'm telling him all this. Maybe it's the fact that, for once, he's actually listening.

He folds his hands in front of him. "Why do you think she's getting restless?"

That answer is easy and obvious. "Ben." I start digging my heel into the floor again. "It's hard enough dealing with three young, confused, grieving kids. Add a lazy, selfish drunk to the mix and the job gets ten times as hard."

"Does he contribute at all?"

Wait... are we having an actual conversation?

"He took my sister's death really hard."

"Is that a no?"

I sigh. "No. He doesn't contribute at all."

There it is: the Oryolov scowl. But for once, it's not directed at me. At least, I'm pretty sure it's not. But just in case I'm wrong, I decide to quit while I'm ahead and excuse myself from the premises.

"Anyway, I'm gonna go fine-tune the guest list for next week's cocktail—"

"Emma."

I have no idea why goosebumps erupt over my arms. It may possibly be because he just slipped and used my first name. I'm always "Ms. Carson" and, as cold as that sounds, at least it's safe. But "Emma"? *Whoo boy*, that's dangerous.

"Yes?" I squeak.

"70-33-40."

"Excuse me?"

"That's the access code to my penthouse. You can use it whenever you need."

I stare at him with my mouth hanging open. What he's saying is not computing. "Your... penthouse?"

He nods. "You have twenty-four-seven access. I want to make sure you have a place to go if you ever need to get away from your deadbeat brother-in-law or any other slimy reporters that may come your way. The kids are welcome, too, obviously. You can change the access code once you're inside for added privacy and protection."

At this point, my eyes feel like they're about to burst out of their sockets. I subtly pinch the inside of my elbow to make sure I'm awake. It hurts.

Yeah, this is real.

"But then you'll be locked out."

He shrugs. "If that's what it takes to make you and the children feel safe, I'm fine with that."

Pinch or no pinch, I'm definitely hallucinating. That's what's happening here. Nothing else makes sense.

"I... I don't know what to say."

"You don't have to say anything. Just accept what I'm offering you."

But that's just it. What he's offering me is so much more than a gesture. It's safety. Security. Peace of mind.

And I'm pretty sure it's an egregious breach of our contract.

Which is why, when I step toward him, it doesn't feel quite so crazy. My heart is beating so hard that the vibrations run down my hands and make my fingers tremble.

I round his desk and stop at his knees. He glances up at me and I realize that I have maybe two seconds to either back out—or commit.

"I want to show you how grateful I am, *sir*," I whisper, trembling as I sink down to my knees in front of him.

His expression remains intimidatingly aloof, but I notice the way his hands tighten around the edge of the armrests.

"Emma..."

I reach for the front of his pants, but I only manage to undo the buckle before his hands come down on top of mine. I'm caught between panic and desire. I'm nervous from the waist up and an utter dripping mess from the waist down.

"Yes, Mr. Oryolov?" I ask innocently.

Those amber eyes scorch my face, but I refuse to drop my gaze. If he wants to turn me down, I'll take it like a grown woman with some semblance of dignity.

His jaw clenches and his fingers tighten over mine. "This is not a good idea."

My disappointment is cushioned by the knowledge that turning me down is not easy for him. That's made obvious by the extremely noticeable bulge pushing up through the crotch of his pants.

As generous as he's being to me, I am not about to make this easy on him. "Should I leave then?"

His eyes run over my face and dip down to my cleavage. "You should fucking *run*," he hisses.

I nod, ready to get back to my feet, but his hand grabs my wrist just before I rise. I descend back onto my knees and freeze, waiting for him to decide what he wants.

His jaw is clenched tight. So is the rest of him. "You dirty little *kiska*."

I can't help but grin shyly. The bright light streaming through the windows offers me a clear view of the way his pupils are dilating, blown wide with lust.

"Go on then. Show me how grateful you are."

Biting my lower lip with satisfaction, I unbuckle his pants and ease his cock free. He's so fucking hard, his tip already smeared with a little pre-cum. The plan is to take it slow, but the moment I taste him, I forget the plan entirely. I suck him into my mouth, swirling my tongue while my hand massages his shaft.

His fingers clamp down hard around my forearm. "For fuck's sake, *kiska*," he growls. "I know you're hungry for my cock, but you're gonna have to take it slow."

I lift my head and hold his gaze for a moment. But I don't stop fisting his thick shaft.

"Gentler," he instructs me softly. His voice is much less gruff, much silkier. I'm all too happy to obey, taking him back into my mouth and savoring the way he throbs along my tongue. "Yes, like that… Mmm, *fuck*…"

His eyes close and he leans back against the black leather chair. "Now, glide your tongue from the bottom to the tip."

I bend my head back down and obey. I start at the base of him, nuzzling the weight of his balls on my cheek, and apply more pressure with my tongue as I glide up toward his head.

"*Fuck*. Yes. Just like that."

I repeat the motion a few times, adding a gentle suckle over that sweet spot that makes him hiss a deep gasp.

"What a good little assistant you are. So fucking obedient. Are you going to stay obedient for me?"

"Yes," I rasp.

"Good girl. Now, suck my dick. Show me how hungry you are."

I thought he'd never ask. I suck on him desperately, my mouth getting used to his size until I'm confident enough to take him deeper.

At some point, his hand finds the back of my head. Tears prick at the corners of my eyes as he presses down gently. He could go harder if he wanted to, though. I'd let him. Hell, I might even beg him to. I'm that fucking desperate for him to fill my throat, to own me in every way possible.

"You're such a good girl," he croons. "You're so fucking beautiful when you take all of me."

I slurp and swallow, refusing to let up even when I think I'm nearing the end of my ability. I can feel his legs tremble on either side of me as he gets even thicker on my tongue and I know he's close. I pull him deeper into my mouth and, just when I feel like I'm about to gag on how huge he is, he jerks violently.

Once, twice he spasms, filling my throat with his cum. I swallow as fast as I can, but it just keeps coming.

Finally, there's nothing left. He pulls out and I gasp, falling back against the cool floor as I try to catch my breath. Ruslan is panting hard, too, and I feel a swell of pride in my chest at the sight of him slumped in his chair.

He just came in my mouth.

He's the first man to ever have the privilege.

And even though I know it's in flagrant disregard of the *Don't you dare catch feelings* clause of our contract...

I wouldn't have it any other way.

33

RUSLAN

The train is officially off the track.

Last week's steamy blowjob in my office pushed it to the edge of the rails. And now, a measly seven days later?

We're an absolute fucking disaster.

For starters, I can't stop fucking her at work. Her mere presence is just one big tease. Every time I walk into the office and find her sitting at her desk like a good, innocent little employee, my balls feel like they're on the verge of exploding. I keep shutting the door on that coquettish smile of hers, trying to resist calling her into my office for reasons that have nothing to do with my meeting schedule or when I want my afternoon coffee brought in.

But day after day, I lose the battle. It doesn't matter if I invent a lie to drag her in or not; it all ends the same way—with Emma spread out on my desk or up against a wall or bent over the chair while I fuck her brains out.

And since we've already established that she's a screamer, it falls to me to keep her quiet. I've experimented thus far with clamping a hand over her lips, burying myself in her mouth, or shoving her panties in while I fist her hair and bend her back so far I wonder if one day her spine might just snap. None of the techniques are particularly effective. I'll have to keep exploring.

Every time she struts into my office with that cheeky little grin on her face, it feels like a challenge. It feels like she's asking me, *What filthy thing are you going to do to me next?*

Maybe that's why I upped the ante by calling her into a meeting with the board last week just so I could finger her pussy under the table while Henrich Stenson droned on about annual sales reports and net profits.

She squirmed so much and turned so red that Henrich actually paused in the middle of his speech to ask her if she was feeling alright. She stammered through an apology, muttered something about a migraine, and then excused herself. I trapped her in my office later that day and punished her for leaving without my permission. She had three orgasms, one of which gushed on my face, before she begged me to stop.

Suffice it to say, this was definitely not the plan.

Every night, I go to bed resolving not to cave the next day. And every morning, I wake up with a raging hard-on and the addictive need to see her again, feel her again, fuck her again. There's just something about sex at the office—the illicitness of it, the knowledge that we're breaking all the rules, even the ones we set in place for ourselves.

A lifetime of strict discipline all crumbles to dust the moment I think about Emma Carson.

Case in point: the Olsen-Ferber charity gala. Emma and I would usually go over final details for any event at the office during a scheduled appointment. But today, we pull up outside Jean-Georges to discuss the particulars over a four-course lunch.

We're shown to our table overlooking Columbus Circle. While Emma admires the view, I admire her. I have to bite my tongue so hard I draw blood while I resist the urge to run my hand up the inside of her thigh in public.

To her credit, she always at least tries to maintain a certain level of professionalism. Like right now, as she pulls out her ivory folder and a matching ballpoint pen. She's all business and she keeps me focused on the topic at hand… for the most part. We spend twenty minutes going over logistics and security concerns before I reach over and shut the file.

"That's enough for now."

She doesn't argue. Her cheeks flush a delicate shade of vermillion. "What would you like to discuss now, sir?"

The little minx. She knows what she's doing. What it does to me. It's in the slight rasp of her voice, even when her words are innocent enough on the surface. My hand settles on her knee under the table as that shy smile of hers perks up in the corner of her mouth. "Are we graduating to exhibitionism?"

I loft a brow and match her smirk. "Are you complaining?"

"I wouldn't dream of it." She takes a sip of her water. "Just asking."

The truth is, as tempting as it would be to finger her under the table, I'm struck by the jarring thought that what I want right now is simply to talk to her.

"How are the kids?"

She gives me a subtle double-take that I find mildly offensive. Is it really that surprising that I care enough to ask?

"They're good." I cock a brow and she sighs. "Mostly. It's amazing how many things kids need. Caroline wants to do ballet, which means she'll need leotards, shoes, all kinds of stuff. Josh really wants to try out for basketball, but that's not cheap, either."

I frown. "I would think you'd have a little more money saved up now." I don't want to come right out and cite our arrangement, but it's more than obvious what I'm getting at.

"I do," she admits. "The thing is..." She's squirming now, her eyes flitting from the view to the table and back again. I squeeze her knee until she stops. "I have to be careful what I buy and how I spend the money. If Ben realizes I'm making more, he's just gonna start asking for more."

"'No' is a complete sentence, Emma."

She's pointedly avoiding my gaze now. "It's not as easy as that."

"He doesn't have a job?" I can feel the pressure in my temples starting to tick up, the way it does whenever we happen to stumble into a conversation about this fucking leech.

"He used to work in a bar near Madison Square Park, actually. He was one of their best. Management track and everything. But ever since the accident..." Her eyes get watery the moment she brings it up. "It's like he gave up on life."

"Is that when the drinking started?"

"Pretty much. I mean, he was always a drinker, but it was mostly just social. He took some time off work after the funeral. About three months, actually. When he went back, he only lasted a couple of weeks before he was fired."

"And after that?"

Her brow furrows and her eyes go hazy and distant. "He basically became a permanent fixture of the apartment. If he leaves, it's either to get drunk or stoned." She stares out the window when the silence stretches. "I know what you're thinking."

I lean back in my chair. "Do you?"

"You're wondering why I put up with it, right?" She idly brushes the condensation off her water glass. "It's because I know what it felt like to lose Sienna. How all-consuming that kind of loss is. How can I fault him for being destroyed by it when it nearly destroyed me?"

"But it didn't." Her eyes fly up to mine and I shake my head slowly. "It didn't destroy you. It made you stronger."

"I have to be strong. For the kids."

"That's *his* job."

Her brow creases. "It's *my* job, too. She was my sister. And she—" Her voice breaks mid-sentence. The sob is right there, dying to be released. But instead, she swallows it and composes herself with a deep breath. "She was my world. For most of our lives, she was my other half. How could I not take care of her kids?"

There's more behind those veiled tears, but her jaw is set firmly and I'm pretty sure she's done talking about her sister.

I can't blame her. It's been more than a fucking decade and I still can't bring myself to talk about the accident that changed my life and the people I lost that day.

I'm beginning to realize I have more in common with my secretary than an office and a sex drive. I'm not sure how I ought to feel about that.

A voice breaks in. "*Emma*?!"

Emma's eyes bulge in horror as she turns to see who spoke. "Fuck me," she mutters under her breath. Then she raises her pitch with a fake enthusiasm that matches her fake smile. "Mom! Dad!"

Her parents?

Interesting.

The older couple makes a beeline straight for our table. Both are dressed to the nines, no surprise there; *Jean-Georges* has a strict dress code for their diners. But it's clear that they have taste, too. Teardrop diamonds dangle from Mom's ears and I note a sparkling new Birkin bag on her arm. Dad keeps adjusting and readjusting his cuffs, just in case anyone missed the Patek Philippe watch shining on his wrist.

Mom's eyes are fixed on me even as she addresses Emma. "What are you doing here, darling?"

There's a tremor in Emma's voice when she speaks that wasn't there just a moment ago. "Just having a business lunch." She nearly knocks over her water when she stands up. I move it out of the way before she turns the table into a splash zone. "Mom, Dad, this is my boss, Ruslan Oryolov. Rus—uh, Mr. Oryolov, these are my parents, Barrett and Beatrice."

"How nice to meet you, Ruslan," Beatrice murmurs, batting her eyelashes at me.

Emma cringes. "Mr. Oryolov and I are just here to go over last-minute details for a charity gala taking place next week."

"Ah, Beatrice and I support a great many charities," Barrett tells me in a self-congratulatory tone. "Which one is this?"

"Olsen-Ferber."

Barrett gives me an approving nod. "Ah, yes, of course. Wonderful charity. Beatrice and I have made many contributions over the years."

I'd bet a testicle he has no idea what the charity actually does, but I'm not about to make Emma feel any more uncomfortable than she clearly already is. She's radiating misery.

"Anyway, we should really—"

"How are my grandchildren?" Beatrice asks, cutting Emma off. "You didn't bring them over last weekend like I asked. I had deviled eggs made especially for Jake."

Emma's fake smile curdles. "Who is Jake?"

Beatrice's own smile falters, too. "Really, Emma?" Her eyes flick over to me self-consciously. "There's no reason to be so rude."

"I was just taken aback for a second because, the last time I checked, your *grandson's* name is *Josh*."

Barrett clears his throat. "For God's sake, Emma. Your mother made a mistake. There's no reason to be so defensive about it."

Emma's vein practically pops out of her forehead. It's the most prominent I've ever seen it. Who knew there were two other people who pissed her off more than I did?

She glares at her mother. "And I'm not sure who you're thinking of, but *Josh* has never liked deviled eggs."

Barrett's thick silver eyebrows knit together. "You're in quite the mood today, young lady."

I clear my throat. That's about all I'm willing to put up with.

I look between Beatrice and Barrett. "Emma has a lot on her plate and not a whole lot of help." My voice is cold as I give them the same venomous stare I offer to any idiot who dares strut into my office with an ego. And since this is a business lunch, that makes this space my office. "I'm sure, as the doting grandparents you so clearly are, you completely understand. Now, if you don't mind, we have more work to do before we need to be back at the office."

Emma swivels in my direction. She looks just as dumbfounded as her parents. I sit back down and reach for my glass of wine.

"Ahem!" Barrett puts his hand on his wife's shoulder. "Come, Beatrice. If you'll excuse us…"

They storm off to the opposite side of the restaurant while Emma just stands there, gawking after them.

"It's gonna be hard for you to eat standing up," I tell her.

Her gaze veers slowly to me. "I can't believe you just… *dismissed them*. You just dismissed my parents." She falls back into her seat. I'm trying to figure out if she's pissed or not when she suddenly smiles in sheer amazement. "No one has ever done that before."

I shrug, enjoying the awe in her eyes a little too much. "Not my first time."

She snorts. "Oh, I know. I've been on the receiving end of the infamous Oryolov dismissal. I know it well." She takes a deep breath and leans back, still shaking her head. "Of all the people to run into here…"

Barrett and Beatrice are out of sight now, but Emma hasn't totally relaxed. The gently throbbing vein on her forehead is proof of that.

"So. You come from money." I watch her squirm a little in her seat, but there's no way we're glossing over that bombshell.

She rolls her eyes. "I haven't taken a cent from my parents since I graduated high school. And I don't plan on starting now, either."

"What about the kids?"

The vein throbs a little harder. "I was thinking of nothing *but* the kids when I turned down my parents' offer to help. Beatrice and Barrett come with strings. They always have."

I want her to tell me more, but she picks up her menu and becomes thoroughly absorbed in it.

And for the rest of lunch, that vein doesn't go away.

34

EMMA

I almost knock over an old lady in my rush to get to Bane. It doesn't even matter at this point; I'm already an hour late. I glance at the dinged-up watch on my wrist and cringe.

Scratch that: one hour and seventeen minutes late.

"Sorry!" I yell at the old lady who I'm pretty sure flips me the bird as I run toward the silver skyscraper.

By the time I get through security and into the elevators, I'm sweating through my light blue blouse. Because of course I just *had* to wear silk today. Another great decision.

I'm on a freaking roll.

And since I am not allowed to catch a break today, the elevator makes eleven slow stops before it finally hits my floor. "Excuse me!" I gasp, shoving my way out of the elevator and racing down the corridor towards my desk.

Maybe he won't notice?

Ha. Right.

I'm not at my desk three seconds before the doors of Ruslan's office open. He stands in the threshold, his gaze directed squarely at me.

"Ms. Carson." He sounds pissed. "My office. Now."

He leaves the door open and disappears inside. A steady stream of *Fuck, fuck, fuck, fuck, fuck* plays in my head as I follow him inside and shut the door.

I start talking before I'm even at his desk. "I am *so* sorry. I know I've said it before, but this *will not* happen again and—"

He holds up a hand and I fall silent in the face of that very large, very intimidating, very callused, very, very capable palm.

"Was there an emergency of some sort?"

"Um… no. Not exactly."

"An accident?"

"No."

"Are you hurt in any way?"

"No."

This little interrogation is not helping my sweat glands calm down.

"What about the kids?"

"Safe and in school."

He nods. "Then I'd like your explanation as to why you're one hour and twenty-seven minutes late."

I take a deep breath and barrel ahead. "I thought I put my phone on the charger last night, but the plug fell out because the wall thingie is broken loose. So it died on me while I was asleep and my alarm didn't go off. By the time Josh woke me up, Ben was gone, so I had to get the kids to school first, which made me miss my train. So I caught the second train into the city which was delayed by seven minutes due to some 'technical difficulties,' because of course it was." I am very aware of the fact that I'm ranting now, but I can't seem to stop myself. "And then I nearly took down an old lady as I ran to the building. And of course, there were, like, a hundred people in the elevator on the way up here. Do you know how slow that elevator is? Can someone look into that? And why is it always so crowded? You would think that a building with so many elevators wouldn't have a crowding issue, but well, anyway…" I glance up at him and notice that raised brow. "Um… here I am."

I'm winded by the time I finish. And now, I'm definitely sweating through my shirt.

Ruslan is silent, staring at me with that inscrutable expression of his.

"I really am sorry, Mr. Oryolov. I promise you, it won't—"

"Sit down."

He doesn't leave me a lot of room to decline. I plonk myself down on a chair and wait for him to fire me.

But instead of reading me the Riot Act, Ruslan just walks across the office toward the door I came through.

My knee starts jumping as I stare unseeingly at the view in front of me. He's gonna fire me. Or worse, he's gonna bend me over the desk, make me forget all about being late, and *then* fire me, just to make that pink slip even pinker.

Would he really do that? After everything we've been through?

Of course, "everything we've been through" in this case just means a lot of sex. An insane amount of sex, if I'm being honest. Which may not be as significant to him as it has been for me.

Serves you right for catching feelings, dummy.

"Idiot," I mutter to myself. "Complete fucking idiot."

I freeze the moment I hear his wingtips on the laminate flooring. His shadow falls across me and I'm seized with the very real fear that I'm about to lose my income.

Please God, no.

"Here."

I stare at the glass of water he's offering me. "Water?"

"It's to drink. Or throw on yourself—whichever you need more. Can't say I'll complain either way."

I accept the glass with a shaky hand. I end up guzzling most of it. Apparently, running a marathon in heels and then working yourself into a frenzied panic can really dehydrate a girl. "Thank you."

He takes the glass from my hands when I'm done and then drags the chair next to mine forward so that it's right in front of me. Sitting down, he pulls out a small face towel from who the hell knows where.

Just when I think he's going to offer it to me, he reaches out to pat it gently against the side of my face himself. I flinch the moment he touches me. He's not even really touching me; the washcloth is firmly between us. And yet it feels so intimate that a tiny gasp escapes my lips.

He must hear it, because he freezes, then drops his hand and hands me the towel instead. "You're sweating."

A few of the butterflies in my stomach go berserk. "Right. Thank you."

He nods as I try to hide my embarrassment with the damp cloth. I pass it over my face twice before I feel brave enough to drop my arm and peek out at him again.

"I really am sorry—"

"Emma."

His voice is firm, but surprisingly gentle.

Oh, God, is he being so nice because he's trying to cushion the blow? Is this the end?

"You don't have to apologize."

Because I'm fired?

"You've been a stellar employee for a very long time. You're allowed to be late to work once in a while."

My mouth drops open. "I'm... what?"

He actually cracks a smile. And by "smile," I mean one corner of his mouth twitches up and his eyes crinkle at the corners.

"You have a lot going on. It stands to reason that you would be late once in a while. That being said, getting a second alarm wouldn't hurt."

I know I'm gaping at him, but I just can't help it. This reaction is such a departure from what I was expecting.

I smile self-consciously. "Thank you. I'll keep that in mind."

He gestures towards the door. "Work awaits."

It's a more abrupt dismissal than I expected, especially considering the last few minutes of gut-churning tension, but I get up and leave all the same. He has a point: we've got a full day ahead and I need to catch up quickly.

I spend the rest of the morning sitting behind my desk doing exactly that. Ruslan doesn't call me into his office once. Not to work *or* play. When he needs me to do something, he either sends me a text or uses the intercom.

The relief I felt when I was in his office dwindles slowly throughout the rest of the afternoon and the blind panic starts to creep back in. Maybe he wasn't as okay with my tardiness or my chaotic life as he let on. Maybe he isn't interested in being that understanding all the time.

What if firing me still isn't off the table? What if I lose this job and all the benefits? The income? It would be a devastating blow to lose all that money.

Who am I kidding? It'd be a devastating blow to lose all that sex, too.

But as I scroll through my personal banking page on my laptop later in the afternoon, I realize that my nest egg has gone from nonexistent to fairly sizable in just a matter of weeks. Ruslan's weekly allowances have been coming in and building up steadily. Even if I were to lose this job, I'd be able to manage for a bit.

I'd be okay.

The kids would be okay.

I exhale slowly. I've been drowning for so long that I forgot what it feels like to breathe.

Now, thanks to Ruslan, I can.

35

EMMA

RUSLAN: *Be in my office in five, Ms. Carson.*

This is the first time he's summoned me all day since my little breakdown in his office this morning. I get to my feet and smooth down my skirt.

"Stay calm, Emma," I coach myself under my breath. "Be cool."

"Mr. Oryolov?" I say when I walk inside. "You asked for me?"

He pulls out a small black device from a drawer in his desk and throws it at me. Thankfully, I have great reflexes developed from little kids running around the house. I catch it with one hand and give it a look.

My eyes snap to his. "This is a car key."

"You have impeccable observation skills, Ms. Carson."

I flush. "Do you want me to schedule a service for one of your cars?"

"No. I want you to take the car that goes with that key and drive it home. And then drive it back here in the morning. And then just keep doing that on repeat until further notice."

My eyebrows feel like they're going to disappear into my forehead. "You... you're giving me a car?"

The moment I say it, I regret it. What if that's not what's going on? What if I misunderstood?

"Once again, Ms. Carson, nothing seems to get past you." His eyes flicker with amusement. "To be clear, it's a company vehicle that is currently registered on loan to you. But essentially, yes, I am giving you a car."

Um... what?

Despite the sudden bout of vertigo, I'm reminded of the little pep talk I gave myself before walking in here. "May I ask why?" I say it calmly. Coolly. Like someone who's definitely *not* about to pass out.

"Because I need you to look and act the part of an important CEO's executive assistant. That's going to be difficult if you're constantly catching the wrong train and missing the empty elevator time. Now that you have a car, there will be no excuses."

It's an extremely plausible explanation. Airtight, really.

So why don't I believe it?

"This is... very kind of you. Some would say too kind."

His mouth hardlines. "I'm not doing it to be 'kind,' Ms. Carson. I'm doing it to make sure you perform your job to the best of your abilities."

I force back a smile and nod. "Of course, Mr. Oryolov."

"That will be all."

I wait until I'm back at my desk to let out the delirious laugh that I've been holding in.

A car. He gave me a freaking *car*!

And he bought the kids brand-new shoes. And he brought me water this morning. And he tried to wipe the sweat off my face. And he offered me the use of his penthouse whenever I wanted.

He could tell me a trillion times that he isn't doing any of this to be kind. None of it's personal. It's all about optimal professionalism. Increased efficiency. Bane's reputation, his reputation, et cetera.

But the tiny little smile playing on his lips as I walked out of his office told an entirely different story. In other words, my quest to stay emotionally detached is completely fucked.

As am I.

The call picks up. "Hey, Amelia, are the kids around?"

"Yup!" the sitter says brightly. "We're just building Legos in the living room."

I am *so* freaking excited. I'm squiggling around in my seat. "Awesome. Can you ask them to come to the window, please?"

"Uh, sure." The line fizzles with a little static. "Hey, kiddos! Auntie Em wants you guys to go to the window. Em, I'm putting you on speaker."

I roll back the Mercedes' sunroof and stick my head out. A second later, Josh's face pops up at the apartment window. Then Caroline's. Then Reagan's. Through the phone, I can hear their little gasps going off like firecrackers.

"Auntie Em!" Reagan squeals, waving eagerly at me.

"*Cool* car," Caroline quips with wide eyes.

"You bought a car?" Josh gasps.

I laugh at their reactions. "I didn't buy the car. It's a company car, but it's mine. So—who wants a ride?"

Again, I'm hit with a barrage of responses.

Reagan: "Me! Me! *Meeee*!"

Caroline: "*I* do! *I* do! *I* do!"

Josh: "Shotgun!"

Laughing, I hold the phone away from my ear. "Amelia?"

She clearly takes me off speaker because the chaos on her side gets cut down by half. Josh steps off to the side and she takes his place at the window. There's a huge smile on her face. "What's up?"

"For the first time ever, I can offer you a ride back home."

"Are you sure?"

"Hundred percent."

"Amazing. Be down in five."

"Five minutes?" I laugh. "Ambitious."

Sure enough, it's fifteen minutes later before Amelia troops towards the car like the Pied Piper with all three kids trailing. She hops in the front while the kids bunch up in the spacious back seat of the deep blue Mercedes.

I ran a quick Google search on the car when I first saw it gleaming out in front of the Bane building. It claims the country's highest child occupant protection rating at a whopping ninety-one percent. Something tells me that wasn't an accident.

Which is enough to make my heart melt in ways it really, really shouldn't.

The kids *ooh* and *aah* over the car the whole way to Amelia's place. She and I don't manage to get a word in edgewise. After we drop her off, Josh jumps into the front seat.

"Auntie Em?" Caroline asks, wriggling underneath the hold of her seatbelt. "Do we have to go home now?"

I pretend to think about it. "Well… tonight *is* a school night."

I'm met with a disappointed chorus of *"awww's."* I twist around in my seat. "Then again…" The girls hitch up their breaths. "It's not every day we get a new car! Let's get ice cream!"

I have to cover my ears as the car erupts with cheers and screams. I'm smiling so damn hard that my face hurts by the time we get to the ice cream parlor just north of Hudson Yards.

It's one of those boujee places with neon signs that say stuff like *"I Licked It So It's Mine"* and a line of eager patrons wrapped around the block more often than not. It's also one of those places where a child-sized cup of vanilla with sprinkles sets you back fourteen bucks—so needless to say, we've never been before.

But if there was ever a day to drop a hundred bucks on a sweet treat, it's today.

Caroline and Reagan's eyes double in size when we walk in. Aside from the delectable smell of melted caramel and cookie dough, the ambience promises all sorts of sugary goodness. The tables sit between swings that are anchored to the floor and the ceiling to keep them in place. The walls are covered in floral arrangements that bloom between framed posters featuring ice cream cones pasted into old Renaissance paintings. The *Mona Lisa* is partial to rocky road, apparently.

We each pick a flavor and settle at the table right beneath a pink neon billboard that reads, *You Can't Buy Happiness, But You Can Buy Ice Cream, & That's Practically the Same Thing.*

Reagan seems to agree. "This is the best day ever!" she declares between licks of her double chocolate fudge scoop.

Josh and Caroline's mouths are stuffed with ice cream so they just nod emphatically. My heart is fit to bursting.

I can't remember when I last felt this good.

I bite another mouthful of salted caramel cheesecake and sigh contentedly. *It can't get any better than this.*

Then Josh gasps. "Oh, Auntie Em! I almost forgot." He reaches around into his backpack and pulls out a thin stack of papers. "It's for basketball."

Dang it. I might've spoken too soon.

My heart drops. It's so much worse this time around because I *can* actually afford to pay for Josh's basketball program. The problem isn't money—it's Ben.

"Oh, honey…"

But he shakes his head and beams. "I have a patron."

I stop short. "I'm sorry, a—what?"

"A patron." He turns to the third page and hands it over to me. "You just need to fill out the rest of the form."

I scroll down to the bottom end of the page where instructions for payment methods are outlined. Sure enough, right there on the dotted line are words printed in thick bold letters: **PAID IN FULL—PATRON.**

No.

It can't be.

Ruslan?

I remember mentioning it to him during one of my word vomit episodes, which—now that I think about it—are becoming entirely too frequent. Is it possible that he not only remembered, but actually *did* something about it?

"Are you my patron?" Josh asks innocently.

"I wish I could take the credit, but no, I'm not."

Caroline gasps. "Maybe you have a fairy godmother!"

"Or a fairy godfather," I mutter. The sudden image of Ruslan in a Tom Ford suit and sparkling fairy wings makes my snorts turn into giggles and the kids join in until we're all laughing so hard we have tears running down our cheeks.

The moment is too good to forget. I take my phone out, open the camera, and switch it to selfie mode. "Okay, everyone: smile!"

Afterwards, the kids gobble down their ice creams and I open Ruslan's thread and attach the picture I just took.

EMMA: *Took the kids out for ice cream in the new car. As you can see, they're over the moon.*

EMMA: *Josh showed us his basketball enrollment form. The girls think he has a fairy godmother and now, I'm imagining you with a wand and a sparkly halo. :laughing face:*

EMMA: *All I can say is—*thank you*! I mean that from the bottom of my heart.*

I'm crossing multiple lines with the texts, not to mention the picture, but I have to say *something.* He needs to know how much this means to us. To *all* of us.

So I take a deep breath and press send.

36

RUSLAN

I unlock my phone the moment I sit down at my desk. It opens to the picture that Emma sent me last evening.

Those four smiling faces stare back at me and I'm struck by how happy they all seem. And for what?

A ten-minute drive?

A little ice cream?

Basketball?

I considered them small gestures on my part, so inconsequential as to be damn near meaningless—but those messages from Emma make me feel like I've transformed their lives somehow.

All I can say is—*thank you! *I mean that from the bottom of my heart.

I don't know what the fuck to call the way that makes me feel.

It's only 8:20 A.M. when Emma arrives at the office. Not that I should be surprised she's here so early; I gave her a car citing that specific reason. She slips into my office and walks right around my desk.

I can barely compute what's happening when she sits herself down right on my lap and wraps her arms around me. Despite my shock, I'm struck by two things right off the bat.

One: this is definitely breaking a rule.

Two: it feels so damn natural. Seamless.

My fingers twitch as they curl around the small of her back. Why the hell is my chest suddenly more alive than my cock?

A little voice at the back of my head laughs at me. *Because this is not sexual. It's something completely different.*

That alone should make me want to push her the hell off. But the mere thought only makes my hand clutch tighter around her.

She drapes an arm around my shoulders. "The kids and I want to thank you properly for yesterday."

I frown. "There's no—"

"You're invited to dinner tonight at the apartment."

I stop short. Dinner? At her place? The last time I was there, I had the distinct impression that she was uncomfortable with me in her space.

Which is why, even though I should be turning her down, I find myself nodding.

It's just curiosity. I want to see into her life. I want to know more. We'll call it "research." And honestly, we've already broken so many rules already.

What's one more?

I show up exactly on time, with three tiny bouquets of flowers in hand. Of course, it's Josh who opens the door for me. His usually somber face transforms into a small, self-conscious smile as he steps aside and invites me in.

I'm barely two steps inside when I hear two little gasps. "Flowers!" Reagan bounces up to my waist. "Are those for me?"

Smiling, I hand her one of the bouquets. "This one is." Then I turn to Caroline. "And this one's for you."

Emma walks out of the kitchen, her face aglow with a soft smile. "Girls, what do you say?"

"Thank you!" they sing in unison.

I'm struck by how Emma looks tonight. No pencil skirts or silk blouses. No high heels and not a dab of makeup in sight.

She walks barefoot toward me, her hair flowing freely over her shoulders. She's wearing a simple white cotton dress with thin tied straps that hugs her waist before flaring out subtly at her hips.

She's fucking beautiful.

I hand her the last bouquet of flowers and she accepts it with a small blush. "You shouldn't have," she demurs, holding the bouquet up to her nose.

Josh is eyeing me from the corner. I pull out the Nintendo Switch that I had Kirill purchase for me and hand it over. It's not a fancy one, purely because I didn't think Emma would appreciate anything too over-the-top for an eight-year-old.

Josh looks surprised. "For me?"

"For you."

He takes it hesitantly. "Why?"

"Because you never show up anywhere empty-handed. My mother taught me that when I was about your age."

It slips out so effortlessly that I shock myself. When was the last time I mentioned her? When was the last time I even thought about her?

"Josh, can I see?" Reagan asks, slapping her hands together like she's about to pray. "Please?"

"I wanna see, too!" Caroline jumps in.

Josh hands over the console without protest. Once again, I'm amazed at how grown-up the boy is. Any other eight-year-old would have clung to it and refused to share.

The girls fall onto the sofa and start mashing buttons, but Josh's eyes remain fixed squarely on me. "Thanks for the present, Ruslan."

"No problem."

Emma walks up behind Josh and rests her hands on his shoulders. "Why don't you take a seat? Josh, how about you bring out the canapés?"

"Canapés?" I smile. "I wasn't aware this was such a highbrow affair."

Emma laughs self-consciously. "Don't get too excited. It's cubes of cheddar cheese on savory crackers. I'm just managing expectations here." She blushes again. "This dinner isn't going to be what you're used to."

"Did you cook?"

"We helped, too!" Caroline quips, abandoning the Switch. "I cut up the sausages all on my own."

"And I stirred the pasta," Reagan adds.

Emma chuckles, sidling a little closer so she can whisper to me, "Don't worry; that's their dinner. You're getting something different."

"Thank God. I was just about to walk out." I wink so she knows I'm teasing.

Her smile grows wider and there's that weird tremor in my chest that feels a little bit like a heart attack. Except it feels… *good*.

Josh comes out a second later, carrying the "canapés" on an off-shaped plate with a bunch of handprints painted all over it. I scan the room, realizing that all eyes are on me. So I make a show of trying one of the crackers.

"Wow." I take my time to chew and savor, just like I would eating caviar at a restaurant. "That's good."

Reagan claps. "You like it?"

"I love it."

Caroline starts jumping on the sofa while Reagan continues clapping. "We're good cookers!"

Laughing, I grab another one just to make them happy. But the smile I most want to see is Emma's. I've never seen her look quite so in her element. It's almost a shame that I keep her so busy at the office when, clearly, this is where she's meant to be.

"Girls!" Emma calls. "Let's go put our flowers in some water. Josh, will you keep Ruslan company?"

Josh nods sheepishly while Emma herds the girls into the kitchen. He walks over to the sofa and sits down opposite me. Gingerly, he reaches for the gaming device the girls have abandoned.

There's just something about this boy. Maybe it's the sad brown eyes that make him seem so much older. Maybe it's the fact that he's more observant than talkative. Maybe it's how, despite his size, he feels the need to protect Emma and the girls.

I can relate to him. And even with full-blown adults, that's not something I feel often.

I gesture with my eyes to the canapé dish. "I like the plate."

He shuffles his feet uncomfortably. "My mom made it in a pottery class when I was three. She had me dip my hands in paint to decorate it." His voice dips low when he mentions his mother. "She died when I was five."

My chest constricts. "I lost my mother a long time ago, too."

He stops shuffling his feet. "Really?"

"Really. I was much older than you, though."

"So you must remember a lot about her."

If it were anyone else, I'd have cut this conversation off at the pass. But the usual melancholy in the boy's eyes has receded somewhat. He actually looks engaged. Interested.

Dammit. I can't not indulge him.

"I remember a lot, yes."

Josh frowns. "That's the problem. I don't."

"Maybe that's a good thing," I hear myself saying. "The more you remember, the more you'll miss her."

His expression ripples and his bottom lip pushes out. "I'm okay with missing her if it means I can remember more of her."

Well, shit. This kid just might be braver than I am.

Giggles erupt all of a sudden and, a second later, Reagan and Caroline slide into the living room with matching grins.

"Bum-bum-BUM! Dinner is served!" Caroline announces.

"*Heyyy*!" Reagan places her hands on her hips and turns to her older sister. "That was *my* line."

"Was not."

"Was too!*"

"Was not."

"Was *too!*"

"Girls! Stop fighting and show Ruslan into the kitchen."

The little pitbulls race toward me and they each grab a hand. They drag me into the kitchen with Josh trailing behind us, fighting a smile the entire time.

"Come sit next to me, Ruslan," Caroline orders, pointing to a chair at the round table crammed in between the fridge and the stove.

"No! Sit next to me!" Reagan wheedles as she quite literally hangs off my arm.

Emma rolls her eyes and lets out a long-suffering sigh. "Girls, can we *please* be on our best behavior tonight?"

Both of them stop short and look at her as though she's deeply offended them. "But we're being so good!" Reagan insists.

Caroline nods effusively. "Super *duper* good."

I nod, backing up the little hooligans. "I agree. They're angelic."

Reagan juts her chin out and braces her hands on her hips, the very picture of sass. I get the feeling this is a pose she strikes a lot. "See?"

Emma holds her hands up. "Alright, I can see I'm outnumbered. Ruslan can sit over here and you can both sit on either side of him. How's that?"

By the time we're all seated, it feels like we've achieved some semblance of peace. I can't seem to stop smiling. Between Emma's maternal clucking and the girls' constant chatter and Josh's stoic patience, this dinner is, as advertised, most definitely *not* what I'm used to.

So then why do I keep imagining myself amidst the pandemonium on a more frequent basis? Not as an outsider, like I am right now, but a member of this chaotic little tribe?

I need to get a fucking grip.

Talking about my mother, thinking about being a part of this family, wondering whether Emma's going to walk into my office tomorrow and sit on my lap like she did today…

I mean, what the fuck is next? I'm gonna decide that knocking Emma up is the right move for her future and mine?

And just like that, I'm imagining a highchair wedged between Josh and Emma. A chubby little baby with her warm eyes and my dark hair.

What.

The.

Fuck.

Before I can decide whether to cut and run or grit my teeth and sit through this dinner, the door in the living room bursts open.

Emma freezes. Josh flinches. The girls jump in their seats.

"What the hell is going on?" The man who appears in the threshold of the kitchen looks at me with bloodshot eyes and a fuck-ton of suspicion. "Who the fuck are *you?*"

37

RUSLAN

Emma jerks to her feet, the color draining from her face. "Ben, this is my boss, Ruslan Oryolov."

I can smell his breath from here. He stinks of cheap booze and cigarette smoke. The moment Emma introduces me, his eyes bulge a little wider. The veins running through the whites of his eyeballs shine a sickly red.

"*The* Ruslan Oryolov?"

I don't like the way he says that. I can practically see his irises turning into two massive dollar signs.

Emma's gaze keeps flicking from the drunkard to me. "Ben, we're in the middle of dinner."

"The hell is that supposed to mean?" he growls. "I'm not invited to dinner in my own fuckin' apartment?"

It's the first time all night the girls have been silent. The bottom half of Reagan's face has disappeared behind the table. All I can see are those big eyes glancing around fearfully. Caroline has moved a little closer to me and she's abandoned her plate of pasta to chew on her nails. Josh is the only one who's sitting up straighter since their so-called father entered the room. But I don't miss how his fists tighten around his fork and knife.

Emma is trying hard to contain the situation. "If you're hungry, Ben, I can get you a plate."

How she manages not to kick this motherfucker out on his ass is a testament to her patience. It's probably also a testament to how much she loves these kids.

He pulls his lips back and displays a set of yellowing teeth. "I don't need a fuckin' plate. I need that damned piece-of-shit car to work properly."

Emma's eyebrows knit together. "What happened now?"

He grunts and moves to the fridge. "Fucker died on me again."

"Ben!" she hisses, lowering her voice. "Stop cursing in front of the kids. And take that car to the mechanic while you're at it."

"I'll talk the way I wanna fuckin' talk." He snatches a can of beer from the fridge. "I'm a grown fuckin' man. As for the damn car, I don't have the fuckin' money to—"

My chair scrapes loudly as I push back from the table and stand. Emma and Ben turn to me at the same time. My hands clench into fists, just like Josh's, and for a moment, the desire to use them is tempting.

But Ben and Emma aren't the only ones who are watching me. Reagan, Caroline, and Josh are staring at me with wide eyes. And everyone is holding their breaths.

I look right at Ben, trusting that he can read the threat in my eyes even if I can't say what I want to say to him. "Where's the car?"

He blinks stupidly. "What?"

"The car. You said it died on you. Where is it now?"

He clears his throat to hide a burp. "Oh, right. Yeah. It's parked out on the curb."

"Then let's go take a look. Lead the way."

Emma's jaw drops. "Ruslan, you don't have to do that."

"It's not a problem. I used to work on cars for a living." I throw Ben a murderous glance before I make my way into the living room. Emma says something to the kids in a gentle voice, but the actual words escape me. I'm too busy imagining all the ways I could beat the shit out of her asshole of a brother-in-law.

I'm almost at the door when Emma catches up with me. "Ruslan!" Her hand floats over my arm, but she snatches it away before she actually touches me. "I'm so sorry about him. The car's a piece of junk, though. It has been dying for a while. You don't need to—"

"If I stay in this apartment with him for a second longer, I will punch the fucking stink right off him." Her eyes widen for a moment, but then they soften. "Let me go down and look at the car. Okay?"

She nods reluctantly. "You've never actually worked on cars, have you?"

"Why do you look like that strikes you as funny?"

She lets out a soft giggle and shrugs. "I just never pegged you —the great Ruslan Oryolov, big bad Bane Corp. CEO—as a grease monkey. Did you also wear grease-stained jeans and muscle shirts? Did you have a mullet?"

I narrow my eyes. "What if I did?"

As her eyes run up and down my tailored pants and designer shirt, she bites her lip. I wonder if she knows she's doing it. If she's aware of how magnetic her attraction to me is—and vice versa. "I'm having a hard time imagining it. Do you have any pictures?"

"None that you're ever getting your hands on."

She laughs. In my face. If we weren't in her shoebox of an apartment with her three little dependents and her one big inconvenience in the very next room, I'd throw her over my knee and spank that juicy ass of hers until it's raw.

"Anyway," I say, clearing my throat and my head at the same time. "I know my way around an engine."

"Can I come?" We both turn to find that Josh has managed to sneak into the living room without either one of us noticing.

I glance at Emma. She looks conflicted for a moment. Then her shoulders sag and she nods. "If Ruslan says it's okay."

In answer, I hold the door open for him. "After you."

Josh doesn't say a word as we walk downstairs. He doesn't say a word when I pop the hood and take a look at the smoking engine, either. He just stands off to the side and watches me work.

"Shit," I growl when I'm done poking around.

"How bad is it?"

I sit down on the edge of the curb just in front of the car. "I'm shocked it's lasted this long with that amount of damage to the radiator." Josh sits down next to me. "Does your dad drive you around in this thing?"

Josh nods. "Sometimes. And Auntie Em, too, if Dad doesn't already have the car."

I shake my head. "From now on, *none* of you are getting in this car. Not until I fix it."

"You're gonna fix it?" I grind my teeth and nod. Josh sidles closer to me. "But Auntie Em has the new company car."

"Yes, but I'm guessing your dad uses this one. He's probably going to keep using it until it combusts in the middle of the road." Josh flinches at the image. "So I'm going to fix it up so that that doesn't happen."

The guy may be an asshole. But he's an asshole with three young kids. Three *great* kids. Despite his flaws, they don't deserve to lose their father after everything they've already been through. And as much as I would like Ben to disappear off the face of the earth, I'm not gonna be responsible, directly or indirectly, for taking away the only parent that Josh, Reagan, and Caroline have left.

Josh's gaze veers over to me. "You're a good guy, aren't you?"

Fuck me.

"No one's ever accused me of that before."

The kid actually cracks a smile. "I know you're the one that paid for my basketball fees this season."

I'm not about to deny it. If the boy is smart enough to have figured it out, then he deserves the truth.

"That doesn't make me a good guy."

He frowns. "What does it make you, then?"

"It makes me the kind of man who refuses to let the people in his life suffer."

Josh's gaze rises to the window of his apartment. I think I have a pretty good idea what he's thinking. Compared to Ben, I probably look like a goddamn saint.

I can't help but laugh at the irony of that. The cold-hearted, violent, soulless *pakhan* of a deadly Bratva is more of a role model to this eight-year-old than his own drunkard father.

Who would've thought I'd be anyone's hero?

"Ruslan, can I ask you something?"

The tremble in his voice should serve as a warning, but I ignore it and nod. "Go ahead."

"Will you come to my basketball game next week? It's the first game of the season."

I stare down at his earnest little face with warning bells tolling in the back of my head. I should grab his shoulders and shake some sense into him. *I'm not a hero, boy. I don't deserve your admiration or your awe. Don't make me into something I'm not.*

But instead of saying any of that—instead of turning him down like I should—I end up nodding. I end up telling him I'll be happy to be there.

The craziest part is…

I mean it.

38

EMMA

"Delivery for Carson."

I blink at the sullen delivery boy in the Uber Eats vest. "I didn't order anything."

He shrugs, completely deadpan. "It was ordered for you. There's a note."

Without further ado, he shoves the two flat boxes into my arms. I'm immediately overwhelmed with the smell of garlic and cheese. The note tacked to the front of the box reads simply, "*So you've got one less thing on your plate today before the game—Ruslan.*"

It's so strange to think that, just a couple of months ago, I thought Ruslan Oryolov was the spawn of Satan. The man hell-bent on ruining my life and putting me in an early grave. But somehow, in a matter of weeks, he's become the knight in shining armor I never knew I needed.

How did he even know about Josh's game?

Well, clearly, Josh told him. But the fact that he remembered? That he considered what my day might look like, only to try and make it easier?

I have genuinely never been this turned on. Sure, the man's hot as sin—but even those amber eyes, those powerful arms, that strong jaw, all that pales in comparison to the turn-on that is an unexpected, thoughtful gesture. If I saw him help a grandma cross the street right now, I'd probably mount him in the middle of the pedestrian path.

I give the delivery guy a tip and a distracted thank you and walk the pizzas into the kitchen.

The moment Ben sees me, his eyes narrow. "You ordered pizza again?"

I set the boxes down on the counter and quickly slip Ruslan's note into my pants pocket before he can see it. "From Phoebe. She wanted to do something nice before Josh's big game."

"What game?"

"Ben, are you kidding me? He's only been talking about this all freaking week."

Ben coughs and snaps his fingers towards the fridge. "Pass me another beer, will ya?"

"It's one in the afternoon. Do you really need a drink?"

He scowls at me. "For God's sake, when did you become such a pain in the ass? You're not my wife. If you're not sucking my dick, you've got no right to nag me, either."

I glare at him furiously. "Now, I *know* you're joking."

"You're the one who started it," he mutters. "Hey—the beer…?"

I ignore him and call for the kids. "Lunch, munchkins!"

Ben tosses me a dirty look and shoves past me to fetch himself another beer. The girls tumble into the kitchen, all knees and elbows, their little noses pointed upwards like hunting dogs on the scent.

Reagan gasps when she spots the pizza boxes on the counter. "Pizza! Woohoo!"

While the girls celebrate with a pizza dance that Caroline invented and takes *very* seriously, Josh strides into the kitchen, already in his team uniform. He sits down opposite Ben, his eyes flitting sporadically to his father before going right back down to his lap.

The moment the girls stuff their faces with pizza, Josh makes use of the temporary quiet. "Dad, do you wanna come to my game today?"

Ben takes a swig of his beer and shifts in his seat. "Uh…"

I grit my teeth and cross my fingers, praying silently. How could he say no to that sweet face? Only a monster would say—

"Listen, kid, I'd really like to, but I've already got a helluva headache and sitting out in the sun isn't gonna help."

Guess that makes him a monster.

I walk up behind Josh and scowl at Ben. "It's an *indoor* court."

His mouth goes stupidly slack. "Still, it's best I sit this one out. I'm not feeling great and you wouldn't want me throwing up all over the court, right, J?" Josh nods silently and Ben lets out a satisfied burp. "Good kid. I'll make the next game."

Then he proceeds to heap his plate with pizza before he leaves the kitchen. A few seconds later, his door slams shut.

I sit down next to Josh. "I bet you're the only kid there with his own personal cheerleading squad." I cringe at how falsely bright my voice is. "Me, Caro, and Reagan—and you know Care Bear has that dance she's been torturing me into learning. Heck, even Aunt Phoebe is joining!"

"I know." Josh gives me a tight smile. "Anyway, I'm not hungry. May I be excused?"

My heart sinks but I nod anyway. I would've stormed into Ben's room and forced his miserable ass to attend the game if I wasn't sure that he would find a way to make the whole evening all about him if he came.

The kids are better off when Ben's not involved in their lives. The only problem is—

They don't know that yet.

"I can't believe you made a sign!" I laugh as Phoebe thrusts her homemade *JOSH THE BOSS* poster into the air as I approach with Caroline and Rae each holding a hand.

"Of course I did. This is a big deal. The rhyme scheme is questionable, but we're gonna overlook that, mmkay?" She puts the sign down so she can squeeze the girls. "Where's our main man?"

I glance around to find that Josh isn't right behind me like I'd thought. "He was right here just a second ago." I inch a little closer to Phoebe while the girls start wobbling her posterboard and giggling at the sound it makes. "Ben didn't come and I think Josh is a little down because of it."

"Down?" Phoebe interrupts. "He doesn't look down to me."

I follow her gaze to the end of the bleachers where Josh is standing with a huge smile on his face. "What is he…?"

I gasp when I realize *who* he's smiling at.

Phoebe grabs my arm so tightly it's actually painful. "Oh my *God!* Is that who I think it is?"

"Pheebs, excuse me for a second."

I leave her with the girls and walk over to Ruslan, trying to look a hell of a lot more composed than I actually feel. His and Josh's heads are close together. Josh says something, Ruslan laughs, they exchange a fist bump, and then Josh joins his teammates on the court to start running through layup lines and warmup drills.

"Ruslan?" I gape at him, still not totally convinced that he's real.

He just nods. "Hey."

That's it. That's all he gives me. *Hey.* So damn casual. "What are you, uh—whatcha doing here?" I'm going for "easy, breezy, *Cover Girl*" vibes, but I think I end up sounding constipated.

"Josh invited me."

"And you *came?*"

He shrugs. "I had some free time."

I glance over at Phoebe, who wags her eyebrows at me and starts doing her weird shoulder dance that she uses as nonverbal encouragement. I turn my back on her, hoping that Ruslan doesn't notice.

"I really appreciate you showing up, but you don't have to stay. I'll talk to Josh and—"

"I'm not going anywhere." His eyes gleam under the bright lights. "He didn't force me to show up; he asked if I would and I made a promise to him. So I'm here and I'm staying for the whole game."

He lifts a hand and waves. I twist around to see Josh stepping up to the hoop to make his layup. It's obvious he wants Ruslan to watch him. It's also obvious that he's nervous. He fumbles the ball a few times and it almost gets away from him.

"Deep breath, Josh," Ruslan rumbles, giving him a loud clap.

Josh nods, takes a deep breath, and shoots.

"YES!" I scream when the ball goes in, my enthusiasm wildly out of proportion to how uneventful warmup drills are in the overall context of things.

Josh side-eyes me with an embarrassed glance, his cheeks going red. I frown and clamp my lips shut. "How did I end up being the embarrassing aunt and how did *you* turn out to be the cool—"

I stop short when I realize I don't know what the hell he is at the moment. Makes sense, really—how should I know what Ruslan is to the kids, when I'm not even sure what he is to me?

What I do know is that Josh's mood has picked up considerably. He's racing around the court with a huge smile on his face, looking like a real eight-year-old for a change. It's enough to make me grateful that Ruslan is here in the first place.

Like I needed another reason...

I gesture for Ruslan to follow me. "Well, come on then. Family and friends section is this way." As we approach, the girls finally look up from Phoebe's poster long enough to notice Ruslan. Both of them start squealing loudly as they make a run for him.

"Shut up," I mutter the moment I'm standing next to Phoebe.

She's grinning from ear to ear. "I didn't say anything."

Ruslan approaches with Caroline and Reagan hanging off him like human accessories. "Phoebe, this is my boss, Ruslan Oryolov. Ruslan, this is—"

"The best friend," she interrupts, sticking her hand out to him. "Phoebe Lawrence."

Ruslan gives her his full wattage smile. It actually annoys me —not because Phoebe doesn't deserve it, but because I think *I* deserve it, too.

Would it kill him to smile at me like that every once in a while?

We find a good spot on the bleachers and I try to shoot Phoebe a warning glare as she rattles off rapid-fire questions at Ruslan.

"How did you start Bane Corp.? How long have you been CEO? Do you ever take time off? Do you have an active social life?"

Her questions go on and on. But I have to give it to Ruslan: he never falters, never betrays irritation or impatience. He sits there, balancing Reagan on one knee and Caroline on the other, and answers every last one of Phoebe's questions.

The only time she lets up is when the game starts and Josh gets possession of the ball. Phoebe holds up her sign, the girls screech, and Ruslan claps loudly.

At some point, in the middle of the game, Phoebe leans towards me. "Okay," she says softly. "I approve."

I'm genuinely surprised. Phoebe's not usually so easily won. Especially when it comes to my boyfriends.

Not that Ruslan is anything of the sort.

"That's it, Josh! Well done!" Ruslan exclaims.

It's hard to miss Josh's beaming smile as he runs past us. My gaze slides over to Ruslan's sharp profile. He's half-covered by Reagan's curtain of hair and Caroline is busy playing with his watch clasp.

I know he's not a "good guy" by any stretch of the imagination. But maybe, just maybe…

He's a good *man*.

39

EMMA

I'm in a happy feelings daze. I'm not quite sure how we went from the basketball game at school to Connie's Creamery, but here we are.

Ruslan is at the counter with the kids, helping them settle on flavors, while Phoebe and I slide into the window table under a sign that reads *Relationship Status: Ice Cream.*

Phoebe shoots me a suggestive smirk. "This is a trippy day."

"You're telling me." Glancing towards Ruslan and the kids, it strikes me that Reagan still hasn't let go of Ruslan's hand. She's been surgically attached to him since we left the basketball game. "I can't believe he's here."

"He's obviously here because he wants to be. It was his idea to come here for celebratory sweets. The man might be a genius.."

I bite my bottom lip. "He's good with them, isn't he?"

"Extremely. Who'd have thought, huh?"

"Yeah." I shake my head with disbelief. "Who'd have thought?"

A few minutes later, Ruslan and his three new appendages join us at the table. Ruslan has to pull up a chair to make enough room for everyone.

I gesture for Reagan to come to me. "Rae, honey, you can sit on my lap."

She shakes her head. "I'll sit on Ruslan's lap," she insists, climbing aboard without bothering to ask permission.

Phoebe suppresses a giggle. "Can't believe you expected her to choose you over a hot guy."

I poke her in the ribs with my elbow, not that it does a damn bit of good. She just keeps on giggling.

Ruslan spends almost a full hour with Reagan on his knee. He doesn't seem at all fazed when Caroline drips her cone on his pants. Or when Reagan spills her glass of water across the table. Or when Phoebe resumes her interrogation of him.

I don't say much. I have this weird churning feeling in my stomach that I can't quite put a finger on. But since no one's paying any attention to me, I decide to explore it a little.

I'm thrilled with how well this day has gone. Not only did Josh get to play his very first basketball match, but he won. More importantly, he looks happier than I've seen him in a long time. As much as I'd like to give the game all the credit, I know that Ruslan's presence has made a world of difference.

It sets a stark contrast to the man we left at home in a drunken stupor. I've tried to explain it to Ben several times in the past: your kids don't care if you're rich or smart or funny or cool. They just want you to *show up*.

Which is probably why, even though I am thrilled about today, I'm also terrified. Because I can't expect Ruslan to show up like this all the time. He's a temporary part of our lives and so the way the kids are looking at him right now freaks the hell out of me.

They've already lost their mother. In many ways, they've lost their father, too. As much as I've tried to fill the holes in their lives, I'm starting to realize that I can't be all the things they've lost. I can't be all the things they need.

And as for Ruslan…

Reagan whispers something in his ear and he laughs. I've never seen him smile so much. He runs a hand down Caroline's long hair and says something back to Reagan that makes her giggle.

It's bad enough that he's handsome and smart and successful. Does he have to be so damn *nice* as well? Does he have to be so damn generous? Kind? Thoughtful?

It makes me think—there has to be a catch, right? I mean, no man is that perfect.

That, in turn, makes me do a double-take. *What am I saying?* Ruslan Oryolov sure as hell is not perfect. He's a cutthroat business mogul who may or may not have ties to the Russian mafia. He may or may not *be* the freaking Russian mafia.

He's also spent the last eighteen months of my life being the bosshole from hell.

The thing is, the more time I spend with him now, the harder it becomes to remember what he was like back then. I guess the only thing I can do is keep reminding myself. Because even though he seems pretty content to play the role of

Temporary Daddy, there's no way in hell it's a role he wants for keeps.

Our contract will end sometime and, when it does, I'm gonna have to move on. And so will the kids.

I'm just hoping he doesn't do anything else between now and then that'll cause my uterus to throw herself at his feet.

Ruslan clears his throat. "Josh, in honor of your first win, I have something for you."

Well, that didn't take long.

"Be right back," Ruslan says, popping Reagan off his lap. "Gotta go get it from the car."

Phoebe glances at me as he strides out of the ice cream shop, drawing plenty of admiring gazes on his way. "Did you know about this?"

"Not a thing."

Josh is peering out the window as Ruslan grabs something from the trunk of his car and walks back into the creamery. "Here you go," he says, handing the thin package to Josh.

The girls help Josh tear the colored blue paper off. I'm so focused on how animated Josh's face is that I don't even look at the present until he gasps, his eyes growing even wider.

"A Knicks jersey!"

Ruslan points towards the bottom of the jersey. "It's signed, too."

Josh looks like he's about to swallow his own tongue. "I-I-I…"

Reagan and Caroline giggle. "Joshie forgot how to speak."

"Thank you," Josh breathes at last. "Thank you so much!"

I try to dab away my tears without anyone noticing, but nothing gets past Ruslan. I catch him staring at me before I turn my face away to hide.

Ruslan claps Josh on the back. "You deserve it. You played well today."

"I'm gonna put it on right now," Josh insists.

"Are you sure, honey?" I ask. "Why not wait 'til we get home?"

Josh's face curdles into a frown. "If Dad sees it, he'll try to sell it, Aunt Em. I can't wear it at home."

Ruslan's eyes meet mine for a second and, even though I can't be sure what he's thinking, I imagine, based on that scorching look in his eyes, it goes a little something like, *That fucking sorry excuse for a father.*

When everyone's done with their ice cream, I take the girls to the bathroom to clean up their sticky mouths and their even stickier hands. On the way back to our table, I notice Phoebe leaning towards Ruslan, her expression earnest. The last time she looked that serious was when I'd told her Sienna was gone.

I have no idea what's been said while I was in the restroom, but I catch the tail end of their conversation.

"… just don't hurt them," she whispers. "Any of them."

Ruslan doesn't move. His expression is hard to read, but he answers immediately.

All he says is, "I won't."

40

RUSLAN

"Good evening, Mr. Oryolov!"

Kirill snorts into his drink while I lean away from the phone in confusion. Hearing Sergey this chirpy is certainly a departure from the norm.

"I'm guessing you have good news to share?"

His breathing, despite his good mood, is still huffy and heavy. Apparently, that's not a nervous thing, just a Sergey thing. "Sir, so far, all the trials we've conducted have been a roaring success. The new formula is performing well, with minimal side effects."

"Excellent. And what about final studies?"

"Close to being completed, sir."

"Final chemical shipment?"

"Due in two days."

Kirill meets my gaze with a satisfied smirk. "We're right on track," he mouths to me.

"I'll check in tomorrow. Keep it up, Sergey."

Kirill punches his fist in the air as I hang up. "You've done it again."

"I'm not celebrating until the launch event is over with," I warn.

He waves a hand dismissively. "You've got nothing to worry about, dude. Our dealers have been hyping up Venera, pushing a couple of 'exclusive' samples to give the public a taste of it. People are losing their goddamn minds over this stuff. And happy customers spread the word to other happy customers. By the time we launch, it's going to be the number one demand on everyone's lips." He cocks an ear to the window and softly chants, "*Ve-ner-a. Ve-ner-a,*" as if there's a crowd of hungry partiers lining up outside to get their hands on a taste of the stuff.

It's hard to temper the sense of victory, but I'm also keenly aware that a lot can change in a matter of days. I'm not willing to fuck things up by being overconfident about this launch. I'll leave that task to Kirill.

"Speaking of the launch party—"

"Got it covered. A sizable 'donation' was made to the relevant authorities yesterday. I spoke to Sergeant Mathison myself. On the night of the launch, he and his men will be looking the other way."

"Good."

"What about our lord high commissioner?" Kirill asks, putting his hands together. "Do we need to approach Hiram Allens?"

"No. He's a last-minute play, if and only if things go wrong and we need some extra pull. As long as I have Jessica eating out of the palm of my hand, convincing Hiram to help us with damage control is going to be a cinch."

"I applaud your confidence."

Something in my second's tone catches my attention. "What exactly are you nervous about?"

Kirill rolls his eyes. "Oh, I don't know—how about the fact that you've been stringing Jessica Allens along for a long ass time now? How can you be so sure she'll jump when you tell her to jump?"

I smirk. "Because that's how badly she wants me."

"Except that you're sleeping with your pretty little secretary."

My fingers curl around the corners of the armrests. "Exclusivity was never part of my agreement with Jessica."

"But it is with Emma, is it not?" I glare at Kirill, who just smiles sheepishly. "What can I say? I like reading the fine print."

"It was necessary," I growl. "I wasn't about to let her fuck around with other men while she's sleeping with me."

"Makes sense." He points a finger at me. "What *doesn't* make sense is the fact that you're going to her kids' basketball games and taking them out for ice cream and fixing her beatdown old car."

"For fuck's sake," I mutter under my breath. "I knew it was a mistake telling you all that."

Kirill laughs. "You have feelings for her."

If he were anyone else, I'd be firstly denying it and second, throwing him out of my office. Instead, I nod. "I feel *something* for her," I admit grudgingly. "I just... don't know what."

"Maybe you don't need to know. Right now, it's just sex and fun right?"

"Right."

"Then don't overthink it. Just keep things the way they are for as long as they feel good. Why put a label on it?"

I nod. Kirill's right. I need to stay in the present and focus on what I'm getting out of my association with Emma right now. The future is blurry and that's okay with me. I don't need her to be anything other than my secretary and my after-hours plaything.

Kirill and I go over the numbers for the current round of trial sessions that Sergey is carrying out. They're the most expensive sessions we've run, given the tight deadline I placed on them, but I'm sure it's a decision that will pay off.

Based on all the preliminary feedback we've received, Venera is going to sell out the moment it hits the market. Which means I'm going to recover my cost in record time.

I'm feeling fucking *good* when I slip into the back of the SUV after the meeting.

"Where to, boss?" Boris asks from the driver's seat.

"The Madison Avenue penthouse today, Boris."

A little peace and quiet is what I need right now. And when that's my goal, the thirty-fifth floor of my place on Madison serves as my safe place.

From the chaos of being *pahkan.*

From the stress of being CEO.

From the pressures of my personal life.

We're halfway there when my mood begins to shift. I still want peace and quiet. I still want refuge. But somehow, the thought of going to my silent, spartan penthouse in Midtown isn't cutting it for me.

"Boris, change of plans. Drop me off in Hell's Kitchen."

I catch Boris's confused expression in the rearview mirror. "Hell's Kitchen, sir?"

"Yes."

He changes course as I grab my phone and pull up the picture that Emma sent me last week, the day I'd given her the Mercedes.

She looked so damn happy, smiling at me through the blurry corner of the picture. It's amazing that she can smile so big when, most of the time, she's pushing a giant boulder up a hill.

Maybe that's why I'm so determined to fix that stupid car of hers. And buy her kids pizza and ice cream and new shoes. I just want to make her life a little easier.

Is that really why? asks a pesky voice in my head. *Is that why you just changed destinations? For her?*

Or for yourself?

I swipe out of the picture and put my phone away as unease spreads through me. I had wanted to be alone tonight. I had wanted peace and quiet. Part of me still does. But another part of me—a part that's growing louder and louder by the day…

Wants Emma Carson instead.

41

RUSLAN

I hope the kids are still awake.

That's the third shocking thought that I've had in the last half an hour. This shit is getting out of hand. I ought to put a stop to it before it spirals even further.

But apparently, that concern isn't enough to stop me from darkening their doorstep at eight-thirty in the evening.

Emma looks stunned when she opens the door and comes face to face with me. "Ruslan?"

I can hear squeals coming from one of the rooms in the back of the apartment. So the little monsters *are* still awake. I wish that didn't put such a goofy smile on my face.

Cut that shit out, I snarl at myself.

"Busy?"

She glances back over her shoulder. The living room looks like a disaster zone. It's covered in clothes and toys and scraps of cardboard and glitter.

"Always." She manages a smile as she turns back to me. "Did I, uh… forget something at the office?"

I shake my head. "No, I just thought I'd take another look at the car."

Her eyes scan my navy blue suit. "I'm not sure you can be a grease monkey in Tom Ford."

"You can do *anything* in Tom Ford."

Her laugh is drowned out as the girls come squealing into the living room, some imaginary monster hot on their heels.

The imaginary monster turns out to be Josh. All three kids stop short when they see me.

Then—chaos.

"Ruslan! Ruslan! Ruslan!" Caroline cries, throwing herself at my waist and nearly kneeing me in the balls.

"Did you bring us pizza?" Reagan asks as she pulls on the corner of my suit jacket.

"Caroline! Reagan! Give Ruslan some room to breathe, for God's sake."

"But Auntie Em!" whines Caroline. "He came to see *us.*"

Ah, the confidence of youth. Josh helps Emma disentangle the girls from me. "He came to see *Aunt Em,*" Josh scolds his sisters.

Both of them pout instantly. Caroline turns to me with knitted eyebrows and Reagan plants her fists on her hips like the five-year-old grandmother she is.

"*Who* did you come to see?" Reagan demands. "We wanna know."

Emma gives me an apologetic look over their heads, her cheeks flushed.

"I came to see the car," I tell the two little she-devils in front of me. The moment their faces fall, I add, "*And* I came to see you guys."

They erupt in cheers while Josh covers his ears and Emma fights a laugh. "So much for getting them to bed early," she reprimands me.

"Add it to my list of sins."

She gives me a helpless little shrug and a smile that makes me want to take her down and strip her naked right here and now. Then she turns to the kids and claps her hands together. "Okay, gremlins, time for bed—" She keeps talking over the chorus of disappointed moans that ensues. "—which means we brush teeth first. You know the drill."

When the girls ignore her, she grabs an elbow each and starts dragging them towards their room. Josh sidles a little closer to me. "Thanks for coming." He blushes a little and takes a deep breath. "It makes Aunt Emma really happy when you come over."

Then, before I can respond, he bolts out of the living room. I stand there, in the midst of Emma's life, staring at everything she's built, with one glaringly obvious observation on my mind.

You don't fit in here.

Shaking my head, I walk towards the mantel. A series of framed photographs beams out at me. Like the rest of the apartment, it's chaotic and mismatched. But *also* like the rest of the apartment, somehow, it works.

Most of the pictures are of the kids. Chubby-cheeked babies, toddlers with skinned knees and gummy smiles. But off to the left, tucked almost out of sight, is a picture of Emma and another young woman who can only be her sister. Both have fake highlights: Emma's hair is an electric blue and her sister's are bubblegum pink. They're both looking off-camera, laughing unreservedly. Something about the scene makes my heart pang uncomfortably.

I stroll down the mantel, running my finger along the edge of it. On the far side is a small wooden music box, nestled between a photograph of a four-year-old Josh smearing birthday cake on his face and the girls blowing bubbles in the park.

I touch the silver crank on the side and look at my fingertip. No dust. Someone comes here and winds the toy up often.

I open the lid delicately and a little figurine of a ballerina rises up from within. When I push the crank, the first few tinkling notes of a song begin to play softly.

"It was Sienna's."

For the first time in as long as I can remember, someone caught me by surprise. I was so engrossed that I didn't even realize that Emma had returned to the living room. She joins me at the mantel.

"She gave it to me when I went off to college," she explains. "I've carried it with me everywhere we've moved since then. It's the first thing I pack and the last thing I unpack."

She turns to me as the silence creeps in between us. She's shared so much of her life with me and still, I'm greedy for more. Greedy for the backstories to every picture on the mantel, for the secrets she keeps locked up tight, hiding behind those aqua eyes of hers.

It's not a fair ask. I haven't given her anything of myself in return.

"Ruslan—"

She stops short at the sound of heavy footsteps in the hallway. I hear the sound of a key being forced into the front door. Then it swings open and Ben stumbles in.

"Oh, God, Ben!" Emma gasps.

He looks like an absolute fucking trainwreck. He makes it half a step into the living room before collapsing against the side of the sofa, an eerily inhuman moan floating from between his lips.

Emma stalks over to the front door and closes it just as a passing neighbor looks in with alarm written on his face. "Wasted again?" she hisses with an embarrassed glance over her shoulder at me. "This is the fourth time this week!"

He presses three limp fingers to his forehead. "I'mma not d-drunk," he slurs.

"You were supposed to take the kids to school this morning! Where were you?"

He looks at her for a moment, before his eyes veer to me. "I had…" He burps mid-sentence before finishing, "… shit to do."

"You promised the girls you'd take them. They were counting on you—"

She breaks off when the kids enter the living room. They take one look at Ben and their wide smiles falter. Josh looks wary; Rae and Caro look nervous. Ben aims another shifty glance at me and clears his throat before turning his sloppy attention toward them.

"Come here, m-my little angels," he says, throwing his arms out wide. "Come give Daddy a kiss."

The girls hesitate for only a moment before they venture warily into his arms. He tickles them until they relax. Then he starts digging into the pockets of his pants. "Guess what? I brought you two a present."

"A present!" Reagan trills. "Yay!"

The son of a bitch proceeds to pull out a dirty lozenge that's been in his pocket for fuck knows how long. He hands it to Reagan.

Caroline stares at him expectantly. "What about me, Daddy?"

He tries to mask his impatience. "Hold on, hold on, hold the hell on." He keeps digging while Emma, Josh and I stand on the periphery, watching this pathetic fucking attempt at fatherhood.

"Aw, shit, looks like it fell out of my pocket." He plucks the lozenge out of Reagan's hand and gives it to Caroline. "Just share, okay?"

"But—"

"Now, go on. Daddy's got a headache."

Reagan tries to grab the lozenge from her sister while Ben fights to control the grimace on his face.

Of course, Emma's right there, already in damage control mode. "Okay, girls, bedtime! Go on. Put your PJs on and get in bed; I'll be there in a second."

Both girls give me shy smiles on their way out of the living room. Josh inches closer to me, his eyes fixed on Ben.

Ben's gaze narrows, but despite the deep downturn in his mouth, he tries to keep his voice upbeat. "J-Man, how was your d-day?"

"Fine."

He's not so far gone that he doesn't realize his son is being intentionally short with him. He glares at Josh, the scowl overtaking his need to put up this half-assed façade for my benefit. He drops it entirely when he looks at me. "Spent the whole day here, did ya?"

"Just got here, actually," I answer coolly. "I stopped by to take a look at the car."

Ben laughs before it descends into a cough. "Hey, you wanna help, you can get me a new car like you did Emma."

Emma's eyes go wide. "Ben—"

"Emma's an employee. You are not. She works for what she has. You do not."

He opens his mouth to argue, then changes his mind and shoves himself back to standing. "I-I'm just gonna… sleep off this headache…" Then he stumbles out of the living room, leaving behind the stink of booze like a toxic cloud.

Emma turns to Josh, her expression confusing me for a second. "Honey…"

Only then do I notice that Josh is shaking. Literally *shaking*. Emma reaches out towards him, but before she can stop him, he snatches up the empty glass on the table and flings it at the exposed brick wall. It bursts like fireworks and shards of glass go in every direction.

Based on Emma's reaction, I'm guessing this isn't the first time something like this has happened. I see it now; I'm not sure how I didn't before. I thought the wreckage of his life just made Josh sad. But now, when I look closer, I see the undercurrent of anger surging beneath it. That anger runs *deep.*

I know the feeling.

Emma ignores the broken glass all over the floor and kneels down in front of Josh. Her voice is calm and soothing when she speaks. "Breathe, Josh. Just breathe. I'm here."

She pulls him against her. The moment his cheek comes to rest on her shoulder, his body starts quaking with sobs.

"I-I'm sorry."

"It's okay, darling," Emma says, rubbing his back gently. "It's okay. You're okay."

"Aunt Emma?" The girls' voices carry through from their bedroom.

Emma glances at me helplessly. "Can you... can you just stay with Josh? I won't be five minutes."

I can only nod silently. She places a delicate kiss on Josh's head and hurries off to make sure the girls are okay.

Josh turns away from me, wiping away his tears and avoiding eye contact. I put a hand on his shoulder and spin him around to face me.

"Talk to me," I rumble.

He still doesn't look at me. "I hate him. I hate him so much and it makes me so... so *angry.*"

His little body roils with the weight of his emotion. I know exactly what he's feeling right now—because once upon a time, I *was* Josh, shaking with anger and frustration, without the faintest idea what to do about it.

I place my hands on his shoulders. "It's okay, Josh. It's gonna be okay."

Finally, he raises his eyes to mine. "How do you know?"

"Because I'm gonna make it that way."

42

EMMA

While the girls run into school, I put my hand on Josh's shoulder. "Hey, kiddo, can you hang back a minute?"

Josh turns those sullen eyes on me and nods. We walk over to the low wall that circles the school garden and sit down.

"Am I in trouble?"

"No, of course not," I assure him. "I just want to talk to you."

When I went back into the living room last night, Ruslan was saying something to Josh in a low voice. By the time I saw Ruslan out the door and come back, Josh had already retreated to his bedroom. I crept in there hoping to talk to him, but he had the covers pulled tight above his head.

Say what you want about me, but I can take a hint.

"About last night?" He's chewing on his bottom lip and pulling at the edges of his cuticles.

Gently, I pry his hand free and weave it through mine. "Yes, about last night."

"I'm sorry."

It breaks my heart how sad he looks right now—almost embarrassed. "I know you are. And I know you're dealing with a lot right now. I want you to know that you can talk to me, Josh. About anything. Even about your dad."

His lip falls out of his bite and quivers. "He makes me so angry."

"I don't blame you. It's okay to be angry, Josh, but you have to try not to let that anger control you. I just want you to be safe. That's all."

He glances at me anxiously out of the corner of his eyes. "So you're not upset with me?"

I wrap an arm around his shoulders and pull him as close to me as possible. "Of course not. You're a great kid. The best kid I know, actually." He gives me a tiny smile and I kiss the top of his head. "So you lost it for a moment. Trust me: even adults lose it sometimes."

He shrugs. "I bet Ruslan *never* loses it."

"I wouldn't be so sure." I poke him in the shoulder playfully. "Ruslan's a person, same as you and me."

He pushes off the stone wall and gives me a smile that makes my heart melt. "I'm glad Ruslan's around. I like him."

I have no idea what to say to that, so I point towards the school. "Go on now; I don't want you to be late." He hugs my waist and races towards the steps.

Great. Just freaking great.

Looks like I'm not the only one who's gone and caught feelings for Ruslan Oryolov.

"Good morning, Ms. Carson."

I spring to my feet as he sweeps down the hall on his way from the executive lounge. "Mr. Oryolov! Good morning. Your schedule is on your desk."

He nods. "And the meeting with the Santino people?"

"Confirmed for 3:00 P.M. this afternoon." He surveys the messy heap of papers on my desk and I cringe. "Um, I was just gonna clean—"

"How's Josh?"

The stern professionalism in his voice drops for a moment. This is his "after hours" voice. The one he uses when I'm "Emma," not "Ms. Carson."

"He's fine." It's an automatic answer and one that Ruslan sees through immediately. He cocks an eyebrow at me. "Okay, maybe not 'fine,'" I concede. "He's struggling."

"I talked to him last night when you were putting the girls to bed. I want to help."

"You want to *what*?"

"The boy is going through a lot and the fact that he's holding everything in is exactly why he's prone to angry outbursts." He fixes me with that unblinking amber gaze. "I'm guessing this is not the first time he's thrown a tantrum like that."

I squirm where I stand. *Would it be a betrayal of Josh to cop to that?* No, I can trust Ruslan.

"No, it's not. Far from it."

Ruslan nods. "He needs an outlet for his anger. He needs someone to help him channel it."

"And *you* want to help with that."

"I'm uniquely qualified to."

I raise my eyebrows. "How do you figure that?"

"Because I've been where he is."

I try to keep my expression stoic, but I'm pretty sure the surprise shows in my eyes. This is possibly the first time he's allowed me a glimpse into his past. And the fact that he's letting his guard down for my nephew—it means a lot.

"What do you say?"

What do *I say?* Excellent question. Because the truth is, what I want to do and what I *have* to do are two totally different things. "He really looks up to you, you know."

"I know."

"And… he's getting attached fast." I swallow back my doubt. "Which is why I have to say no. I'm sorry, I really do appreciate the offer, but I can't keep exposing Josh to another person he stands a chance of losing."

I hold my breath, waiting for some pushback. It's gotta be coming, in a particularly angry fashion, in three, two, one…

"I understand."

Um—what?

He doesn't even look annoyed. Just shrugs calmly. "I can respect that. Just know that if you change your mind, the offer still stands."

With that, he brushes past me and walks into his office. The door snaps shut. And—that's it.

I plonk myself down behind my desk and try to rein in the rollercoaster of emotions that's hurtling through me.

I'm surprised by how easily he accepted my decision.

I'm touched by how willing he was to help my nephew.

I'm honored by the tiny little window he gave me into his past.

And all that adds up to… is a shit-ton of attraction that I have no idea how to process.

Worse yet… no idea how to stop.

~

"Reagan, honey, eat your peas."

"I *hate* peas."

I fix her with a stern glance. "We don't use that word in this house."

Her bottom lip sticks out and Josh drags his chair a little closer to her. "Eating peas can be fun, Rae. Look." He grabs a pea off her plate and tosses it in the air. Then he leans forward with his mouth open and it plops right in. "See?"

Reagan's face twists into delight. "Do it again!"

He shakes his head. "You gotta try it this time."

She gives her plate an uncertain grimace but she takes a pea. Of course, the first one lands on the table instead of her mouth. But, three tries later: "I did it!" she cries while Josh,

Caroline, and I applaud like she just won Olympic gold. She chews happily and hums a song.

I snort with laughter and give Josh a grateful wink. It never ceases to amaze me how tactful he is with the girls. More like a parent than an older brother sometimes. It's even more apparent after dinner, when the girls run into the living room to crawl into their pillow fort while Josh stays in the kitchen to help me clean up.

His head barely reaches over the sink. But there he stands, balancing on his tiptoes as he rinses out the plates.

"Hon, I can manage. You don't need to wash up."

He shrugs. "I don't mind."

No, but I do.

"Hey, Josh?" He glances over at me and grunts that he's listening as he continues to scrub silverware. "What do you wanna do this weekend?"

With a shrug, he mumbles, "I dunno. Whatever the girls want to do."

I toss him the dish towel and gesture for him to join me at the kitchen table. "We're always doing things that the girls want. I believe that pillow fort in the living room was their idea. And I'm ninety-nine percent sure you weren't the one who suggested the tea party last week. So this weekend is your weekend. You get to pick."

He just shrugs again, completely noncommittal. I blink at my eight-year-old nephew as a rogue tear comes to my eye. Where did the happy boy go? Right on the mantel is a picture of him, a fat-cheeked Josh with a huge, toothless grin as he swatted at a balloon tied to his stroller. Where's that boy? Who is this solemn little man standing in his place?

When did I lose him?

"What if we went to the park and had a picnic, all of us together?"

Josh's eyes go wide. "Dad, too?" There's an edge of panic in his voice.

"Oh, well, I wasn't necessarily thinking of your dad. Unless you *want* to ask—"

"No!" he says fiercely. "I don't want Dad to come."

His hands are balled into fists, his entire body wound tight with tension. Something about it just feels so wrong to me. He shouldn't have feelings this big, this thorny, this dark.

"Then we don't have to invite him." I put my hand on Josh's shoulder. His trembles run through me as his eyes dart to mine, then away again. "He's not invited, okay?"

He nods and I bite down on my tongue to keep the tears from spilling over. "Why don't you go get ready for bed, sweetheart? I have a quick call to make and then I'll come tuck you in."

The moment he leaves the kitchen, I grab my phone and scramble through the window onto the fire escape. I dial in Ruslan's number—embarrassingly, I know it by heart—and wait for him to pick up. I start babbling as soon as he answers.

"He doesn't know how to be a kid! He's forgotten how to be an eight-year-old and that's completely my fault because I haven't *allowed* him to be an eight-year-old. He's had to shoulder the burden of his fuck-up dad; he's had to look after his sisters; and I didn't notice because I was just... I was so damn *busy.* But tonight, I saw it so clearly. I fucked up, Ruslan. I've fucked him up and—"

"Emma."

That's all it takes to shut me up.

"You inherited three children, a drunk, and a fuck ton of debt. You were trying to *survive.*"

He's not wrong; it just doesn't really make me feel better. "He's so *angry*, Ruslan. And how could I blame him? He has every right to be angry. He lost his mother to a drunk driver, he lost his father to grief and booze, and now, he's forced to be an adult for his sisters. It's not fair!"

"You're right—it's not fair. But Josh is a strong kid. And he has you."

"I'm not sure that's enough anymore." I take a deep breath. "Ruslan, I'm taking you up on your offer to help him."

"I thought you might."

"Am I that predictable?"

His dark chuckle does a little something to my knees. "No. You just love the boy that much."

Okay. That *does* make me feel better.

"I'll pick him up after school tomorrow," he says. "That okay?"

I nod gratefully. "Yes. I'll inform the school. Thank you, Ruslan. I just—thank you."

"Goodnight, Emma."

Josh is pouring himself a glass of water when I crawl back through the window. He raises his eyebrows and I give him a guilty smile. "Busted."

He giggles and the sound warms me from the inside out. I'm not gonna stop until I hear that sound every freaking day, five times a day. Ten, if I can manage it.

It's not too late to save him.

"Guess what, kiddo?" I wait until I have his full attention, though I can't keep the goofy grin from my face. "Ruslan's gonna be picking you up from school tomorrow."

His eyes go round and his jaw drops. "Ruslan? Really?"

"He wants to do something with you. And I think it might be fun. What do you say?"

"I-I… *Yeah*! Okay!" He runs towards me and grabs me around the waist. "*Thank you,* Aunt Em!"

That night, after all three kids are in bed, I slip into the shower. My tears are lost under the running water when I think about that worshipful look in Josh's eyes when I told him about Ruslan. He used to look at Ben like that, once upon a time. Sienna would be heartbroken if she could see the state her family is in now.

I'm sorry, Si, I sob silently as the cold water numbs my skin. *I'm doing the best I can.*

43

RUSLAN

"… already got him set up with our most advanced security system. Remote-controlled CCTV cameras, complete with infrared sensors for all the doors and windows."

I glance at my watch. It's getting late and Vadim doesn't seem to be in any hurry to wrap up this meeting. I'm about to crawl out of my skin with impatience.

"I've also suggested a biometric gun safe with rapid release."

I nod distractedly. "Sounds great. So what's the problem?"

My uncle scowls. "The problem is that this fucker is paranoid, nephew. Even with the audio-enabled cameras and digital keypad access, he's not satisfied." He raps a knuckle on the client file open on the desk between us. "He wants *more*. He wants—"

"What he wants will have to wait," I snap, shoving the client file towards Vadim. "I've got somewhere I need to be."

Vadim's eyebrows fly up nearly to his hairline. "He's requested a meeting with you."

"I'm a busy man and I'm not in the habit of meeting every client we sign. He'll have to make do with you."

Vadim's lips purse up, his eyes gliding over to the Rolex on his wrist. "We still have twenty-three minutes left in our meeting."

"You might. I do not. Something came up last-minute."

Vadim's pinched scowl turns into a suggestive smile. "A woman?"

"With all due respect, uncle: fuck off."

He twirls a pen between his fingers as he leans back in his seat. "I can't imagine you would cut out on business for any other reason."

"Then clearly you don't know me as well as you think you do."

I get to my feet and Vadim follows suit. "I'm hoping you took my advice the other day to heart. Making the Oryolov Bratva heirs should be your top priority."

My jaw clenches but I swallow the irritation. At this point, Vadim is just a thorn in my side. Easy enough to pull out, but easier still to ignore.

"I'm sure you can cinch this deal without my help. Or do you need me to hold your hand through the process?"

"Try not to use a condom."

I shut the door on him and give Emma only a cursory nod when I walk past her desk. There are too many people milling around to justify a conversation, as bad as I want to stop and ask her about everything and nothing at all. *How was your day? How are the kids? What are your deepest fears, your darkest secrets, the ones you've never told another soul?*

Just before I get into the car, my phone pings.

EMMA: *If you or Josh need anything, please text or call. Have fun today!*

Three little typing dots appear and flash for a while before disappearing again. I can sense her anxiety through them.

I don't blame her for being nervous. Adoptive or not, she doesn't seem like the kind of guardian who'd just hand her kid over to a stranger. Although at this point, "stranger" seems a little off the mark.

I mean, fuck, I've had dinner in her home.

I've bounced her girls on my knees.

I've been *inside* her.

Still, the fact that she okayed this in the first place tells me that she's just that worried about Josh. And she has no idea how to deal with it on her own.

The boy is standing outside by the school breezeway entrance when Boris pulls up in front. The brick facade is weathered and the concrete spiderwebbed with cracks. It's seen better days. I open the door and Josh's face lights up. But the smile only lasts a second before he runs towards the SUV.

"Am I late?" I ask when he slides into the back seat next to me, all business with his clenched jaw.

"No."

"The girls?"

"Amelia picked them up already."

"Good. How was school?"

He fidgets with the seatbelt. "Fine."

He's usually a little chattier than this, which gives me pause. Emma led me to believe that Josh liked the idea of spending some time with me, but he's showing no sign of enthusiasm now. I'm starting to second-guess myself—which is the first time in my entire fucking life that *that* has happened.

I glance over. He's pulling at his seat belt and avoiding my gaze altogether.

"Is there something bothering you?" I ask quietly.

I get nothing more than a fleeting glance and an evasive shrug before he turns his eyes back out of the window. Surreptitiously, I pull up my phone and text Emma.

RUSLAN: *He's quiet.*

Emma's call comes in almost immediately. I decide to put her on speakerphone. The moment Josh hears her voice, he perks right up. "Aunt Em?"

"Hey, buddy," she croons, her voice staticky and indistinct. "How're things going?"

He shoots me a wary glance. "It's fine... When will you get off work?"

"Not for another couple of hours honey. Why do you ask?"

"It's just—the girls are at home alone."

"Alone?" Emma repeats. "They're with Amelia."

He keeps fidgeting. "Yeah, I know."

Of course. I'm a fucking idiot. "Emma, we've got to go. I'll let you know what time I'll be dropping Josh off."

"Uh, okay?" She seems nervous to hang up, but she does anyway. Immediately after, I call Kirill and transfer the call to speaker once again.

"'Sup, boss?"

"I need you to drop whatever it is you're doing and stand guard outside Hell's Kitchen until I drop Josh off this evening."

There's a beat of silence on Kirill's end. "I must've misheard you. You want me to drop what I'm doing and…?"

"Right now."

"Even if it's important?"

Josh is staring at me with his mouth hanging open. "It's not more important than this," I say without breaking eye contact.

"Alrighty then. You're the boss."

The moment I hang up, Josh blurts, "Why did you do that?"

"You were worried about your sisters, weren't you?"

He nods.

"Well, now, you don't have to worry anymore. If your father causes problems, Kirill is right outside. He'll make sure your sisters are safe."

"And Aunt Emma? When she gets home?"

"Of course. Aunt Emma, too."

He flops back against the seat and, for the first time since he got into the car, he leaves his seat belt alone. "Okay." Then he spares me a shy sideways look. "How did you know?"

I smile. "Because that's how I would have felt in your place. You need to know that your people are safe. It's the hallmark of a good leader." He sits up a little straighter and I can't help adding, "It's the hallmark of a good man, too."

We spend the rest of the drive in companionable silence. It's amusing to me that at no point has Josh asked where we're going or what we're going to do. It's only when Boris parks outside the sleek Midtown gym that Josh starts asking questions.

"This is a gym?"

I chuckle at the confused expression on his face. "Something like that. Come on."

Josh follows me into the locker rooms. Some of the other patrons gawk at the sight of this gangly young boy in their midst, but when they see who he's with, they decide to mind their own fucking business. Good call.

We find an empty nook and I push a package into his hands. "What's this?" he asks tentatively, toying with the edge of the plain brown paper wrapping.

"Only one way to find out."

He sets the package down carefully on one of the benches and frees the tucked-in flap. When he pulls out the crisp new pair of boxing gloves, his face transforms from confusion to elation.

I grin and wink. "It's time we got some of that pent-up frustration off those little shoulders."

His face scrunches up instantly. "My shoulders aren't *little*!"

Laughing, I pat him on the back. "They are compared to what they will be soon. Go on then—try them on."

He scurries into them and I help him lace them to proper tightness. I hold up my hands so he can give my palms a few exploratory jabs. "Ready?" I ask him.

He nods fervently, eyes gleaming bright. "Ready."

We make our way towards the punching bags in the far corner of the gym. I coach him into a stance—knees bent, elbows tucked, fists guarding either side of his face. He listens attentively, his gaze following my every movement.

"It should look like this," I explain. I drop into my own crouch, then unleash a right hook into the heavy bag.

The chains clack and groan, the leather pops, and a thin shower of dust descends from the ceiling tiles above. Josh's jaw drops to the mats at our feet.

"*Whoa!*"

Laughing, I give his arm a mock punch. "You'll be able to do that one day."

"Soon?"

I shrug. "Depends on how committed you are. Come on— let's see what you've got."

Josh gulps and staggers a couple of steps back. "No… I don't think I can do it." His gaze veers around the rest of the gym. No one else is watching, but by the fear in his eyes, you'd think he was on stage in front of thousands of critics.

I squat down in front of him. "Josh, look at me. You can't be perfect on the first try." My vision blurs for a moment and I hear those words again, but it's not my voice that says them.

It's his.

Leonid's.

Something twists in my chest. I'm so used to experiencing that throbbing burst of pain that this different kind of simmering ache takes me off guard. Thinking about my dead brother isn't quite as painful as it used to be and I have no fucking clue why.

Focus, idiot.

"There's a learning curve, Josh. We've all been through it. Even me. Hell, *especially* me."

He chews at his bottom lip. "But… what if I suck?"

"If you suck—which I very much doubt you will—then fine, you suck. But if you *do* suck, you will be confronted with a choice: you can continue to suck or you can get better. And if you choose the latter, then that's exactly what will happen. But you can trust me on this: you'll never get anywhere if you don't try first."

I can actually see the resolve settle into Josh's clenched jaw. He nods curtly and straightens up. "I'm ready."

I pat him on the back. "Brave man."

I teach Josh the same way that Leonid taught me. Silently encouraging, unfailingly patient, ridiculously determined. For me, boxing has never been about releasing suppressed aggression. Well, never *just* about that.

It is about finding your own power. It is about *owning* that power.

Josh boxes like an eight-year-old boy who's mad at the world. That is to be expected. But as we approach the end of the hour, I can see the beginnings of something resembling skill in the force of those tired punches. *Control.*

He looks drained when we get back into the SUV dripping with sweat, but there's a newfound confidence in his step. He doesn't fidget and he doesn't avoid my gaze.

"I'd say we've earned some ice cream, wouldn't you?"

Josh hesitates. "Can we take some back for Aunt Emma and the girls?"

"Of course."

Only then does he nod his approval.

On our drive to the creamery, I try to figure out this strange feeling spreading over my chest. I keep going back to the picture Emma sent me of her and the kids eating ice cream. The smile on her face, the happiness in her eyes—they both felt foreign to me at the time. I was an outsider, looking in.

But now?

Now, I think about Emma's joyful smile and it hits me—I *feel* the way she looks in that picture. I've stolen a little slice of her world for myself and it's forced me to remember what mine once revolved around.

Before I was *pahkan.*

Before I was grieving.

Before I thought building barriers to keep people out was the only way to live.

44

EMMA

"There's freaking tissue paper, Em! Gilt-edged tissue paper!"

I lean away from the mirror above my sink so that I can see Phoebe through my open bathroom door. She's holding the lid of the package in her hands and she's staring reverently at the tissue-paper-wrapped contents on my bed.

It arrived half an hour ago, precisely three hours before tonight's Olson-Ferber charity gala. The courier didn't have a sender's name, but he didn't have to—this has Ruslan's fingerprints all over it.

"Just open it," I chuckle before I go back to applying my eyeliner.

"Respect must be paid, Em! This is like foreplay; you can't just charge right in. Did you see the label on the top of this baby?"

I'm trying not to laugh but that's just making my hand shake even harder. Abandoning my eyeliner, I join Phoebe in front of the sleek black box. It's embossed with a cursive *Vivienne Westwood* stamp.

Phoebe puts her hands over her heart. "It's gorgeous. I'm swooning."

I frown. "You haven't even seen the dress yet. Save the swoon for when it counts."

When I pull apart the leaves of tissue paper, Phoebe gasps. "Red! That is *so* your color."

"You would have said that no matter what color it was."

Phoebe fingers the fabric and sighs longingly. "He's a keeper. The man is a gift from the angels above."

I cock an eyebrow at her. "What ever happened to 'protect your heart' and 'don't get sucked in with over-the-top, expensive gifts'?"

Phoebe gestures to the dress. "It's *Vivienne Westwood!*" she repeats for emphasis. "Also, are you aware that you've only lined one eye? If it's some kind of statement, then you do you, girl, but if not, in the interest of honesty, it's kinda terrifying."

Rolling my eyes, I head into the bathroom again to finish my second eye. Phoebe follows me and leans against the threshold, letting her euphoria drop for a moment. "Re: protecting your heart—at this point you know the stakes. I'm not gonna beat you over the head with lectures and cautionary tales."

I try to keep my hand steady while I ring my second eye with dusky charcoal. Phoebe's right—I *do* know the stakes.

The problem is that it doesn't seem to matter.

Ruslan and I have been sleeping together now for almost five months. Between the hours of nine-to-five, I'm a constant, dripping mess with near-permanent rug burn on my knees. And as if that weren't enough, twice a week, we leave the office together and go to his penthouse on 48th. He offers me a drink and then he fucks me to within an inch of my life.

We've christened the living room, all the bedrooms, the kitchen, even the bathrooms. He's had me up against the windows, the walls, bent over the sofa and the table, sprawled out across the kitchen counter. Standing, sitting— you name it, we've done it.

And the crazy thing is—*he only keeps getting better.*

The moment his tongue hits my pussy, I turn into a goopy puddle of need. The oral sex is great, but every other kind of sex we've had has been equally incredible. I leave his apartment practically levitating off the ground every time.

But I do leave. Given my precarious emotional position, I've been constantly telling myself that I need to be diligent about leaving the apartment right after the sex. It's just… that it isn't always so easy to do. Especially when he asks about the kids. Which he does. Often.

So to recap the whole shebang: my boss and I are having amazing sex on the regular, although he almost always wears condoms now.

He is taking Josh out twice a week for their one-on-one male bonding outings and it's making a world of difference to my surly eight-year-old.

He brings ice cream home for the girls every time he drops Josh off.

He wiped out all my debts in the blink of an eye.

He keeps making all these sweet, thoughtful little gestures or doing random odd jobs around the house just to make my life easier. Like fixing the car. Or sanding down the legs of our lopsided coffee table so that we don't need the coasters to hold it up anymore.

And sometimes, every so often, I catch him looking at me with this strange expression on his face. The naïve fool in me keeps hoping that it means that maybe he might be catching feelings, too.

Because, despite my best efforts, I've gone and fallen hard for the one person who I'm *contractually obligated* not to fall for.

It never fails to amaze me how things can be so great and so terrible at the exact same time.

Once my makeup is done, Phoebe helps me wiggle my way into the dress. I have to suck in my breath as she zips up the corset, but after a little effort on my part and a lot of grunting on Phoebe's, I'm zipped up and feeling just a little bit fabulous.

Phoebe claps her hands to her cheeks the moment she circles around to face me. "You look *gorgeous*, Em. In your movie starlet era."

I don't have a full-length mirror to take advantage of, but I do *feel* amazing. The Bardot neckline and the thigh-high slit have me feeling sexy, but the structured corset and the subtle A-line silhouette provide just enough coverage to make me feel elegant, too.

"What's wrong?" I ask when I realize that Phoebe has her head tilted to one side as she frowns at me.

"The nude lip is nice, but I think you need to go bold for this dress."

"Not my red lipstick."

She smiles. "I think you *have* to."

"It'll be too much."

"Um, hello? You're going to be on the arm of the hottest bachelor in New York tonight. You need to bring the fire."

"I don't know…"

She waves away my hesitation and grabs the seduction red lipstick from my threadbare makeup bag. "Well?" she asks, holding the lipstick up like it's a weapon. "Go big or go home, right?"

Laughing, I nod. "Alright then. Lay it on me."

"Yesss!" She keeps snapping her fingers. "Girl, *slay*! He won't be able to take his eyes off you!"

Yeah, I think to myself with that mix of self-loathing and fluttery hope that's come to feel all too natural lately. *That's what I'm hoping for.*

And that's exactly the problem.

When I walk out of my bedroom, everyone freezes. Amelia and the kids are sitting in the middle of the living room floor, having shoved aside the coffee table to make a sprawling Lego city populated by Barbies galore—another present from Ruslan.

Caroline just gasps. Amelia wolf whistles. Josh's jaw drops and Reagan jumps to her feet. "Auntie Em! You look like Cinderella when the Fairy Godmother made her a dress."

Phoebe giggles. "Hit the nail on the head, Rae."

Reagan frowns indignantly. "I didn't hit anything, Aunt Phoebe."

While Phoebe tries to explain that expression to a five-year-old, Josh and Caroline skip over to me.

Caro strokes the dress with the tips of her fingers. "You look like a princess, Aunt Em."

Josh nods. "You look beautiful."

I'm gonna have to try doubly hard not to blush tonight. I don't wanna blend into my dress too much.

"Thank you, my loves. Now, be good for Amelia and Aunt Phoebe. Go to bed when you're told. No negotiations, okay?"

"Aw, can't we come down and say hi to Ruslan?" Caroline pleads.

"Not tonight, honey."

She hits me with her trademark heartbreaking pout, but I kiss her hard, leaving an imprint of my lips on her forehead.

"I want a kiss like that!" Reagan insists immediately.

I brand the girls with matching lipstick marks on their foreheads and blow kisses to everyone else. I take the stairs slowly, still getting used to the three-and-a-half inch—yes, Phoebe measured—Manolo Blahniks that Ruslan sent along with the dress.

When I finally reach the ground floor lobby, I take a deep breath. Ruslan's SUV is parked out front, exactly on time as usual, but I need a second to collect my nerves.

This is your Cinderella moment, Emma. Just enjoy it.

"Okay. Here goes—"

I'm reaching for the front door of the apartment building when it flies inward, nearly taking my hand out. "Jesus! Caref—"

I catch the overpoweringly rancid scent of beer, smoke, and throw-up, and I freeze.

Leave it to my brother-in-law to ruin everything. As usual.

Ben takes a moment longer to recognize who he nearly clobbered with the door. When his eyes land on my face, they go wide. Then they trail over the length of my body. Twice.

"What the fuck are you wearing?" he blurts at last.

I clear my throat. "It's called a dress. Now, if you'll excuse me—"

When I try to walk around him, he blocks me. "Where the hell did you get the money for that get-up?"

I narrow my eyes. "If you must know, Ruslan gave it to me."

"Oh, *Ruslan* gave it to you," he sneers. "What else has he been giving you? I've got a guess."

"Ben, I really don't have the time for—"

"Did he pay off all your credit card debt, too?" Ben demands. "What about the basketball program Josh is in? Or the new shoes all the kids have suddenly? I've got guesses for all that shit also."

I don't want to answer the bastard, but it's my best chance of getting out the door sooner. "Yes," I grit out, "Ruslan helped with some of those things. And I paid off the rest."

"How?"

"I've been putting in a lot of overtime lately, okay?" He's moving a little closer to me and now, my sweat glands are really kicking it up a notch.

"Overtime, huh?" He leers. "Is that code for 'working on your back'?"

"Asshole!"

I'm tempted to slap the hell out of him. Instead, making use of his unsteadiness, I bolt around him and rush through the door before he can stop me. Unfortunately, the rank turd follows me outside.

"I'm not done talking to you!"

"Well, I'm done talking to you!"

I'm in the process of flipping him the bird when he grabs my arm. "Listen here, you—"

Suddenly, Ben is yanked right off me. I turn to my savior, expecting to see Ruslan. But instead, it's Kirill who's got Ben by the front of his soiled t-shirt.

"W-who are you?" Ben demands.

"Right now? Your worst nightmare."

I raise my eyebrows. Under normal circumstances, a line like that would be a cringe-inducing cliché. But apparently, with the right delivery, it's surprisingly effective. Ben seems to agree—he goes deathly pale and his twitching kicks up a notch.

"There are better men than you that have their eyes on Ms. Carson. And I won't hesitate to pluck yours out if you *ever* lay a hand on her again. Understood?"

Ben nods obediently, his eyes wide with fear.

Kirill shoves Ben back. His heel catches the curb and he lands with his ass on the pavement. Kirill flashes me a charming smile and offers me his arm.

"Shall we, madam?"

It's not exactly the fairytale departure I'd hope for.

But this Cinderella's gonna take what she gets.

45

EMMA

"Where's Ruslan?"

I'm busy adjusting my seatbelt so it doesn't mess with my dress, so I miss Kirill's facial expression. "He'll be on his way to the gala now as we speak."

I raise my eyebrows. "Oh. Does he have press to do on his own or something?"

Kirill's forehead wrinkles. "Press?"

I'm starting to feel a little hot despite the fact that the air conditioning is blasting. "Well, um, I mean, I thought we were supposed to walk in together. Doesn't he usually enter these galas with his dates?"

His eyebrows rise but he gives me only a nod. "Usually, yeah, he does."

Am I missing something?

"Sorry, I don't mean to sound like a country bumpkin or anything. It's just that this is my first gala and I'm not sure how it all works. I was kinda hoping Ruslan would be with me to talk me through the whole thing."

Kirill shifts to the side and clears his throat. "Well, the thing is, there's a certain… protocol at these kinds of events."

"I know. That's why I'm asking."

He gives me a glance that I can't quite read. Is he nervous for me? Does he feel sorry for me? Does he think Ruslan made the wrong choice in choosing me as his date?

"The crowds at this type of thing are different than what you're used to, Emma," he explains gently. "Ruslan will be forced to be different, too."

I have no earthly idea what that means. Is he trying to tell me that Ruslan's not gonna be all lovey-dovey with me in public? 'Cause if so, I've got news for him—Ruslan's not really lovey-dovey with me in private, either.

"I know. Ruslan's an important man. People want to meet him."

Kirill nods. "I'm happy to keep you company, though."

I smile uncertainly. "Thanks."

Again—weird.

A legion of luxury cars is queued up in a single file line as we near the Met. Photographers line the red carpet just outside the museum's elegant entrance and flashing lights pop every other second.

"Oh, God," I breathe, my anxiety clawing its way up my throat. "I'm gonna bust my ass up those stairs for sure."

Kirill gives me a reassuring wink. "I've got you. Don't worry."

When our Escalade finally gets to the front of the line, my door is thrown open and I'm hit with a frenzy of flashes. It's almost enough to make me cower into the back of the SUV and refuse to come out.

The overwhelming thought in the back of my head is, *I wish Ruslan were with me right now.*

Then Kirill walks around and offers me his hand. I take it gratefully and we walk into the museum together.

"You didn't trip," he whispers to me. "Bravo."

Feeling slightly more relaxed now that we've cleared the throng of reporters and photographers, my confidence rises.

That and I catch a glimpse of myself in the full length mirrors that line the foyer.

And *damn*, I do look good.

The Onyx Ballroom is aglitter with shimmering lights and shimmering people. It's enough to blind me. I scan the room from side to side, hoping to catch a glimpse of the man I'm here for. Kirill sticks close to my side and escorts me through the ballroom. I assume he's leading me towards Ruslan, but then I catch a glimpse of him on the other side of the room.

I thought I looked good, but I don't hold a candle to him. Neither does any other man in this place. Not the politicians or the movie stars. No one wears a tux like Ruslan Oryolov.

"Wait, Kirill. Ruslan's over—"

I stop in my tracks. I can practically feel the color drain from my face. "I-is that… Jessica Allens next to him?"

She's not just next to him; she's practically part of his outfit, hanging off his arm in her sequined champagne cocktail dress. She's laughing exuberantly, massaging his bicep possessively, glancing around to make sure everyone knows who he's with.

My gaze veers slowly to Kirill and the look on his face makes everything clear.

Pity.

That's what I saw back in the car.

"So why am I here then?" I ask Kirill miserably. "The call girl, kept close by for convenience's sake so he has an easy lay when the night's over?"

He runs a hand through his hair. "You're his assistant, Emma. You're here in case he needs you."

I scoff. "Right." I zone in on the bar, which, thankfully, is on the opposite side of the room, far from where Ruslan and his witch of a date are mingling. "Well, if our boss *needs* me, I'll be at the bar. Consider it my address for the rest of the night."

I zoom off in the direction of the bar and grab the first empty stool I see. But because I'm a masochist, I pick the stool that offers me a bird's-eye view of Ruslan and the botched Botox version of Miranda Priestley he's with.

Had I actually been confident when I came up here? Did I really think that putting on a pretty red dress and *come hither* lipstick would change a damn thing between Ruslan and me? Dress or no dress, I'm still just the lowly assistant, the hired help. He's still the playboy billionaire with the endless roster of options. I'm nothing more to him than a plaything.

A distraction at best.

A charity case at worst.

I flag down a bartender who's wearing a scarlet bow tie the same color of my dress. *Fitting.*

"What can I get you, ma'am?" he asks.

"A cab home would be great."

"What was that?" he asks distractedly.

I clear my throat. "Gin and tonic, please. And if you go heavy on the gin, I won't complain."

It's not my usual drink of choice, but I need something to jolt me out of the funk that I'm sinking into. I need to drum up at least enough energy to get me through a couple of hours of this thing. Either that or enough apathy.

The moment the drink is set down in front of me—on a crystal coaster no less—I pick it up and take a big and very unladylike sip. The burn scours its way down my throat but it doesn't do a damn thing to lighten the heaviness in my chest.

Jessica is smoothing out Ruslan's collar now. I can't see his face clearly, but I know him well enough to know that he's not the kind of man who likes being groomed in public.

"That's a hefty pour there, *chica*."

I roll my eyes as Kirill takes the stool next to me. "I can do what I want. No one's paying attention to me."

"Emma, you look ravishing tonight. Half the men in this room are locked onto you."

I give him a skeptical glare. "Is this flattery you overcompensating for the fact that your boss is a total douche?"

"Two things can be true at once."

I take another sip of my G&T. "I don't need you to babysit me tonight, Kirill. I'm a big girl; I can take care of myself."

"Fair enough." He holds up his hands in self-defense. "I'm just here for the free drinks."

I take another sip. "Urgh." I scowl directly at Jessica Allens. "She's *awful.*"

Kirill raises his glass once the bartender brings it over and we cheers to that. "He's on the clock right now, Emma. I wouldn't take it personally."

"I wouldn't have if he'd just *told* me. He had weeks to break it to me and instead, he made me believe that *I* was gonna be his date to this thing."

Kirill cringes. "I'm sure he just assumed that—"

"I know he's your boss and all, but I really, really need you to not defend him right now."

Kirill nods and buries his face behind his drink. After he's done, he pops off the stool. "I'll check back in a bit."

"You don't need to do that."

He gives me a wink that says he'll do it anyway and disappears into the crowd. When I tear my attention away from Jessica and Ruslan long enough, I notice that he was right: I *am* getting a few looks. Women who are admiring my dress. Men who seem to be admiring me. It gives me a little burst of satisfaction that I'm fully aware is horrifically petty, but at this rate, I'll take more of whatever helps me get through the night.

"Hello there."

The man at my back is standing a little too close to be Kirill. He glides around my stool and takes the empty spot next to me. "Can you help me solve a little mystery?"

I arch an eyebrow and brace myself for a cringey pick-up line. "I can try."

He smiles. He's not unattractive. In fact, with his slicked-back white-blonde hair and hollow cheekbones, he's working the whole *Game of Thrones*, Targaryen vibe. "I've been watching you for a few minutes now—"

"Hm, not creepy at all. Go on."

"—and I can't for the life of me figure out why a woman as gorgeous as you is sitting all by herself with that permanent frown on her face."

As pick-up lines go, it's not *bad*.

"Guess I'm just not in the mood for—" I gesture to the ballroom. "—all this hoopla."

"I can't blame you. These functions tend to be a lot of pompous, self-aggrandizing millionaires, each one desperate to outdo the other. Either that or insufferable social climbers."

"Which one are you?"

He chuckles. "I'll give you the chance to figure that one out while we dance."

I stare at the hand he's offering me. "I don't know. I kinda like my quiet little stool in the corner."

"Oh, come on. You're far too pretty to be sitting here all by yourself."

I glance past the dancefloor and catch Ruslan's back. Jessica, of course, is not far away from him. Her hand glides over the back of his coat before she loops it through his arm.

I've been sitting here for more than an hour and he hasn't so much as glanced my way. Not even once. It really does feel like a "gotcha" moment. *Here's a beautiful red dress and a gorgeous pair of shoes, Emma. Now, come sit and watch while I tote around New York's most obnoxious daddy's girl while I ignore you completely.*

Yeah, well—I don't have to sit and watch. I don't have to play the wallflower. If I have to endure this evening, I can do it on the dance floor with a man who seems more than willing to shower me with the attention and compliments that Ruslan is cruelly withholding.

I slip my hand into his and give him a decisive nod. "Fine. Let's dance."

46

RUSLAN

"I must say, the two of you make a wonderful couple."

Fyodor coughs discreetly while Vadim flashes me his biggest smile. He only totes that cheesing smirk out at events like these. I've come to hate it with a fucking passion.

"*Aren't* we, Vadim?" Jessica trills as she reaches up to adjust my collar yet again.

Does the woman think I'm some thumbless ape that can't adjust his own outfit? Every time I move out from under her reach, she finds a way to latch onto me again. Bloodsucking fucking ghoul. I can't wait to be rid of her.

Vadim ogles us with a suggestive smirk. "I can just imagine what the kids will look like."

He's so full of it. No one can imagine what the kids will look like—mostly because, at this point, no one can even remember what Jessica's original face looked like.

"Oh, they'd be *so* gorgeous, don't you think so, Rus?"

My head swivels in her direction. Did she just call me *Rus?*

I drop my arm from around her waist and reach for another flute of champagne. It's my third glass of the night already, but this weak shit will not suffice. Spending any length of time with Jessica Allens requires hard liquor. Lots of it.

I catch a flourish of scarlet from the corner of my eye and I turn automatically. I've spent the last half an hour double-taking at every woman dressed in red. Then I catch a whiff of citrus and I *know* it's her.

And my fucking God, she looks stunning.

I've imagined this very dress on her a hundred times already, but my imagination didn't come close to doing her justice. Emma in real life is more than I could've ever dreamed. The fabric drapes smoothly around her body, highlighting her slim waist, her gorgeous breasts, the flush of her perfect skin.

And her *lips.* They're painted with a deep, dangerous crimson and just begging to be wrapped around my cock.

My immediate reaction is desire. Hot and dense, shot through with need.

My second reaction is *rage.*

I've spent my whole life practicing the art of control. In my line of work, if you lose it, you die. But now, in the fucking crucible, with allies and enemies swarming on every side... I'm too pissed to rein it in.

There are too many eyes on her. Too many second looks, too many lingering glances. The women are largely tolerable, but the *men*—I'm tempted to write down every single name so that I can personally pluck out their eyes later.

"Darling, what're you looking at?"

When I don't immediately look at her, Jessica floats her fingers across my cheek. It takes every last fiber of discipline I have not to flinch away from her touch.

Jessica Allens does *not* belong on my arm.

Emma does.

And now, I've lost her amongst the crowd.

"Don't mind him, Jessica. He's just in boss mode still." I hate that I'm letting Vadim make my excuses, but at least someone is keeping the she-devil at ease. I can't even muster up the energy to lie to her convincingly.

"All work and no play makes Ruslan a very dull boy," she quips, laughing hysterically at her own bad joke. Then she gasps. "Oh my God! Lola, is that you? Excuse me for a minute, darling; I have to go say hello."

"Take all the minutes you want," I mutter under my breath. The moment she clears my space, I feel a hundred pounds lighter. "Thank *fuck* for Lola." I remind myself to donate something sizable to the woman's charity later.

Fyodor fixes me with a penetrating gaze. "You'll have to make a choice soon, my son."

He doesn't say anything else—but Uncle Vadim, of course, can't leave it there. "The Allens girl has amazing connections and enough money to rival your fortune."

I scoff. "No amount of money is worth procreating with that banshee. I'd rather lose a testicle."

My father lets out a weary sigh. Vadim just clicks his tongue with disapproval. "Wisdom is wasted on the young."

I'm about to tell him exactly where he can shove his wisdom when Jessica appears again, all too soon. But since the appendage she's pulling towards me is a man I might need one day, I put on my most charming smile.

"Commissioner Allens," I say to her father. "How nice to see you again."

He gives me a hearty handshake. "Ruslan! Pleasure, pleasure."

While he's greeting Vadim and Fyodor, I spot a mirage of red off in the distance. I shift an inch to the side and catch Emma sitting by the bar.

Except she's not alone.

The fury turns my vision spotty when I realize *who* she's talking to.

Adrik fucking Makarov.

If I thought I was pissed before, it doesn't hold a candle to the inferno burning through my veins right now. I'm seconds away from going absolutely berserk if that fucker doesn't move away from her right fucking *now*, when—

"Ruslan?" Hiram Allens's deep voice cuts through the sharp edge of my anger.

Goddammit. I swallow hard and turn to him, forcing the smile back onto my face. "Will you excuse me for just a minute, Commissioner? I've got some business I need to see to."

I'm not so blinded by rage that I don't see the incredulous looks on Jessica's and Vadim's faces when I excuse myself from Hiram's company. Even Fyodor looks mildly surprised and he rarely concerns himself with the politics anymore.

But I can't concentrate on charming the head of the NYPD when that slimy motherfucker has his sights set on *my woman.*

I start carving my way through the crowd towards the bar in the far corner. But before I can get close enough to Adrik to strangle him, Kirill inserts himself right in my path. "Whoa, let's take a breath there, brother. I know where you're going and, trust me—that's not a good idea."

"You were supposed to be taking care of Emma tonight." I'm this fucking close to pushing him aside and just barreling my way down to that bar. "Why the fuck didn't you run interference?"

"Because the moment I do, Adrik is gonna know that Emma is a weak spot for you."

Those two words.

Weak spot.

Fucking hell, are they sobering.

But they get through to me. It's bad enough that Remmy honed in on Emma. If Adrik were to do the same, that would be a hell of a lot worse. It would put Emma in danger. It would put the kids in danger. It's the whole damn reason I couldn't bring her as my date tonight: the moment people saw her on my arm, they'd know she was important. They'd start digging into her life, her past, her relationships.

And I won't stand for that.

"He's here tonight to piss you off. This is about Lees International."

My eyes snap to his. "You closed the deal?"

Kirill nods. "The board of directors agreed this morning. Bane Corp. will be buying up Lees International and there's not a damn thing Adrik can do about it. The decision was unanimous."

Lees International is only one of Adrik's subsidiary companies, but it will still be a significant loss. Especially considering who he's losing it to. This would have been great news if it weren't for the fact that Adrik is now offering Emma his hand.

And she *fucking takes it.*

Kirill looks back over his shoulder. "He's trying to get a rise out of you by screwing with your assistant, that's all," he cautions. "Do not give him the hint that she might be more. And most of all, don't give him the satisfaction."

My gaze narrows as Adrik wraps an arm around Emma's waist and pulls her close. Of course I'd picked out the sexiest dress I could find for her. And now, that son of a bitch gets the benefit of it.

She should be mine.

"Okay," I spit through gritted teeth. "So be it."

"Don't worry," Kirill assures me. "I'll keep an eye on them."

I force myself to walk back to my group. On the upside, Hiram Allens is in the same spot I left him. On the downside, so is his daughter.

Hiram gives me an approving nod. "I admire a man who never stops working, Ruslan. But you have to know when to stop and smell the roses, too."

He looks right at his insufferable daughter when he says it. She curls her hand around my arm. "Ruslan's busy building his empire, Daddy."

I glance over Jessica's shoulder but I can't spot Emma and Adrik. There are at least two other red dresses cavorting around on the dance floor, distracting me every time they pass through my line of sight.

I'm only vaguely aware that Jessica is speaking. "Is someone interested in a dance?"

I see her then—being spun around the dance floor by that grotesque little weasel. She's got her back to me. Adrik's hand rests just above her ass.

I'm gonna kill that fucking bastard.

I raise my eyes—only to find that *his* are aimed right at me. He gives me a brazen smile and a wink that's just begging to be ripped off his face.

"Rus?" Jessica tries again.

Yeah, that's the *wrong* way to get me to respond to anything.

"Ruslan." The curt displeasure in Hiram's voice gets my attention. "You seem very... distracted. Unforgivable, really, when you consider the beautiful woman you have on your arm."

I suppress my gag reflex for her father's benefit and try to get my head back in the game. I need Hiram Allens' loyalty; therefore, I need to keep his daughter happy.

But I'm not about to let Adrik's machinations go unanswered, either. There's no way he can put his hands on what is *mine* and get away with it.

I know damn well why I've kept Emma a secret from the world. For her sake, for the kids' sake, that's been the best move. But there is a beast in me that says to hell with that. I can handle the consequences. I can keep her entire family safe even if every last man, woman, child, and animal on this planet tries to take her from me.

But mark my words: one way or another, come hell or high water, by any means necessary...

By the time this night ends, every fucking soul at this gala is going to know *exactly* who Emma belongs to.

47

RUSLAN

When dinner is served, I see that Adrik has been assigned to a seat at the reject table way in the back of the Onyx Room, which is satisfying enough. But right now, I'm more concerned with the seating situation at my own table.

"Did you switch the name cards on our table?" I growl the moment Kirill walks over to me.

"Of course. Emma's sitting on your right."

I'm tempted to make Kirill rearrange it so that Jessica is sitting far away from me, but that would be asking too much. I leave Jessica gossiping with a gaggle of her equally nauseating friends and march straight for where we'll be seated in the position of honor at the front of the ballroom.

Just in time to catch a certain woman in red trying to switch around the name cards so that she's *not* sitting next to me.

"Is there a problem, Ms. Carson?"

She lets out a startled gasp and nearly drops her placard on one of the decorative candles adorning the centerpiece. Her cheeks flush a bright red, only a shade lighter than her dress. She looks even more ravishing up close.

"I just figured you'd prefer to be sitting next to someone more important," she bites out.

"I'll make do with you."

Her jaw clenches tight as she sits herself down and angles her chair away from me.

The little siren is in quite the mood tonight.

Me being here with Jessica has her all riled up. I wonder if that's the reason she chose to dance with Adrik—to make me feel what she's feeling. Not that she could have known who he is. What he's done.

"Oh, what a lovely table!" Jessica cries as she appears from nowhere and claims the seat on my left. "So elegant."

Of course, her eyes land right on Emma. She's the only outsider at this table. That and she *does* stand out.

That dress was made for the spotlight. And she was made for that dress.

Jessica leans around me. "Hello there." When Emma tries to ignore her, Jessica actually flutters her hand in Emma's face. "Helloooo."

Emma affords her a tight smile. "Hi."

"I'm Jessica."

"I know."

Jessica's smile falters just a tad, but she manages to pick it right back up. "That dress is just *gorg!* Is it Carolina?"

"Um, I believe it's Vivienne Westwood."

"Of course! It's *so* Vivienne." She's laughing a little too often —a surefire sign that she's feeling insecure as hell. "I'm sorry; I didn't get your name."

"It's Emma, Ms. Allens. We've met several times."

Jessica purses her lips and taps one manicured nail against them. "Have we?"

"I'm Mr. Oryolov's assistant."

Jessica's smile freezes. She stares at Emma, then glances at me, then back to Emma. "You're the... assistant?"

"I am."

Jessica's smile drops instantly and she leans back against her seat. "Why is your *assistant* at our table?" she hisses at me under her breath.

It makes me want to slice her tongue right out of her mouth, but I sheathe my instincts and give her only a cursory glare. "Because I asked her to be."

She must've actually caught the menace in my voice because, for once, she shuts up. However, the moment the appetizers land on the table, her hand lands on my inner thigh, too close to my crotch for comfort. She squeezes and laughs distractedly at something Mrs. Pelham, the wife of a prominent city councilman, is saying from across the table. I put my hand down on hers and she sucks in a breath, probably assuming that I'm being affectionate.

Then I remove her hand from my leg and her smile dies on her lips.

I turn my attention to Emma. She's thrown herself into a conversation with Reggie Schaffer. The man owns a chain of high-end exotic resorts around the world and is fresh off the grand opening of his new flagship in Bali. He's a charmer, but I also happen to know that he has been happily married to his second wife for the last forty years. Which is why he was intentionally seated on Emma's right.

"… just a little intimidating, these events," Emma says shyly, leaning towards Mr. and Mrs. Schaffer.

Mrs. Schaffer gives Emma a sympathetic smile. "Oh, honey, trust me: I've been there. You get used to it."

"I don't have to get used to it. This is not my world. I'm just the help."

Reggie looks skeptical. "This may not be your world, but you certainly look like you fit in."

Emma laughs and places a friendly hand on his arm. The man is pushing eighty and Emma's touch doesn't linger for more than a second, but it still pisses me off. I'm jealous of every smile, every laugh, every conversation she exchanges with anyone that isn't me.

Across the table, a developer named Brady Sanchez drapes an arm around his twenty-two-year-old date and flashes me an enthusiastic smile. "Oryolov! I can't tell you how glad I am that we're sitting at the same table. You're a hard man to wrangle, you busy bastard."

I contain my smirk. Nothing about the seating chart had been left to chance. But as long as it has the appearance of coincidence, it works in my favor.

"I've got a new luxury skyrise apartment complex coming up in Manhattan and I need to get it decked out with all the fixings. I want that place locked down *tight*."

This is shaping up to be the easiest sale of my life. Sanchez is a trust fund baby who has never met a dollar he didn't immediately want to spend.

Then I hear laughter to my right and I completely lose my train of thought. The Schaffers are chuckling at something Emma's just said. Even Dennis Carlisle has joined their conversation. That smarmy finance *mudak* is sitting next to his mistress in public while his third wife molders at home and he *still* has the audacity to look at Emma like she's a juicy piece of fruit, ripe for the plucking.

"So what do you say, Oryolov?" Brady presses when I don't reply. "My skyrise is a forty-story behemoth. And I'm gonna want every single apartment wrapped in Bane's finest bells and whistles."

Another burst of laughter to my right. Instinctively, my hand finds Emma's leg under the table. She stiffens, her smile faltering for only a moment. Then she shoves my hand right off her thigh. It's enough to make me laugh, too. When I try again, she repeats the process, keeping her face angled away from me the whole time. All I can see is her jaw vibrating with tension.

"Only the finest for you, Brady," I murmur.

Apparently, I've *really* pissed her off tonight. It's gonna take more than a little under-the-table feeler to thaw my sexy little *kiska*.

Lucky for me, I enjoy a good challenge.

Of course, not all challenges are quite so enjoyable. I'm reminded of that when Jessica's hand finds its way back to my own thigh. I give her five seconds to reconsider and then I peel it off again. She interprets that as an excuse to sidle a little closer to me. I ignore her and focus on the little glacier in red sitting on my right.

This time, when I palm Emma's thigh, grateful as ever for the slit that offers me contact with her naked skin, she's ready for me. She grabs my hand and digs her nails in. It takes some effort not to burst out laughing.

The little hellcat is all claws tonight—literally—and I'm fucking loving it.

"I hope that glint in your eye means you're the one who's going to handle this account." Brady folds his arms haughtily. "I'm not willing to accept anyone else." His gaze veers to Fyodor and Vadim, the latter of whom hides his scowl behind his champagne flute.

I keep my face straight as Emma digs in a little harder. Any deeper and she'll start to draw blood. Still, I refuse to remove my hand.

"I wouldn't dream of giving you to anyone else."

"Excellent." He lifts up his champagne glass and we cheers to the new alliance.

But despite the fact that I've managed to score Bane Corp. a new contract worth millions before the main course has even hit the table, I'm more interested in closing the deal with the siren on my right.

I slide my hand up her inner thigh and pry her legs open. She jerks violently, causing her newfound friends to raise their eyes in alarm.

"Are you alright, dear?" Mrs. Schaeffer asks.

"Mhmm," Emma grits out, trying desperately to push away my hand without being obvious about it.

"Is something bothering you?" Dennis Carlisle chimes in. It looks more like he's talking to her cleavage.

"Fine," Emma answers tightly. "Just, um… hungry."

Yeah, I bet you are, my little minx.

The main courses hit the table and I take the opportunity to dive in a little deeper. The clinking of cutlery drowns out Emma's fevered gasp as my fingers make contact with the thin fabric of her panties.

I tease them to the side, exposing her pussy before running my fingers along her slit. Just as I suspected: she's wet.

But not wet enough for me yet.

"Why don't you eat, sweetheart?" Mrs. Schaeffer suggests thoughtfully. "You're looking a little flushed."

I push a finger inside her and Emma lets out a tiny gasp that she tries to turn into a cough. Her cheeks flush a deeper shade of scarlet and, suddenly, she's pushing off from the table and excusing herself.

A more patient man might have waited a few minutes before excusing himself, too, but I'm rock-hard and at the end of my tether. I'm keenly aware of Jessica's eyes on my back as I follow Emma out of the Onyx Room, but at this point, I don't give a fuck.

I'm done pretending she's anything but mine.

The hallway outside the ballroom is empty except for Emma. She's racing towards the restrooms when I catch up, grab her arm, and twist her around to face me. She collides with me, all breathless and panicked.

"What the hell are you doing?" she gasps. "That was not funny!"

"No," I growl, pushing her up against the wall. "No, it was *not* fucking funny."

I silence her with my lips, stealing the kiss the only way I know how. No negotiations, no conversation. Just demanding and greedy and fucking no-holds-barred. I slide my tongue into her mouth and I feel the moan in her chest.

I'm gonna make sure the whole fucking world knows who she belongs to.

But first, I'm going to remind *her*.

48

EMMA

My head is spinning fast.

My heart feels like it's about to burst out of my chest.

He's got my leg hitched up around his waist and I can feel his cock, rock-solid and possessive, pushing at my panties, demanding entrance.

When he pulls his lips from mine, I'm pretty sure he's wiped the lipstick clean off. I gasp for air, trembling as he leaves a trail of kisses down my neck.

"R-Ruslan—*stop!*"

He just growls. "There's no stopping this now, *kiska*." He pushes his hand through the slit in my dress and rips my panties right off. The fabric gives way beneath his brutish hands.

"No, we... we're out in the... *ahh*... open...!"

"I don't give two fucks." His lips sweep over the tops of my breasts. I hear the screech of his zipper and my heart stops for a moment. "Ruslan—"

He plunges himself into me and just like that, all conversation comes to a screeching halt.

"Did you enjoy dancing with him?" he snarls as he drives all the way in. I'm pressed between the wall and him. I can barely breathe, much less move, and I'm so lost in the feel of him filling me to the max that I can barely register what he's saying, either. My answer is lost in a sea of moans and gasps.

"Do you think *he* could ever make you feel like this?"

"Mmm, Ruslan… *fuuuck!*"

"I didn't think so. Only *I* can make you feel like this. Only *I* can make you come like this. Isn't that right, my naughty little *kiska*?"

"Yes," I gasp. I don't have any earthly idea what I'm yessing, but I tell him what he wants to hear. I'd do anything he wants me to do. All my anger and hurt has turned to pleasure and passion.

At this point, I'm completely his.

He pulls at my earlobe with his lips and sucks on my neck, his thrusts getting more and more frantic. Every one bucks me back into the wall. A shower of dust rains on us from the ceiling tiles above. I wouldn't be surprised if he took the whole damn building down. I doubt he'd care.

"You're *mine*, Ms. Carson. You know that."

"Yes," I gasp. "Yes."

"Tell me."

"I'm yours… *ahh*!"

I cling to his broad shoulders as the orgasm tears through my body. He releases himself inside me at the exact same moment, our bodies fusing together in a whole new way, unleashing delicious new sensations.

Coming down from the high is both sobering and completely terrifying.

While I grip the textured walls to hold myself up, he zips himself up and slips my torn panties into the pocket of his pants. "A little memento," he murmurs to himself.

I'm pretty sure my hair's a hot mess, as is the rest of me. But before I can retreat to the ladies' room to compose myself and process what just happened, I hear a sob from the open door of the Onyx Ballroom.

"I cannot fucking *believe* this!"

I jolt with shock when I realize that Jessica Allens is standing a few feet away from us, her eyes wide with hurt, her mouth curled in anger.

How long has she been standing there?

"You—you *bastard*!" she turns her fury on Ruslan. "Everyone in there heard the two of you rutting out here like animals!"

I cringe, embarrassment flooding through me.

"Good."

My jaw drops as I turn to Ruslan. Did he just say "*good*"?

Apparently, that's exactly what he said, if the way Jessica's jaw hits the floor is anything to go by. "Y-you're not even going to *apologize*?" she screeches.

Ruslan takes a small, possessive half-step towards me. "I was always honest with you, Jessica. Our arrangement was simple and we both got something out of it. I got a plus-one I wasn't required to fuck. And you got the reputational boost of being seen with Ruslan Oryolov. It's not my fault you decided you wanted more."

I cringe internally. *It's not my fault you decided you wanted more.* That one hits a little close to home.

Jessica turns her blazing eyes on me. "You may think you're special, but you're just his latest whore." She gestures towards the door of the Onyx Room. "And now, the whole world knows it, too. At least *I* never compromised my dignity."

Ruslan's expression turns ice-cold. "Not for lack of trying."

Jessica rears back as though she's been slapped. "I can't believe I ever wasted my time on you. You're just a... a—"

The second set of doors to the Onyx Room open and Hiram Allens exits with his plus-one and his bodyguards.

I wonder if it's possible for me to blend into the wallpaper.

"Jessica!" her father snarls. "Don't waste your time on that bastard. Let's go."

Jessica sniffs in Ruslan's direction, throws me a withering glare, and then storms off to join her father. I've never been very clued in to all the social circles that Ruslan runs with. But I know enough to know that Hiram Allens is a very powerful man with very powerful connections.

The moment they disappear into the elevators, I turn to Ruslan. "Oh, God—I'm so sorry."

He looks amused. "Why are you apologizing? I'm the one who followed you out here and fucked you against that wall."

He's not wrong. Add that to the list of inexplicable decisions I've made tonight. I'm convinced that I'm slowly blending into my dress at this point.

"And—" Ruslan walks right up to me until his lips tickle my ear— "I don't regret it."

I stare at him in disbelief. "How can you say that? You just pissed off Hiram Allens! Even *I* know that man controls half of New York."

I can't detect even a modicum of panic in Ruslan's unwavering gaze. "You know who controls the other half of New York?" His eyes gleam. "*I* do."

He moves in and I'm forced to take a step back. He keeps going until my back is flush against the wall, right back in the position we started in. Pretty sure I've left indents in the wallpaper with my nails.

"Ruslan—"

"You've been introduced to only *one* side of my life, Emma. You know the businessman, the CEO. What you don't know is the *other* part of my life. The dangerous part."

My palms are sweating now. All those rumors floating around about mob ties, cartels, and illegal underground dealings start floating to the forefront of my mind. "H-how dangerous?"

"Dangerous enough that bringing you as my date to an event like this would have been foolish."

My mouth pops open. "*That's* why you chose Jessica?"

He nods, running a delicate finger along my bottom lip. "I don't give a shit about Jessica Allens. She's merely a prop. But *you*—you are different."

I'm trying to resist his honeyed eyes, his hypnotizing words. But there's a swoon on the horizon that's every bit as dangerous as Ruslan is saying he is. I'm falling in all the wrong ways. The smart thing to do would be to tell him to leave me alone forever. I open my mouth to do exactly that. What comes out instead is:

"How am I different?"

"I wanted to hide you before. For your own good. But now… fuck that. You're different because you're *mine*." His breath is sweet in my face. "And since you're *mine,* you will never again accept a dance with any man. Especially not *that* man."

My eyebrows pull together as I try to remember anything beyond the last couple minutes. "Are you talking about the blonde guy I danced with?"

"His name is Adrik Makarov."

From the bite in his voice, I can tell there's no love lost there. "What is he, your mortal enemy or something?"

I'm mostly kidding but Ruslan doesn't crack a smile. "I wouldn't call him my *mortal* enemy. But 'enemy' is pretty damn close. Especially after tonight."

"I am beyond confused right now. Who is he?"

He sighs and strokes his chin, eyes going hazy with memory. "Way back when, Adrik and I used to be friends. Things changed when I took over the family business. We went from friends to rivals and there have been moments over the years when that rivalry has gotten out of hand. He was here tonight to piss me off."

I run my fingers along his jaw. "It seems like he succeeded."

"Fuck him." Ruslan shakes his head angrily. "The next time he bothers you, come straight to me. Promise me that."

I nod because what other choice do I have? I knew from the start that getting involved with Ruslan meant playing dangerous games. Now that he's showing me just *how* dangerous, I can either try to figure it out on my own…

Or I can choose to trust him.

"I'd like a promise of my own," I blurt suddenly. He raises an eyebrow and waits for me to elaborate. "I understand why I couldn't be your date tonight. I get why you brought Jessica. But… I still don't like it. I'm not sure I can handle another night like this one."

Both his eyebrows lift this time and I hold my breath. What I'm asking for isn't exactly part of our contract. In fact, I'm pretty sure most of this conversation breaks at least one of his intractable rules.

"Okay."

My eyes go wide. "Okay?"

Ruslan nods. "No more superficial plus-ones. No more fake dates with other women. Just you."

Have sweeter words ever been spoken?

49

EMMA

Updated recap: I'm not gonna be dancing with any other men in the foreseeable future.

And Ruslan won't be taking fake dates to his social events anymore.

That's what I call a successful night.

I can't help doing a little shoulder shimmy in the bathroom mirror. I thought I'd be a total mess when I rushed in, but apart from smudged lipstick and mild sex hair, I don't look that bad. It takes a few minutes to apply a fresh coat of lipstick and comb out the knots in my hair with my fingers. Once that's done, though, I look like the picture of class and elegance.

If you can forget the fact that I'd indulged in some very public sex with my boss while his entire social circle listened on.

Which you can only believe if you believe Jessica Allens.

Which I'm hoping no one does.

Once I've made sure my dress is on properly and nothing is peeping out—going commando and thigh-high slits are not a great combo—I stare at my reflection in the dazzling water-ripple mirrors that take up half the bathroom wall.

I can't miss the glow on my cheeks, the brightness in my eyes. It's hard not to feel like you're walking on air when the man you've been pining for basically claims you as his own.

The feminist in me puts up a half-hearted fight—but the romantic in me is giddy with joy.

Emma and Ruslan sitting in a tree...

I have to stop spending time with Caroline and Reagan. Those two are a bad influence.

I scowl at myself in the mirror with all the seriousness I can muster. I'm a grown ass woman and I need to conduct myself accordingly. To that end, I'm thankful I haven't gone off birth control. Ruslan has been diligent about wearing condoms lately, but he'd definitely forgone the wrapper this time.

Not that I'm complaining.

A startling image pops into my head. One that includes me and Ruslan—and a baby that looks like a mix of both of us.

My ovaries promptly do a backflip.

I push the thought right back out of my head, because it doesn't belong anywhere in this emotional zip code. I'm not even technically *dating* him. Thinking about babies is, at best, laughably premature. At worst, it's a complete fucking nightmare.

I take three deep breaths and head out of the bathroom with my head held high and my big girl pants on, metaphorically speaking.

"Well, well, well…"

I whirl around, taken aback by a nasal voice I'd hoped I'd never have to hear again. "Remmy," I hiss.

The reporter ogles me with a wide grin that makes my whole body pucker up. "Missed me?"

"What the hell are you doing here?"

He's wearing a sad gray suit and a purple bow tie, both of which have seen much better days. His face has, too—I can still see fading marks where Ruslan did God knows what to him. He pushes himself off the wall and walks over to me with a blustery confidence that he certainly didn't have last time we interacted.

"Isn't it obvious? I'm a reporter—and I'm here for a story."

I shake my head. "There's no story here."

"Funny. That's exactly what your boss said the last time we spoke. Right before he beat the shit out of me and drove me across the border in the trunk of his lackey's car."

That does explain the bruises.

"Seems like a pretty dumb move for you to be here at all then, don't you think?"

He shrugs, pulling out a small recording device from his inner jacket pocket. "Sometimes, the risk is worth the reward. It could be for you, too."

"If you think I'm gonna give you an interview, then you're out of your—"

"You're putting those kids in danger by associating with him," he interrupts. "You know that, right?"

Fear rips through me. Not because of what he's said; more because he's mentioned the kids at all. "You stay the *fuck* away from them!"

He holds up his hands. "I don't mean them any harm."

"If Ruslan knows you're here, he'll kill you." My attempts to scare him into leaving don't seem to be working. But the mere thought of him laying his grimy paws on Rae's hair makes me taste bile. "Just… just leave me and my family the hell alone, Remmy. I want nothing to do with you. I'm not gonna give you what you want."

He sneers down his newly crooked nose at me. "Disappointing. But I suppose I shouldn't be surprised that you won't rat out Ruslan Oryolov. Why would you? It's not easy to fuck over the guy you're fucking." I stiffen instantly and his chuckling leer becomes all the more pronounced. "I must say, fucking your secretary is wholly unoriginal. I would have expected more from Ruslan."

Since I'm not about to deny it, I decide to walk away.

"I have a tape!" he blurts.

That has me stopping in my tracks. I slowly pivot on the spot. "What?"

He laughs without blinking—creepy—and holds up the recording device. "Let me take you back to a few minutes ago. You and Ruslan. Moaning and groaning against *that* wall —" He gestures over to the wall Ruslan took me against. "— fucking like rabbits."

A tiny zip of panic unsettles my stomach. But it's gone as soon as it comes. "So if I don't give you dirt on Ruslan, you're gonna make that tape public?"

"You're a smart one."

I squint at the device he's wiggling in my direction. "Wish I could return the compliment." His smile vanishes. "That's an audio recorder, am I right?"

His hand drops. "Yes."

I shrug. "How can you prove it's me on that tape? Without visual evidence, how can you prove it's *Ruslan* on the tape?"

He bares his teeth. "People trust me—"

I scoff. "I think you'll find that you don't have the reach or the reputation that you seem to believe you do. You want to put that tape out there? Go right ahead. Frankly, I don't give a damn."

The last traces of his smug smile disappears completely. He glares at me with wide eyes and flared nostrils. "Wait... wait!"

I walk away without glancing back. But I do give him a parting warning over my shoulder. "I suggest you run, Remmy. Run now. Run fast."

I don't make eye contact with anyone when I enter the Onyx Room and veer straight towards my table. I know I'm the center of attention right now, and perhaps not for the right reasons—but I'm finding it hard to care. The only person whose eyes I *want* on me are Ruslan's.

I have that from the moment I step inside.

And, the moment I sit down, his hand finds its way onto my thigh. That's right where it belongs, too. He smells like me, his usual oaky musk underlined by the faint scent of citrus.

"You took longer than I expected."

I ignore the eagle-eyed gaze I'm getting from Ruslan's uncle and lean towards him. "I was stopped by someone outside the bathroom. Remmy."

A shadow passes across Ruslan's face. He's too composed in public for his jaw to drop or his eyebrows to fly up his forehead, but I know where to look and so I see all the signs of a murderous rage. "Remmy?" he rasps. "You're sure?"

When I nod, Ruslan snaps his fingers to get Kirill's attention. The two of them whisper back and forth for a few seconds. I have no idea the specifics of the order that Ruslan gives Kirill, but I'm willing to bet it's along the lines of "take out the trash; burn it if you have to."

I expect him to take off with Kirill, but Ruslan stays right where he is.

His hand never leaves my knee.

50

RUSLAN

I'm scrolling through the photo gallery on my personal message history with Emma. It's not the first time I've wasted endless minutes doing exactly this. That's why I know there are fourteen pictures from the last few weeks. I've got them all memorized.

Most are of the kids. Bike rides in the park. Ice cream at Connie's Creamery. Reagan's crayon doodle of me, a masterpiece currently housed on Emma's refrigerator. But once in a while, there's a picture that includes Emma, beaming from the corner of a photo almost like an afterthought.

I've been combing through this gallery a little too often lately. But that's only because an idea entered my head a few days ago and now, it won't budge.

"Brady Sanchez's team reached out. He wants a meeting with you to discuss the contract for his new building."

"Hm."

"I checked with Emma. You have some time next week to schedule a meeting."

"Hm."

I flick to a particularly cute picture of all three kids together. Josh is sitting cross-legged on the grass with Reagan on his lap and Caroline kneeling behind him with her arms around his neck. He's smiling for once. I see the faintest traces of new muscle filling out the sleeve of his t-shirt. He's been working hard in the gym during our sessions together. The other day, one of his punches jostled some dust loose from the ceiling and I think he still hasn't stopped grinning about it.

Kirill clears his throat. "Drafting the next great American novel?"

Scowling at him, I put my phone away. "Just going over the trial results that Sergey sent me."

Kirill cocks an eyebrow. "Bro—you're sitting in front of reflective glass. You were looking at pictures of those kids."

Fuck. It's bad enough knowing you have a problem. It's so much worse when you're called out.

I leave the chair by the window and move to the sofa. This apartment used to be my bachelor pad. It's decked out with a game room, a theater, and a gym. Kirill usually crashes here when he's too lazy to trek downtown to his own apartment. It's also become our go-to hangout spot when we're looking to unwind, away from people and loud music and sleazy fucking reporters with long lens cameras.

"This thing with you and Emma… How serious is it?"

I clench my jaw. "The contract still stands. That part hasn't changed. It's just more... exclusive now."

"A contracted girlfriend."

"She's not my girlfriend," I snap.

Kirill smirks. "She's your *something*. Why else would you spend so much time with her and those kids when you don't have to?"

He's got a point. But it'll take a damn army to make me admit that. "Because I had an idea recently and, the more I think about it, the less crazy it seems."

Kirill sits up a little straighter. "Intriguing. What's this idea?'"

Once you say it out loud, there's no going back...

"Well?" he presses. "You gonna keep me in suspense or what?"

"I was thinking about adding an addendum to the contract."

His eyebrows rise. "Scheduled sex four times a week instead of two?" he asks. "Doggystyle *and* missionary required in every session?" His chuckle dies when he sees the look on my face. He clears his throat. "Okay... so this is a *serious* addendum?"

"I don't say this often but Vadim's right: I *do* need to start thinking about heirs."

Kirill nearly sprays my designer sofa with a mouthful of gin. He sets the glass back on the liquor cart and slides up to the furthest edge of his seat.

"Brother, are you saying what I think you're saying?"

"She's a good mother. And I can work with her."

"By 'work' with her, do you mean raise children with her? Because that and what she does now are two *very* different jobs."

"I'm not interested in doing things traditionally—"

"Thanks for clarifying; I wasn't aware."

"—so this is the perfect solution."

Kirill frowns. "I think *'perfect'* is the wrong word."

I'm jonesing for another drink but I fight the urge. "I know it's crazy—"

"A *baby* clause?" he murmurs, dumbfounded. "Or would it be a surrogacy clause?"

"Surrogacy implies she would have no connection to the child after she pushes it out. She's a good mother, Kirill. I've seen her in action."

"So what you're suggesting is an additional clause to be engineered into the existing contract that involves you having a baby with your secretary and then raising the child together."

"You can ax the tone," I snap. "I know how it sounds."

Kirill falls back into his seat. "It's fucking *madness*. Especially for you."

"Why especially for me?"

"You've never wanted a child! You've never really thought about it."

I clench the arm of the sofa. "Maybe that's because I never met a woman I could see being the mother of my child. With Emma, it's... different."

He rests his chin on his fist. "So then why keep the contract at all?"

"Because I'm not interested in romance. I don't want marriage. I'm not saying I want a family; what I want is an *heir,* specifically. So far, my arrangement with Emma has gone smoothly. Why shouldn't this be any different?"

"Oh, I don't know—maybe because it involves the creation of a *human being!*"

I expected Kirill to be surprised. But his blatant shock is pissing me off. "If I do this, it'll shut everyone up once and for all. Once I have an heir, I don't ever have to listen to Vadim's nagging again."

"At least until you give the Oryolov Bratva an heir and a spare."

"Let's start with one baby first, shall we?"

"You're serious about this." Kirill's eyes go wide and he whistles softly. "She'll have no idea what she's getting into, Ruslan. She doesn't know everything. She doesn't know who you really are."

He's got me there.

But like the rest of my second's inconvenient observations, I don't tell him that.

"I don't plan on tricking her into anything. She will have all the facts before I put a new contract in front of her."

I'm a thousand percent certain that Kirill is underestimating her. All he sees is a shy woman who blushes every time anyone looks at her sideways. But I see more than that. I see the steel behind the self-consciousness.

She walked back into the gala ballroom the other night with her head held high. I'm sure she heard the whispers, saw the curious eyes following her through the rest of the evening, but she never once buckled under the weight. She smiled, she made conversation, she dazzled the room despite the scrutiny she was under.

She may not have been born to this world—but there's a chance she's made for it.

Despite that, there's nothing superficial about her. Her charm ripples with sincerity, which is exactly what makes her so irresistible. Not that any man dared look her way after she returned to the ballroom. I'd gotten my message through loud and clear. Hell, I may as well have tattooed *Ruslan Oryolov* right on her skin. Come to think of it, the caveman in me likes that idea.

Just not as much as the idea of Emma's belly growing bigger and bigger with my child.

"Have you thought this through?" Kirill asks.

I blink myself back to reality. "She's the kind of woman I want raising my children. End of story."

"But is she the kind of woman you want to tie yourself to for the *rest* of your life? Because that's what having a baby will do, whether you like it or not." Kirill meets my eyes. "I can see you're set on this. Just promise me one thing: take some more time. Really think about it. Once you bring this up with her, there'll be no going back."

It's annoying how many good points he's making tonight.

"Very well," I acquiesce. "I'll give it a little more time."

Kirill's right; it's the smart thing to do. A necessary step to ensure I'm not making a huge mistake.

But the caveman in me doesn't like waiting at all.

51

RUSLAN

It's taken me seven days of brooding, but I'm finally sure.

I don't want a wife—not after I saw what losing one did to my father. But I do need an heir.

And Emma is the perfect solution.

There's only one problem: how do I package this in a way that will prevent her from slapping me and walking out on our entire agreement?

She's sitting on the bed right now, balancing her wine glass in one hand while she admires the view. The first few buttons on her white silk blouse are undone, giving me a bird's-eye view of her sexy black bra. Her breasts are practically spilling out of them.

There's a nagging worry in the back of my head. One that's warning me that this night might be our last night together. If Emma finds my proposition insulting, there's nothing I can do to stop her from shredding our contract and leaving.

That's the last thing I want.

"You're deep in thought tonight," she remarks. She puts her wine glass down and leans back on the bed with her elbows.

I walk over, my eyes never leaving hers. "I'd rather be deep in you."

"Cringe!" she laughs. Then her smile turns into something sly and seductive. "Well? What are you waiting for?"

She sits up and starts unbuckling my pants. She strips me down, peeling off each layer until I'm standing naked in front of her. She swallows hard, her hands running over my abs. I grab her wrist and pull her to her feet, switching places with her.

She stands between my legs like the sultry, obedient goddess she is and waits patiently while I undress her. I go slow. Take my time, enjoying the rustle of fabric over her skin as it's bared to me inch by delicious inch. I twist her around before I remove her skirt and then watch with my breath caught in my chest as I pull the zipper down one tooth at a time.

When she's naked, I drop my lips to her ass cheek and give it a little bite. She yelps but I hold her in place and press my lips against the same spot to smooth away the pain. She shivers, her eyes finding mine over her shoulder. I wrap an arm around her waist and pull her down onto the bed with me. When she tries to turn around, I stop her.

"No," I growl. "You're going to ride me like this."

I stare at her perfect ass, adjusting her so that her pussy is poised over my cock. She's already wet but I tease her with my fingers from behind until she's dripping. It's a perfect fucking view—that pink, perfect pussy framed by that gorgeous ass of hers, her knees planted on either side of my hips, the long, smooth expanse of her back glowing in the moonlight through the window.

When my fingers are coated in her juices, I grab her hips and guide her down onto my cock. She cries out, wriggling against my girth. I slap her ass hard.

"Take it slow, baby," I command. "Ride me."

Her ass bobs up and down, back arching while she moans. If it weren't for my fear that this might be our last night together, I could come right now. Instead, I grab her hair and pull it back until she's forced to change her rhythm, thrusting her hips back and forth. She chases down her orgasm and when she explodes on my cock, her ass jiggles with the strength of her tremors.

She dips forward as I pull out of her but I'm not interested in giving her a moment to catch her breath. I flip her onto her back, haul myself on top, and bury my face between her legs.

"*Ruslan!*" she cries as her hand lands on my head.

I push my tongue into her pussy and drag it up until I find her clit. Then I bear down, circling and sucking until she's screaming and slamming her fists against the bed.

"Fuck, yes, yes… *ahh,* Ruslan… I can't… *fuck…!*"

I don't let up until she's coming, her body tightening with every swirl of my tongue. By the time I wipe the wetness from my mouth, her eyes are fluttering closed, her breasts heaving up and down, her skin flushed and peppered with goosebumps.

Only when I mount her do her eyes flare open. There's a dreamy look in them when she smiles at me. She brushes the back of her hand against my jaw. "You're so handsome…"

I push her legs apart with my knee, my cock sliding up and down her dripping pussy. She shudders. "Ruslan…"

"Yes, baby?"

Her eyelashes flutter. "I don't think I can handle another orgasm."

"Hm…" I run my lips over her jaw, along her neck and towards her ear. "I'm afraid you don't have a choice."

I bite down on her lobe as I push inside her again. Her mouth pops open into a perfect O. She's probably not gonna be able to walk tomorrow.

Good. She can sit down and think about my proposition.

Either way, I want her body sore and aching for days after this night. I want to leave my imprint on her body; I want to leave my scent on her skin. I want to show her exactly what she's giving up if she chooses to walk away from this.

I watch her tits bounce as I pump into her wildly. "Who do you belong to?" I demand through gritted teeth.

She's so busy moaning and screaming that she doesn't answer. So I repeat myself, louder this time.

"I'm not gonna stop until I hear you say it. *Who* do you belong to?"

Her eyes find mine. She looks wild, completely undone. Hair flying untamed, eyes bright with lust, cheeks flush with fire. "*You,*" she gasps. "Only you."

"Good girl," I growl, increasing the speed and strength of my thrusts as reward.

Her screams spur me on faster and faster. I'm not sure how, but somewhere between her orgasm and mine, I find our hands interlinked, fingers entwined together, gripping tight. I'm balls-deep inside of her—and yet holding hands is a million times more intimate. It reminds of the first night we did this, when I kissed her while we fucked. There's a line being crossed. One I never saw coming, but I'm helpless to stop myself from soaring right across it.

When I finish coming, I collapse, careful not to put all my weight on top of her.

"Good Lord," Emma gasps. "That was… intense."

She's right. It *was* intense.

But it only makes me greedy for more.

"This ice cream is straight-up *sinful.*"

She's wearing one of my t-shirts, her legs stretched across the sofa towards me. I'm tempted to take her feet and plop them on my lap, but like the hand-holding when we were having sex, the consequences of a gesture like that is giving me pause.

It's not that I don't want to do it.

It's that I know that I already let my inner beast out of the cage at the gala and it ended up in a fucking headache. Fuck knows what kind of consequences it would bring if I unhooked it from its leash again.

"Okay!" Emma slams the lid back on the ice cream container and hands it to me. "Take it away or else I won't stop."

After the first three orgasms I'd given her, we took a half-hour break. Then I'd fucked her mouth before carrying her into the kitchen to spread her out on the marble counter. We ended up in the living room where, two orgasms later, she informed me that she was in danger of fainting if she didn't get some sugar in her body immediately.

Strangely, despite the workout I've just had, I'm not hungry at all. The only thing I'm craving is her.

Still.

"I should get going—"

"No."

She falls back against the arm of the sofa. "No?"

"There's something I want to discuss with you before you leave."

One eyebrow drifts upward. "Okay. Discuss away."

"But before I tell you what's on my mind, it's important that you know exactly who I am. And what I do."

She nods slowly, hesitantly. "Should I be nervous?"

"I'd just be attentive."

She tries to return the smile but doesn't quite manage. "Go on."

"Bane Corp. was founded by my grandfather almost seventy years ago. It was a tiny security company that he was hoping would be the perfect façade to hide what the family *really* did. What we still do."

She gulps, pulling her legs up to her chest and wrapping her arms around them. "Oh my God… the rumors are true then?"

I shrug. "Depends on which rumor you're talking about."

"The ones that claim you're somehow tied to the mafia."

"Yes and no. Our roots are Russian. We aren't mafia; we're Bratva. We don't have dons; we have *pahkans.* And I'm not 'tied to the Bratva'; I *am* the Bratva."

She stares back at me. The color has drained from her face and all breathing has come to a screeching halt.

I give her a moment. It's the kind of revelation that requires a little processing time.

"B-Bratva…" she repeats as if she's trying the word on for size. "Wow, that's really… something."

I snort. "That's all you have to say?"

She throws her hands up. "Well, I'm not sure what the correct response is when the guy you're sleeping with tells you he's a mafia don!"

"Bratva *pahkan.*"

She takes a deep breath and then starts chewing on the inside of her cheek. The last time she did that also happened to be the first night we kicked off the contract. I'm hoping this isn't a book-end sort of situation.

"I guess… it's not a *huge* shock," she admits. "Like I said, there were rumors. I didn't really pay them all that much attention. Now, I wish I had."

"I *am* a dangerous man, Emma. I won't deny it." I make sure to look her in the eye. "But I just want you to know that I'm not dangerous to *you.* Or your family."

She holds my gaze and nods. "I think I already know that." Her voice is barely above a whisper.

There it is—that burgeoning sense of hope. That naive little voice saying, *This could work...*

"Thank you for telling me," she says.

"I had to tell you. I wanted you to have all the information before you made your decision."

The anxiety is back. I can tell from the new lines on her forehead. "What decision?"

I decide to just tear off the bandage. "I want to add an addendum to our contract."

She stiffens. "What kind of addendum?"

"Given my role as *pahkan*, I'm required to ensure the continuity of the Oryolov name." She doesn't really move, but her eyebrows twitch. She looks confused. *Rip off the fucking bandage, you coward.* "I want to add a baby clause to our contract."

"I'm sorry—did you just say '*baby* clause'?" Her mouth drops. She and Josh definitely have that in common, that same *you-have-got-to-be-fucking-kidding me* face. "Y-you... you want me to have your baby?"

"As I said, I need an heir. And since our contract has worked well so far, I figured I'd put it to you and see where you stand. Just so you know, if you agree to this, I will make sure you and the baby are well provided for. That goes for the kids, too. Josh, Reagan, and Caroline will want for nothing as long as they live. I'll take care of their education, their medical bills, their clothes and shoes and whatever else." She's blinking rapidly, her eyes darting over my face again and again. I wonder if she's even getting half of what I'm throwing at her. But since this might be my only chance to convince her, I keep going. "In addition, I will set you up in a new place. Somewhere large enough that every child has a room of their own. Somewhere with space for them to run. I will also give you an additional monthly stipend until the baby turns eighteen to use as you see fit. It will not be an insignificant amount."

She exhales sharply. "That is… a lot to process."

"You don't have to give me an answer now. Take some time and think about it."

She meets my gaze for a fleeting moment. "And what if I say no?"

I try not to let my body betray me. So I force myself to remain relaxed, unbothered, even though the caveman in my chest is beating a drum and howling like a fucking lunatic. "Our original contract will still stand whether you accept this new clause or not."

She nods.

"But—" That causes her to flinch, her eyes colliding once again with mine. "—should you decide you want out of the contract altogether, I will release you with the promised severance package. I will even help you get another job."

Her eyebrows knit together and her mouth comes down at the corners. She doesn't seem wild about the fact that I'm willing, at least on the surface, to let her go so easily.

Hope kindles in my gut.

Maybe that can work in my favor.

Maybe there's a way for me to get *everything* I want.

52

EMMA

A week has passed since the offer that rocked my world on its axis. I'm still pondering. Still dreaming. Still waking up breathless.

I need a distraction. But riding the elevator up towards Ruslan's penthouse feels more like a recipe for disaster. I'm in no fit state to meet him. I'm in no fit state to meet *anyone.*

Today of all days...

It's the whole entire reason I called in sick to work today. Of course I'd forgotten that we had a rendezvous scheduled for this evening and, instead of canceling like I should have, I decided to make use of the fact that Amelia was babysitting tonight.

So here I am, wearing my first-date dress.

Because the truth is, despite my mental state right now—I *want* to see him.

Even after he proposed the baby clause addendum to our contract. Because at this rate, what's another clause, huh? What's another contract?

This one just so happens to include a *child*. One that would be half his and half mine. I wonder if the fact that I'm here at all means that I've already made my decision.

No. Stop it. You're too emotional today.

If there's one thing that Sienna had taught me, it was that you never make big decisions when you are riding too high or too low.

I find Ruslan in the living room in all his shirtless glory. He's got a wineglass in one hand and a book in the other. As distractions go, he's a pretty good one.

"Whatcha reading?" I ask. He snaps the book shut and holds the cover up for me to see. "Alexander Pushkin, huh? Is he any good?"

Ruslan chuckles. "Only one of the greatest poets to have ever lived."

I smile as I sit down on the couch next to him. "I didn't realize you were into poetry."

"I like beautiful things." He sets his wine aside. "How are you feeling, *kiska*?"

"You don't have to worry about catching anything from me, if that's what you're asking."

He arches one eyebrow at my outburst of feistiness. "I'm asking how *you* are feeling?"

"Fine," I say without meeting his eyes. "I'm fine."

He accepts that wordlessly. "Then come here."

I hike my dress up and slide onto his lap, straddling him like always, but the usual needy throbbing that accompanies any kind of proximity to Ruslan is glaringly absent today. I swallow the lump in my throat and place my hands on his shoulders.

Distraction, distraction, distraction...

I lean in and kiss him, my tongue circling his, waiting for the pool of desire to knock me off my feet like it always does. But I'm too aware of everything. I feel clumsy and self-conscious. I feel the lump in my throat settle over my chest. And it hits me: I don't need sex; I need to cry.

And just like that, a giant, ugly, uncontrollable sob escapes out of my mouth—and lands on his.

He pulls back, startled. "Emma?"

Oh fuck, oh fuck, oh fuck...

"Are you crying?"

"N-n-n-no."

"What happened?"

"Oh God," I whisper through my tears. "I'm so s-sorry."

I sure know how to spice up sexy time.

"Did I hurt you?" The fact that he even asks makes me sob harder. "Emma, what's wrong?"

I just shake my head, unable to speak. I know that, if I try, everything will just come out in a warbled mess of unintelligible sounds. And I've already embarrassed myself plenty for one night.

I yelp, taken aback when Ruslan gathers me in his arms and gets to his feet. I cling to him as he walks me into the master bathroom and sits me down on the chaise lounge that sits opposite the gigantic drop-in tub.

As he starts filling the tub with water, I try to compose myself. That turns out to be a mistake in its own right; I just end up sobbing harder. I catch the scent of rosehips and hibiscus and, when I look towards the tub, I see a gentle pink foam bubbling on the surface of the water. Ruslan extends his hand out to me and I slip my fingers through his without even thinking about it.

He says there can't be any romance here, but this feels like love I can fall back on when I'm not even sure I can stand upright on my own two feet anymore. I'm so beyond confused by Ruslan Oryolov. In the morning, I know I'll look back on this and be confused even further.

But for now, for tonight…

I need him.

He pulls me to my feet and starts undressing me. I stand there, biting my lip, trying to get my game face on. But once we're in the tub—him at my back and me staring at the pretty little foam bubbles that caress my skin—he doesn't make a move.

He keeps his hands thrown over each side of the tub, while I lie nestled between his legs, my bare back pressed against his naked chest. By the time I stop crying, the foam has dissipated somewhat and the silence has gone on so long that it's become comfortable.

When I finally break it, my voice comes out all croaky. "Today is… Sienna's birthday. Or… it would have been."

His right arm leaves the edge of the tub and wraps around my waist.

I rest the back of my head against his shoulder. "I don't know why this day hit me so hard this time around." I sigh. "I guess it was a few things. I came home late last night expecting to find the kids asleep. Amelia had gone home an hour earlier and Ben was supposed to be with the kids…"

"He wasn't?" There's a tiny little snap in Ruslan's voice.

"No, no, he was. He just happened to have thrown up on the living room floor and passed out on the sofa."

Ruslan's arm tightens around my waist.

"I walked in to find Josh on his hands and knees, cleaning it up. His eyes were swollen, so I knew he'd been crying. I thought the kids would be okay with Ben for that hour. It was just *one* hour." Thankfully, I'm all cried out. And I'm finding that saying all this out loud is really helping. "I helped him clean up but he barely said a word the whole time. He was just so… out of it. Even when I put him to bed, it was like he was looking *through* me." I shiver with the weight of my failure. "I wanted to make Sienna *proud*. I wanted to be the best stand-in mother I could be for her kids. But…" My breath hitches up but I force myself to say it, the thing I've suspected for quite some time now but never dared utter aloud. "… I don't think I'm a very good mother."

It would have been the *only* gift she'd have wanted today. And I couldn't even give her that.

"Emma. You *are* a good mother."

I flinch. "You're just saying that."

"I never 'just say' anything."

That almost makes me smile. "Well, you wouldn't say it if you knew what goes on in my head sometimes."

"Try me."

I mean, I'd just admitted that I'm not a good mother. Why not back it up with some solid proof, huh? I've opened Pandora's box, so why not let the secrets fly?

Also—those arms of his are making me feel like I can say anything and he'll hold me together through it all.

"Sometimes, I think about accepting my parents' offer to help."

"And that's a bad thing because their offer comes with strings?"

"Exactly."

"Which are?"

I swallow my hesitation. "They're willing to provide for the kids, but only if I grant them custody first."

Ruslan gets very still all of a sudden. "And you don't want to lose them?"

"It's not that. I mean, of course I'd hate to lose them. I love those kids with every fiber of my being. But if they were going to be well-looked after, provided for and loved, then I would give my parents free rein. But Barrett and Beatrice's idea of raising children involves fancy private boarding schools, foreign nannies, and mandatory attendance at horrible social events. Sienna fought so hard so that the two of us didn't have to endure that life forever. She wouldn't want her kids to have to go through the same thing. If she knew I was even considering it, she'd be so disappointed in me."

Suddenly, I feel air flood my back as Ruslan pushes me off him. He twists me around so that we're face to face.

"Emma." His voice is gentler than I've ever heard it before. "You've considered it—but you haven't done it."

Sniffing back my tears, I nod. "I know I can't give them everything, but at least now, they have each other. They have *me*."

"Trust me, Emma: money isn't everything. You didn't have to uproot your life for those kids. You didn't have to take care of their father, either. You don't *have* to put up with Ben and his demons—but you do all that anyway. Because you don't want those kids losing their father as well." My eyes connect with his and now, I can't look away. "You have made every possible sacrifice for those children. You'd do anything for them and they know that. If that's not a good mother, I don't know what is. *That's* why I wanted to add a baby clause into our contract. Because I want my child to have the comfort and benefit of your kindness, your love, your patience."

My eyes go wide as he speaks. *Am I really hearing this?* It almost feels like I'm dreaming.

"I could easily hire a surrogate to carry a child for me. But that requires raising a child on my own and I don't have the inclination or the skill set to do it alone. I want my child to have a real mother, a *good* mother. And I happen to believe that you are a great one."

Those scorching amber eyes of his are softer tonight, buoyed by a tenderness that I've never seen in him before.

"I… I assumed you picked me because I was close and… and convenient."

He shakes his head, his jaw clenching firmly. "I chose you for *you*, Emma Carson. For your character, your compassion, your capacity to love. I chose you because there's no one else in this whole fucking world I can see myself raising a child with."

I breathe out slowly, captivated by his words, by the look in his eyes.

And somehow, that changes *everything*.

53

RUSLAN

This is the first time she's let me in.

And instead of being wary, like I probably should be, I just feel grateful. I'm glad she's finally opening up to me. I'm glad she's pulling down her walls and letting me see inside.

Even though all it does is make me greedy for more.

"I'm sorry—I just threw up all over you. Emotionally speaking."

She blushes hard and the need to kiss her is so bad that I don't bother denying myself. Her lips shiver against mine, soft and feather-light.

"I just… I don't really have anyone I can talk to," she admits when I pull away. "My parents are barely human, my best friend has her own shit to deal with, and my sister died on me…" Her eyes flutter up. "I really appreciate you listening to all my drama. But please feel free to tell me to shut up at any time."

"You're allowed to grieve your sister. You're allowed to miss her. You're even allowed to be angry with her."

Her eyebrows rise a notch. "How did you—"

"Because I've been there. I've grieved my own losses. I still am. Grief isn't something that just goes away on its own. It doesn't come with an expiration date."

She opens her mouth, then shuts it. I can understand her hesitation. I haven't exactly encouraged these kinds of vulnerable conversations in the history of our relationship. But now that we're here, it doesn't feel quite as threatening as I would've guessed.

"It's okay. You can ask me."

Her gaze softens. "Who did you lose?"

When was the last time I *chose* to talk about them? When was the last time I willingly thought about them? Their memories live in a dark, locked box in my heart and that's where I thought they'd always stay. But as soon as Emma asks the question, the lid of that box goes flying open and I'm talking before I even realize it.

"My mother and my brother."

"Both?" she gasps.

"At the same time. Car accident."

She shivers from head to toe. "No…" When she grabs my hand, warm droplets of soapy water splash onto my face. "That's how I lost Sienna."

I happen to know exactly how her sister died. It was all in the file that Kirill handed me months ago when I requested an in-depth background check on Emma. But I still want *her* to tell me. Facts on a sheet of paper—*single-car collision, one death, young female pedestrian*—don't do it justice.

"You don't have to tell me if you don't want to," I rasp.

Emotions are warring on her face. The things that are hard to say fighting against the things that need to be said. Her lips move without making sound for a while.

"She was on a pedestrian crossing and... and..." Her eyelids close and she grips my hand a little tighter. When her eyes open again, they're full of tears. "And there was a truck. It was orange, I remember that. An orange pick-up truck barreling around the corner towards us." A tear glides down her cheek. "I heard the screech of tires and I froze. And Sienna, sh-she pushed me out of the way." Her fingers are trembling. "She joked once that, when she said she'd die for me, she didn't mean it literally. But she *did*. She literally died to save me."

"Emma." She lifts her eyes to mine. "You and I have a lot in common."

"What do you mean?"

"The car accident my mother and brother were involved in... *I* was the one who was supposed to be driving. It should have been me in the driver's seat of the car that day. Not Leonid."

She slides a little closer to me, her hand falling against the curve of my neck. "You blame yourself?"

"Don't you?"

She bites her bottom lip. "Every single day."

"Like I said—we have a lot in common."

She laughs miserably. "I wish it had been something fun. Like being double-jointed or matching birthmarks or something." Her hand never leaves my neck. The water is getting cold at this point and the soap suds are almost gone, but she doesn't seem to notice. "I'm sorry it's this instead," she whispers. "But I'm glad you told me."

The craziest thing isn't that I did in fact tell her, although that's insane in its own right. It's that telling her felt *good.* Cathartic. Healing.

"Is that how you inherited the, um… family business or whatever you call it."

I nod. "I was seventeen at the time. Far too young to take control of either Bane or the Bratva. I just assumed that, after my father, my uncle Vadim would take over. It made sense. He was the one who held the whole operation together after the accident. But in the end, my father chose me. To this day, I still don't know why."

The furrow between her brows deepens. "Your dad seems… quiet."

"The accident destroyed him. He might as well have died in that car with my mother and Leonid."

"Sometimes, I think the same thing about Ben," Emma confesses. "That stupid orange truck killed everything human about him, too. I suppose it's the price you pay for loving someone that deeply."

The bath salts feel like they're burning my skin all of a sudden. But it's got nothing to do with the water; it's got everything to do with Emma's words.

It's the price you pay for loving someone that deeply.

It's a price I swore to myself that I would never pay.

"Ruslan?" Her voice pierces through a dozen different thoughts raging around inside my head. Those beautiful aqua eyes are deep with emotion. Emotion she's carrying for both of us now. Her loss as well as mine.

I want her.

I want her more than I've ever wanted any other woman in my life.

And while that terrifies me, it terrifies me less than letting her go. Because now that I've had a taste of Emma—her beauty, her playfulness, her compassion, her vulnerability—I know that I want to be the one to take care of her. I want to be the one to give her what she needs. I want to be her savior and her protector.

It's a heady feeling. Strange and unfamiliar. I've never wanted to be *responsible* for someone like this before.

Is this what Fyodor felt when he first met Mama?

"Hey." Emma cups my face and pulls herself into the circle of my arms. "Come back to me."

I focus on her face—that delicate button nose, the swell of her cheeks, those luscious lips—and I feel a sense of calm that I haven't felt since before Leonid died. That was the last time I was blanketed in any kind of comfort, any sense of security.

And since the lines are blurring slowly, I decide to make them clear.

This is not love.

It can't be.

"What happened to my father… I never want to lose myself that way, Emma. I can't afford to."

She gulps. "I understand."

I'm not so sure she does, so I hold her a little tighter and continue. "I can't give myself to you completely. Whatever this is between us—you will only get parts."

I'm aware of how selfish the offer is. It's wholly one-sided. And yet she doesn't scowl or scoff. She runs her fingers along my jaw, her eyes trailing along after them.

"I'll take any piece of you I can get, Ruslan."

When she kisses me, my entire body curls around her. The water is cold but our bodies heat it right back up. She's the one who straddles me, grinding herself right against my cock. It takes only seconds before I'm hard and desperate to bury myself inside her.

I'm not sure that's what she wants, though. At least not until her hand curls around my length and squeezes gently. I raise her hips and pull her down on it. She whimpers, her back arching away from me so that I have a full view of her gorgeous breasts. I knead them while she rides me slowly, waves lapping at her thighs. The sex is slow today. It's considerate and passionate, each moment punctuated by everything we've just shared with each other. All the little parts of ourselves we have allowed the other to see.

I kiss her breasts, her neck, her lips. I run my hands over her slick body, losing myself in her beauty, and when we come, we come together.

We've had sex so many different times, in so many different ways. But this time stands out. This time feels different.

Everything feels different.

54

EMMA

"Josh?

The apartment is eerily quiet.

"Rae? Caro?"

Amelia had a last-minute emergency come up so she couldn't be here today for the evening shift. I'd called Ben while I was at work and begged him to take care of the kids. *Sober.* I stressed on that stipulation until he told me to "stop fucking nagging."

Once he agreed, I spent the remaining two hours of my workday sweating through my green blouse.

I hate leaving Ben alone with the kids. But some days, it's unavoidable.

"Guys?"

The moment I hear the *pitter-patter* of little feet, I breathe a sigh of relief. Then Caroline and Reagan round the corner at Mach 10, slamming into me like blond bullets. Their giggles are strangely muted, though, and when Reagan lets out a panicked little squeal when I try to tickle her under the arms, Caroline slaps a finger over her mouth and stares at her sister with wide, reproachful eyes.

I plop down on the arm of the sofa. "Guys, what's wrong? Why are you being so quiet?"

"'Cause Daddy's sweeping," Reagan whispers in her baby voice.

"*Sleeping*," Caroline corrects haughtily. "Daddy's sleeping and he told us that if we made any noise, he'd drag us into his room by our ears and beat our butts until they were black and blue."

Reagan looks at me with her bottom lip sticking out. "I don't want my bottom to be black and blue, Auntie Em!"

"He really said that to you?"

Both girls nod in unison. My lip curls up into a furious sneer. *I'd like to beat their father until he's black and blue.*

"Where's Josh?" I say instead in as controlled a tone as I can muster.

"He's making dinner. We're having pasta with cut-up sausages!" Reagan whoops. That earns her another glare from Caroline. Then the girls scurry into the kitchen, gesturing for me to follow them.

I find Josh at the stove, prepping the pasta. "Josh?" I ask as we approach. "You okay?"

The way his shoulders stiffen and the fact that it takes him a moment to turn around tells me that he's very far from okay.

"Girls, why don't you go wash up and get ready for dinner?" I suggest. The moment they're gone, I walk over to Josh. "What happened?"

He's not meeting my eye. He just keeps stirring the pasta unnecessarily. I clamp a hand down on his wrist, forcing him to stop.

"Josh, honey, talk to me."

"Nothing *happened.* It's just the same old shit as always." As soon as the uncharacteristic curse flies out of his mouth, he flinches and his cheeks flood with red shame. "I-I'm sorry…"

As his face crumples, I grab him and pull him to me. "Hey, it's okay. It's okay, little man." I keep whispering softly to him. "Everything's gonna be alright."

He pushes back a little and frowns at me. "Do you really believe that?"

I take a deep breath and gesture for him to join me at the table. "I know things have been bad lately. Your dad's just… in a dark place. He's lost right now, but he does love you guys."

Josh's nose gets red, a sure fire sign that he's fighting tears. "No, he doesn't," he snaps flatly. "If he really loved us, he wouldn't threaten to beat us over every little thing."

My jaw clenches. I could kill that asshole right now.

"I could take him, you know. If he tried."

I stare at my eight-year-old nephew. His eyes are thin slits, his nostrils flared, his fists clenched and trembling at his sides. He looks like he's ready for a fight.

"Josh—"

"Ruslan's been teaching me what to do. I could protect the girls from him. I could protect you, too."

I put my hands down on his quivering shoulders. "Sweetheart, I appreciate that; I do. But it's not your job to protect me or the girls. It's *my* job to protect *you*. Listen—"

Before I can finish my sentence, the girls rush into the kitchen, whisper-shouting that they're hungry. Sighing, I stand and go to get them situated.

I fill their bowls with pasta before slipping out of the kitchen under the pretense of changing out of my work clothes. On the way, I detour into Ben's room and find him lying face down on his bed, drool forming a dark stain around his mouth.

Wrinkling my nose in disgust, I grab a pillow that he's kicked to the floor and whack him with it. He doesn't so much as flinch, so I keep at it until he stirs.

He snorts awake all at once, his eyes flickering open. He nearly chokes on his own saliva as he struggles to right himself.

"Jesus," I mutter. As always, he reeks of booze and bad decisions.

"What the hell are you doing?" I growl through gritted teeth. "Those children out there *need* you."

His eyes focus on me and he frowns. "Sienna…"

I freeze. *Is this a joke?* If so, it's crueler than I thought even he was capable of.

He blinks a couple of times and then lets out a loud burp that has me cringing a few steps backward. Judging from his breath and the way his eyes flicker erratically, he's still wasted.

"Si…"

He's screwing with me. This is some sick prank.

But Ben has never been that good an actor. He's got this longing, desperate look on his face. His bloodshot eyes swing wildly over my body as he stumbles closer to me.

"Si… I'm so fucking sorry… I forgot your b-birthday…"

"Ben," I say firmly. "It's me. Emma. I'm not Sienna."

He frowns, hiccupping as he reaches for me. "I've missed you so much, baby…"

He tries to touch me but I recoil from him. *"Ben!* I'm Emma. Snap out of it. Are you so far gone that you can't even tell—?"

I gasp when he grabs my arm and reels me against him. For a guy who's half-asleep and half-drunk, he's got a surprisingly firm grip.

"Ben! Stop!"

I'm vaguely aware of the door swinging in on its hinges but I'm too worried about Ben's wandering hands to pay much attention to it. At least not until Ben grunts with pain, his back arching. He stumbles to the side to reveal Josh standing there, his hands balled into fists.

Did Josh just punch *his father?*

"Fucking hell, you little bastard!" Ben hisses as he wakes up from whatever intoxicated hallucination he was caught in.

"You get the hell away from her!" Josh orders, glaring at his father with a fury that belongs on a much older man.

Ben shakes his head from side to side in stupefied disbelief. "You little shit! Did you just hit me?"

"You were scaring Aunt Emma!"

Ben's eyes veer to me for only a second before they fall back on Josh. He's wearing a venomous glare that doesn't deserve to be aimed at any eight-year-old, let alone your own son. "I don't care what the fuck I did; it's not your place to—"

I step right between him and Josh. "Ben, stop it. You're out of control. You have—"

He shoves me roughly out of the way and lunges at Josh. I trip and fall to the side, aware of Josh racing out the door from my peripheral vision. Ben chases after him and, for the first time since that orange pickup truck changed everything, I'm actually scared of what Ben is capable of.

I hit hard, cracking my head against the wood floor, but I'm back on my feet again as fast as I can manage it. I rush into the living room where Ben is circling the couch, trying to claw at Josh.

"Ben! Have you completely lost your mind? He's a child! He's your *son!*"

"Exactly!" he yells. "My fucking son. And he's got to learn *respect!*"

Startled, the girls scream. I catch their terrified little faces peeking out from around the kitchen, pale as ghosts.

"Ben, I will call the police!" I yell right back.

He turns on me, hair mussed, eyes wild. I've never seen him look so unhinged. But despite that, all I feel is relief. At least his attention is on me now, not Josh. *Let him beat me black and blue. As long as the kids are okay.*

"What the fuck did you say?" he growls.

I square my shoulders. "You heard me. I will call the damn cops if you don't settle down right now. You're scaring the kids!"

He takes a menacing lurch towards me and that's when I notice Josh dart out from behind the couch. I only have the time to gasp before his little fist connects with Ben's ribs for the second time in as many minutes.

"Fuck!" Ben roars. "What the—" He whirls around, hand raised and before I can stop him, he grabs Josh by the front of his t-shirt.

"BEN! STOP!"

Caroline's small voice cuts through the heat of my panic. "D-daddy! Please don't…"

Ben acts as though he can't hear any of us. He flings Josh against the coffee table. It's not a violent throw, but Josh's too-thin little body makes a dull *thwacking* sound as he careens into the furniture. He grunts low with pain and even that heartbreaking sound doesn't seem to snap Ben out of his fugue state.

"You bastard!" I scream at his back while he storms out the door and slams it on his children's tears.

I rush to Josh and pick him up off the floor. It's not until I have him in my arms that I realize he's not the one that's shaking.

I am.

"Josh," I gasp, cradling him like I used to when he was a toddler. "I'm so sorry. I'm *so* sorry." He clings to me, his chest heaving with silent sobs. All I can do is hold him. "It's okay.

Go ahead and cry. You deserve to cry as loud as you want for as long as you want."

"J-Joshie...?"

I look up to find Caroline and Reagan still hiding behind the kitchen wall, tears streaking down their cheeks. I gesture for them to come over and they run to me, their heat engulfing me from both sides as we all huddle together.

"It's okay," I whisper. "We're gonna be okay, I promise. I'm gonna make sure we're all okay..."

I thought having Ben around was important for the kids. I thought it was necessary. Despite all his shortcomings, I didn't want them to lose their only living parent. But after tonight, I have to face the fact that having him around is doing them more harm than good. Maybe we're all better off without him.

Which leaves me with only one path forward and, of course, it won't be easy. My heart beats wildly, even as my resolve hardens.

From now on, I have to be their mother *and* their father.

I have to strip Ben of his parental rights.

I have to adopt these kids.

Once that's sunk in, I hold onto the kids just as tightly as they're holding onto me. And then—

I let myself cry, too.

55

EMMA

Be calm.

You don't know what your chances are.

And if this doesn't work out, then *you can kill him.*

My leg has been bouncing erratically since I sat down in Isabel Costa's empty office to wait for her. I could have cornered her in the lunchroom, but I didn't want to have this conversation in public.

"Emma?"

I spin around in my chair. "Hi, Isabel."

The lawyer is standing on the threshold of her door, looking at me with arched eyebrows. She seems to get the measure of the situation in seconds because she walks in and closes her door.

Isabel *never* closes her door.

"What's up?" she asks, sitting down next to me instead of behind her desk.

"I know you're not in the habit of handing out free legal advice—"

She smiles. "Let's consider this personal advice then, shall we?"

I nod gratefully. I've always liked Isabel, always felt like we could be good friends whenever we happened to end up sitting at the same lunch table at work or crossing paths at the firm's Christmas party. We might have been, if it weren't for the fact that I was too busy trying to keep my head above water to put any energy into developing new friendships.

"Sure. Personal." I try to return her smile, but mine is weak, with more tears waiting if I get too deep in the weeds. "Before you came to Bane, didn't you used to work in family law?"

"Ten years of it," she confirms. "Is this about your nieces?"

"And nephew." I take a deep breath and jump right in. "I want to legally adopt them. And I also want to strip their father of his rights."

Isabel's eyebrows hit the roof of her forehead. *Not a good sign.*

"It's possible, isn't it?" I press desperately. "It has been done before?"

"It has. But rarely. It is extremely difficult to get a biological parent's rights stripped while they're still in the picture, Emma. It can be hard for the *other* parent to do it, let alone an aunt. And the only way a court would even consider it is if you can prove that your brother-in-law is a danger to those kids."

I laugh bitterly. "I can do that."

It's a credit to her professionalism that she doesn't wince or look surprised. She just nods and sighs. "Well then, that will make a difference. Is he abusive? Violent?"

"He drinks a lot. And lately, he has been getting violent. H-he… pushed Josh last night."

I'm angry with myself for how this is all coming out. I'm making it seem like a non-incident when it was anything but. He *broke* those kids last night. All three had clambered into my bed and it took five bedtime stories before they felt soothed enough to fall asleep.

"Does he have a history of that kind of behavior?"

"Last night was the first time it got that bad," I admit. "But he does sometimes threaten to hit them. He's been getting more and more belligerent. And the drinking has increased, too."

Isabel sighs. "Emma, I'd love to be able to give you some positive news, but this sounds like it's going to be a long, drawn-out court case. Unless of course your brother-in-law is willing to sign over his parental rights to you."

I bite my lip. "I doubt he'll agree to that."

"Then you're looking at a custody battle and that's gonna take time and money."

The nest egg that I've built in the last few months is significant. But it's nowhere near enough to cover the kind of legal fees that a case like this would require.

"I don't have enough of either of those things," I mutter.

"Does he?"

"No… but he knows where to get the money," I admit.

I call them Mom and Dad. They'd help him in a heartbeat.

Isabel fixes me with a sympathetic expression. "Listen—if you're determined to go down this road, I can recommend a good lawyer. In fact, when it comes to child custody cases, she might just be the best."

The anxiety is setting in something fierce right about now. I *need* the best. But I can't afford the best. The mere thought of lawyer bills hitting my inbox gives me the chills. "I'm gonna have to think this over a little."

Isabel nods. "You do that and let me know if you need that contact."

I thank Isabel and head out into the corridors of Bane Corp. feeling like I've just been spat out by a tornado. My heart is clamoring against my chest and it feels like I have only a few options left.

Plan A was the court system, but that seems like it might be out of reach right now. Plan B is drop a piano on Ben's head and, as satisfying at that might be, I'm just not that type of person.

Which means all I have left is Plan C.

And Plan C goes by the name of Ruslan Oryolov.

The new contract. The baby clause.

The thought alone gives me hives. I get a concerned look from a passing intern, so I duck into the nearest restroom and splash some cold water on my neck.

I'd be lying if I said I hadn't already been considering Ruslan's new contract. Especially after the conversation we had on Sienna's would-be birthday. It was a lot, though, and the thought of something that big, that permanent, was terrifying enough for me to throw up an instinctive, automatic *Hell, no.*

But now?

Now, I have another reason to consider it. A bigger, more important reason. Now, it's not about personal choice—we're talking *necessity*. We're talking *survival*.

And in the deepest recesses of my mind, where all my darkest secrets lie hidden away, one thought tunnels through to my consciousness.

I can have my cake and eat it, too.

Because let's face it: if I were to look at the list of things I want, saying "yes" to this amended contract is the only way to get them all.

Cue quick mental checklist:

I want custody of those kids.

I want to strip Ben of his parental rights.

I need enough money to do both those things.

I need enough money to provide for those children once I have them.

I've always wanted a family of my own.

I've never felt about a man the way I feel about Ruslan.

Signing his contract would give me all the above. Of course, the downside is that I'd be signing a contract to start a family with a man who isn't even really my boyfriend. Who explicitly warned I'd never get all of him. And I'd be exchanging my body—again—for money.

It really is a slippery slope.

But as I stare at my reflection in the mirror, it occurs to me: I'm prepared to slide right down. I'm ready and willing to deal with whatever consequences await me at the bottom of this slope.

For the kids, if not for myself. They deserve everything I can give them.

Okay, Emma. It's now or never.

Riding the high of my new resolve, I march towards Ruslan's office. I don't even knock before I enter—guns out, barrels blazing.

Ruslan takes one look at my face and throws a sharp "Out" at Kirill.

When the door closes behind Kirill, I face Ruslan and I put all my cards on the table. "I need to get my kids away from Ben. I probably should have done it a long time ago, but— well, you know why I didn't. The thing is, I'm looking at a long, drawn-out custody battle because Ben's not gonna give those kids up without a fight. And he's probably gonna have my parents in his corner, which means I need to find the money to pay the best custody lawyer I can find."

I'm not taking what you'd call a "normal amount of pauses." I'm not taking what you'd call "a normal amount of breaths," either. But now that I've started, I can't stop.

"I know this is probably not what you wanted. Picking someone else would be a hell of a lot simpler. But you should know what you're getting into, which is why I'm telling you all this up front. Going with me is gonna mean a fuck-ton of drama, a protracted court battle, and a hell of lot of tears. But —if you're up for it, I am, too."

The moment I stop talking, I'm engulfed in fear.

Way to sell yourself, Emma.

Ruslan's expression is unreadable. There isn't so much as a line on his forehead. He gets to his feet slowly and walks around his desk. "Was that your way of telling me you're willing to sign my new contract?"

I gulp. "Was that not clear?" He smirks and I cover my face with my hands. "I'm sorry," I say into my palms just before I drop them. "Yes, I am willing to sign your new contract."

He doesn't say a word. Instead, he grabs a folder from his desk and hands it to me.

I let out a low whistle. "You had that one locked and loaded."

"I've had time to think about this."

"Sure, but I just hit you with a lot of new information. You sure you're willing to sign up for the drama?"

He still doesn't so much as blink. "I want to have an heir with someone I like and respect. If drama is part of the deal, then so be it."

"You like and respect me?" I mumble stupidly.

He rolls his eyes. "Just take the damn contract, Emma."

A bubble of laughter escapes me. This feels so *weird.* Surreal, almost. No, not almost—it *is* surreal. It is completely, certifiably crazy.

But it also feels like the right thing to do.

I take the contract and hold it to my chest. "I'll have it back on your desk by this evening."

Talk about déjà vu.

"Actually," he says suddenly, "I have one more tweak I want to make before I let you take it. I'll have Kirill deliver it to you in an hour or so. You can return it to me tonight—at the penthouse."

"Tonight's not our usual night."

"No," he agrees in a smooth, suggestive baritone rumble, "it's not."

I pass the contract back to him, feeling my cheeks heat up. "Okay then."

Our eyes meet and I try to suppress the shiver that threatens to run down my spine. I'd expected fear. Wariness. Nervousness, at the very least.

But all I feel is excitement.

Rae, Caroline, and Josh are going to be safe.

Ben is going to be shoved out of the picture.

Ruslan and I are going to have a baby.

56

RUSLAN

I have an off-site meeting in the evening, so Emma's already at the penthouse when I walk in.

The amended contract is sitting open on the dining room table and she is pacing barefoot between the windows and the bar. The first thing I notice is how beautiful she looks with her hair down. The second thing I notice is the pen sitting next to the open contract.

So she hasn't actually signed it yet.

She stops short when she sees me. "You don't have to do this."

"Some context would be nice," I reply, even though I have a pretty good idea I know what she's talking about.

She points at the open page of the contract. "I read through the amended section. You *do not* have to take care of all my legal bills. What you already offered is enough."

"I know that. I want to."

She stares at me, her eyes wide and disbelieving. "But… it's not your fight, Ruslan. It has nothing to do with you."

"If you sign that contract, you will be carrying my child soon, Emma," I remind her. "And from then on, if anything affects you, directly or indirectly, it *does* have something to do with me."

She swallows, her eyes flitting from me to the contract, then back to me. "It's too much."

It's not nearly as much as you deserve.

"I'll be the judge of that."

Her bottom lip trembles before she bites down on it. "I… I don't know what to say."

"You don't have to say anything. You just have to sign on the dotted line—*if* this is really what you want."

She walks over to the table and picks up the pen. Her eyes hover on me for a moment. Is that hesitation in her eyes? Fear? Doubt?

"This is a big deal, isn't it?" she whispers.

I nod. "You have to be sure."

She exhales and closes her eyes. I resist the urge to touch her. But all I can think is, *She has to sign. I fucking* need *her to sign.*

Because if I don't put a baby in this woman tonight, *I'm going to go fucking insane.*

When she opens her eyes again, she looks calm. "I *am* sure." She proves it by scribbling her signature confidently at the bottom of the page. "There. It's done."

"It's done."

She blushes. "So… now what?"

"Now, I need your purse."

"My *what?*"

I hold out my hand. After a few moments of hemming and hawing, she passes it over and I promptly start rooting around in it. I catch her perplexed expression from my periphery.

"Didn't anyone ever tell you that you never go through a lady's bag?" I ignore her. "Ruslan, what are you looking for?"

I finally manage to find what I'm after in the excess of random junk she's got stuffed in her purse. I pull it up for her to see.

"My birth control pills," she breathes, staring at the small pink case. "Wow. We're really doing this?"

I head into the bathroom just off the living room and start popping each pill into the toilet while Emma lingers to the side, watching me give each dose its own send-off.

"Dramatic, much?"

Dramatic? Yes.

Turned-on? Very fucking much so.

"You did promise me drama. I'm just returning the favor." I step aside to let her come closer. "Care to do the honors?"

She takes a deep breath and reaches out. Her fingers tremble as they come to rest on the silver lever. She takes one more breath for good measure, then, holding the exhale, she pushes down on the flush. We watch the pills disappear into the whirlpool and despite her tease earlier, it really does feel necessarily dramatic. We are officially "trying."

How the fuck this came to be, I'm still not entirely certain.

I grab hold of her and pull her against my chest. "You're deep in thought."

Emma nods distractedly, her cheek rustling against my shirt. "I was just thinking…"

"I've warned you not to do that."

She pokes me in the ribs. "I was just thinking how that flush signified the end of one part of my life and the beginning of another." We're so close that I can see the flecks of gray in those blue eyes of hers when she looks up at me. "It's the—I mean, the—shit, it's *really* hard to concentrate when you're looking at me like that."

"Like what?"

"Like you want to take a bite out of me."

I smile. "Funnily enough, that's *exactly* what I was thinking." I grip her chin with my fingers. "You're *mine* now, Emma Carson."

"I was already yours," she whispers.

Those words rush straight down to my cock. She yelps as I scoop her up into my arms and carry her into the master bedroom. I throw her onto the bed and she bounces on the mattress until I steady her with one hand on her hip and another lightly banded across her throat. My lips find her neck first, then her chest, and she shudders when I use my teeth to rip off the buttons of her blouse.

At this rate, I'm gonna have to buy her a whole new wardrobe.

I don't mind. It's the perfect fucking excuse to spoil her rotten.

There are so many things I want to do for her. So many things I want to give her. Her pride would have said "no" before now. But once she's carrying my child, it'll be a whole different ball game.

My tongue lashes out over her breasts, circling her juicy nipples until they're hard and pert. I suck on them as she bucks against me, nails digging into my back, then I kiss my way down her stomach while she writhes and whimpers. I peel her clothes off and lick her pussy until she's dripping all over the sheets and then I haul myself back up, ready to fill her.

"You ready for me, *kiska?*"

She bites her lip. "Mhmm."

"You want me to fuck a baby into you?" She nods, her eyes wide, all the blood gushing through her cheeks. I fist a handful of her hair. "Let me hear you say it."

"I-I want your baby," she moans as I rub the head of my cock along her drenched slit. "Fuck me, Ruslan. Please… I want your baby."

I slip two fingers between those luscious lips and, while she's sucking on them, I thrust myself inside her.

"Ahh!"

I pump hard from the get-go, silencing her moans with my fingers until she's biting down on them. "Hm, my vicious little *kiska*. I'm gonna fill you up. I'm gonna cover you in my cum. You'd like that, wouldn't you?"

Her breasts bounce with the strength of my thrusts. "Y-yes," she gasps. "Fuck yes. Fill me up. Fuck me good... yes, *yes, YES!*"

I fuck her harder, deeper, faster. Every moan out of her mouth makes my cock hungrier and greedier for more. Even when my lungs feel like they're about to cave in on themselves, I keep pumping, spurred on by that sound of flesh on flesh. The thunder of my pelvis as it bears down against her slick pussy.

And the whole time, all I can see in my mind's eye is her growing belly. The child that will come into existence because of this night, or tomorrow night, or a night like this one. I can't wait to fuck her when she's pregnant. Her breasts will be so much bigger, her stomach ripe with our baby. I have to grit my teeth to stop myself from coming.

Not yet, not yet...

"Fuck, *Ruslan!*" she screams. "I can't take it anymore... *fuck!*"

"Oh, you can take it. That tight pussy of yours was made for me. Can you feel it?"

"Yes," she moans. "*Yes.*"

"You want me to come inside you?"

"Yes, please... please..."

I bend down and swipe my tongue inside her ear. She bucks, her hips thrusting upwards into me.

"You're mine now," I growl. "*All. Fucking. Mine.*"

Even when she falls apart in my arms, I don't stop fucking her. All I can think about is the child we're going to make together. Once she's pregnant, it'll change everything. I can take care of her the way I was meant to. I can protect her. I can give her the life she deserves.

Once my baby's in her belly, she'll be tied to me forever. It's the only excuse I'll need to do this again and again.

Until then—I'm gonna savor every fucking moment of trying.

"*Ruslan*!" she gasps, jerking forward. "Please!"

"What are the magic words?" I snarl.

My hips feel like they're going to give out at any second. *Mind over matter.* I will fuck her for as long as it takes.

"I'm yours!" she cries out. "All fucking yours!"

That's all it takes for me to erupt.

57

EMMA

What did I come in here for?

Oh, that's right—a last-minute appointment reschedule.

I can't really remember who I was supposed to reschedule. I can barely hear myself think above the sound of Ruslan's hips slamming hard against my ass as he fucks me for the fourth time today.

I'm just gonna say it: the sex is getting out of hand.

Which would be terrible if I didn't enjoy it so damn much.

But really, it's actually interfering with work now. Even my body has gotten conditioned to the new status quo at the office these days. Every time Ruslan asks for me, my pussy starts throbbing and I get wet. Half the time, I don't even know what he wants. Doesn't matter—I get wet anyway.

Of course, more often than not, even if it starts off as work, it ends up as sex.

In his chair.

Against his desk.

Up against the windows.

And it's not just at work, either. If we're not having sex at the penthouse, he sneaks into my apartment after the kids have gone to bed. He has to fuck me with his hand over my mouth because, as we've established before, I'm a screamer.

We almost got caught last weekend when Reagan had a bad dream and tried to inch into my room. Thankfully, I'd had the foresight to lock my door. Ruslan hid in my bathroom while Reagan crawled into my bed with a disgruntled look.

"Why was your door locked?"

"Um, I must've locked it by mistake, honey. I'm sorry."

"Don't do it again," she warned me solemnly with her eyebrows all scrunched up.

We laughed about that the next day—right before Ruslan forced me to my knees and made me swallow his cock. Of course, he'd followed that up by coming inside me. Because *all* sex now involves him coming inside me.

He is a caveman about it, too. If I so much as reach for a tissue, he gives me a stern glare and forces me to put my panties on instead.

"You can walk around all day with my cum dripping down your thighs. Don't worry about cleaning up—I'll lick you dry later."

With a promise like *that*, how could I not listen?

As far as downsides, they're not nonexistent. As intoxicatingly, deliciously, amazingly exciting as all the sex is, my pussy is always sore. Come to think of it, *all* of me is sore all the time now.

Ah, the perils of a healthy sex life.

Phoebe would be so proud—that is, if she knew just how much sex Ruslan and I were having. The thing is, I didn't want to tell her the contractual reason we are having so much sex, so it's been simpler not to mention anything at all.

Simpler—though not easier.

Ruslan collects my hair into a loose ponytail and pulls hard as he starts thrusting even harder. I'm biting down on the heel of his palm, trying to keep the screams from alerting the entire floor of our new addiction. But when he gets that Neanderthal gleam in his eye and revs up the speed to maximum intensity, all self-control goes out the window.

I spasm forward as a fresh orgasm rockets through me, upending a stack of paperwork that I spent all morning on. I'm gonna be pissed about that later, but right now, I couldn't care less—he just keeps ramming into me, his breaths getting shorter and shorter as we both reach our final peak.

Just when I see little blue stars pop up in front of my dizzy eyes, I feel him release, filling me with his hot cum.

Wonder if we made a baby this time...

Then again, I've been thinking that every time we've slept together the last few weeks. He straightens up and passes me my panties.

I can already feel the cum drip down my thighs but I ignore the tissue box and slide my panties on.

"People are gonna wonder why I smell like you all the time."

Ruslan rounds the table and starts picking up the papers I upended. "If they have to wonder, they're fucking stupid. It's obvious."

"Obvious to *who?*" I balk.

Ruslan smirks. "You've never spent this much time in my office, Ms. Carson."

"Oh, *God.* I'm the whore of Bane Corp. The Hester Prynne of New York City. Might as well get a scarlet A embroidered on all my blouses."

Ruslan just chuckles. "Red does look good on you."

I launch a paper clip at him. "Not funny."

Still laughing, he steps over and smooths a wayward hair out of my face with a tender stroke of his fingers. "Who cares what people are saying, *kiska?* No one knows about the contract and that's all that matters. And anyway, you'll be pregnant with my baby soon. If they haven't figured it out by now, that'll certainly do the trick."

My mouth drops. "I hadn't thought about that."

"Well, you've been distracted lately."

I roll my eyes while trying to suppress a smile. Then I gather up the schedule I brought in here, which is now ripped down the middle thanks to the way Ruslan grabbed me the second I walked in and bent me over his desk.

"I'll go print out another one of these."

Knock, knock, knock.

I glance towards the door. It's a very pointed knock. Also a very familiar one. Kirill has made more than one joke about wearing a bell on a collar around his neck so we can hear him coming.

"Come in," Ruslan calls.

Kirill walks in, stops at Ruslan's desk, and glares at the two of us, knowing without having to ask what just happened. "For fuck's sake." He wrinkles his nose. "*Again?*"

Ruslan just chuckles and dismisses me with a wink and a nod. I hurry out, doing my best to hide the blush on my cheeks.

I'm not at my desk ten minutes before my phone *pings.*

RUSLAN: *I've got a club event to go to next week. I need a plus-one.*

EMMA: *And you want me to go with you?*

RUSLAN: *Yes.*

EMMA: *And just so we're clear—I'd be your date. Your only date.*

RUSLAN: *That is correct, Ms. Carson.*

It is extremely hard not to go straight into my happy dance. But a few junior execs are milling around right now and I don't need people gossiping about me any more than they already are. So I suppress the excited butterflies fluttering around in my stomach and focus on my phone

EMMA: *Hm. I'll think about it.*

RUSLAN: *Wanna come back in here so I can help you think about it?*

EMMA: *You are an animal!*

RUSLAN: *Don't you forget it.*

EMMA: *Fine. I'll go.*

RUSLAN: *That's what I thought.*

Look at us, flirting and everything. Like a normal couple. It's enough to make me giddy. These last couple of weeks have me in a constant good mood. So good that I can't help thinking the same question that inevitably crops up whenever life happens to look this beautiful for any stretch of time.

When will the other shoe drop?

58

EMMA

"What about Russy?"

I hide my snort of laughter behind a cough when Ruslan shoots me a glare. Then he turns his attention back to the two little goobers who have been heckling him for an endless, relentless thirty minutes.

"No."

"Can I call you Ru-Ru?"

He looks pained. "Not if you want me to respond."

Josh is setting the table with a huge smile on his face. It's so great to see him like this. Sometimes, I feel like the only time I see that smile is when Ruslan's around.

And he has been *around* recently.

At least two nights a week, he drives me home and entertains the kids while I get dinner ready. Sometimes, he helps them build pillow forts in the girls' room; other times, the evenings are devoted to Lego castles on the living room carpet. And then there are the nights, like tonight, when everyone is congregated around the kitchen table, talking over one another about nothing at all.

It's true that I'm not his girlfriend and he's not my boyfriend.

It's true that we have a legally-binding contract that goes into explicit, excruciating detail about every facet of our relationship.

It's true that he's offering me money in exchange for whatever he expects of me.

It's also true that he's never said he loves me and he probably never will.

But the thing is, he's *amazing* with my kids. He's taken to them and they've taken to him in a way I would never have thought possible. I genuinely believe he cares about me. Enough to want to take care of my debt and my legal expenses and all the little stresses of my day-to-day life.

He's got a wall up around his heart, but he *told* me why. And I'm willing to bet that opening up to anyone isn't something that Ruslan Oryolov does very often.

Most importantly, we are monogamous.

So in the end, why would I get hung up over a title? Why would I care about not being enough when he's paid me the unique compliment of wanting me to be the mother of his child? Sure, it's not traditional.

But hey—traditional is boring, right?

Reagan descends into violent giggles as Ruslan grabs her, hoists her onto his lap, and starts tickling her on the sides of her belly. I watch them for a few minutes, feeling a sense of calm that surges through me whenever the five of us are together.

It's starting to feel less like an experiment and more like a family.

I don't need to be his wife. I just need *this*.

Which, of course, is when I hear the thundering slam of a door and the hideous, unwelcome thump of two heavy feet. One thought and one thought only races through my head.

I spoke too soon.

Reagan buries her face in Ruslan's chest, Caroline shifts to cower at his side, and Josh tosses me a nervous glance that he quickly shifts towards the door.

Ever since the incident, Ben has kept his distance. He comes home late, long after the kids and I go to bed, and he leaves around midday, when I'm at work and the kids are at school. None of us are expecting him here at this hour.

"Why don't you excuse me for a bit, guys?" Ruslan stands up and props Reagan back on his chair. "I have something I'd like to discuss with Ben."

My eyes go wide with panic. "Ruslan…"

He ignores me completely. "I won't be long."

He doesn't wait for me to tell him all the reasons why talking to Ben would be a bad idea. He leaves the kitchen, clapping Josh on the back on his way out.

"Josh, stay with the girls, okay? We'll be right back."

Then I rush into the living room behind Ruslan. Ben is already sprawled out on the couch, looking like he's crawled out of some dank, smelly hole.

His eyelids burst open when he sees Ruslan emerge. "What the—"

"Get up," Ruslan rumbles.

That tone. Good Lord. It's got the hairs on the back of my neck standing on end. I can only imagine what kind of effect it has on Ben.

Enough, apparently, to get him on his feet.

"You and I are going to go downstairs and have a little talk," Ruslan continues.

Yeah, okay, maybe it was a mistake telling Ruslan about the incident with Josh the other night. I'd just been really upset and talking to him made me feel better.

Until right now, of course.

Now, I wonder if I'm about to witness a murder.

"W-why can't we talk right here?" Ben gulps.

I used to think of Ben as a big man. He's six feet tall and built well. But next to Ruslan, Ben looks like a hobbit. And he looks *afraid.*

"Because I don't want to upset the kids. You've done enough damage as it is."

Ben looks at me. "Emma?"

Does he actually expect me to help him out here?

Ruslan slides in between us and points for the door without breathing another word. Ben scowls, but he stumbles to where Ruslan is directing him and the two of them slink out.

I turn back to make sure the kids are staying tucked out of sight. Josh gives me a brave thumbs up, then drags his sisters back onto the couch.

With a sharp inhale, I follow the men out.

Ben has followed Ruslan to the sidewalk. The street is quiet and empty of people, except for the line of cars parked along the curb. I keep my distance.

"Okay," Ruslan says, turning to Ben. "I'm gonna speak slowly so you can understand. Lay a hand on any of those kids ever again and I'll cut it the fuck off and feed the birds with it. If you won't protect them from the world, then you leave me no choice but to protect them from *you*."

Ruslan's so focused on Ben that I'm sure he misses the subtle flash popping off at regular intervals. I glance in the direction of the flash and catch a shadowy figure darting behind one of the cars on the opposite side of the street. I know that figure.

Remmy.

Ben, of course, chooses this moment to try his hand at being an alpha. "L-listen, buddy: I'm their *dad.* This is none of your business."

"I'm *making* it my business, *yebanyy mudak.*" He advances towards Ben, who backs into the bricks and shrinks.

I rush to Ruslan's side. "Ruslan," I whisper, *"Remmy's here. Across the street."*

His hands stay curled into tight fists, though. He continues to glare at Ben as though he didn't hear a word I just said.

Ben tries to remain unbothered but the red spots forming across his cheeks are betraying him. "L-listen—"

"No, *you* listen." He takes another step forward and I genuinely believe he's going to beat the shit out of Ben. "You come within five miles of those kids and I will make your life a living hell. Do you understand?"

Back down, Ben. For the love of God, back down!

"Fine," Ben snaps. "I don't need this shit."

He storms off towards his car—the same one Ruslan fixed—climbs in and drives off. When he's gone, Ruslan turns to me. "Remmy?" he mutters, moving closer to my side and looping a strong arm around my shoulders.

I look over at the car Remmy was hiding behind, but he's nowhere to be seen. "He's gone…"

"Good fucking riddance." He pulls me in close and presses a tender kiss to the soft space behind my ear. "Are you okay?"

"Sure," I lie. "Yeah. Of course."

But the truth is, I'm rattled.

Ben and Remmy in one night—it's too much. Why can't things just be good? Then I catch a whiff of Ruslan's oaky scent and that sense of calm settles right back over me. It's getting to be familiar now. I'm coming to rely on it—which is dangerous in its own right, but we're long past the point of no return.

Ruslan steers me towards the apartment. "Let's go up to the kids."

From his lips, nothing has ever sounded sweeter.

59

RUSLAN

"I'm hearing lots of strange rumors, *moy syn*."

It's rare for Fyodor to start a conversation. It's even rarer to see him outside of the comfort of his gardens. He's come to abhor the inner city—probably because he remembers a time when he was happy in it.

I push the pastry basket towards him. "You don't usually pay much attention to rumors, Otets."

His gaze veers to the stunning view of Manhattan but he might as well be staring at a blank canvas for all the interest he's showing.

"I do when they involve my son."

I pick at my Spanish omelet, trying not to think about what Emma and the kids are up to this Sunday morning. She'd told me she was planning on taking them to the aquarium but so far, I haven't gotten any pictures.

"What have you heard?"

"That you're sleeping with your secretary."

I raise my eyebrows. "Are you going to call me unoriginal?"

Fyodor's mouth turns up slightly. He almost looks animated for a change. "So it's true?"

I shrug. "It just… happened."

"And the children—did that just happen, too?"

"It was sort of a package deal."

"And that didn't dissuade you?" he asks shrewdly. "We both know you aren't very interested in fatherhood. At least, you weren't."

I glance down at his plate. "You've barely touched your French toast."

He pushes the plate away from him. "It's too dry. Not enough sugar." I suppress a sigh. That's not the reason he doesn't like the French toast and we both know it. The real reason is… "Your mother used to make the best French toast."

"Mama's not here, *Otets*."

His eyes flash angrily. "You don't need to remind me of that."

Sometimes, I intentionally try to piss him off. It's the only indication I have that there's still some life left in that hollow shell he's dragging around.

"Try the salmon then."

He grunts. "I'm not hungry."

He never is anymore. He eats to survive; that's it. In the past, when I wasn't pitying the poor bastard, I resented him.

Today is the first time I actually feel like I *understand* him.

The thought of losing Emma or one of those kids drives me insane. I lie awake at night trying to think of all the different ways I can keep them safe. On bad nights, I find myself thinking about all the different ways I could lose them.

It's a special kind of madness.

So if what I'm experiencing now is even close to what my father has endured, I'm willing to give him credit for dragging himself away from his gardens at all.

Fyodor fixes his milky blue eyes on me. "You're avoiding my question, son."

"I couldn't explain it even if I tried," I admit. "I stumbled into this situation and now, I don't know how to get myself out of it."

Fyodor raises his eyebrows. "Do you want to?"

"No. I don't."

He doesn't exactly smile but he doesn't look quite so morose anymore, either. "It won't always be easy. But trust me—it'll be worth it."

Until one of them dies and you spend the rest of your life a walking ghost...

I banish that thought before it can even begin to manifest. I have to make sure history doesn't repeat itself. I *will* make sure history doesn't repeat itself.

I clear my throat. "The launch for Venera is next week. Will you be there?"

Fyodor nods noncommittally. "I hear that the soft launch was an outstanding success."

I can't help a smug smile. "It was adequate."

"I have to admit, when you first told me about this venture of yours, I thought it was insanity. I thought you'd struggle and dump the idea before it even got to development. But you proved me wrong. You actually saw it through. You did it."

It takes a big man to admit that he was wrong. Just like Fyodor, Vadim had hemmed and hawed his way through my entire proposal, but hell would freeze twice over before he ever acknowledged his doubts now.

"It does look like we're on track to make a killing."

At the moment, there are no obstructions or misgivings in sight. The road ahead is clear and everything is going according to plan. The city is abuzz with talk of the new magic drug on the market. Bane Corp. is doing better than ever. And things with Emma and the kids are perfect.

It's all too fucking good to be true.

My father was once in the same position I'm in now. He was sitting on the top of the world—respected businessman, feared *pahkan* of a powerful Bratva, devoted husband and father.

And then it all came crashing down.

I was with him when the news reached us. Vadim brought it to our doorstep himself. I still remember the way my uncle hugged Fyodor first before he ever said a word. Almost as though he knew that his older brother would need to be held together.

"Brother," he whispered, "be strong. The next few months will test you."

I couldn't hear the exact words Vadim used to tell Fyodor the details of what happened; I just saw my father's legs buckle. I saw the color drain from his face. Before that moment, I had never seen him show so much as a single trace of weakness. And in seconds, he went from ruthless Bratva *pahkan* to a shattered shell of a man.

There was a lesson in that moment and it taught me one thing: *we are all just one tragedy from our knees.*

"You have done far more than I thought was possible." Fyodor's listless eyes grow a little brighter. "Leonid would have been proud."

He doesn't mention my brother often. Maybe that's why it hits so hard when he does.

"That's what I strive for every day," I rasp. "To be the kind of *pahkan* Leonid would have been if he'd only had the chance."

Fyodor's eyes glitter with unshed tears. "Leonid was smart and cunning. But he was a politician, not a titan. He would never have grown the Bratva like you have. Claim your victories for yourself, Ruslan, not for others."

There are moments, like now, when I see flashes of the man he used to be. The *pahkan* he used to be. It ought to make me proud. Instead, it just makes me mourn for what he once had and lost.

"I should be going."

He pushes up from his seat and I follow suit. I walk him to the elevators but before I can push in the access code to open the doors, he stops me with a hand to my shoulder.

He's gotten stooped with age. There's a slight hunch where once there was a steel spine. "Your mother would have been proud, too," he adds softly.

I raise a skeptical eyebrow. "Mama never cared for Bratva life. She cared about *us*; that was all."

Fyodor nods in agreement. "That she did. The only thing she cared about was her family. Which is why she would have been so glad that you've found yours."

I tense, racked with an immediate sense of anxiety. But before I can correct my father about the nature of my "family," he makes eye contact. He stopped doing that so long ago that I've forgotten what it feels like to be seen, really *seen* by him.

There were moments back in the dark days when it felt as though, where *Otets* was concerned, I had disappeared right alongside Mama and Leonid.

"Even as a child, you were always strong. Strong, stable, and capable. You are a better man than I, my son. And you will be a better father than I have been. Those children are lucky to have you."

I'm not sure what to say to that. Thankfully, Fyodor doesn't seem to require a response. He pats me around the neck like he used to do when I was a boy and gestures towards the access code pad.

"Now, you gonna let me out of this stuffy building or what?" he demands. I predict the next words out of his mouth before he says them. "I've been away too long from my gardens."

And just like that, he's back to the human ghost. A walking shell.

But even after he's long gone, his words ring in my ears. *Those children are lucky to have you.*

So why do I feel like the lucky one?

60

RUSLAN

I'm thinking either Per Se or Le Bernadine for lunch today. Emma's partial to the latter but we ate there last week and I want to see her face when she tries the *Oysters & Pearls* dish. It'll blow her mind.

But my appetite dies an instant death when I open my office door to find Adrik standing over Emma's desk, leaning towards her with a sickening leer on his face.

Motherfucker.

Emma's smile is polite but forced. She's leaning away from him, the vein in her forehead throbbing gently like a warning flare.

"Adrik," I snarl, "is there a reason you're harassing my assistant?"

I expect a scowl but instead, he offers me a simpering smile. "I wasn't aware having a conversation with her qualified as 'harassment.'"

"It does when your breath reeks like you just tongue-fucked a graveyard."

Emma pushes off from her desk, face pale as though caught in the crossfire of this conversation is the last place on Earth she wants to be. "I've got some work to do in the copy room. Excuse me."

She hurries off and Adrik has the audacity to watch her go, eyes locked on her ass *right in front of me*. The *mudak* knows exactly what he's doing.

"Is there a reason you're here?" I spit, if only to draw his attention away from Emma.

He doesn't look at me until she's turned the corner. "I was in the neighborhood."

There's that smile again. The one that's hiding an ulterior motive. "And you decided to stop by and see what a successful business looked like?"

That earns me a scowl. "So funny, as always."

I dip my head. "Here all week. Now, what are you *really* doing here, Adrik?"

"I wanted to ask you out to lunch."

"You're not my type."

Another scowl. "I'm trying to be the bigger man here, Ruslan. This lunch is meant to be a celebration. To commemorate the sale of Lees Industries finally going through."

I raise my eyebrows. "So you're here to celebrate the fact that you lost one of your subsidiaries to me?"

"Like I said, I'm trying to be the bigger man."

"That would be a first."

He shrugs nonchalantly. "I took a peek at your schedule when I was also admiring your assistant's cleavage—" He grins a little wider at the black look I skewer him with. "—and I happen to know that you're free for lunch."

I could tell Adrik to eat shit. Or I could use this to my advantage. Maybe I can try and suss out what he really wants during the course of this lunch. Because one thing I know for sure—he's got a plan in motion.

I just need to figure out what that plan is.

"Fine. We're going to Per Se. You're paying."

He rolls his eyes but sweeps an arm toward the elevators. "Lead the way, your highness."

～

The walk down to the front of the building is quiet. I can practically see the wheels in Adrik's head spinning. His car is parked on the curb just outside the building's canopy. "Meet you there," he drawls with a sarcastic princess wave goodbye.

I watch him drive off first before Boris rolls up in the SUV. I text Emma from the backseat, already annoyed that we can't have lunch together like I'd planned.

RUSLAN: *Change of plans, I'm having lunch with Adrik.*

EMMA: *Wow, I'm being dumped for a man? I didn't expect that.*

RUSLAN: *Just so you know, I'm rolling my eyes.*

EMMA: *:crying laughing face emoji: You're supposed to actually use the rolling eyes emoji. That's what it's there for.*

RUSLAN: *Did he hit on you?*

EMMA: *Umm—no...*

RUSLAN: *Emma.*

EMMA: *He mentioned our dance once. Said he enjoyed it. That was it. And I shut it down, okay? It was literally, like, two minutes of small talk before you walked out.*

My hackles rise instantly. Two minutes of small talk is two minutes too fucking long. And I don't like the fact that she wrote "our" dance.

Our.

Like they had some sort of shared experience. Something that meant something to her.

The rational part of my brain tells me that I'm overreacting but the caveman in me is banging his fists against his chest and howling, already desperate to go back to the office just so I can remind Emma who all her dances belong to now.

EMMA: *Ruslan? :eyes emoji:*

RUSLAN: *I'll see you back in an hour. I expect to find you in my office, panties dropped.*

EMMA: *Yes sir.*

I smile and breathe. *That's a good girl.*

The food at *Per Se* is phenomenal. The company? Less so.

Adrik and I spend the first hour lobbing questions back and forth. It's typical business small talk that has my head pulsating with boredom.

I could be feeling up Emma under the table right now. Instead, I'm stuck with this dipshit.

At the start of the second hour, I can see the light at the end of the tunnel. But I'm also wondering when Adrik will get to the fucking point. He didn't invite me out to lunch for the pleasure of my company.

"So, Ruslan—since I have you here…"

Fucking knew it.

"You want something?"

He raises his eyebrows innocently. "This is business, of course. I would pay."

"For what?"

"I want to book out Alcazar for one night next week to host an exclusive event."

I humor him. "Booking out Alcazar will cost you half a mil. Excluding food and beverages."

He shrugs. "I've got the money."

"You also have a club of your own," I point out. "Hosting your event there would cost you nothing."

"As you've pointed out numerous times before: despite my best efforts, my club doesn't seem to have the same appeal that yours does."

There's definitely a trap in place. I eye him carefully, but he is the picture of innocence. "What night are you looking at?"

"The thirteenth of August."

I grit my teeth.

The next day I believe in a coincidence will be the first. In my world, there's no such thing—there's just plans in motion and fools too stupid to see them tightening around their throats.

Because the thirteenth of August is the date of the full-scale Venera launch. And there isn't a fucking chance in hell that Adrik doesn't somehow know that.

Outwardly, I play it cool. "Unfortunately, booking Alcazar for any kind of event requires at least three months' prior notice. I'm afraid your date isn't available."

"I figured that, since I know the owner—"

"You figured wrong. We're booked."

He eyes me over his whiskey. "Oh? Big event?"

I keep my face calmly apathetic, even as I daydream about throttling this bastard here and now. "Every event at Alcazar is a big event." I get to my feet. "Now, if you'll excuse me, I have meetings to get to."

Adrik remains seated. He doesn't seem miffed that I've denied him the use of my club, which is making me even more suspicious.

It's a relief that lunch is over but I'm also hard-wired to sense when something is not right. Right now, all my senses are blaring red alert.

Kirill is in the foyer of the Bane skyscraper when I walk in. He makes a beeline straight for me. "What's this I hear about a lunch with Adrik?"

"Just managed to get away."

He narrows his eyes. "What did the bastard want?"

"He wanted a venue for some event. Alcazar on the thirteenth of August."

Kirill's scowl captures exactly how I'm feeling. "That can't be a coincidence, can it?" I shake my head and his scowl deepens. "If it's not a coincidence, that can mean only one thing."

"Yeah," I snarl with a grimace. "Adrik knows too much."

61

EMMA

"I cannot get over this look!" Phoebe declares as she follows me into the living room.

The kids are already asleep so we're both talking softly and walking slow. Well, *I'm* walking slow. The three-inch Prada heels I'm wearing weren't exactly made for running.

"And, wow, not to bury the lede here, but your ass looks *amazing* from back here."

I spin around for her benefit. The truth is, I feel pretty dang good. And not just because of the sequined Valentino mini I'm wearing. Tonight is my club date with Ruslan and I'm all squidgy inside with excitement.

We're actually going to be out in public together—a couple for the world to see.

It's about freaking time.

"If only I had a camera on me. We need to memorialize this moment so that you can look back forty years from now and remember what a hot bod you had."

I roll my eyes. "Don't you worry. I'll have a hot body forty years from now, too."

"Ooh! I like the confidence. This new Emma is definitely an upgrade."

"New Emma?"

"Oh, brand *spanking* new." Phoebe wags her eyebrows at me. "Let's face it: you've transformed these last couple of months. You went from a stressed, tired, worried little caterpillar into a confident, happy, sexy sequined butterfly clothed in designer like it ain't nothin'."

I cringe. "He keeps buying me expensive clothes—"

"And you need to keep accepting them. For my sake, if not for yours. I'm borrowing this dress when you're done with it, by the way."

I laugh. "No prob—"

I stop short when I see Ben's shadow come up behind Phoebe. She steps to the side with distaste, making no secret of the fact that she barely tolerates his presence. That makes two of us.

His eyes land on my dress. "The fuck're *you* going?"

"Out," I snap shortly.

His eyes veer to Phoebe. "What's she doing here?"

"*She* is staying over to look after *your* kids," Phoebe retorts before I can answer.

Ben doesn't even acknowledge her. I wonder if he forgets that Phoebe was Sienna's friend, too. That she lost Si, just like he and I did.

If he does remember that, he shows no sign of it. He just refocuses his glare on me. He's been a little extra abrasive since the night Ruslan threatened to cut his hand off, though he's kept his distance.

"I need to talk to you," he growls.

"I'm about to leave, Ben."

"Well, this is important. I need—"

The *knock-knock-knock* at the door has his mouth clamping shut. Phoebe gives me a satisfied smile. "Ruslan has excellent timing. Another point in his favor." She wiggles her fingers at me. "Have an amazing time, Cinderella."

She shoots me a wink and disappears down the hall towards my room. I walk over to the door but pause before I open it. "What did you wanna talk to me about?"

He scowls. "That him?"

"Yes."

He blanches and backs away towards his room. "We'll talk later then."

Suppressing a smile, I open the door and walk right into Ruslan's arms. I drop a kiss on his lips and, when I turn to close the door, Ben's already disappeared.

"You look sexy as hell," Ruslan rumbles as he curls an arm around my waist. "I might have to get a taste of you right here and now."

"Right back atcha." I finger his open collared shirt as I lean close and add in a seductive whisper, "But if you think I'm letting you get me naked in this roach-infested hallway, you've lost your mind."

He laughs and nips at my neck, then we make our way out of the building and out into the heart of the city. I really must look sexy because he doesn't take his hands off me. With the exception of getting in and out of the SUV, he has at least one palm on my waist at all times. You'd think the possessiveness would be claustrophobic, but I can't stop smiling.

His club is understated on the outside. I particularly love the dark tunnel adorned with black and whites of old New York City. But the moment we enter the body of the beast, it feels like I've stepped from the past into the future.

Neon. Bass. Roving lights, dancers on high pedestals, so much to see and hear and smell in every direction that I don't even know where to begin.

Ruslan's arm only winds tighter around me as he drops his lips to my ear. "What do you want to do?"

"Mr. Control Freak is asking *me* what *I* want to do?"

His grin is intoxicating. "Thought I'd mix things up for once."

"Then I want to dance!"

Cheesing from ear to ear, I drag him onto the middle of the dance floor. A huge, studded disco ball revolves overhead, bathing us in strobe lights as the music intensifies.

When was the last time I was in a club? When was the last time I danced? It's been so long ago that the last dancing partner I can remember is Sienna. I brace myself for the usual pang that comes up whenever I think of her—but for once, I don't feel sad that she's gone.

I'm just grateful I got those wild, carefree moments with her, however brief they were.

I keep a hand on Ruslan's shoulder while I roll my body into his. The music is so loud that I can feel it in my bones. The only way to communicate is through body language. Luckily, Ruslan knows exactly how to communicate with his. I shouldn't be surprised, really—the man is good at everything.

He spins me around, pulling me close enough to slide his hand up my skirt. The way his hands glide over me, touching and caressing without ever lingering for too long—it feels like a dance in and of itself. A dance meant to drive me crazy. Every time his fingers run up my inner thigh or snake over my breasts, I shudder with longing, wondering just how far his public sex fetish is capable of going.

I'm pretty sure the answer is, *He'd fuck you right here if you let him.*

At one point, I tease him right back by flicking my tongue over his salty neck. He answers by pulling me against him so tightly that I can feel his erection at my thigh. He slides his own tongue into my mouth and the music kind of fades into the background. When he finally pulls back, I'm breathless and completely wet.

On second thought, fuck the games. I need more.

"Restroom," I mouth to him. "*Now.*"

He smirks and nods once. I bite my lip suggestively and walk backwards off the dance floor, making eye contact with him the whole time.

The restrooms on the bottom floor are packed, dozens of women queued up for their turn. So I head up the stairs to try my luck with the bathrooms on the second mezzanine. Maybe they'll afford us a little more privacy. Before I can even locate the bathroom, I feel his presence behind me.

Hm, he's following more closely than I thought. Someone's eager...

But when he grips me tight around the elbow and whips me around, my excitement turns to dread. His smell is wrong. His presence feels different. This touch promises pain, not pleasure.

Then I realize that it's not Ruslan who followed me at all.

"*Remmy!*" My eyes bulge with shock.

"You look sexy."

It's amazing how the exact same compliment can give you two completely different reactions. Ruslan made me feel like I was the only woman in the world.

Remmy is making me feel like I'm cornered prey.

"You need to get a fucking life!"

I reach for my phone so that I can call Ruslan but Remmy slaps it out of my hand. When I reach down to get it, he twists my arm and yanks me into him.

"What the hell is wrong with you? *Get off me!*"

"*No*," he hisses. "Not until you give me what I want."

I would scream if it weren't for the fact that the music is so damn loud and not one solitary soul in this building will hear me. Which leaves me with two options.

Option one: wait for someone to pass by so that I can get their attention.

Or option two—fight back.

I like the second option better.

Summoning up all my courage, I push Remmy back as hard as I can and try to race around him. He stumbles momentarily, but he still manages to grab me by the waist and reel me backwards before I can get away. Reacting blindly, I stomp down. My heel digs into the toe of his wingtips and he howls in pain.

These Prada heels may not have been made for running. But they work pretty damn well for fighting.

I take advantage of his wild hopping and kick him in the balls. I don't even realize how close we are to the staircase until Remmy loses his balance and starts to fall.

Finally. A fight I fucking won *for a change.*

The relief stops at my throat—right when his hand grabs a hold of my ankle. "No—!" I get the wind knocked out of me as he pulls me down with him and we both go soaring into the air above the staircase.

First, there's fear.

Then there's pain.

Then there's nothing at all.

62

RUSLAN

"Alert security," I growl. "She has to be here somewhere."

Kirill eyes me warily. "When did you lose sight of her?"

"Just a few minutes ago. I was following her—" *Desperate for the fuck that we were both teasing each other with all night—* "and then Kostya intercepted me and got in my face about some unruly son of a bitch in the VIP section. By the time he finished talking, she was gone. She was heading to one of the bathrooms."

"Bathrooms. Got it. I'll start with the one on this floor."

I stride towards the first mezzanine. She was probably put off by the crowds on the ground floor. I'm trying as hard as I fucking can not to panic but there's this gnawing feeling in my gut that's eerily familiar.

It's the same one I had the day of the accident.

Something's not right. She should have returned from the bathroom by now. More importantly: I should never have let her out of my sight.

"Ruslan!" Kirill reappears and trails me to the second mezzanine. "The bathrooms on the base level are clear."

I follow an empty corridor off to the left. It leads to a few private rooms that VIPs can book at their discretion. As I walk, I try calling Emma again. The ringtone is loud and clear—and echoing down the corridor.

Kirill and I run towards the sound… only to find her phone face down on the floor.

"Fuck," I growl.

"It's possible she dropped her phone."

"This is not a fucking accident, Kirill," I snap. "This is someone's doing."

I keep walking until I hit the staircase. I freeze at the landing when I see her body crumpled at the bottom of the steps.

"Call an ambulance," I yell. "*Now!*"

In my head, one thought beats like a fucking drum.

No.

No.

No.

Not again.

63

RUSLAN

The drive to the hospital is a blur of traffic and frantic phone calls. I bark orders on the phone without ever letting go of Emma. She doesn't so much as stir through any of it. The gash I found on her forehead keeps weeping blood.

"They're checking security footage now," Kirill informs me when I call him.

"Comb through every inch of the club. I want the motherfucker who did this so I can kill him with my bare hands."

The paramedic gives me a startled look but I don't give a shit what she thinks. The only thing I'm concerned about right now is Emma. I take comfort in the fact that she's still breathing. But every time I notice a new bruise on her skin, I want to fucking tear the whole of New York City apart until I find the asshole responsible.

This kind of rage is new to me. Boxing has taught me discipline, especially where my emotions are concerned. My anger has always been restrained. But right now, it feels out of control. It feels *wild*. Even *I'm* not sure what I'm capable of doing.

"Sir…" The paramedic has deep blue eyes that are a similar shade as Emma's. "You're holding her a little too tightly."

She reaches out to adjust my grip, but I pull Emma out of her grasp. "Don't even think about it."

The woman freezes, then lets out a soft sigh.

"You found your wife like this?" she asks.

Wife. That word makes me shudder. Not necessarily in a bad way, either. "Yes."

The paramedic's eyes slide down Emma's body. Assessing. Observing. When they pass over her waist, something twinges.

I don't like that shit at all.

"What?"

Her gaze jerks to me. "Nothing."

"Say it."

Another sigh. This one more labored. "Will she need a rape kit at the hospital?"

I go cold. *Rape kit.* This is a fucking nightmare. I'll kill the man who did this. I swear to God I'll kill him—as slowly and painfully as any man has ever been put to death before.

When we get to the hospital, the nurses have to pry her out of my arms. The only way they manage to get me to let go is when the blue-eyed paramedic puts her hand on my arm and whispers, "They're just trying to help her. Let them. For her sake."

So I let go, though nothing has ever been harder. As I watch them transfer her onto a stretcher, for the second time in my life, I feel utterly and completely helpless.

"It's never easy to see someone you love hurt," the paramedic advises in more of that same soft whisper. "Have faith."

Faith? Fuck that. Faith has never been a part of my life. Neither has love. And for good cause—because the way I'm feeling right now is the exact reason why getting too close to Emma was a bad idea.

Love destroys you.

Faith ruins you.

I follow the gurney up to the second floor. A nurse tells me they're going to run some tests, but I barely hear any of what she's saying until the very end. " ... you her husband?"

I swallow and focus on her. "No."

The nurse raises her eyebrows. "Boyfriend?"

"Something like that."

She accepts that and nods. "Does she have any medical conditions we should know about?"

"Not that I know of."

"Is she allergic to anything?"

I'm coming up blank. "Not that I know of."

"Is she pregnant?"

I feel my heartbeat slow for a second. "I don't know... She might be. We've been... trying."

"Very well." She scribbles something on a clipboard. "We'll run a blood test."

"I want to be with her when you do it."

I turn and march toward Emma's door while the nurse still has her nose buried in her clipboard. Emma's gash has been stitched up, but her bruises have only darkened. Her forehead is a mottled collage of black and blue and there's a nasty purple gleam on her thighs.

They're prepping her hand for an IV when she stirs. The vein in her forehead starts pulsing erratically as she moans.

But all I feel is relief. *At least she's awake.*

I grab her free hand. "Emma? Can you hear me?"

She blinks her eyes open, squinting against the fluorescent light searing down on her. "W-where am I?" she asks hoarsely.

"You're in the hospital. You're safe."

She doesn't seem convinced. Her blinking is fast, her breath hitching up every few seconds. The nurse on the opposite side of the bed grabs her shoulder and pins her down.

"Miss, you're going to be disoriented for a while. I need you to calm down."

Emma turns to me, wracked with fear. "R-Ruslan?"

"I'm here." She doesn't look disoriented so much as scared. *Why the fuck did I let her walk away from me?* This is my fault. *This is all my fucking fault.* "I'm right here."

I sit at her side, practically without breathing, while they take blood samples and check her for signs of internal bleeding.

The whole time, she clings to my hand tightly and refuses to let go. That's fine by me—I'm not letting go of her, either.

"Ruslan…" she whispers when the nurse excuses herself to go get the ultrasound machine. "What happened?"

I've been biting my tongue this whole time but her question finally gives me permission to ask. "I was hoping you'd tell me."

She frowns. The vein in her forehead comes back with a vengeance. "I remember the… club. We… we were dancing. I went to the b-bathroom. I thought you were right behind me."

My jaw clenches. "Did someone attack you?"

She cringes as though someone's just shone a bright light in her eyes. "I… I can't remember. *Someone* was behind me. I just remember… falling."

Someone's gonna fucking die for this.

The nurse reenters the room, pushing a large machine on wheels. "Excuse me. I'm going to perform the ultrasound now."

Emma turns to me with alarm. "Ruslan…?"

"Don't worry. It's just to rule out any internal damage."

But her frown doesn't ease. "I… What if I'm pregnant…? I fell so far…"

The nurse chimes in, "If you are, the ultrasound will help us determine if the baby is alright. If there's even a baby in the first place." She steps forward holding a thin metallic probe. "Ma'am, the best way to get the clearest view of your uterus at this stage would be transvaginally. With your permission,

I'll insert this and begin scanning." She holds up the probe. "You'll feel mild discomfort at first."

Emma just nods but her forehead vein is throbbing hard.

"Don't worry," I whisper, drawing her eyes to me. "It'll be over soon."

She keeps her eyes on me, flinching and sucking in a sharp breath when the nurse inserts the probe. I hold my breath as the nurse squints at the monitor with an eagle eye. A part of me wonders if this is how Emma and I learn we're going to be parents. It's the first time my thoughts on fatherhood haven't centered around the Oryolov Bratva, around heirs and successors and doing my duty.

It's the first time I've thought simply, *I want this for* this. *For her. For us.*

"Hmm."

Emma's breath catches in her chest. "Was that a good 'hmm' or a bad 'hmm'?"

The nurse flushes and she clears her throat self-consciously. "There seems to be an anomaly on the ultrasound. This will need a doctor's expertise. I'll be right back."

She looks at me helplessly. "She didn't say if it was a good 'hmm' or a bad 'hmm.'"

"We'll deal with it—whatever it was—together."

I want to be her rock now, because God knows she needs that. But my words fall on deaf ears. She's already chewing on the inside of her cheek and, no matter how hard I grip her hand, the vein in her forehead doesn't stop thudding.

When the doctor walks in a few minutes later, Emma uses my arm to tow herself upright.

"How are we doing today?" the gray-haired doctor asks with the kind of false cheery tone that inspires nothing but doubt.

When no one answers him, he turns his attention to the ultrasound. Emma doesn't give him long. "W-was I pregnant, doctor?" she stammers. "Did I lose the baby?"

The doctor turns to her with pursed lips and a carefully constructed mask of professional sympathy. "Ms. Carson, I'm... I'm afraid there was no baby to lose."

"Oh." Her face drops instantly.

"I understand you've been trying. The thing is... it might be difficult for you to get pregnant at all."

This time, it's my face that drops. "What do you mean?" I bark. "Explain."

"The ultrasound shows a blocked fallopian tube."

Emma sucks in a breath. "You mean... I can't get pregnant?"

"No, no," he answers quickly, fidgeting with the stethoscope around his neck. "It's not impossible. It's just... not going to be *easy*. The odds are not in your favor."

I notice the tear running down her cheek. I understand her sadness; I understand her disappointment.

What I don't understand is *mine*.

Up until a few months ago, fatherhood was a curse I did my damndest to avoid. Until just a few nights ago, it was a duty I wanted to run from.

When did it become something I actually *want?*

64

EMMA

When I'm finally discharged from the hospital, Ruslan insists on taking me back to the penthouse.

It feels weird coming here when sex is off the table. Almost as though it's a waste of the apartment. Somehow, it all feels like a waste now.

Does all that incredible sex we've had mean nothing if nothing comes out of it?

Does he regret choosing me?

I'm aware that I'm not thinking rationally. My head hurts. My ankle hurts. My heart hurts. *Everything* hurts. But I can't pull myself out of the downward spiral.

I sit at the edge of his bed, staring out at the view, trying to imagine what my life will look like if I never get to carry a baby of my own, never raise a child of my own. Is this ache in my chest permanent? Will it ease with time or will I have to learn to live with it?

"Emma."

I accept the glass of water Ruslan's offering me but I don't take a sip despite how parched I am. It feels like every inch of motion requires energy I just don't have. And then, beneath that, it feels like I don't deserve the water, or his affection, or anything but this thudding, pounding, grinding ache in my chest.

He takes the glass off my hands but just when I think he's about to set it down, he brings it to my lips instead. All I do is swallow; he does the rest. When I've finished every last drop, he unzips my dress and pulls it off me. He strips off my underwear, too.

I'm struck by how different this experience is. Ruslan has undressed me a hundred times in the past. But this time is different. He's gentle. He takes it slow. He doesn't touch me except for when he needs to. The half-crazed look of passion and hunger that I'm used to seeing in his eyes is gone. Instead, his eyebrows pull together, his lips pursed down as if he's concentrating. I can only guess at what he's feeling.

He has to be disappointed, too, right? He was counting on me to give him an heir.

But instead, he got stuck with the dud woman and her dud fallopian tube.

I bet he's regretting that new contract now.

Then again, Ruslan Oryolov always thinks ahead. He probably has a hidden clause in our contract for just such a circumstance. *In the event that Party B (henceforth known as "The Dud") is unable to fulfill her contractually obligated duties as set forth in the preceding sections, Party A (henceforth known as "The Boss") will kick The Dud to the curb and replace her with a woman who possesses a functioning fallopian tube (and no gag reflex).*

He pulls the duvet over my naked body and suddenly, I'm sobbing all over his Egyptian cotton sheets.

As if he doesn't already have enough reasons to get rid of me.

"Emma…"

A moment later, his cool chest hits my back and his arms engulf me. The coldness subsides in seconds and I'm swimming in his oaky scent and his warmth.

"Y-you don't have to do this," I whimper.

"Sleep now," is all he whispers to me. "Just sleep."

His voice betrays nothing. I can't see his face and, even if I could, I'm scared of what I might see there. Yes, he's spent this whole ordeal by my side, but guilt doesn't necessarily equal affection. And kindness doesn't equal hope.

"Ruslan—"

"*Shh.*"

His voice is gentle. It's almost enough to make me believe that he's here because he cares about me. But I signed a contract that said that that would never happen. I don't want to be *that* girl. The girl who dared to hope for more even after she was explicitly told that more was not an option.

"Sleep now. In the morning, I'll take you back."

Is he stamping *"Return to Sender"* on my forehead? Are those words the kiss of death? I want to ask but I'm swallowed up in a cocktail of drugs, fatigue, and failure.

Might as well succumb to sleep now.

I'll still be a dud tomorrow.

65

EMMA

He's sitting on the chair by the window, his features twisted up with melancholy. At least I think it's melancholy. I might just be projecting. My mood feels a little bit like a sinkhole. The more I try to snap out of it, the deeper I fall in.

I watch him for a few minutes before he realizes I'm awake. He's so damn beautiful—all the more so now that I know the kind of man that hides behind that steely exterior.

The kind of man who cares enough about an eight-year-old boy to help him overcome his anger issues.

The kind of man who takes two little girls out to ice cream because their own father can't be bothered.

The kind of man who takes care of a broken woman because she clearly can't take care of herself.

His gaze flickers to me. "You're awake."

I nod and force myself upright.

"How are you feeling?"

"Tired."

"Breakfast will help."

Just the thought of eating makes me want to throw up. As does the thought of staying in this apartment any longer. It's too big a reminder of everything I can't do, everything I'm in the process of losing.

"I need to get home."

He doesn't argue. He probably wants to get me back home himself. Playing nurse really doesn't seem like Ruslan's style. And yet, as with everything else, he does it so well. He carries me to the bathroom despite my protests; he helps me get dressed; he even insists that I eat an apple before we leave.

I'm expecting the SUV to come to take us to Hell's Kitchen, but Ruslan ends up driving himself. The whole ride is marked by a heavy silence that I don't have the strength to break. I just sit there, wrapped up in a pair of sweats and one of Ruslan's sweaters. I have half a mind to pull the hood up so that I can hide beneath it.

I want to disappear.

When Ruslan parks, I stare up at the window of my apartment as a new sense of dread settles in. It's a Saturday, which means the kids will be at home all day.

I can't do this...

"Emma, are you okay?"

"Fine," I mumble without looking at him.

He doesn't try to touch me and for that, I'm grateful. I'm tired of being a charity case. And he's already done enough.

First, it was clearing my debt. Then it was giving me a lifeline in the form of the contract. After that came taking care of the kids, putting up with my family drama, fixing the car, dealing with Ben... The list goes on and on.

"Emma."

I clear my throat. "I should go in."

He's already at my door by the time I manage to get it open. He helps me down from the car and supports my weight all the way up to the apartment, no matter how many times I insist that I'm fine, that I can do it myself, that he doesn't have to come with me.

When we get closer, I can hear the girls' soft chatter, Phoebe's loud laugh. They're all in the living room.

Might as well get it over with.

The moment we walk inside, everyone freezes. Phoebe unfolds to her feet slowly, her eyes focused on my bruises. "Em? What happened?"

I manage to force a smile for the kids' sake. "I just had a little accident last night. Slipped and fell down the stairs." Josh sidles closer to me while the girls just gawk at the bandage on my head. "I'm fine, though. Totally fine."

God, I sound fake.

Phoebe's gaze veers from me to Ruslan but she doesn't say anything. Caroline drags her feet a little closer. "Does it hurt, Auntie Em?"

Everything hurts.

"No, sweetheart," I say cheerily. "I just need some rest. That's all."

"I know what will make you feel better, Aunt Em!" Reagan says enthusiastically. "A hug!"

She wraps her arms around my waist and squeezes tight. Caroline does the same and Josh puts his hand against my arm. I can feel the tears well up without warning. *Oh, God.* Another minute and I'm going to be bawling all over all the children.

Keep it together, Emma. Keep it the fuck toge—

"Kids." Ruslan's doing a much better job than I am of pretending everything's alright. "Your aunt needs some peace and quiet right now. How about I take you guys to the park for a couple of hours? Maybe we can get lunch afterwards."

"And ice cream?!" Reagan asks excitedly.

Ruslan spreads his hands wide like the answer is obvious. "What would the weekend be without ice cream?"

With the promise of sweets on the horizon, the girls release me and run to get their shoes on. I swallow my tears and plant a kiss on Josh's head to stop him staring at me. He's not as easily distracted as his sisters.

"I'm okay," I whisper to him. "Have fun with Ruslan."

When he goes to grab his shoes, I meet Ruslan's eyes for perhaps the first time all morning. "Thank you," I mouth to him.

He doesn't say a word. Just grazes my cheek with the back of his hand. It's the softest of touches and it only lasts a moment. Fleeting enough that, once he and the kids have waved goodbye and walked out of the apartment, I wonder if I imagined the whole thing.

"Emma…" Phoebe's hand strokes my back.

I turn around, throw my arms around her, and start sobbing hysterically. She doesn't say a word. She just lets me cry. She holds onto me the entire time as I completely fall apart and she does the kindness of simply letting me.

At some point, we end up on the couch with a box of tissues clutched in my lap and eventually, the tears dry up.

But the heaviness on my chest persists. Pheebs doesn't ask me a thing. She waits until I'm ready to talk. But when I finally open up, I can tell her only parts. The club, the fall, the possibility that someone I can't remember pushed me down that staircase.

It's a horrible story, but it all pales in comparison to what I really lost last night—the chance at a family of my own. The chance to be a mother.

The chance to give Ruslan what he wants.

"Emma, I know this is hard, but you still have one functioning fallopian tube. You could still get pregnant, if that's what you really wanted."

I shake my head. "It's gonna be so hard now. And it might take a very long time. I let him down, Phoebe. After everything he's done for me, I'm letting him down."

Frowning, she squeezes my arm. "Hey now, none of that. I'm sure Ruslan is disappointed, too, but that's not gonna change anything between the two of you."

I desperately wish I could tell her about the contract. It's hard to explain this situation to anyone who doesn't know the stakes.

"I'm afraid it will."

"Emma, I've seen the way he looks at you," Phoebe says gently. "You're not just the woman he's sleeping with. You're *his*. *That's* how he looks at you."

"He deserves better."

Phoebe's mouth turns down at the corners. She looks angry now. "Don't say that. Don't you dare even think—"

"It's *true*. From the beginning, it's been one thing after another. I'm a fucking mess, Phoebe. All I've come with is debts and grief and bills. A dead sister, a nightmare brother-in-law, three dependents, and now, a defective fallopian tube."

Her voice gets really soft. "Sweetheart, you are so much more than your problems. You have got to stop feeling sorry for yourself."

I grab a pillow and bury my face in it. I take a couple of deep breaths, then steel myself. "You're right. The kids will be back soon and I need to be strong for them."

Phoebe frowns. "No, that's not what I—"

"I might as well put all my focus and energy on the three of them. They're the only children I'm ever gonna have."

I ignore Phoebe's sigh and mope towards my bedroom. As grateful as I am for her company, what I really need right now is to be alone.

66

RUSLAN

I thought seeing her at the bottom of those stairs was bad.

I was wrong.

Watching her fall apart is worse.

Especially because she doesn't fall apart like she needs to. All messy tears and furious denials and angry conversations with God. No—she recedes into herself as though she's ashamed of her pain.

She barely meets my eyes. She barely smiles and sleepwalks through every conversation.

I understand why. She needs to put on a brave face for the kids. But every time she has to pretend like she's okay, I know how much it's costing her.

Which is probably why she kicked me out right after we returned from the park outing. *"I'm fine. I just need rest, Ruslan. I'm fine. I'm fine."*

She repeated those two cursed fucking words way too many times for me to believe them.

Now, I've somehow ended up back in the penthouse on 48th, buried deep in a bottle of my finest gin. I'm dangerously close to being drunk right now but it's been a while since I've indulged like this. I figure I'm allowed.

I'm pretty sure I'm hallucinating when I see Kirill walk in and do a double-take.

"Brother?"

Not a hallucination. *Dammit.*

"I forgot I gave you the access code to this place."

Kirill's eyes narrow. "I've been trying to contact you all night."

I shrug. "Haven't been... looking."

"Jesus, man, are you *drunk?*"

I scowl, contemplating throwing the almost empty bottle of gin at him. "I don't appreciate the judgment."

Kirill sits down heavily next to me. "It was Remmy. He was the one who got into an altercation with Emma. He didn't push her down the stairs—*she* pushed *him*; he just took her down with him."

I squint hard until all three versions of Kirill refocus into one. "Okay." I get to my feet, wobble, right myself. "He just signed his death warrant."

Kirill blocks my path with a hand to my chest. "Where do you think you're going?"

"Gonna go find the motherfucker. Then I'm gonna kill him."

"You're in no fit state to leave this apartment."

"Who's the *pahkan* here?" I growl.

Kirill doesn't move. He grabs the mostly-empty bottle of gin that I'd forgotten I was holding. "How fast did you get through this bottle?"

"Who the hell do you think you are? My *father*?"

"Okay, pause. Can we rewind for a second?" He takes a deep breath. "What the fuck *happened*?"

"I really need to change that stupid access code again. This is supposed to be *my* fortress of solitude," I mumble through fat, uncooperative lips.

He cocks an eyebrow and gestures for me to sit down. "It's not. This *was* your fuckpad. Most recently, it's been your Emma pad."

At the sound of her name, my knees buckle and I collapse on the sofa so hard that I'm pretty sure I hear some of the springs break. Kirill perches on the coffee table in front of me.

"Brother…" He sighs. "Talk to me."

So I tell him. About the ultrasound and the doctor's revelation. About Emma's reaction to all of it. By the time I'm finished, I'm fiending for another bottle of gin. Kirill seems to know exactly what I'm thinking, because he tucks the bottle behind him.

Little shit.

"I'm sorry, *sobrat*," he says quietly.

I look away from him. "It is what it is."

"So the chances of you having a baby with Emma are slim?"

"Slim to none, according to Dr. Dead-in-the-Eyes. Yes."

Kirill balances his elbows on his knees. "And if it turns out that you can't have a baby with Emma... what then?"

I frown. "What do you mean?"

"I mean, what's the next step?"

I have no idea what exactly he's asking me. But it forces me to think about the next step. If Emma and I can't have a baby together—what then?

I need an heir. And if she can't give me one...

"It won't change a fucking thing," I croak.

Kirill's eyebrows rise. "But you need an—"

"The kid is strong. And capable. And *smart*. He's already got the makings of a great leader. It won't take much to mold him into a great *pahkan*..."

Kirill rubs his temples in confusion. "What are you talking about? *Who* are you talking about?"

My eyes lock on him. "Josh. I'm talking about Josh. I could make him my heir." Kirill's jaw drops, but I'm flying too high with this idea to care. "He's a good kid. They all are. And they deserve more than the shithead of a father they've got. Emma's trying to strip Ben of his rights. I could help her adopt them. Fuck—I could adopt them myself. It would lend legitimacy to Josh's appointment. And then—"

"Ruslan. Stop."

Kirill's voice is soft but earnest. I hear that tone so rarely that I'm forced to stop for a moment and listen. All that gin is making it a little difficult, though.

"This is a *big* decision. One that affects more than just you. You're gonna need to think about it. Preferably while sober."

I wave away his concerns. "There have been worse marriages of convenience, Kirill—"

"Oh, are we talking about marriage now?" he scoffs. "I thought that was off the table."

"It's for appearances' sake," I snap impatiently. "If I'm making Josh my heir, then adopting him makes sense. Marrying his mother makes sense. It's pragmatic. I'm being fucking pragmatic."

Why doesn't he see how fucking perfect this is?

"I like her and I respect her. I care about those kids. I can take care of all of them. And I know Emma will agree—"

"Of *course* she'll agree!" Kirill cries out, throwing his hands up. "She's *in love* with you." He leans in a little closer, his voice dipping low with urgency. "Ruslan, you can talk about convenience and practicality all you want—but feelings don't give a fuck about pragmatism."

I sit back, head spinning. "We have a contract."

Kirill exhales wearily like he's exhausted of my bullshit. "That contract means jack shit, man. It's just a paper shield to protect your heart. To try to keep her out of it. But guess what? It's too late for that."

I'm feeling a lot more sober than I was a few minutes ago.

And that's not necessarily a good thing.

"What do you mean?"

"I mean, when are you going to cut the bullshit and admit to yourself that you're in love with Emma, too?"

I grit my teeth. "If you were anyone else, I'd punch the fucking teeth from your head."

He smiles cheekily. "Luckily for me, I'm not anyone else. I'm the man who's been at your side from the very beginning. I *know* you, Ruslan."

I shake my head. "I can't be in love with her, man. I just... I fucking can't..."

"Because of your contract?" I narrow my eyes at him and he chuckles. "Let me ask you this; if Emma decided to walk out of your life today, would you fight for her or would you let her go?"

I open my mouth. A second later—I shut it.

I run a hand through my hair.

I breathe out sharply.

"*Fuuuck!*"

Kirill smiles. "Yeah. I thought so."

67

RUSLAN

RUSLAN: ARE YOU AWAKE?

EMMA: *Yes.*

RUSLAN: *Come to the door.*

EMMA: *Why?*

RUSLAN: *Because I'm outside.*

A few moments later, she opens the door, ensconced in baggy sweats and a thick sweater. Her puffy eyes betray the fact that she's been crying. Her tangled hair betrays the fact that she's been tossing and turning in bed for a while.

"Ruslan, it's late."

I grab her hand and pull her out into the hallway. The recessed staircase lights are on but the only other light coming through is from the streetlamps and the moon streaming in through the windows above the staircase.

"I need to talk to you."

She sighs, crossing her hands over her chest. "It's been a really long day, Ruslan. I'm tired. I want to sleep."

"It's past one, Emma. If you wanted to sleep, you'd be asleep."

She bites her bottom lip and turns towards the door. "Okay, so maybe I just want to be alone," she snaps. "I appreciate everything you did for me today but honestly, it's not necessary. I can take care of myself."

"Can you?"

Her eyes narrow instantly. That's not how I meant it to come out. Coming here when I was less than a hundred percent sober may not have been the best idea, but it's too late now; I've already jumped down the rabbit hole.

"You need to leave."

"I'm not going anywhere until you hear me out."

Her eyes go wide. "Does playing the hero make you feel good about yourself, Ruslan? Because I'm not interested in being the victim. I'm not interested in being your charity case, either. What I need right now is *space*."

"If that's what you really want, then I'll accept it. But first, I need to say a few things."

Her mouth turns down at the corners and her gaze gets more distant. *What is she anticipating?* She sighs. "I'll give you five minutes."

"I only need one." I meet her eyes. "I'm not going anywhere, Emma. I meant what I said: you're *mine*. And I'm gonna take care of you. And those kids. If they're the only children we ever have together, that's alright with me."

Her eyes get wider as I speak. Her cheeks flush with color until it overtakes the bruise on her face.

"Y-you... really mean that?" she asks in barely a whisper.

"I never say anything I don't mean."

She takes a deep breath. "I... um... That's a lot to process."

I take her hand. "Take your time. Just know that I'm right here. I won't let you push me out the door again."

Her fingers return pressure. She's quiet for a moment, chewing at her lip and looking at me, at the moon, at the floor, at me again. At last, she whispers, "Do you wanna come in?"

"Only if you want me to."

She meets my eyes. "I do."

68

EMMA

So many things have changed since the night Ruslan showed up at my door.

For starters, this is the first time I've ever initiated a meeting at the penthouse. Ruslan seemed confused earlier when I called him to ask if it was possible. He was quiet for a while. Hesitating? Considering refusing? I'm not sure. But in the end, he'd sent Boris to collect me from the apartment.

I don't quite know why, but I'm nervous as hell when I step through those shiny silver doors. Probably because we're moving into uncharted territory here. A few months ago— hell, a few *weeks* ago—I'd never have expected Ruslan to show up outside my door, determined to be a part of my life despite the fact that I couldn't give him what he wanted.

Something's shifting between us. It's not just sex anymore. It's sex *and feelings.*

And all the messiness that comes with it.

The penthouse living room is empty, so I try the bedroom instead. He's lying on the bed in his boxers, looking incredibly comfortable.

And incredibly sexy...

Focus, Emma.

"Hey."

He sits up and gestures for me to come over. I slide into the bed beside him and take a deep breath. "I wanted to say something to you."

He raises his eyebrows. "I'm listening."

"I wanted to say... *thank you*. For taking care of me like you did. For staying with me. For looking after the kids. And most importantly, for choosing to stick around. Even now."

He exhales a soft, raspy rumble. "Where would I go?"

There's an anxious trembling in my heart. I'm on the edge of happiness; I'm just terrified to fall.

I glance over to the chair by the window. His Armani suit is draped over it and it reminds me of what's happening tonight.

August thirteenth.

"Oh, *shit*! You have a big event at Alcazar tonight, don't you? That's why you were hesitant on the phone—*shit*—I'm so sorry—" I jerk upright, ready to get off the bed.

But he grabs my arm and pulls me back down. "Emma. Calm down. It's okay."

"I should have remembered. I haven't been to work in three days and I've already forgotten everything."

His chuckle soothes me. He coaxes me closer to him and runs his fingers down my face. "The bruise looks better."

I nod. "The cut is healing nicely, too. Had my stitches checked this morning." I glance at the suit again, shining a moody navy in the evening sunlight. "I'll get out of your way—

Ruslan doesn't loosen his hold on me. "I've got some time. And you've come all this way…"

He gives me a smile that makes me blush right down to my toes. "Are you sure?"

He squeezes my ass as he hauls me into his lap and grinds his erection against my heat. "What do you think? Do I feel unsure?"

I cup the side of his face and kiss him. I go in hot and heavy, my tongue pushing into his mouth, desperate to have him claim me the way he likes, the way I love. His hands slide up and down my back but it's more of a caress than a *I'm-gonna-rip-your-clothes-off* pawing.

Tenderly, he pushes me backwards onto the bed and rains soft little kisses along my face and down my neck.

Strange. He's never *this* gentle.

I arch my hips up until I can feel his hardness. I rub myself against him, desperate for some friction. While he plays with my earlobe, I reach down and wrap my hand around his cock.

"Fuck me, Ruslan," I whisper in his ear. "I want you to fuck me hard."

He laughs, his breath fanning out over my face, sweet and cool. "I'm happy to fuck you… but we're gonna take it slow today."

I pout. "Why?"

He rears back and looks at me with a half-smile on his face. "Emma, you spent the night in a hospital only three days ago, remember?"

I just push my hips into his groin a little harder. "I can take it."

He shakes his head. "I've created a monster."

"Then maybe you need to tame me."

"Oh, I plan to," he says with a fierce snarl. Then he sighs and it smooths out again. "Just... not tonight."

He silences me with a kiss, his fingers pushing my skirt up and my panties aside. My heart is thrumming softly as he glides his fingers over my clit. Usually, the sex is so explosive that I can't think straight.

This is different.

I *am* thinking. About how good this feels. About how gentle he's being with me. How easily it would be to misconstrue his tenderness for love.

When he finally enters me, I gasp, my gaze connecting with his. Those scorching amber eyes are brighter than I've ever seen them. His thrusts are so controlled. The slow build is in some ways more intense than the heated, button-ripping, breathless-gasping sex I'm used to having with Ruslan. Everything feels so much more heightened.

Unbroken eye contact and synchronized breathing and the way his lips ghost over mine, as if I'm the most precious thing in the world.

Careful, Emma...

I told myself that it didn't matter what he called me. I didn't need a title or for him to say he loved me. *This* is what matters. This crazy, cosmic, powerful connection that we're experiencing together—this is all I need.

But still... it would be so freaking amazing to hear it all the same.

When I come, it takes my breath away.

Afterwards, as I'm struggling to put my skirt back on straight, he grabs me. Tender again. Soft. "I'm going to be busy the next couple of nights. But if you need me, just call. I'll be there."

I smile. "I'll call."

～

Ben is standing in the living room facing the door when I walk in.

"*My God!*" I gasp, holding a hand to my racing heart. "Creepy much?"

"Where've you been?"

"None of your business." I glare at him as I drop my purse on the kitchen table. "Are the kids all in bed?"

"Amelia's putting them to sleep right now," he says dismissively. "Did you forget that I needed to talk to you?"

I sigh. "What did you need to speak to me about, Ben?"

My body goes cold at the nasal voice that emerges from just around the corner. "About what a bad, *bad* girl you've been."

"What the—"

Remmy steps into the living room, his arms folded over his chest, that skin-crawling leer on his lips. "Hello there, pretty woman."

I look between Ben and Remmy as horror scours through me. "What the hell is this?"

Ben moves to the sofa. "I think the better question would be, what the hell is *this*?" He plucks out something from behind one of the cushions.

I freeze. I recognize that sheaf of papers.

The contract.

"Where did you get that?" I whisper.

"The glove compartment of your car, of course. Where you *hid* it," he sneers at me.

"What the hell were you doing in my car?" I'm shaking now. If I don't resort to anger, I'll be reduced to tears.

Ben just shrugs. "Figured, since you were outta commission for a few days, I'd make use of the new wheels. Turns out that was a great decision. Who knew I'd strike gold?"

"You fucking bas—"

"Now, now, Emma, there's no need to get emotional," Remmy chides, pushing himself off the wall. "I did warn you."

I try to lunge for the contract but Ben holds it out of my reach. Chuckling, he passes it to Remmy, who starts *tut-tutting* in my direction. "Who would have thought, hm? The pretty little assistant, no better than a two-bit hooker on the side of the road."

"That is *not* what this is!"

"Oh, no?" Remmy asks with arched eyebrows. "Because there's a whole clause in this contract that details how you will be paid an exorbitant sum of money every month for spreading your legs two nights a week in a luxurious penthouse with Ruslan Oryolov."

I want to kill Ben, but since Remmy's the one with his finger on the trigger, I focus my energy on him.

"Remmy, *please*—don't print this."

He shrugs, eyes gleaming like lit coals. "If you had come clean with me in the beginning, I'd have found a way to protect you. I could have blacked out your name in this contract, protected your identity. Now, though…" He shrugs again. "Now, I couldn't care less about your reputation."

He really thinks I care about *my* reputation. The only reputation I'm thinking about right now is Ruslan's.

I'm this close to a panic attack. If only I had the luxury of succumbing to one. "Okay. Okay. What do you want?"

Remmy smiles. "Oh, *now*, she asks."

"Money—is that it?" I press, looking between the two scumbags in front of me. "I can get you money. Just, please, bury the story."

Remmy shakes his head. "Sorry, honey. No amount of money will sway me. My only goal is destroying Ruslan Oryolov. You just happen to be collateral damage." He drops the contract onto the coffee table. "You can keep that. I have plenty of copies." He slams the door on his way out.

I turn slowly to Ben. "Do you realize what you just did?"

His fists knot up at his sides, but his eyes are weirdly hazy and distant. "I'm not sure the whore should be casting judgment. I saw an opportunity and I took it. It's not like you were gonna share all your dirty money with me."

I swallow my tears. My hands are still trembling. I shouldn't feel so betrayed, but I think a part of me was still clinging to the hope that Ben could be saved. For his kids' sake, if nothing else.

"The difference between us is that I took Ruslan's money for those children." I jab a quivering finger down the hall where they're sleeping. "You took Remmy's money for *yourself*. And you screwed me and the kids over in the process."

"Oh, boo fucking hoo."

When he tries to walk past me, I get right in his face. "What the hell *happened* to you?" I scream, stabbing my finger in his chest. "What happened to the man my sister married?"

The scowl on his face freezes. His mouth drops and his eyebrows arch and those hands vibrate even faster at his sides. For a moment, I think he might actually hit me. "That man died when she did."

Then he pushes past me and disappears into his room.

I let out a strangled sob. *What do I do now?* But the answer is obvious. There's only one thing I can do.

I need to tell Ruslan. I need to explain what's happened so we can fix this. I grab my car keys and race back out...

Hoping against hope that this won't be the last straw for him.

69

RUSLAN

KIRILL: *Where are you, bro? You gonna miss your own party?*

RUSLAN: *On my way.*

I start driving, feeling incredibly confident about the launch. This drug will be the crowning jewel in my Bratva empire. Even if I live to a hundred, I don't think I'll ever achieve anything this big again.

I've only been driving for a few minutes when my phone starts ringing. Kirill has the patience of a fucking gnat sometimes. I'm so sure it's him that I don't even check the name on my screen before I press accept through the steering wheel.

"What do you want?"

"R-Ruslan?"

Immediately, all my sensors start pinging. She sounds distraught. "Emma, what's wrong?"

"I-I'm so sorry to call. I know you're busy tonight—the big launch and e-everything…"

"Are you crying?"

My hands freeze up on the wheel. I didn't expect to get a call from her less than an hour after she left the penthouse. Which can only mean one thing—something's gone very wrong, very fast.

"Um… I… need to talk to you. It's better if we—" She pauses and I hear the screech of tires and a few obnoxious honks. "—we talk face-to-face."

"Emma, are you driving?"

"I'm coming to your penthouse."

"I already left."

"Oh, *shit*. Ruslan, I'm so sorry. Everything's a fucking mess —*aah!*" Her scream is drowned out by more grating tires, more honks.

"Fucking hell," I snarl. "Emma, listen to me. Pull the car over right now. You are in no fit state to be driving." She only sniffles in response. "Once you've parked, send me your location. I'll drive to you."

"A-are you sure?"

"I want you off the road this instant. You hear me?"

"Yes," she says in a small voice.

"I expect to receive your location in the next two minutes."

The call drops and I pull to the side myself and wait for her to send me her coordinates. A million different thoughts are running rampant through my head.

Is she rethinking our contract?

Does she want more out of our agreement?

Is she backsliding into depression about her fertility?

Whatever it is, I won't be able to concentrate on the launch until I know what's going on with her. I fire off a quick text to Kirill.

RUSLAN: *Running late. Something's come up. Will be there in an hour or so.*

Immediately after I send the text, Emma's location comes in. Thankfully, she's only ten minutes from where I am. I make a quick U-turn and hit the gas.

Eight minutes later, I pull in behind her Mercedes with my tires smoking. She's pacing the pavement, hands crossed over her chest, brow furrowed down in a sharp V.

The moment she sees me, she runs right into my arms. "I'm so sorry," she blubbers.

I have no idea what she's apologizing for, but I need to ensure first things first. "Where are the kids?"

"They're home in bed. Amelia's with them."

I nod with relief before focusing on the tears streaking Emma's face. "What happened in an hour to cause this reaction?" I ask, wiping her tears away with my thumb.

She's staring at my suit. "God, you look handsome…"

"Emma."

She blinks, squeezing out two more fat tears. "I went home and—"

HONK. HONK. HONK.

"Fucking *hell*," I growl. "We can't be parked here. Get in my car. I'll have one of my men pick up the Mercedes and drive it back to Hell's Kitchen."

The vein is pulsing softly in her forehead as she gets into the passenger's seat. I send Boris a quick text and then drive us out onto the road.

"I know the timing is horrible—"

Ring. Ring. Ring.

Since my phone is connected to the car, the ringtone blares louder than normal. Emma jumps in her seat and I cut the call without answering.

"It's just Kirill calling to nag me about being late. Go on."

Her eyebrows turn down. "Oh, God..."

Sighing, I try to rein in my frustration. "It doesn't matter, Emma. Just tell me what's bothering you."

"M-maybe it can wait until—"

Ring. Ring. Ring.

Kirill again. *What the fuck?* He's not usually this annoying persistent. I reject it. "You were saying?"

This time, she doesn't even get the chance to get a single word out before my phone starts up *again*.

I'm not about to ignore this many calls from my second. *Something's up.*

"Kirill?"

"*Ruslan!* Where the fuck are you?"

"I told you something came—"

"Yeah, well, something's come up here, too. And it's not good." He's normally unflappable. Nothing is a big deal to him. So to hear the panic in his voice right now…

"What's going on?"

"Are you alone?"

My gaze slides to Emma. She's sitting there quietly, hands tangled together, chewing on her bottom lip.

"Emma's here but it's okay. You can tell me anyway."

Kirill hesitates for only a second. "We started circulating the Venera a little over an hour ago. Everything was going smoothly. Everyone's mood was up. The samples were doing their magic. And then—"

And then…

"—we had five people O.D."

I nearly crash into the car in front of us. Emma screams and grabs my arm instinctively. I just barely manage to veer away in time to avoid the collision.

The only thing better than my reflexes are my instincts.

And they're telling me that there's foul play at work here.

"Venera's not that kind of drug. It's an aphrodisiac. Basically just an oyster on steroids. It's not even fucking *possible* to overdose on it."

"Brother, I'm looking at five bodies right now that say otherwise."

Emma's eyes are wide, fearful, and aimed right at me.

"Get one of the men to pick Sergey up," I order. "Go yourself if you need to. I want him at the club fucking immediately. I'll be there soon."

Emma doesn't say anything when I hang up. But a second later, she moves her hand to my knee and squeezes it gently. It's amazing how much of a difference one small gesture can make. The fear I saw in her eyes earlier is not *because* of me.

It's *for* me.

"I have to go handle this."

"I know. Of course you do. I can just get a cab back—"

"Absolutely the fuck not," I growl. "I'm dropping you off at my place. I'll be back once I've got the situation under control."

She accepts that wordlessly. At least until we arrive outside the sleek thirty-five floor luxury skyscraper. Then she turns to me with a frown. "This is Madison," she says. "Not 48th Street."

"Penthouse #1. The access code is 23-28-37."

She seems flustered when she exits the SUV and gives me a half-hearted wave as I drive off. I'll have to worry about Emma after tonight. Right now, I need to focus on the botched Venera launch.

Ping. I chance a quick look at the text I've just received from Kirill.

KIRILL: *Sergey's missing.*

Fuck.

70

EMMA

The Inner Sanctum.

That's how the penthouse on Madison is referred to around the water cooler at Bane. People have more factual information about Atlantis or Narnia, though. If the rumors are to be believed, Ruslan paid a whopping three hundred and thirty million dollars to purchase it a few years ago.

No one has ever seen the inside of it.

Until now.

First of all, it's *breathtaking*. Like a palace in the sky. Even my frazzled brain is capable of noticing just how beautiful every single detail of this place is.

But that's not why I like it. I like it because it *smells* like him. That familiar oaky spice is everywhere and it's absurdly comforting.

How did I end up here?

Not only had Ruslan spoken freely to Kirill in my presence while we were in the car, but he'd given me access to the Inner Sanctum? To the untrained eye, they may have seemed like small gestures, but I know how significant they are. He's sending me a message with those gestures.

He's choosing to let me into his life.

He's letting down his walls bit by bit.

He's telling me he trusts me.

And *this* is the place I'm gonna have to tell him that I've fucked it all up. That, soon, the world will know about our dirty contract. That my dumb ass has gone and pressed the self-destruct button without even realizing it.

I leave the entry gallery and venture towards the stunning views that overlook Central Park. The furniture is minimalistic, but I love every piece I see, including the curved white sofa that takes up an entire side of the living room. It looks like he plucked a literal cloud right out of the sky.

I follow his scent around the apartment. Most of the rooms look untouched. The master bedroom is the only one that feels like it's truly finished. I note a desk next to the bed, a pair of shoes tossed casually aside, a few of Ruslan's shirts strewn over the divan.

I recognize the baby blue shirt that he wore just yesterday. I pick it up and bring it to my nose, inhaling sharply. Like an addict taking a hit for the first time in years.

If only I could bottle that smell...

I'm gonna want to remember it once this all blows up in my face.

I end up stripping down to my underwear. Then I pull the baby blue shirt on and crawl into his bed. There's that smell again, clinging to the bedsheets. I lie in the middle of the mattress, curled up into a ball. I just stare up at the ceiling and do my best not to think of anything at all.

After I've spent an hour spacing out, I check my phone to make sure he hasn't tried calling or checking.

Nothing. Nada. Zilch.

I'm not sure if I'm waiting for him to return—or dreading it.

I'm on the verge of falling asleep when I finally hear a sound from beyond the room. I jerk upright instantly, wide awake all of a sudden. Before I can go investigate, Ruslan strides in. He's already discarded his coat somewhere and he's unbuttoning the front of his shirt.

He doesn't acknowledge me apart from a small nod in my direction. His eyes are hollowed-in, dark circles circling them and making his sharp cheekbones even sharper. I've never seen him like this before.

Angry? Of course.

Frustrated? Definitely.

Annoyed? More times than I can count.

But *tired*? The kind of tired that sits on your shoulders and drags you down toward the earth? Never. Not even once.

"Ruslan—"

I'm on my way out of the bed when he holds up a hand to stop me. "No. Stay right there."

He strips his shirt off, then his pants. He discards both on the floor and climbs into bed with me. He lies on his back, his face aimed at the ceiling just like mine was a moment ago, and closes his eyes. Only after a few minutes of silent breathing does he finally speak.

"*Fuck.*"

I scoot a little closer and balance myself on one elbow as I look down at him. "What happened?"

He doesn't open his eyes. "We had to shut down the launch and send everyone home. It was the worst thing that could have happened. And of course, Sergey has disappeared into thin air and I have no clue if he was taken or he chose to run."

I'm surprised that he's talking about it at all. I start tracing my fingers along his arm. "Who's Sergey? And why would he choose to run?"

"He's my lead chemist. He has complete control over my formula. If he chose to alter it before the launch…"

"But why would he do that?"

"Because someone offered him more money than I did."

A little shiver runs over my body. This is the first time we've really spoken about his other life and the work it involves. I'm getting a sense of just how huge it all is.

"So you had him invent a… a drug?"

His eyes finally open. They veer to me, more gold than amber right now. "Venera is a drug, yes, but it's meant to be a poppable aphrodisiac. We conducted months of trials to ensure that its effects weren't harmful or addictive. We were so thorough. Except now, five people are dead and my whole venture is over before it even started."

I've never heard him talk like this. The defeatist attitude is not him. I move even closer, cup his face with my palm, and force him to look at me.

"*Nothing* is over," I insist. "You're Ruslan fucking Oryolov. There's nothing you can't fix."

"I can't bring people back from the dead."

My face drops. "Right. No, of course not. I'm sorry—that was a stupid thing to say."

He doesn't smile but his expression softens, just a little. His eyebrows relax and his mouth isn't quite so severe a straight line.

"How much trouble are you in?"

His jaw sets firmly. "Nothing I can't handle."

"Now, *there's* the Ruslan I know."

He laughs bitterly and I keep running a hand over his jaw, his arms, his abs. I'm not quite sure what to do in this situation but I do know that now is not the right moment to tell him about Remmy. I desperately *want* to. But it's too much in one night. He needs the peace of this apartment.

Maybe he even needs *me*.

"Can I get you anything?" I ask softly.

His eyes graze over my face. "I have everything I need right now."

Then he kisses me. Soft and slow, his lips feel like they're caressing mine. I always seem to lose myself in him, but this is the first time I feel like he's trying to lose himself in me. I try to memorize how it feels, smells, looks, sounds.

I have to remember it all.

Growling into my lips, his hands scour my body, tugging at my panties before he's even gotten my shirt off. He buries his face between my breasts, kneading my nipples with his tongue while he slides his fingers in and out of me. I cling to him, intoxicated by the strength in those arms that still manage to be so gentle.

I writhe on his hand, desperate for the orgasm he's promising. But tonight, I want to give him what he gives me. I want to erase all possibility of thought from his head until it's just him and me—two naked bodies minus all the noise.

I have to push him off me. His irises are dilated, his gaze intense. But before he can pull me back against him, I slide down to his waist and pull his boxer briefs off. I slide my tongue over his tip, lapping up the drop of pre-cum.

Cupping his balls, I run my tongue down the length of him, honing in on the most sensitive parts of him that I've discovered over the last few months. I like knowing what makes him moan, what makes him sigh, what makes him stiffen and buck and bite his lip. I suck him slow, deeper and deeper, inch by inch.

"Fuck," he moans. "Fuck—Emma…"

I don't let up. Even when tears bead up in the corners of my eyes, I keep going. I swallow his cock as my hands work him up and down until his twitching intensifies, his breath shortens, and then he comes.

"Fuck!"

He explodes in my mouth and I swallow every last drop until he has nothing left to give. Wiping my lips, I rise back up and catch my breath. His chest rises and falls, little droplets of sweat dancing along his pecs. I climb on top of him and start licking each one of them off.

His eyes flutter closed as he lets me tend to him. Then, when his breathing has steadied, he grabs me unexpectedly and flips me to my side while I let out a sound that's halfway between a gasp and a squeal. He tucks me underneath one arm and wraps the other around my waist.

I feel his lips at my shoulder and then, seconds later, his breath tickling my neck. "Ruslan...?"

But I already know he's asleep. That's another first, another indication that he's getting more comfortable with me. He never falls asleep first.

A part of me is relieved. But an equally big part of me is terrified.

I'll tell him about Remmy first thing tomorrow.

No excuses.

71

RUSLAN

I'm jolted awake by a pinch on the arm. I jerk up and spot Kirill at my bedside. Emma is draped over me, so I have to move slowly and carefully to untangle myself from her and the sheets before I can get out.

Kirill backs off to the doorway while I pull my boxers on. I check to see that Emma is still sleeping and then I follow him into the living room.

"What are you doing here?" I growl.

"Sorry. I tried calling, but you didn't pick up."

"Did you find Sergey?"

"Man's still missing. But the security team did find something else that I think you'll want to know about."

Kirill's lips are pursed together. He's also cracking his knuckles a lot, which is a sure sign that he's got bad news for me.

"What is it?"

He clears his throat and gestures towards the thin brown envelope sitting on the dining table. "I'm sorry, man."

Those are ominous words. I rip off the top half of the envelope and pull the contents out. It's a sheath of photographs. The first one is a blurry picture of Remmy Jefferson leaning against a very familiar-looking wall. Just beyond is a woman with her hair pulled up in a bun. The picture quality is low but I recognize Emma immediately.

I glance up at Kirill. "What the fuck is this?"

"It looks like Remmy visited Emma last night."

Last night? Is that why she was so frazzled? She was borderline hysterical. Goddammit, why the fuck hadn't I just slowed down for two seconds and let her say what she'd called me to say?

Oh, right—*five dead bodies.*

I move onto the next photograph. It's more of the same. Remmy standing in Emma's apartment, the two obviously engaged in a conversation. Of course, there's no way to know the nature of the conversation. But the fact that it took place in her apartment is troubling.

When I look up again, Kirill is staring back at me with wary eyes. "I hate to say it, brother… but I think she might've conned you."

I shake my head. Even in the face of photographic evidence, I'm willing to give Emma the benefit of the doubt. Pictures can be doctored. And even if they haven't been, there has to be another explanation.

"She wouldn't do that."

"Look at those pictures, bro."

"I'm fucking looking, *bro*," I snarl. "And I don't fucking believe them. I trust her; she wouldn't—"

"That's not all."

I feel like I'm turning to stone. "Go on."

He cracks his knuckles again. His tendons must be shredded to nothing at this point. "Our contact in the newsroom gave me a call this morning. He wanted to give us a heads-up. They're getting ready to run a story about you soon. He preempted the conversation by saying there was nothing he could do to stop it."

Just like that, my heart drops. "What story?"

Kirill shuffles from one foot to the other. "A story that involves a sex contract between you and your assistant."

Breathe.

Fucking breathe.

One.

Two.

Three...

"*FUCK!*"

Kirill takes a step back. "I know this is a lot but we're gonna have to get in damage control mode real fast. It's bad enough we have the botched Venera launch to deal with. But a sex scandal on top of that…"

I barely hear him. How have things gone from absolutely perfect to absolute shit in a matter of seconds? How is it possible that she was able to fool me so completely?

Months. I've devoted *months* of my life to this woman. I made her a part of my life. I immersed myself in hers.

I fucking *trusted* her.

The proof is in the fact that she's here at all—in my place of solitude. The place I come to when I want to get away from everything. The place I swore no woman would ever see the inside of.

"How do you want me to handle this?" Kirill asks.

"First, *I* have to handle it."

I snatch up the pictures and storm into the bedroom. The moment I walk in, I realize what a huge mistake I've made. Her scent is everywhere—honey and citrus and sweetness and *lies*. Now, every time I walk into this room, I'll imagine her sprawled across my bed, one slim, bare thigh peeking out from beneath the covers.

No.

Slowly but surely, I have to start expelling every trace of her from my world.

And it starts right fucking now.

She's stirring when I approach. "Ruslan...?" she mumbles sleepily.

"Get up."

Her eyes dart open and the sleep drains from her face the moment she looks at me. "Ruslan, w-what's wrong?" Her eyelashes flutter and her cheeks flush. "Is this about last night?"

"Apparently, last night was the least of my problems." I fling the pictures at her. She flinches back and the photographs scatter, fluttering around her like flakes of ash at the end of the world.

"What…?"

She picks up one of the photographs. Her eyes go wide and she pales. "Ruslan—let me explain—"

As it turns out, that's all the explanation I need. "Get your clothes on and get the *fuck* out of my apartment."

She stares at me as though she's having a hard time recognizing me. *Well, that makes two of us.* "R-Ruslan…" Her voice is barely above a whisper and still, it claws at me.

I turn from her. "You've got two fucking minutes or I'll throw you into that elevator ass naked."

She scrambles off the bed. I can't even bear to look at her. I hear a hint of a sob from behind me but I clench my jaw and dig my heels in. I was a fool to let her in so deep. I was a fool to trust her at all. I knew it was a mistake but I let myself be convinced. And for what? A sweet smile and easy pussy?

"Ruslan, please. I told you I wanted to speak to you last night—"

I whip around. "So you could come clean about your dirty deal with Remmy Jefferson?" he growls. "It's too fucking late to make amends now, Emma."

She's breathing fast. "You don't even know—"

"All I need to know is that you *betrayed* me. I don't care about the reasons."

"I—

"KIRILL!" I roar.

She recoils back, hurt blanketing her face. "You're not even gonna hear my side?"

"*You* were the *only* one who was supposed to know about that contract!" I roar. "If you didn't fucking talk, how the fuck did Remmy Jefferson get his hands on it?"

The redness on her cheeks has spread to her chest. "I was a fool—"

"Not the word I'd use." I turn my back on Emma when Kirill appears at the door. "Make sure this woman is wiped from my life. Make sure her desk at Bane Corp. is cleared, make sure our contract is severed, make sure I never have to see her again after this moment."

"Ruslan, *please*. You need to listen to—"

I whirl on her. "I'm done listening. And I'm done with you. Our agreement is officially at an end, Ms. Carson." She flinches when I backslide into her surname. "Your services will no longer be required."

I'm almost at the door when she grabs my arm. "I just need *two* minutes! Please!"

I twist out of her grasp and shove her against the wall. She stumbles backward, a strangled scream escaping her lips. I step forward and tighten my hand around her throat.

"You know exactly who I am now," I snarl at her. "What you should also know is that I'm a *pakhan* first and a CEO second. If you cross me again, I will destroy you. Do you understand?"

I put just a little bit of pressure on her throat. Not enough to hurt her but plenty to scare her. Her eyes go wide and I get what I'm after.

Fear.

"I asked you a question, Ms. Carson. Do. You. Understand?"

She nods slowly.

"Good." I release her and sweep out of the room. "Kirill... get rid of her."

I hear her sobs even as the elevator doors slide shut. I try to block out the sound but even after the doors spew me out onto the ground floor, I can still hear her. I can still feel her. Even now, after everything I just discovered, she's everywhere.

On my tongue.

Under my skin.

In my fucking soul.

72

EMMA

I didn't just imagine it, did I?

Wasn't it just a few days ago that we were talking babies? Planning a future together? Merging together two worlds that somehow made sense even though they shouldn't?

I cry for most of the ride back to Hell's Kitchen. I figure I might as well get the tears out now, right? I can't exactly break down in front of the kids.

The kids.

"Oh, God," I whisper, covering my face with my hands.

I've been silently crying this entire time to try to preserve my dignity in Kirill's presence. But the moment I think about those kids, I think, *Fuck it*. What dignity do I have left that I need to preserve?

I start ugly crying, loud, snotty sobs breaking through the silence of Kirill's car. For the most part, he ignores me. Right up until he parks outside the apartment and I realize that he's got the baby lock on, trapping me inside. I wipe my tears and turn to him. He's looking at me carefully, like he's not sure what to make of me.

"Can you let me out or did your boss give you instructions to humiliate me some more?"

His brows arrow downward. "I thought you were better than this."

I can feel my cheeks burn up. "Excuse me?"

"Selling Ruslan out for money? It's below you, Emma."

I bite down on my anger. "You know what? Fuck you. And fuck your boss, too. I didn't rat him out for money. I would never do that and, one day, Ruslan's going to figure that out. But it'll be too late. By the time he realizes it, I'll be long gone. Now—" I pull at the handle of the car violently. "—let me out of this damn car!"

The locks click open and I practically soar out of the vehicle. I run into the building and watch Kirill drive away from the corner window.

Is this it then?

The roar of Kirill's engine feels like the severing of my last tie to Ruslan.

I wipe my face dry as I take the stairs up to the apartment, but I'm still on shaky ground. I have no idea how I'll respond if one of the kids asks me about Ruslan.

What I want to do is force a smile and answer evasively.

What I'll probably do is burst into fresh tears.

No—you're stronger than that. You can do this, Emma. For the kids. For Sienna.

Josh, Rae, and Caroline swarm around me the moment I walk through the door. I give them all big hugs and sloppy kisses and take comfort in the fact that there are at least three little people who still think I'm a decent human being.

Of course, all three of those little people also think having ice cream for breakfast is a great idea. But right now, I'll take what I can get.

I relieve Amelia of her nannying duties and, after we send her off, I sit on the living room floor and pretend that I'm invested in a game gone wrong that includes competing tea parties that Reagan and Caroline are hosting against each other. Any other day and I'd have been splitting my side, laughing at their sibling rivalry, but today—

Well, fake it 'til you make it.

"Aunt Emma?" Josh asks, venturing over to my side. "If you're feeling tired, I can look after the girls."

I wrap an arm around Josh and kiss him on the forehead. "Thanks, kiddo, but I'm fine."

He doesn't seem convinced. He keeps looking at my face as though he can will away the bruises if he just concentrates hard enough.

"Auntie Em!" Reagan cries, clearly upset about the fact that Mr. Bunny has chosen to go to Caroline's tea party instead of hers. "Whose tea party are you coming to?"

"I'm coming to both."

Reagan puts her hands on her hips. "You have to *choose*."

"I can't choose between my two favorite nieces. I love you both equally."

Caroline's attempt to lure me to her side comes in the form of old brown playdough. "My tea party has chocolate swiss rolls."

Despite my dark mood, I find myself chuckling. The chuckle dies in my throat when Ben rounds the corner looking... halfway presentable?

What the fuck is happening?

His shirt is free of stains, his jeans are free of holes, and everything he's wearing is clearly brand spanking new. My eyes pop when I notice the shoes on his feet.

"Are those *Yeezys?*"

He lifts the shoe up so I can get a better look. "Pretty damn snazzy, huh? I liked 'em so much, I got the same pair in white. Can't believe they're selling these things for like five hundred a pop."

My hands ball into fists. "Girls, can you take your tea parties to your room, please? I need to speak to your dad."

Josh gets up right away and starts hurrying his sisters along. The moment I hear the door close, I turn to Ben in a fury. "You spent five *hundred* dollars on a pair of shoes?"

"Did you not hear me say I bought two pairs? Or are you just really bad at math?"

I put my hands on his chest and shove him. Hard. He's so startled, he trips backwards and lands on the armchair. "So you're spending the money you screwed me over for on *yourself?*" I screech.

He struggles upright. "Oh, for fuck's sake—here we go again."

"Do you know what you just cost me?"

"Don't worry; you'll find another fuck buddy soon enough."

This isn't the first time I've found myself thinking that some murders are justified. *For four to live, one must die.*

A bubble of crazed laughter bursts out of me. It startles me just as much as it startles Ben. "What the fuck? Are you losing it or some shit?" He picks himself off the sofa and smooths down his Yves St. Laurent t-shirt.

"You know, I just may be losing it. And you are the reason!"

He rolls his eyes. "You really know how to bring the drama, don't you?"

"You cost us our last lifeline, Ben," I whisper. "Now, I'm fucked. *We're* fucked. I don't have an income anymore!"

He shrugs. "You'll find something. It just better be soon, 'cause I saw another pair of shoes that I like."

"You motherfu—" He grabs my arm all of a sudden and reels me towards him, so close that I can smell his breath. *Urgh.* Garlic and beer. "Let go of me!"

He glares at me, his eyes shot through with scaly red veins. "I am fucking *done* with your nagging and bitching. I am the man of this house and I expect you to start *respecting* that."

He twists my arm just to make his point but, despite the pain, the very idea of respecting Ben seems laughably ridiculous.

Which is why I laugh.

Right in his face.

He drops my arm as though he's been scalded. His eyes go wide with disbelief. Then his cheeks color and I know the anger isn't far behind. But still, I can't stop laughing.

Until—

He slaps the fucking hell out of me.

Gasping, I clutch my cheek. I hadn't even seen it coming and even now that it hurts, I still don't quite believe he did it. It stings. No, it's more than a sting. This is *agony*—more emotional than physical, although the reopened cut on my forehead from my tumble down the stairs with Remmy adds some blood to the mix.

Still, holding my cheek I look at Ben with my mouth hanging open. But instead of regret, his face is contorted into a mask of black rage. He takes a step towards me and it forces me back.

"*I'm* the boss now," he growls. "I'm done being pushed around, treated like a second-class citizen."

"You have no right to touch me. Or any of those kids. If you put a hand on me or any of them again, I will—"

My words are swallowed up in another gasp as he snatches me by the front of my blouse and throws me down hard. Except he's not aiming for the sofa like I did when I pushed him.

He's aiming for the coffee table.

Which happens to be made of glass.

I lose my voice in shock as I fall backwards. The glass shatters under the force of my weight and I go right through. Pain screams up and down my arms as those cold shards rip my skin open.

Fear clogs in my throat and all the fight leaves my body. Ben stays put, though. He squats down beside the coffee table and looks right at me.

"I don't give a fuck how you do it, but you *will* get yourself another job and you *will* support me. Work two jobs, clean toilets in the mall, fuck your way through New York—I don't give a shit *how* you do it. I just expect it to be done. And if you don't start falling in line right fucking now, I'm gonna take those kids and make sure you never see them again."

I'm shivering when Ben walks out the door, taking the keys to the Mercedes with him. It's partly because of the fear, partly because of the pain. I've been cut up pretty bad by the glass, but it's nothing compared to the weight on my chest and the knowledge that I'm cornered. And there's no one I can turn to anymore.

I can't rely on my parents.

I can't turn to Ruslan.

It's just me. I'm the last line of defense between Ben and those kids. And I *will not* let them down.

I will not let you down, Sienna.

I swear.

73

EMMA

"A-Aunt Emma?"

"Hiya, Josh."

I sound stupidly cheerful, considering I'm sitting in the middle of our broken coffee table covered in scrapes and bruises while fresh blood wells all along my arms and legs.

"W-what happened?"

"Um, I just—fell. I'm okay, I swear."

He circles around slowly. His bottom lip is trembling but he's trying hard to keep it together. Which is why the trembling is getting so much more pronounced. I can't even try to comfort him with a hug because I don't want any of the glass slicing him.

"You fell?" he repeats.

"Yep. Whoopsie-daisy!"

It takes some careful maneuvering to get up out of the glass pile. I end up using the coffee table's frame to tug myself up onto my feet. Glass crackles around me and Josh's eyes bulge wider.

"You're hurt."

"I'm fine. Nothing a little Neosporin won't fix."

"Aunt Emma." Josh's voice is trembling now, too. "You need to go to a hospital."

"No! I just need to clean up and—

"If you don't go to a hospital right now, I'm calling Ruslan."

I freeze. Did I just get threatened by an eight-year-old? Better question: is the threat *working?* "Josh, honey, there's no need to involve Ruslan."

"Then go to the hospital yourself," he insists.

Stubborn much? *He gets that from Sienna, too.*

"Okay, okay, I'm going. But first, let me call Aunt Pheebs. She'll need to stay with you guys while I go to the hospital."

Josh doesn't look appeased. "We'll come with you."

I walk gingerly over to the sofa where I left my phone. "No honey, it's okay. Really—"

"Did he do this?"

Thankfully, my back is to Josh and he doesn't see my cringe. I manage to compose it just before I turn back around with my phone in hand. "It was an accident, honey. You know how clumsy I can be."

Josh isn't buying it. His eyes fill with tears. "He's a *monster*."

My heart breaks. "Sweetheart…"

"He's a monster and I'm gonna kill him."

"Josh, *no*. You are a better man than that. You're a better man than him. Don't sink down to his level, okay? Trust me—it's not worth it."

He starts chewing on his bottom lip but he gives me a tiny nod. I have to be satisfied with that as I type a quick text to Phoebe. It takes some effort to keep my fingers from shaking.

EMMA: *Hey hon, I know this is super last minute and I understand if you can't make it, but can you maybe watch the kids for a couple of hours?*

She starts typing back almost immediately.

PHOEBE: *So sorry babe. Just got in a meeting. Bossman is here so I can't get out of it. He's a hard ass, too—just not in a fun way like your boss man.*

It's funny how her words send this weird stabbing pain straight through my heart.

He's not my man anymore. In fact, he's not even my boss anymore.

PHOEBE: *What's going on? Is everything okay?*

Since she can't do anything right now, there's no sense in worrying her.

EMMA: *Everything's fine. I'll figure something else out. Not a big deal.*

It is unbelievably hard to keep myself together but Josh seems like he's close to falling apart. Which means I definitely can't afford to do the same.

"Okay, hon. Change of plans. Aunt Phoebe is at work and she can't get out of it, so—"

"You still have to go to the hospital," he says firmly.

I sigh. "Alright then. Guess you're all coming with me. I'm gonna go—" I look down at myself. "—clean myself up a bit. I don't wanna scare the girls. Can you get them ready?"

He nods and heads to their room while I limp towards mine. My tiny little bathroom mirror shows that I'm more torn up than I thought I was. I'm hurting so much from head to toe, inside and out, that it's like my brain isn't even bothering to register it as pain anymore. Just numbness radiating through me.

Josh is right, though—I do need to go to the hospital.

I swap my clothes out for long pants and a long-sleeved shirt that covers most of the damage. I actually look halfway presentable when I walk out. The girls are *oohing* and *ahhing* over the shards of broken glass.

"Girls, walk around the table, please, and make sure to keep your shoes on. Let's go."

We have to take Ben's busted Chevy because the Asshole Extraordinaire took the Mercedes. Turns out, driving while you're bleeding from fifty different places on your body is quite a challenge. Every time I spin the steering wheel, my right underarm stings with sharp pain.

Once we get to the hospital, I have to fill out an endless parade of forms. *Any allergies? Am I on any medications? When was the date of my last period? Cause of injury?* It makes my head spin.

After I get assigned an appointment, we're sent to the emergency room lobby to wait. Forty minutes go by and I can't decide if it's the longest wait of my life or if it passes in a blink.

When they call my name, I leave Josh with the girls and step into the doctor's office for my appointment. I have to strip down and let her examine my cuts.

"You mentioned in your forms that this was a… fall?" Dr. Nara asks with a raised eyebrow, emphasizing her skepticism in the last word.

I shrug, which hurts. "I'm clumsy."

The doctor's dark brown eyes bore into mine. "Ms. Carson, I've seen my fair share of 'clumsy' women walk into this hospital. I can tell the difference between an accident and abuse."

I answer a little too fast. "I'm not being abused. I fell."

Dr. Nara sighs. "I know how hard it is to leave an abusive relationship. Especially with three children and one on the way, but—"

I flinch back, causing her to pull back the little tweezer she's holding to pick out the microscopic glass shards that have apparently been embedded in my skin.

"Careful, Ms. Carson."

"I'm sorry, it's just… *What* did you say?"

"Denial is very common among young women who are suffering at the—"

"No, not about that. About the three-children-and-one-on-the-way part?"

She frowns and then consults her clipboard. "You've mentioned the date of your last period as June. That was two months ago."

"Oh, that… I couldn't really remember my last period. I just put in the date that I could remember."

The doctor's brow pinches together. "If you can remember June, why not July?"

"The human brain works in mysterious ways?"

Dr. Nara gives me a sympathetic nod. "As I said, denial is common amongst women who suffer from abusive relationships. I'm sure another pregnancy is less than ideal for you right now but—"

I sigh. "It's not that. I have a blocked fallopian tube. The chances of me getting pregnant are basically zero. And those three kids are my sister's, not mine. I've never been pregnant. I doubt I am right now."

She cocks her head to the side. "You have one defective fallopian tube?"

"Yes."

"And the other one?"

"Excuse me?"

"Is your second fallopian tube blocked also?"

"Um, well, no. I mean, not that I know of. But the way my luck's been going…"

The doctor nods. "Maybe we should do some tests, just to rule it out?"

I swallow. "Sure."

"I'll clean you up first and then we'll get the bloodwork done."

I spend the next half an hour staring up at the fluorescent lights until I start seeing weird patterns dancing in front of me. Somehow, they all look like babies.

"Alright, Ms. Carson. We have your test results back." I jerk upright and wince. "Whoa there—let's take it easy, shall we? You've been cut up pretty bad. Those wounds will take a few weeks to heal completely."

"T-the results?"

She gives me a look that I can't quite interpret. Is that sympathy? Pity? Apology?

"You are in fact pregnant, Ms. Carson."

Pity. Definitely pity. The buzz of the overhead lights suddenly sounds like a baby's cry.

"How… h-how is that even possible?" I stammer. "I had a test done, like, just a few days ago. That was when they caught my blocked tube."

"Things change quickly. There could also have been some malfunctioning equipment or a faulty reading of the results. But there's no denying this, Ms. Carson. You're pregnant."

Goosebumps erupt all over my arms. *I'm pregnant.* I don't know whether to laugh or cry. I don't know whether to feel happy or sad. I don't know what the fuck I'm supposed to do now.

"Ms. Carson…" I look towards the doctor, hoping that she might have the answers. "You are still in the early stages of your pregnancy. As a rule, we don't normally encourage this, but—you don't necessarily have to *stay* pregnant if you don't want to."

I frown. What is she saying? *She's offering me a way out…*

My first instinct is NO.

My second instinct is—*hell fucking no.*

I force my eyes to the doctor's and my resentment of her suggestion ebbs slightly. All she's seeing is a victim of domestic abuse with three children to raise. She's trying to help me.

But she doesn't know the whole story.

She doesn't know that this baby was born from something real. That I happen to love the father of this child even if he doesn't love me and *despite* how he has treated me. She doesn't know that I've wanted this baby from the moment I saw my sister become a mother. She doesn't know that I have *always* taken my miracles where I can get them. Inconvenient or not.

"I'm gonna keep this baby," I say firmly.

And I'm gonna save my other babies. It's up to me now and there's only one path forward.

We have to leave this city.

For good.

74

RUSLAN

Kirill bursts into my office, his cheeks flushed as though he sprinted all the way here. "I've got news!"

"You found Sergey?"

"No," he pants. "This is about Emma."

I scowl. "Why would I care about that news?"

"The security team is still on her. She ended up in the hospital with all three kids."

Before I realize what I'm doing, I'm on my feet. "Are the kids okay?"

Kirill frowns. "The kids are fine. It's Emma that's hurt."

"Can she walk?"

"Uh, I think so? She drove to the hospital herself."

I sit back down and concentrate on the barrage of legal paperwork in front of me. "Then she's not that badly hurt, is she?"

I'm being pulled in two directions. On the one hand, I fucking loathe that she might be hurt, badly or otherwise. On the other hand, her problems are no longer mine.

I've spent the morning dodging calls from *The Brooklyn Gazette* asking if they can get an exclusive statement from me. A quote, maybe? Fuck them all.

And fuck Emma, too.

"Ruslan, I know you're pissed at her—"

"'Pissed' doesn't begin to cover it. I'm done talking about her."

"There's something you need to—"

"We need to double the number of men looking for Sergey. He can't have just disappeared into thin air."

"I got my hands on Emma's files and—"

"I've managed to suppress news of the botched launch getting out there. So far, the incident has been printed as a 'good time gone bad' incident. Nothing has been traced back to Alcazar itself or to me by association, but rumors are circulating. We need to expedite the investigation so that we have a story we can spin to the press."

Kirill is glaring at me with his jaw clenched. "That's the third time you've cut me off."

"If you didn't insist on talking about Ms. Carson, I wouldn't have to cut you off."

"This is *important*!"

"*You* were the one who brought me the news, remember?" I growl. "You were the one who shoved those pictures in my face and told me that Emma and Remmy were working together."

Kirill bristles. "Meaning what—this is a 'kill the messenger' kind of situation?"

"Whatever you have to say about Emma is immaterial to me now. So if you want to keep talking about her—" I jab a finger toward the door. "—you can get the fuck out and find someone who cares."

He has the nerve to open his mouth again. Thankfully, my phone starts to ring. I pick it up pointedly and answer the call without checking who it is.

"Hiya, buddy. How're you doing?"

Jesus Christ. I can't catch a fucking break anymore.

"What do you want, Adrik?" I ask impatiently.

Kirill's eyebrows leap up on his forehead as he listens.

"Oh, just wanted to see how you were doing. Can't imagine Alcazar is doing all that well, considering all the bodies it's turned up lately."

"Ah, you called to gloat."

"Not at all! I called to sympathize. Personally, I think you should capitalize on your notoriety. Maybe change the name from Alcazar to The Grim Reaper? This game is all about marketing after all."

"It was simply a case of overindulgence. It's happened before. The incident will be forgotten soon enough."

"Overindulgence, huh? That is the *perfect* branding for the magic drug you're pushing. Tell me: how long do you think it'll be until the press gets wind of the fact that five dead bodies turned up the same night that you decided to launch Venera?"

I grit my teeth. "I don't know what you're talking about. I have no connection to Venera and, if I did, I would definitely take the credit."

Adrik chuckles darkly. "Is that how you managed to seduce that pretty little secretary of yours? Slipped her some Venera at the water cooler?"

If only he were standing in front of me now. Nothing could stop me from punching the smirk off that weaselly little cunt.

"If you're done—"

"Why was she at the hospital today? You two had a little fight, did ya? You know what they say: you can't have it all."

I freeze. That's why he's calling. He's not just trying to needle me. *He's trying to let me know that he's got eyes on me.*

"Adrik, a little word of advice: get your nose out of my fucking business and mind your own. Maybe then you'll be able to make at least *one* of your ventures successful."

I hang up without waiting for his reply. My eyes are focused out of the window, but I'm not seeing anything there. "That fucker is watching Emma."

Kirill pulls out his phone immediately. "According to the report I got earlier, the doctor advised that she stay at the hospital overnight for observation. She should still be there..." He puts the phone to his ear. "Maksim? You at the hospital... Yeah... I need you to..."

I turn back to the window while Kirill coordinates with the security team on Emma's tail.

How could I have been so stupid? I brought Emma out into the public sphere with me. I exposed her to the whole damn world. Which means I'm the one who made her a target. I may be done with her, but Adrik doesn't know that and, even if I told him, he would never believe me.

I'm still pissed at her but not enough to justify feeding her to the dogs. Definitely not enough to risk those kids in the process.

"... *what?* What the fuck do you mean... Where... When? *Damn it*, Maks! Okay. Fucking hurry. Hell's Kitchen." Kirill cuts the line and swipes a hand over his hair. "They can't find her."

"I thought you said she was supposed to stay overnight for observation."

What do they need to observe? What happened? I hate that I don't know. I hate that I want to know. I hate everything about this situation.

"Yeah, well, she was. Apparently, she opted not to."

"Stupid," I mutter. "As per fucking usual. Maksim and the team are heading to Hell's Kitchen?"

"As we speak."

I clench my fist around a fountain pen hard enough to bend it. "Where else would she go?"

Kirill doesn't look as confident about that and I have no clue why. But asking him might just encourage him to start talking about Emma and, as much as I want to make sure she and the kids are safe, I do not want *that*.

"We need to get a team on Adrik, too. The motherfucker knows too much."

Kirill frowns. "Do you think he might know something about Sergey's disappearance?"

"I have a feeling he might. He knew about the launch date. And he's the only one who stands a chance to gain through my failures."

"So we know that Adrik has something to do with the botched launch. My question is, *How?*" Kirill starts cracking his knuckles. "This launch was airtight. Only our inner circle knew the details. Only the inner circle even knows that you're behind Venera in the first place."

"Sergey's disappearance feels convenient, don't you think?"

I'm just thinking out loud, but Kirill shakes his head. "Sergey? You think Sergey's the mole?"

"He has all the information."

Kirill frowns. "Still—either the preexisting samples of Venera were tampered with prior to the rollout or those unfortunate five were given a different dose altogether. Either way, Adrik had someone inside Alcazar that night fucking with the Venera samples."

My jaw clenches. "I'm missing something…"

Ring, ring, ring.

Kirill picks up the call and puts it on speaker. "Maks?"

"We just got to Hell's Kitchen, sir," the soldier reports. "It looks like she came here but then… she left again."

Kirill and I exchange a glance. I lean in towards the phone. "*Soldat.*"

He clears his throat. "Yes, *pakhan?*"

"I want you to stay there until she comes back home."

He clears his throat again. "Sir, if I may… It doesn't look like she's coming back."

I freeze. "What do you mean?"

"We've got a long lens camera aimed at the inside of the apartment. She seems to have packed up the majority of her belongings."

Blyat.

"Keep watch," I snarl. "I'll be there soon."

Kirill follows me as I run to the elevators. There's a wariness in his face that I don't care to decipher right now. My head is pinging with warning flares. *Why did I think it would be as easy as cutting the cord?*

Maksim is parked outside Hell's Kitchen when Kirill and I arrive. While Kirill stays behind to talk to the soldier, I dart upstairs. It doesn't take me long to break the lock and let myself into the apartment.

The first thing I notice when I walk in is the broken coffee table. Glass shards litter the center of the living room and I spot little flecks of blood drying on the sharpened edges.

What the hell happened here?

Their clothes are gone. Their shoes are gone. The apartment seems empty compared to its usual comfortable chaos. The only mess is the broken coffee table, which feels ominously symbolic right now. All the little things that are so precious to each child are noticeably absent.

Reagan's favorite soft toy, a stuffed rabbit she named Mr. Bunny.

Gone.

Caroline's cloth doll with the handmade dress that Emma crocheted herself.

Gone.

Josh's boxing gloves. The ones I gave him. The ones I taught him to lace up.

Gone.

As if for added confirmation, I turn towards the mantel. The pictures are still standing in their mismatched frames, Sienna's smiling face shining out at the center. But there's an empty square of dust where something used to be and Emma's words are ringing in my ears.

It's the first thing I pack and the last thing I unpack.

Her sister's music box is gone.

TO BE CONTINUED

CRUEL PARADISE is Book One of the Oryolov Bratva duet. Ruslan and Emma's story concludes in Book Two, CRUEL PROMISE.
Click here to check it out now!

Made in the USA
Las Vegas, NV
12 October 2023

78966490R00305